SHADOWLANDS

ERIN FARWELL

TATE PUBLISHING
AND ENTERPRISES, LLC

Published by Tate Publishing & Enterprises, LLC
127 E. Trade Center Terrace | Mustang, Oklahoma 73064 USA
1.888.361.9473 | www.tatepublishing.com

Tate Publishing is committed to excellence in the publishing industry. The company reflects the philosophy established by the founders, based on Psalm 68:11,
"The Lord gave the word and great was the company of those who published it."

Published in the United States of America

ISBN: 978-1-61862-889-3
1. Fiction / Mystery & Detective / Hard-Boiled
2. Fiction / Historical
12.03.06

For Mike and Willow, whose support made this book possible.

Also in fond memory of John Wenzlaff and Gert Davidson,
who shared their stories of Silver Beach with me and
helped me to bring this wonderful place alive again.

ACKNOWLEDGMENTS

Thanks to Daryl Schlender for sharing his research of the history of Silver Beach with me. Any discrepancies are either author error or author prerogative. Also thanks to John Wenzlaff for his extensive assistance by sharing personal experiences both of Silver Beach and St. Joseph, Michigan, as well as providing an introduction to Gert Davidson, whom I also thank for her assistance.

Roberta Farwell, Jerry Farwell, Harriet Farwell, and Jodi McKinley served as first readers for this book, and I thank them for their patience and assistance. I also thank my father, Jerry Farwell, for also serving as my lovely research assistant.

I would also like to thank the staff of the St. Joseph Historical Society for their assistance in the early phases of this book.

Finally, thank you to Kalyn McAlister for her expertise and support in the final stages of writing this book.

CHAPTER ONE

The hurdy-gurdy calliope music of the carousel faded until it blended with the night sounds of the riverbank. Kittie slipped behind the old bait shop and moved through the dark alley toward the passenger docks. Until last week she had skipped along this route, knowing that Gary would be waiting for her on the gangplank. Now fear, guilt, and the new-moon darkness had her creeping forward, fingers brushing the rough planks of the building to guide her way. Biting her lip to keep from crying, Kittie moved quietly on the sandy ground toward the closed souvenir shop near the ship landing.

The passenger dock led to nothing; the last ship had left at five o'clock to return to Chicago. Further down the river and on the opposite shore, the Central Docks glowed with light and pulsed with activity. Although it was too far away to see more than ships and moving shadows, the flow of the water brought with it the sounds of men talking as they worked loading fruits and vegetables to be sold in the markets of Milwaukee and Chicago tomorrow morning. Kittie turned away from the river and looked back toward the lake. Silver Beach was close enough to see the lights of the airplane ride and the cars of the roller coaster racing along its tracks, but the amusement park felt as if it belonged to another time, another life.

Kittie shivered in the cooling midsummer air, knowing that it wasn't the temperature that chilled her. Laughter from the fishing pier caught her attention. A few men fished off the far end of the pier, their light and presence too far away to offer any comfort. She stood a moment longer until she imagined her mother's rebuke, "Stop your dawdling, girl. If you don't get started, you can't get done." Tamping down her guilt, for she had never lied to her mother before, at least not about something important, she stepped onto the creaking boardwalk and moved as quietly as she could past the closed storefronts.

When she reached the souvenir shop, she paused to catch her breath. Her heart raced as if she had run for miles, and she wondered once again if she were doing the right thing. Closing her eyes, she thought of Gary. With his sandy blond hair and easy smile, he was more cute than handsome but wonderful just the same. He would want her to be brave. She would do this for him.

Calmer now, she grasped the polished metal doorknob. Taking one more deep breath, she turned the knob. The door swung open without a sound. Filled with dread, but determined to learn why her Gary had died, Kittie stepped into the store.

Darkness had stolen the familiar, leaving behind hulking forms and monstrous shapes. Kittie stifled a sob.

"Close the door."

She jumped at the man's voice, but it had broken the horrible spell, and so she did as he commanded.

A match hissed, and soon a flame burned near the back of the store. Kittie sighed in relief, now able to recognize the candy counter, trinket displays, and pennants hanging along the walls. Returned to her known world, Kittie moved quickly toward the candle and the man who had left the strange summons for her at the carnival booth where she worked.

She reached the counter and the light, but the man had moved into the darkness. He was tall, she could tell, and he blended with his shadow to form a hulking figure that loomed over her. His hat was pulled low, hiding his features.

"Who are you?"

"Someone who knows about Gary."

His voice was cold but somehow coaxing. A strong voice, Kittie decided. Here was someone who could help. "Can you tell me who killed Gary? Please, I need to know." Her voice shook with grief and rage. The papers had dismissed Gary's murder as one of the hundreds that occurred on the streets of Capone's gangster-filled Chicago every year. But Gary wasn't a gangster. He was a musician who had played the trumpet in the Wayne Sherman Band, and he had loved her.

"There is something I want from you first. Did you bring it?"

Kittie nodded and slipped her hand into her pocket. "Your voice is familiar. Do I know you?"

She heard a grunt that might have been a laugh, but he said nothing. With a shrug, she held out her hand. The silver bracelet Gary had given her sparkled in the candlelight.

"You stupid bitch."

The words hit Kittie like a slap across her face. Fear danced down her spine and settled in her belly. "But you said to bring the important thing that Gary had given me."

"Idiot." His voice shook with rage. "He gave one of those things to every girl he met. You little fool. You didn't think you were the only one, did you?" His harsh laughter shattered the last bits of Kittie's heart.

Clenching her hands to her ears, she backed away from the truth, sobbing, until she reached the candy counter and there was nowhere else to go. "But he said," she gasped through her tears.

"'But he said,'" the man mocked with a nasty sneer. "Of course he said he loved you. That's what men say when they want a girl to lift her skirts for him."

With a wail of despair, Kittie flung the bracelet at the man as she turned to run away.

"Wait," he said, his voice now cajoling. "Don't you want to know who killed Gary?"

"No," she shouted even as she turned back toward her tormentor. "Why should I care if what you say is true?"

The man was silent for so long Kittie wondered if he was going to answer. Finally, he said, "You loved him. Isn't that reason enough to want to know?"

His truth rooted her to the floor. "What do you want?"

"Didn't he give you anything else? Something important? I know someone who would pay a lot of money to get it back."

Kittie shook her head, confused. "No." And he hadn't. Nothing that anyone would want, just... "No," she said again. "Only the bracelet and a few carnival prizes." She wasn't sure why she lied, except that she was afraid of this man who refused to step into the light.

"You're sure?" Anger had returned to his voice.

"Yes." Her voice trembled, and she wondered if she should tell him the truth, but it was such a small thing, how could it be important?

The man's weight knocked her to the floor before she realized that he had moved. His fingers grabbed her neck and tightened. Kittie kicked against his shins and slapped at his hands, but he only squeezed tighter. Clawing at them, fighting for breath, she realized her mistake, but it was too late. She tried to tell him, to make him stop, but he wouldn't let go, wouldn't let her breathe. As blackness crept around the edge her vision, his hat fell off, and she found the answers to her questions, though they no longer mattered.

CHAPTER TWO

St. Joseph, Michigan
July 17, 1927

Stock prices had risen again. Cabel Evans set aside the business section of the Chicago newspaper. In his opinion the market couldn't sustain such optimism much longer. He would place a call to his broker and put in a sell order on his Archer Holdings stock, which had risen about as high as it would go.

Although he no longer held a role in either the company or his family, Cabel was curious about the value of his shares in Evans Manufacturing, but as a privately held company, it wasn't listed in the paper. All he knew was that healthy dividend checks were consistently deposited into his account and operating reports were regularly received, though never read. As much as he wanted to know how the company was doing, it would be too painful to read of its success, knowing he had no part in it.

Cabel owned thousands of shares in the family business outright and thousands more were held in a trust that would vest to him in a few years. Why did he keep them, these slips of paper that tied to him people who wished he'd never been born? Maybe it was time to end his torture, and theirs.

Shying away from his grim speculations, he focused on the things he could manage. His broker would be unhappy to receive another sell order for the Archer Holdings stock, but the man would make the deal and that was all that mattered. Sometimes Cabel laughed at his own obsession with the business world that he had once been a part of, but in his darker moments, he knew it was his last lifeline. What would happen when it, too, slipped from his fingers?

Marta stepped onto the back porch, all motherly bosom and flour dust. She hurried to his chair, bringing with her the scents of vanilla and cinnamon, which were as much a part of her as her checked apron and faded floral dress.

"You have a visitor, Mr. Cabel."

He looked up, startled. Her pale blue eyes were bright with excitement and hope as she waited for his response. He had known Marta Voss since he was a boy and hated to disappoint his housekeeper yet again, but he had no desire for companionship of any kind. "Whoever it is, please send him away."

Marta shook her head. "He says he's from your old unit and he needs to speak to you. I couldn't turn away one of our veterans. He's in the parlor." She walked back into the house before he could voice his protest.

Cabel sat frozen in time and place. A veteran had come to call. For the rest of the world the Great War had ended almost ten years ago, but for him it remained a daily hell. He would not go into the parlor and risk inviting that hell further into his soul.

The squeak of the screen door was his only warning that Marta had violated his seclusion. Her quick steps were followed by a more measured cadence.

"You were right to want to meet on the porch instead of the parlor. The garden is looking particularly lovely today." She hovered nearby as a man took a seat in the wicker chair across from Cabel. "I'll just bring out some tea," she said as she brushed wisps of gray hair away from her face with the back of her hand. With a nod of approval, she returned to the kitchen.

Cabel couldn't raise his eyes to meet those of the man across from him, afraid of what he might see. Instead he focused on the rose bush just coming into bloom, as if memorizing its details would somehow save him from whatever was to come.

The man seemed content to sit and wait. Birds chirped from the fruit trees, and bees worked busily at the flowers that bloomed in the bed that ran along the porch. Marta returned with a tray, which she placed on the table between the two soldiers, humming as she left.

Cabel wondered if she truly understood the danger of her actions, if she fully appreciated the destructive violence his anger could unleash.

As if reading his thoughts, the man across from him said, "That's a brave woman."

Cabel grunted, nodded, then took a deep breath as he turned to face his past. The man wore the white cotton shirt and dark wool pants of someone who worked hard for a living, clothing of the type that Cabel had worn himself for a few years. He was suddenly conscious of his own wardrobe and realized how much effort Marta made to assure that he was prepared, superficially at least, for his return to society. His anger ebbed.

The man across from him studied Cabel just as openly as he had been studied. Cabel wondered what the intruder saw then decided he didn't want to know.

The visitor spoke again. "Everyone in town knows that you want to be left alone, but I need your help, so here I am."

Cabel let the silence lengthen. It had to be better than whatever words would come.

"You probably don't recognize me, but I was a private in your unit, Lieutenant, I mean Captain."

Cabel flinched at hearing his former rank, especially used with such respect. He closed his eyes and said, "I'd rather you not call me that."

"You're right. It was a long time ago. My apologies, Mr. Evans, but that's just how I knew you. I heard about your promotions, we all did, I mean those of us who were still… Anyway, we were proud of you."

Cabel nodded with clenched teeth. Proud? He wanted to howl at the absurdity. All he had done was lead men into hell over and over again on the orders of his superiors. What had he to be proud of?

"My name is Walter Arledge. You and Lieutenant Warner were fine men, and I was honored to have served under you." He paused, seeming to wait for something, some acknowledgement of their shared horrors, but Cabel had nothing to offer this man.

Arledge cleared his throat and squared his shoulders, ready to declare whatever he had come to say. "I'm here because I need help and there's no one else to ask." His face twitched like a man fighting to hold back tears. His eyes slid from Cabel to the whitewashed planking of the porch.

If the man wanted money, Cabel would pay it gladly just to send him on his way. Whatever the amount, it would be worth the price for the return of his solitude.

Without looking up, the man continued. "My eldest daughter was killed, you see." His voice broke, and he paused a moment. When he finally raised his head and their eyes met, Cabel wished he could look away, but the depths of this man's misery held him hostage. "They tell me she drowned in the river, but I know that's not true." Arledge reached into his pocket and brought out a crumpled piece of newspaper. He smoothed it carefully on the edge of the table before holding it out to Cabel as if offering a chalice or holy relic.

Every part of Cabel's being rebelled at the thought of taking the paper. He wanted to order the man from his house, or walk away without a backwards glance, but something in Arledge's dignity, combined with the inherent bond of men who had seen combat and survived, had him reach out and accept the offering. The article was clipped from the local St. Joseph, Michigan, newspaper, which was why Cabel hadn't seen it, although it was doubtful he would have made the connection to his former private in any case.

Dated July 12, 1927, the brief article stated that the body of Kittie Arledge, age sixteen, had been found floating in the St. Joseph River near the boat docks. The reporter went on to speculate that perhaps she had lost her footing in the dark and had fallen, unnoticed, into the water. She hadn't been found until the next morning. The coroner had ruled it a death by misadventure, and the matter was closed. This had occurred five days ago.

Cabel looked up at Mr. Arledge and waited.

"Kittie's my oldest, and she worked at Silver Beach, but she wasn't working that night. I talked to her boss, Joe George, and he said that she had asked for the night off to stay home and help with the rest of our kids, but that wasn't true and it wasn't like her to lie."

Cabel said nothing, but remembered his own sixteenth year as a time of unspoken desires and secrets. He pushed away memories that threatened to break through his well-constructed barriers.

"Her mother and I, we thought she had gone to work, but when she didn't come home after the park closed, I went looking for her."

"Maybe she met someone, a boyfriend?"

"No, sir, it wasn't that." Arledge sighed and rubbed his hands over his face. "She thought we didn't know, but she and her sister Anne told each other everything, so we heard their secrets, not that most of them mattered. We knew she was seeing a boy who played trumpet in one of the dance bands that comes through here. I checked up at the boarding house where they stay, and Mary Davidson told me that the boy was okay. Anyway, I let Kittie think that her secret was safe but kept my eye on things all the same."

"So why don't you think she met him that night?"

"He was killed, gunned down in Chicago a week or so before Kittie died. She took that real hard." His voice faded away as his own sorrow took hold again.

Cabel tried to ignore the other man's pain even as his own rose to the surfaced. He hadn't been in Chicago by personal choice and family exile in almost five years. His own failures had kept him away, but he read the newspapers. Sensational headlines gave the impression that there were speakeasies on every corner, gangsters in every shop and that Al Capone ran the city. Maybe it was true.

"Please, Mr. Evans, I came here to ask you to help me find out what really happened to my girl."

Cabel looked down at the clipping in his hand then back to the grieving man. "I thought she drowned. What else did you want to know?" He knew his words were harsh, but rather than flinch, Arledge straightened, his eyes hard with resolve.

"I'm not wealthy like you, but I know when someone's handing me a load of manure and telling me its daisies." His voice rose in anger. "The doctor who looked at her when she came out of the water, he was at the funeral parlor, and so was the chief of police. They told me how sorry they were and how it was best to remember Kittie as she was and not see her all drowned and all." Arledge's voice broke again. He paused a moment then stood and walked to the porch railing.

Cabel picked up a sweating glass of iced tea and took a sip while he waited out the wave of grief that had engulfed the near stranger who stood on his porch.

Arledge returned to the chair but didn't sit. He paced in front of Cabel, walking faster with each turn. "My wife, Kaye, was nearly broken and trying hard not to let the children see, and the kids, they were crying, so I thought I'd just take the doctor's advice, let it be; but something about the chief had me wondering. The doc and the chief were helping my wife out of the room, so I walked over to the box—we couldn't afford much..." He swallowed hard. "I opened the lid and saw my little girl." Rage replaced grief. Arledge looked Cabel in the eye as he struggled to control his fury. "She had bruises on her neck, dark, purple bruises. I'm no doctor, but I've seen enough death to know the difference between someone who drowned and someone who was killed." He leaned over Cabel, gripping the arms of the chair. "Someone choked the life out of my baby, and the police won't help me find out who did it, so I came to you."

Stunned, Cabel could do little more than blink. There were so many layers of desperation on the porch, he was surprised that it didn't suffocate the both of them.

Arledge turned and leaned on the railing. Behind him, flowers swayed in the gentle breeze and birds flitted in the branches of an ancient cherry tree. Cabel counted the birds until the band around his chest loosened enough for him to speak.

"What do you think I can do?" he asked, surprised at the calm in his voice.

"You're one of them, wealthy and educated. Your grandfather built his summerhouse here and supported this town. They'd listen to you. I want to know what happened to my girl."

The fallacies in Arledge's assertions were stunning. Cabel was no longer one of them. He'd lost that claim five years ago and didn't want it back. While it was true that his grandfather had been respected here, Cabel doubted that the town's leaders would extend the same courtesies to the prodigal son who had returned from war only to destroy his family, and himself.

"I know what they say about you, the people in town," Arledge said in a deadened voice, still looking out over the yard. "They think that the war made you wrong inside, but I don't know any man who went into that hell and came out the same. Some say you only come out at night. There are people who think you're scarred and ashamed to be seen. But others think you're just crazy." Arledge turned back to study him. "I can see that you don't have scars or bad lungs from the gasses. I don't know what you've done that makes you want to hide away like this, and I don't care. I need your help."

"You don't understand. I can't help you."

"My wife told me you'd say that. Said I was a fool to come and see you, but I promised her that I'd get justice for our girl, and I mean to do it." Arledge reached into his pocket and brought out a small, shiny medallion on a sterling silver chain. It dangled between them, turning gently in the breeze. "We found this after you'd been taken down to the medic station. We knew you'd want it, but with the fighting and all, we couldn't get it to you. We passed it from man to man, keeping it safe."

Cabel stared, mesmerized by the religious medal that glinted in the sunlight. A roaring filled his ears. He shut his eyes, but visions of war flowed through his mind, unimpeded and unstoppable. Tightness in his chest returned, threatening to steal his breath. His mind began to slip from the hard edge of sanity when a hand rested on his shoulder. He opened his eyes and saw Arledge's face inches from his own. The compassion and understanding in the man's eyes had Cabel jerk his shoulder from the other man's grip. Arledge stood back, giving him room to recover.

When Cabel's breathing slowed, Arledge held out the medallion again. "We tried to keep track of you, and when we'd hear that you were assigned to some regiment or attached to a unit, we tried to find you. I was the last one to have this, and I've kept it for you, figuring you'd return to St. Joe one day. In December, when you came back, I would have brought it to you, but you made it clear that you wanted to be left alone." Arledge took a deep breath. "All of us in the unit knew how close you and Lieutenant Warner were, and we knew you'd want to have this back. I always meant to just give it to you, but right now I've got to use whatever I have to find out what happened to my Kittie. This little silver thing is my last hope."

Arledge gently lowered the medallion onto the newspaper clipping that lay on the wicker table then stepped off the porch, leaving through the side yard.

CHAPTER THREE

The morning was cool, as the hour was early, and thus belied the heat of the coming day. The still air carried only the muffled clatter of the looms from the Cooper & Wells factory that stood at the base of the bluff. Cabel kept his mind focused on these small things as he walked along the sidewalk at the top of the bluff toward the Whitcomb Hotel.

The hotel itself was not his destination. At this hour only the kitchen staff and porters would be about their duties. On a nearby street corner, a child of no more than six sold newspapers. Although they'd only exchanged a few words in the eight months since Cabel's return to St. Joseph, he'd found a kindred spirit in the small boy who wore well-patched clothes and whistled in the predawn darkness to hold his fears at bay.

As Cabel approached the corner, he saw the child kneeling, sorting his papers. Alerted by the sound of Cabel's shoes on the brick street, the boy straightened and turned. The overhead streetlight cast a shadow, rendering the child faceless. Cabel stumbled over a paver but righted himself quickly. The boy stepped forward, becoming human once more.

"You okay, mister?"

"Yes, thank you." Cabel's heart raced, but he knew his façade remained in place. Reaching into his pocket, he found three pennies and handed them to the boy.

Wordlessly, the boy accepted the coins and handed Cabel a copy of *The Chicago Tribune*.

Their transaction complete, Cabel walked away. As he turned the corner, he heard the faint notes of whatever tune the boy had begun to whistle.

A false dawn shimmered in the eastern sky, giving a dim outline to the buildings that comprised the town. Toward the west, Lake Michigan still clung to the night, a dark, horizonless abyss. Cabel walked down Lake Street with the strange sense of being caught between them, the dawn and the night.

He stopped at the Fountain Aquarium and listened to the water splashing in the marble basin. The fountain had once graced the Columbian Exposition in Chicago, but now stood here, on the other side of the lake, a fellow refugee in their mutual exile. Dew slicked the benches that encircled the fountain, but Cabel sat anyway, letting the damp seep through his trousers, allowing him to feel something besides fear. He rested the newspaper across his knees, knowing he would need it later.

The religious medallion in his pocket felt as if it was made of lead rather than sterling, and it dragged him down to places he had forsaken long ago. The temptation to heave the thing into the lake was so strong that Cabel stood and pulled it from his pocket, ready to throw it over the side of the bluff. If only he could toss aside the obligation it represented just as easily. In his hand, St. Sebastian, patron saint of soldiers, smiled benignly. Cabel slipped the medallion back into his pocket with a small, disgusted laugh. God knew he had tried to throw his own medal away more times than he cared to remember. Why did he think he could pitch Jon's into the lake without a second thought?

His mind shifted to Arledge rather than risking further thoughts of Jon, dead and buried in France. Anger slipped in, and Cabel didn't shy from it. Arledge had no business asking anything of him, certainly nothing as strange as the investigation of his daughter's death. Who did Arledge think Cabel was, anyway, some detective in a penny dreadful novel? His self-righteous anger felt good, and he indulged himself a moment longer before letting it simmer down to hopelessness.

As dawn tinted the eastern sky, the first hints of blue shimmered on the tips of the waves below. Less than sixty-five miles across the lake, hidden from view but ever present, Chicago towered over its own shoreline. Cabel knew that redemption for the sins he had committed there was impossible to achieve, but perhaps he could repay his debt to Arledge.

A vague pain shifted through his chest, as if his acceptance of this obligation had awakened something that was stretching its muscles after a long sleep. Cabel sighed. If he did look into the girl's death, there would be nothing to find, nothing to learn, and the debt would be easily paid. Yet to do as Arledge asked, even a token effort, would require Cabel to step into the world once again. He would be risking his sanity, maybe his life, not that these things mattered to anyone but himself, and he valued them less with each passing day.

A breeze from the lake carried the fresh smell of water and sky. Staring across the now-blue expanse, Cabel recalled a favorite adage of his grandfather's. "A debt unpaid is a dishonor." Turning away from the lake, Cabel tucked his newspaper under his arm and began the short walk home as he considered the price of honor.

|||||

Two days later Cabel found himself following a brisk young nurse down a brightly lit hall. She stopped at a door, knocked once, then opened it, gesturing for Cabel to enter. Closing the door behind him, she left him standing alone like a naughty schoolboy in the headmaster's office. Cabel's nerves, already stretched thin, now throbbed with the desire to turn and run. When had his self-imposed isolation become a necessity?

Earlier that morning, Marta had fussed over him like a mother bird waiting anxiously for her chick to fly from the nest. He had little appetite but ate what his housekeeper placed in front of him, only to vomit it into the toilet as he tried to dress. With shaking hands stuffed into his pockets, Cabel had walked down Lake Street, the deep blue of Lake Michigan on one side and the homes of St. Joseph's elite on the other, pretending that he belonged.

Now he waited for Dr. Lewis to acknowledge his presence. The old man's office smelled faintly of medicinal alcohol and peppermint. Old hunting prints hung above shelves crammed with books and papers. The man fit the room. Reading glasses, slightly smeared and tilted, perched at the end of his nose. His thick mane of white hair fluffed out at odd places, as if the good doctor frequently ran his fingers through it and then forgot to smooth it down. His white coat nearly blinded the eye, pressed and starched, yet seemed as if made for a bigger man, or that the man who wore it had shrunk with age.

Dr. Lewis closed the medical journal that lay on his desk and started to rise to greet his visitor. Partially standing, he froze and stared at Cabel. He blinked slowly behind his thick spectacles then smiled broadly as he completed his efforts to stand.

"I'm sorry, but for a moment I thought I was seeing your grandfather as a young man again. I always knew you'd grow up to be like him in more ways than one, but I never expected that you would be so close of a physical replica. You're tall, like him, same dark hair and blue eyes. I used to tease him that there must be some Irish in his background, but he said his family back east was too snobbish to allow such a travesty."

Cabel forced himself to smile, to push rusty manners back into use. "I'm afraid I'm not even close to being a replica of my grandfather, but thank you for the compliment."

Dr. Lewis studied Cabel a moment then shook his head. "You're wrong, my boy, you're more like him than you realize. But please, pardon my manners and have a seat." He gestured for Cabel to sit and waited until he had before lowering himself into his well-worn leather chair on the opposite side of the large oak desk. "I can't tell you how wonderful it is to see you. I knew you've been back for several months, but you've kept to yourself. I'm sure you needed some time to adjust to being home, but I'm glad you're here now. Maybe you'd like to have dinner with Mable and me this Sunday? She cooks a lovely roast, and I know she'd be delighted to see you."

Cabel opened his mouth to speak but no words came forth. His head spun with thoughts and feelings he could barely identify, except for fear. That one was an old enemy, so close to him as to almost be a friend.

He looked up to see Dr. Lewis observing him as if he were a patient.

"Don't worry, my boy. Life works best one step at a time, eh?"

Cabel nodded as he shied away from the look of sad understanding in the old man's eyes. He cleared his throat. "I appreciate the invitation, but perhaps another time would be better."

"Yes, of course. Now, what brings you to my office today?"

Cabel shrugged but met the doctor's eyes. Here was surer footing. With a few brief words from Dr. Lewis, Cabel would fulfill his obligation to Arledge and return to the now-questionable sanctuary of his home. He leaned forward and placed the crumpled newspaper article on the blotter in front of the doctor.

The old man picked it up and scanned the headline before quickly setting it aside. Something in his manner brought forth long dormant skills. Cabel's grandfather had told him that he was better at knowing some men's thoughts than they were themselves. This talent had been exceedingly useful in the boardroom and on the battlefield. Cabel leaned across the wide expanse of scarred oak and picked up the scrap of paper. He looked at it as if memorizing the words, all the while observing the good doctor twitch in his chair as he fiddled with his pen.

Feeling as if he were stepping off a cliff, Cabel looked at the doctor and asked, "Why didn't you tell the family the truth?"

This time it was the doctor who opened his mouth only to find that the words had fled.

"This girl's father looked into the coffin and thought he saw bruising on her neck. Not common in drowning victims I should think." Why was he pushing the issue? Cabel sent a silent curse to Arledge and one to his grandfather for good measure. "And then there was the chief of police. What was he doing at the funeral parlor of a dead sand bunny? People up on the bluff still call the folk who live in the cottages near the lake sand bunnies, right?" he asked, deliberately goading the old man and wondering why.

"Yes, and it's a horrible term to use." Dr. Lewis stood as if to end the interview, but Cabel waved him back into his seat, surprised at his own tenacity and even more so by the doctor's obedience.

"I'm sorry, sir, but I really need to know what happened to this girl." Cabel leaned forward and waited until the doctor looked up. Finally, their eyes met. "Her father served with me, and I owe him a great debt," he said by way of both explanation and apology. "Did she drown?"

The old man's shoulders slumped. He pivoted his chair toward the window. His mouth worked as if he chewed something unpleasant, but he didn't speak. Cabel sat back in his chair and waited.

Never taking his eyes from the window, Dr. Lewis said, "No, she didn't drown. I believe she was strangled, murdered."

"Why did you let the family believe otherwise?"

"Politics," the doctor spat out, turning back to Cabel. "Even in St. Joseph, politics and money hold sway."

"Is there a difference?"

The old man snorted. "In this case, no. The mayor and the chief of police were concerned that a murder on the river, so close to Silver Beach, would discourage Chicagoans from crossing the lake. Or if they did come, they would go straight to the House of David Amusement Park rather than stay in town. They want people to spend their money here in St. Joe, not across the river."

Money and greed were motives that Cabel understood well. His grandfather had taught him to respect the power that came with the first, and his father had tried to mold him with the seduction of the second. "Why did you go along with the ruse? Didn't you think of the girl's family?"

"No." Dr. Lewis turned and glared at Cabel, challenging him. "I was thinking about my own. My son, Bradley, has taken over my practice. He's married and has a child, a boy. Bradley humors me by letting me keep my office and see the odd patient or two." He smiled for a moment; then his eyes grew hard. "Mayor Delong made it clear that if I didn't cooperate with their deception, my son's practice would fail, and he has the power to make good on his threat." He turned away again, his shaking hands resting in his lap. In a quiet voice, he added, "If you investigate this matter further, you could ruin my son."

Cabel sighed. Another burden he did not want to acknowledge or carry. He briefly considered lying to Arledge, but knew that wasn't possible. There was no real choice but to see the matter through to the end. A faint tingle of excitement slipped through his body, surprising him. He didn't want to care.

"I'll keep you out of this if I can," Cabel said, rising. "I don't see why anyone would need to know that you told me anything."

Dr. Lewis nodded.

"I do have one more question. Have there been other deaths or problems that Mayor Delong and the police chief are covering up?"

"No, at least none that I'm aware of. St. Joe's is a safe place. It's just that the House of David has been cutting into the tourist trade at Silver Beach and in town to the extent that Delong doesn't want to risk losing more money to those religious fanatics."

Cabel understood the business reasoning, but it didn't justify the lies. Without integrity, a man is forever adrift, as his grandfather was fond of saying. He had never told Cabel, though, that if a man were to become adrift, how he could regain his course. "Thank you for your time," Cabel said, standing. He reached across the desk and offered his hand. Dr. Lewis rose, shook Cabel's hand, and then called for the nurse to see him out.

"Be careful, young man."

Cabel nodded and took his leave. Once outside the office building, he stumbled to the nearest bench, suddenly exhausted beyond measure. His breathing labored and his hands shook. A passing woman in a light summer frock and matching hat eyed him nervously before continuing on her way. After a few minutes, Cabel struggled to his feet and moved slowly along the crowded sidewalk, pushed forward by the knowledge that blessed solitude waited for him on his back porch.

⁞⁞⁞⁞⁞

Contacting Arledge took more effort than he had expected. After returning home from his meeting with Dr. Lewis, Cabel stumbled to his room and slept until dreams of mud and death intruded. He woke and spent the rest of the day on the back porch, ignoring Marta's offers of food and drink. Arledge deserved to know what he had learned, but there were no answers, only more questions, and with them more responsibility than Cabel wanted. The weight of the medallion in his pocket, along with its twin that had now joined it, kept him on a path he did not wish to travel.

Arledge didn't have a telephone, but Marta soon located an address for him on Pine Street, near the lake. In the end, Cabel wrote a note and hired the young paperboy to deliver it the next afternoon. The boy had been pleased with the responsibility and extra coins. Less than an hour later, he returned with a reply.

The neat printing on the scrap of brown paper read:

Thank you. Please let me know what else you learn.

W. Arledge.

The task was set, and Cabel knew his next campaign into the world would send him to Silver Beach.

CHAPTER FOUR

Sunlight filtered through lace curtains that did little to keep the late afternoon heat at bay. In his bed Cabel stretched, refreshed by a sleep that held no nightmares, a rare gift since the war.

Relaxing against the crumpled sheets, he let his mind drift with the shifting shadows on the ceiling. In his dreams, he and Jon were boys again, playing on the banks of the St. Joseph River. Cabel smiled, remembering their games of settlers and Indians or pretending to be the explorer La Salle and his men, living in Fort Miami and trading with the natives. Neither boy had questioned why they traded with the Indians one minute and fought with them the next. Their greatest game had been to reenact the ambush of the settlers by Indians who had crossed Lake Michigan by canoe. In reality, the Indians had forced the settlers to retreat to Fort Niles and even then only a few had survived the battle at Berrien Springs. In their version though, Cabel and Jon bravely fought the Indians at the base of the bluff and forced the red men to retreat to their canoes, never to bother St. Joseph again.

Cabel gave himself a mental shake and returned to a world where battles were both lost and won and Jonathan Warner lay buried in a French grave.

He rose, dressed, and headed down the stairs. In the three days since he had met with Dr. Lewis, Cabel had worked at his courage, bolstering it for the task ahead. He had slept often and unusually well, as if his nightmares had sensed his resolve and allowed him a brief respite from their nightly horrors. This afternoon he felt rested and as ready as was possible to attempt a visit to Silver Beach.

The aroma of fresh-baked bread drew him to the kitchen. Through the window above the old metal sink he could see Marta working in the vegetable garden. Instead of heading for the back porch as usual, Cabel grabbed some of the warm rolls that sat cooling on the counter and walked back through the house. Soon he was out of the front door, feeling like the naughty child he had once been after a successful raid of the kitchen.

He walked down Lake Street eating his pilfered rolls, ignoring the few curious glances that came his way. Families picnicked on the bluff while couples strolled along the sidewalk, all of them immersed in their own lives rather than his, a fact for which Cabel was profoundly grateful. To keep his mind focused and his hands steady, he reviewed, probably for the hundredth time, his meeting with Arledge.

The man had assumed that Cabel had a formal education, probably a college degree. While it was true that he had attended elite primary and secondary schools in Chicago and had graduated near the top of his class, college had not been a part of his life. His grandfather believed that the best education came from experience, and as a result Cabel's business acumen had been acquired in the factories and offices of Evans Manufacturing. His grandfather had died when Cabel was fifteen. A few years later a barely eighteen-year-old Cabel had left for army officers' training and then to war. Upon his return, Cabel's father had pushed him to take an active leadership role in the family business—a decision that had destroyed them both.

Neither the war nor his business experience gave Cabel any idea as to how to go about investigating what had happened to Arledge's daughter. He wasn't a police officer or a Pinkerton agent. He did not want to be forced back into the world he had turned away from five years ago. With a rueful shake of his head, Cabel once again regretted speaking to the family lawyer who had tracked him down in New Orleans.

There was a long queue for the moving staircase. Cabel shuddered at the thought of joining in the crush of people who waited for a ride to the beach below. Before memories of crowded trenches could solidify, bringing with it clostrophobia and panic, he turned away from the moving stairs and found the start of the winding path that descended the bluff. He breathed deeply as he walked, keeping his attention focused on the ever-changing surface of the lake. At the base of the bluff, he skirted the clamorous diversions of Lake Michigan and Silver Beach, heading instead toward the river.

Many things had changed since Cabel had last been along the strip of muddy blue water, though others were just as he remembered as a boy. The rickety bait shop near the fishing pier still stank of rot and fish guts while a few yards away, the well dressed and those from the lower classes ascended the gangplank of a steamer preparing to return to Chicago. Across the river, the north pier jutted into the lake ending with the new lighthouse that marked the channel to the river and the docks. On this side of the river, the long wooden fishing pier defined the southern edge of the channel and was filled with men and boys with poles and bait. A few families strolled there as well, the women shaded by parasols and the men and children as uncovered as decorum allowed.

The lake stretched endless and blue in all directions. Deceptively calm, it had claimed more than its share of lives. Many ships, some passenger, some freight, lay beneath its sparkling surface. Cabel's family had lost several members when *The Tourist* sank in bad weather in the fall of 1898. Although this happened a year before his birth, Cabel had grown up hearing the stories and had an aunt who had refused to set foot on a ship from that time forward.

Cabel turned to look at the high bluff that rose behind the Cooper & Wells textile factory. The Whitcomb Hotel stood in a place of prominence on a part of the bluff that curved out between the lake and river. Its location offered a panoramic view of the lake and its beaches, one that he and his family had often enjoyed while dining in the hotel's fine restaurant. The grand hotel gleamed against the blue sky while the old stone lighthouse a few blocks away stood empty and deserted. The rest of the bluff consisted of a long stretch of green parkland dotted here and there by colorful flowerbeds. Although hidden from view at this angle, mansions and stately homes lined the other side of Lake Street, his own included.

Without conscious thought, Cabel walked the sun-bleached planks of the fishing pier until reaching the end. Standing on the worn timbers, with the sound of the water lapping at the pilings below, he felt as if he stood on the deck of a ship that held the possibility of sailing anywhere in the world. This had been a favorite game of his as a boy and was one of the reasons he had selected the city of New Orleans as his original place of exile. Wherever there was water, ships, and crews, there existed the chance to escape.

He stood for several minutes letting the clean air blow around him before turning back toward the shore. As he walked, he focused on Silver Beach. Even from a distance, he noticed the many changes that had occurred in the years since he had last visited the park. The roller coaster had been moved and expanded, and the old dance hall was now a fun house. But the airplane ride still spun in its circles, as did the merry-go-round, with its hand-carved horses and the calliope that had come all the way from Germany nearly thirty years ago. The newest addition to the park was also the closest to the pier. The Shadowland Ballroom was a large, circular building that replaced the smaller dance hall at the opposite end of the boardwalk. Cabel only knew the particulars because there had been an article about it in the *Chicago Tribune*.

Although the ballroom had opened just a month ago, it had booked many famous bands, as well as lesser-known ensembles and local groups looking for a chance to perform.

With a deep breath, Cabel left the pier, stepping onto the boardwalk that led the way to Silver Beach. The pathway took him past the ice cream parlor, the high-striker challenge, and several other games of skill or chance. Hawkers called from their wood and canvas booths, trying to lure players for their games and wares. Music from the carousel's calliope drifted over him only to be drowned out by the rumble of the roller coaster. Children squealed and dodged between the adults who strolled among the amusements.

The sticky-sweet smell of cotton candy competed with frying onions at the sandwich shop. Further down, a man roasted peanuts and called out to the crowed, "Buy your freshly roasted, highly toasted Virginia goobers here!"

Memories mingled with the present. Much had changed, yet the core of Silver Beach remained as it had always been. Cabel found this to be a precious gift.

Beyond the food concessions, people tried their luck at the games of chance that lined this section of the boardwalk. Cabel strolled past the colorful booths and stepped into a nightmare.

Shattered trees clawed at the night sky. Flares blazed the path to the enemy. Bodies tangled in the barbed wire that marked no-man's land. The stench of blood and rot settled into the trench like a noxious fog. Cabel shouted to his men, straining to be heard above the clamor of a nearby 37-mm gun. A few yards down the trench, Jon rallied his own troops. For a brief moment Cabel locked eyes with his best friend then, with a final shout, led his men over the top and into hell.

|||||

"Mister Cabel, sir, are you all right?"

Cabel took a gasping breath, which eased the heavy weight on his chest. Keeping his eyes closed, he concentrated on breathing and bringing his shaking limbs under control. The smell of canvas and closed air made him wonder if he was in a medic tent near the front, but there were no screams, no mortar blasts. That war was long past.

"Mr. Cabel, sir?" the man asked again. The deep voice, with its thick, Slavic accent, slipped through Cabel's memory but refused to settle into place.

"Let him be for a moment," a female voice chastised. "He must rest."

A small, calloused hand wrapped around his. Its warmth calmed him. Tentatively he opened his eyes and looked up to see a young woman leaning over him. Her heart-shaped face was framed by a heavy fall of dark brown hair, and he silently thanked the stars that it wasn't bobbed in the current fashion, for that surely would have been such a sin as to make the angels weep. Her black eyes and tawny skin reminded him of some of the Greek officers he had served with. Smiling, she brushed the hair from his forehead. "Welcome back." Her voice, as dusky as her skin, hinted at exotic places and sensual pleasures.

An older man appeared over the girl's shoulder. "Ah, Mr. Cabel, it is good of you to return to us."

The man's face and accent were familiar, though it took another moment to remember. "Joe George."

Joe George gave a booming laugh. "You see, Mama, I knew he would remember us. Yes, I am Joe George, king of the gypsies!" He thumped his barrel chest with a ham-sized fist and laughed again.

Cabel struggled to sit. Although he was still light headed, he preferred to risk fainting than to remain prone and vulnerable in front of these people he barely knew. An older, once-beautiful woman with thick, graying hair plaited down her back, and dark, serious eyes replaced the young beauty in the chair beside him. Confused, Cabel didn't object when the woman took his hand and placed it in her own. She studied his palm intently, tracing her fingers along the lines she found there. After a moment, she placed her hand on Cabel's chest and stared into his eyes. His soul shrank from her scrutiny. The examination ended as abruptly as it had begun.

"You are haunted by many things," she said softly. Her accent was as thick as the man's, though feminine but somehow deeper, as if it traveled a great distance to reach her lips. "You are haunted by many horrors, many regrets. You must forgive yourself and lay your ghosts to rest." She patted his shoulder as she rose, leaving him cringing at her words. There was no forgiveness, no mercy for his sins.

As the woman stood, Cabel took stock of his surroundings. He sat on a wide bench along the wall of a wood-frame and canvas structure. One of the Silver Beach booths, he realized. Mysterious symbols, stars, planets, and all-seeing, all-knowing eyes were painted on the canvas walls and ceiling. Recognition flared.

"You're Bessie George, the fortune teller," Cabel said, wondering at his stupidity.

The woman chuckled. "Yes, fortunes, loves, secrets, I see all," she intoned with mock seriousness. The others laughed as if this were an old but appreciated joke. Bessie's face grew solemn. "Much time has passed since you last come here, before the Great War, I think." Not needing a reply, she asked, "Do you know what happened just now?"

Cabel shook his head both in answer and in a vain attempt to clear his thinking. "I was walking along the boardwalk and then…" How could he tell them the truth? One moment he was enjoying the park and the next he was reliving the horrors of France. They would think he was insane. He feared it was true.

"You fall on boardwalk, near shooting gallery," Joe George said. "I see this from my fish pond booth and come help you."

"Thank you," Cabel mumbled. Yes, he had smelled cordite from the rifles just before his collapse. A shudder racked his body.

Like a sniper's bullet, a smell or a sound would hit, sending Cabel back to the trenches. These attacks weren't memories or dreams, though he wanted to dismiss them as such. No. In those brief moments he returned to specific places and times in battle. He could hear men shouting, feel the rifle in his hands and smell the rotting corpses in no-man's land. His greatest fear was that he would be flung back into that hell and not be able find his way home.

Bessie looked into his eyes again and said. "You need much healing but are stronger than you know." She stepped back, and her long gypsy skirts swirled around her legs. "You have had enough today, I think. Now you go home and rest. You can ask questions tomorrow."

"Questions?" How did she know?

"Yes, about the girl, Kittie. Is this not why you come to Silver Beach?"

"Now, Mama," Joe George said, "why he come here to ask about poor girl?"

Cabel looked at the fortuneteller, with her colorful scarf and heavy necklaces and remembered why he, Jon, and many of the other children who roamed the park at will, did whatever they could to avoid crossing her path.

"Actually, I am here about the girl." Joe George looked surprised for a moment then shrugged as if to say that he should have known. "Her father asked me to look into her death."

Joe George nodded slowly. "Walter is good man, and his daughter, she was nice girl, hard worker. All is very sad, but what can you do about this?"

Cabel started to answer, but Bessie cut him off. "No, Papa, the boy has had enough for now. Let him come back tomorrow."

"Yes, he should rest now," the girl said, stepping forward. Cabel searched his memory, but she was not familiar. Even with Elizabeth by his side, he would have noticed this exotic beauty. "It would be best if someone saw him home. I will walk with him to top of bluff." Her accent and her voice were softer than the others' but just as strong.

Bessie shook her head. "You must restock prizes in booths for tonight, Daniela. Eddie will walk him up the bluff."

Daniela's face set in a pout, but she didn't protest. Bessie lifted a flap at the front of the booth and called to her eldest son, who appeared moments later. A few words were exchanged in their native language, creating sounds Cabel remembered from childhood but could not place. Eddie looked doubtfully at Cabel then shrugged and walked away.

Suspecting this was all of the invitation he would receive, Cabel rose and stepped into the sunlight.

"Come back tomorrow, Mr. Cabel," Bessie George called. "We talk then."

CHAPTER FIVE

Night sounds played like a symphony. Crickets and cicadas provided the quiet yet constant base while spring peepers lent their sporadic melody. The questioning hoot of an owl added drama and tension until the hunter flew off in search of prey.

Cabel sat in the midnight darkness, his mind festering with shame and embarrassment. His collapse at Silver Beach proved once again that he had no place in society. Although he knew this, had known it even before boarding the troop ship that had carried him from France to New York, the truth still pained him. Shell shock is what the doctors called it, such a benign phrase for the horrors the condition inflicted. He had never admitted to anyone the tricks his mind played—how could he? Few could understand, and others would either shun him or lock him away. Perhaps that would be for the best.

That is why he stayed away from others, those who were untainted by the war, not wanting to see their disbelief—or worse, their pity. How could he meet his obligation to Arledge when he couldn't leave the house for fear of what might happen?

The breeze cooled as the night deepened, but in his hand the two religious medals pulsed with heat. Elizabeth had given identical medals to "her two dashing officers." They had all laughed, but secretly Cabel had wished that Elizabeth would single him out, just once, before he and Jon left for New York and officer training. He knew that Jon had felt the same.

Cabel's chest tightened with deep grief and a fearsome rage as he thought of his best friend. Why the hell had they gone to fight in a war that wasn't even theirs? How could their parents have pushed them to do their duty and have their glory with no thought to the cost? Why couldn't Jon be sitting here now, safe and whole, instead of the shattered vestiges of the man Cabel had once been?

He felt himself slip into a blackness deeper than any night. Rather than fight against it, he leaned back in his chair and let the darkness pull him down. Pictures flashed through his mind like so many postcards scattered across a table. The pictures slowly ordered themselves and became a moving picture show.

|||||

Cabel met Jonathan Warner for the first time at the park near Wabash Street where the neighborhood boys played baseball. Jon, lanky and tall, stood watching, baseball glove in hand and longing in his eyes. Cabel walked past him on the way to the slab bench that served as their dugout and slapped him on his shoulder. "You're with me," he had said, and their friendship began.

Both were children of wealthy, privileged families with homes located near Chicago's Magnificent Mile just a few blocks away from Lake Michigan. Together they attended select schools and all of the trainings and events required of them. Most were tedious lessons in manners and decorum, but every once in a while Cabel's grandfather would insist on something "more manly" like fencing or boxing. Both boys excelled at sports and studies, and together they roamed their Chicago neighborhood at will, often with Cabel's younger cousin Jim tagging along at their heels.

In the eighth grade, Cabel and Jon shared their first crush on Dolly Sinclair, vying for her attention with gifts and antics, anything to make her notice them. She ignored their efforts and took up with Howard Maxwell instead. In the wake of that disappointment, Cabel and Jon made a solemn oath never to let a woman come between them again, and they kept their word through other crushes and first, stolen kisses. Then they met Elizabeth Gish.

Cabel and Jon were standing near the drinks table at a cotillion held in honor of Jon's oldest sister's engagement. The ballroom of the Blackstone Hotel held a crush of people. The open windows and slow-moving fans could not alleviate the late summer heat trapped in the room. Everyone look wilted and uncomfortable, especially the girls in their ruffled dresses and drooping coursages. Cabel had decided that it was time for him and Jon to slip away when a girl, blonde, brown-eyed, and as flawless as a silent movie star, came to the nearby table and requested a glass of punch. Without thought or planning, Cabel and Jon flanked her and introduced themselves, ignoring the rules of etiquette requiring a chaperone to perform that service.

Elizabeth blushed and stammered, embarrassed by the attention the boys gave her. Soon her charm and intelligence began to show, and both boys were entranced. Throughout their last two years of high school, the three of them were rarely seen in the company of others, as if together they were complete. Elizabeth, funny and gracious, never chose one boy over the other, even when she needed an escort for a dinner or event. Polite society was amused and tolerant of the threesome they made. Everyone assumed that soon Elizabeth would pick one of the boys as her beau, and Cabel and Jon waited with hope and dread to see which of them it would be.

While Cabel, Jon, and Elizabeth enjoyed their youth, Kaiser Wilhelm and his cronies marched their way across Europe. In the midst of Cabel's senior year, the American Expeditionary Force was created. America would help her allies beat the Germans. Cabel's grandfather, James Cabel Evans, had commanded forces for the Union Army during the Civil War, and served with honor and distinction. Cabel's father, Edward, forever lamented the fact that he had no war in which to fight and prove that he was a true Evans. Cabel would do so in his stead.

With their combined connections, Jon and Cabel's parents secured places for the boys in the army officer-training program at Plattsburgh Barracks, New York. Their sons would be officers, as befitted their station.

Their high school graduation celebration also became their going-away party, and it was considered one of the best events of the season. Everyone believed that once America joined the fight, the war would be over in a matter of weeks, months at the most. Parents weren't sending their sons off to fight, but merely to put the Germans in their place. Cabel and Jon would leave as boys and return in a few months as men, officers, and heroes.

Amid the gaiety of the party, Elizabeth presented the religious medallions to the boys. On one side was the depiction of Saint Sebastian, the patron saint of soldiers. The other side was engraved with their names, all three on each. Elizabeth joked that while none of them were Catholic, she would convert if it would help bring her men safely home. Cabel was proud to be called a man, especially by Elizabeth. Jon's chest swelled as well.

Soon they boarded a train to New York, and once there they excelled in their training and were commissioned lieutenants. In Langres, France, all American officers received additional training, and this was where the boys first glimpsed the ravages of war. The French officers who worked with the Americans had nothing but contempt for their naivety and lack of experience. They scoffed and said that President Wilson had sent them babes, not men, and certainly not officers who understood what lay before them. The truth of their words was brought home to Cabel the day he realized that the officer who was the harshest and most condescending was only two years older than Cabel himself. With graying hair and haunted eyes, Cabel had assumed the man to be in his thirties, rather than a mere twenty.

Training complete, Cabel and Jon were assigned to the same unit within the Second Division and quickly had set about working with their men and meeting the demands of their superior officers.

When the call came for the regiment to deploy to the front, the bored and anxious men cheered and climbed into the trucks. As they neared the battle zone, the roads became clogged with men and horses, trucks and carts. Their own trucks became mired axel-deep in the mud and muck. The men waited, listening to the distant sounds of battle as the day wore on. They sat on the hard benches of the trucks for more than six hours before the road cleared and they continued their journey.

Cannon fire grew louder, and the ground shook from mortar strikes. Finally the trucks stopped and the men were ordered out. As they disembarked, a unit of men came down from the trenches, filthy and exhausted. Cabel and his men cheered for them, only to receive sour looks. One of them yelled, "You're fools, the lot of you."

Cabel and Jon organized their men, but it was well after dark when they were ordered into the trenches. The starless night made it impossible to see where they were going, forcing each man to walk with his hand on the shoulder of the soldier in front of him. The darkness hid many things, and Cabel quickly learned that if someone quietly called "body" he needed to pick up his feet to avoid stepping on the dead. The dark couldn't hide the stench, though, and it clung to them as they shuffled forward.

Movement through the trenches was slow, and bodies grew in number until the men were called to a halt. Here the trenches widened, and the men they were relieving silently filed past. "My God, where are the rest of them?" someone asked as the last of the departing soldiers was swallowed by the night. With sudden, horrible insight, Cabel knew the answer, and a cold, hard fear settled in his belly, where it would remain for the next two years. Orders were given, and Cabel led his men down the long narrow trench that would become their own piece of hell for the next three weeks. Jon walked past him, squeezing his arm to let Cabel know that he, too, felt afraid.

His unit fought hard that night and many died, and Cabel understood why it was his father, not his grandfather, who spoke of the glory of battle.

For six months Cabel and Jon faced this nightmare together. Their commander quickly realized that the two worked better together than apart, and he sent them and their troops over the top of the trenches time and again. The young lieutenants and their men distinguished themselves and earned commendations, many of which would be presented to grieving families. New recruits filled the vacant slots left by casualties, and Cabel and Jon did their best to make them soldiers rather than cannon fodder.

In the midst of the blood and gore, death and disease, two things kept Cabel fighting to survive: his friendship with Jon and letters from Elizabeth. When his name was shouted at mail call, Cabel's heart would skip while he raised his hand and waited for his letters to be passed to him. Any mail was a godsent diversion, but the ones from Elizabeth were cherished. She wrote delightful, cheery letters, sharing stories of her life in Chicago and passing along bits of gossip she thought would amuse him. The world she wrote of was distant, a near forgotten dream that he had lost hope of ever recapturing. Some of her letters were flirtatious, sending his pulse racing with unrelieved passion while others were almost sisterly, and he would ache with despair for days. Jon also received letters from Elizabeth. This was the one thing they never discussed.

In spite of their unspoken rivalry for Elizabeth's love, Jon and Cabel's childhood friendship was forged by war into a bond that had no words. Hardships, fears, responsibilities, deaths, each strengthened the ties between them until it was difficult to know where one of them ended and the other began. Their men sometimes referred to their superior officers as "Lieutenant Warnerevans," which Cabel and Jon found amusing and never corrected. Knowing Jon was leading his men into battle gave

Cabel the courage to do the same. Knowing that Jon felt the same gave Cabel pride.

Battles were fierce and bloody. Often the night ended with only a few inches of ground gained or lost but at the price of thousands dead on both sides. Cabel and Jon also fought the sense of futility that rose within the ranks and within themselves.

Dysentery was another enemy that had taken its toll in the trenches, and no one was immune.

After receiving orders for predawn raid, Cabel and Jon kept back half of their men for the morning battle. During the night Jon fell ill with bloody diahrea and high fever, the unmistakable symptoms of dysentery. Despite his affliction, Jon wanted to stay with his men while Cabel argued that he needed to go to the infirmary. As a compromise, Jon agreed to stay in the trenches and help with the wounded while Cabel led the raid alone.

Cabel rallied his men, gave the order, and prepared to fling himself over the side. As he reached the top of the wooden steps, a mortar shell hit the edge of the trench, sending deadly shrapnel in all directions. Men flattened themselves on the ground, and the screams of the injured filled the air. Cabel found himself lying on the body of a young recruit who had caught a piece of shrapnel in his chest. Pushing himself away from the mangled body, Cabel stood to assess the damage to himself and his unit.

He saw Jon sitting against the opposite wall of the trench, hands folded in his lap. Cabel felt a rush of relief and started over to his friend when he realized that Jon's neatly severed head lay a few feet away, eyes wide with shock but empty of life.

Cabel felt a cold so deep that it froze his soul. He rushed forward, tripping over other casualties as he made his way to his friend. Through the haze of shock and denial, he grabbed Jon's head and tried to put it back on his body, all the while lecturing Jon that he needed his head and shouldn't have let it get away so easily. Cabel's hands were slick with blood when his men dragged him, screaming, from Jon's corpse.

The next few days were a blur of nurses and medications and solemn-faced priests. He knew he was in the infirmary but couldn't understand why no one would answer him when he asked how Jon's surgery had gone. It was in this haze of drugs, with the screams of the injured and dying constant in his ears, that the horror of Jon's death became real. His screams of rage and agony joined those of the other men until no other sound existed.

|||||

Cabel leaned over the porch railing and vomited into the rose bushes. Emptied of everything but pain, he threw back his head and howled to the stars.

Soft arms wrapped around him.

"Shhhh, shhh, you're all right," Marta crooned in his ear as she drew him to her. Cabel buried his face in her shoulder and sobbed. She held him tight against her chest, rocking in an ageless rhythm, which promised that, somehow, everything would be right again.

CHAPTER SIX

Honeysuckle and jasmine scented the cool breeze that slipped across his body. Church bells chimed in the distance. Cabel opened weary eyes and saw familiar shadows playing across the ceiling. Marta's husband, Jorge, must have helped him upstairs last night after his breakdown. God help him.

Cabel rubbed his hands over his face, feeling the stubble and grime. Embarrassment would come, he supposed, and guilt and shame, but he didn't have the energy for those emotions yet. Instead, he felt—quiet. It was the only word that came to mind. Not peaceful, there was too much waiting under the surface, but there was a stillness in himself that he couldn't remember feeling before.

His body ached, as if recovering from a long illness and his raw throat demanded water. He forced himself onto shaky legs, which steadied as he made his way to the bathroom. Along the way he shed his clothes, leaving the stink of vomit and sweat behind. He washed, shaved, and dressed, taking his time and feeling more himself with every step of his ablutions. Jorge and Marta were at church, so he wouldn't need to face them yet. As was the household's Sunday routine, he knew a simple breakfast waited for him downstairs.

Surprised to find he was hungry, Cabel went to the kitchen and ate the rolls and cold ham that Marta had left for him. Restless, but not ready to face either the back porch or the public, he roamed the house.

Turrets, gingerbread trim, porches, and ornate railings festooned the exterior of the house his grandfather had chosen for his summer residence. Like many of the homes along the bluff, it had been built at the height of the Victorian movement, and James Evans had whole-heartedly joined in the process. The house was the only bit of whimsy that Cabel had ever known his grandfather to demonstrate.

The interior of the home, however, held the imprint of his grandmother's personality. The parlor, overstuffed yet comfortable, had been her primary domain. The scent of lily of the valley haunted the room, as did memories of his grandmother presiding over formal teas flanked by her daughters-in-law. She had a piercing glare that she used to keep him and Jim from squirming when they grew bored of the grown-up activity and wanted to play outside.

Bric-a-brac cluttered every flat surface: tables, piano, and mantle, as was the style several years ago. He preferred clean, spare surfaces, but he wouldn't change anything. The house may be legally his, but it was still his grandparents' summer home.

Looking more closely at the odds and ends that had collected in the room over the years, Cabel was surprised to find a faint layer of dust covered many of the figurines and vases. He knew Marta worked hard to keep up the house and wondered why she had neglected this room.

Frowning, Cabel walked down the hall, past the downstairs water closet, and stopped in front of the closed door of the study. He hadn't opened it since he'd returned from New Orleans. The room where his grandfather had lived and worked, despite complaints from the women that they were in St. Joseph to relax, held the best memories Cabel had of the great man. Grandfather had insisted that while the boys, Cabel and his younger cousin Jim, should have the full advantage of the lake, parks, and fresh air, there was no reason to stop learning just because it was warm outside.

Jim had hated these lessons, Cabel remembered now, tracing the carving on the door with his fingertips, but he himself had loved them. School had been a necessary drudgery that supplied no understanding of why anything taught there mattered beyond its walls. It was here, in this study, that Cabel had learned about the real world of business and how to apply his knowledge to important matters.

The day-to-day running of a business was more work than Cabel, the boy, had ever realized. At his writing desk he learned about costs, fixed and variable and how to control them. The importance of reliable suppliers of raw materials and parts as well as a strong distribution system was drummed into his head, and he had understood. In Chicago, his grandparents were too busy to spend much time with their grandsons, but St. Joseph was a magical place where there was time enough for everything. Cabel had thrived under his grandfather's tutelage much to his parents' joy and his cousin's disdain. In the summer of 1914, his grandfather had pronounced Cabel to be a born businessman, destined to take over the family holdings. In that moment, Cabel felt he'd become a man.

Now he leaned his head against the door, his hand resting on the knob, and grieved anew for his grandfather, lost to a stroke that following winter. He was grateful, though, that the great man had never witnessed the disgrace that his favored grandson had become. Cabel often thought that if his grandfather had lived, things would have turned out differently. Straightening, he turned away from the door and the futile thoughts of "what if."

Wandering back into the kitchen, he noticed that the room was exactly the same as it had been when he was a boy. The rest of the house had been modernized with running water and electricity. His grandmother had despised the fact that the conveniences she enjoyed in Chicago were unavailable in the small town of St. Joseph. As soon as power lines sprouted from their poles, Grandmother had insisted on updating the house.

Toilets were installed upstairs and down, and the outhouse had been unceremoniously dismantled and filled with fresh dirt. Hot water from the new heater was piped upstairs for the sinks and tubs, allowing Grandmother her scented baths.

The kitchen, though, remained unchanged. An ancient icebox squatted near the back door, a small pan underneath catching the drips. The old hand pump and rusting metal sink filled the northern wall and the wood-burning stove and oven stood nearby. Cabel knew that most farmhouses still had kitchens like this, since electricity had yet to make its way into rural areas, but he was shocked that his grandmother hadn't thought to modernize this room. Of course many new machines and conveniences had only recently come onto the market, but piped water, hot and cold, should have been added a long time ago. He was writing notes on the back of a piece of butcher paper when Marta and Jorge came in.

Jorge smiled at him before disappearing into the couple's small apartment that opened off of the kitchen. Cabel wondered if those rooms had been modernized, or if they needed attention as well. Since his grandmother never entered those rooms, the kitchen either, for that matter, she probably hadn't considered the need for changes or simply felt that such things as running water and electricity were luxuries the servants didn't need. His grandmother had been a proud and gracious woman, though when it came to the servants, Cabel thought she would have fit in well in the pre–Civil War South.

"How are you this morning, Cabel?" Marta asked as she checked the icebox to be sure he had eaten his breakfast.

"Fine," he said, surprised to find it was true. "And, about last night…"

Marta turned and smiled.

"I just want to say…"

His housekeeper waived away any further attempts on his part to offer his thanks and express his embarrassment. He gratefully accepted her kindness.

"Jorge and I are going to our daughter's family for dinner. Would you care to join us?"

Jorge appeared in the doorway, having changed out of his church clothes into comfortable-looking shirt and pants. He seemed relieved when Cabel said, "No thank you."

Cabel looked down at the list he had been writing before the elderly couple had walked in. "If you have a moment, though, there is something I would like to discuss with the both of you."

Fear filled Marta's eyes, but she held his gaze and said, "Of course."

Confused by her emotion, Cabel looked back down at the paper and then around the room. "This place is hard for you to keep up," he began.

"Marta works very hard for you, young man. Maybe she can't do as much as she used to, but she does what she can. We both do."

Until this moment, Cabel didn't think he'd heard Jorge speak more than three words in a row in his entire life, but now he had an explanation for their fear. "You're right, of course." Cabel faced the old man who stood defiantly next to his wife, a protective arm wrapped around her shoulders. "I would never replace you or Marta." How could he when they were the only thing passing as family that he had left in the world?

Cabel cleared his throat and looked back at his paper. "What I want to do is modernize the kitchen, and your apartment, too, if it needs it," he said, looking at Marta. "I was making a list of the things I thought we should change. The hand pump needs to go, and we can install some descent plumbing. That old icebox should be replaced with one of those new electric ones."

"A refrigerator," Marta whispered in awe.

"Yes. And I thought one of those new stoves and ovens would be easier to manage than that cast-iron relic."

"I'm not so sure about the stove, Cabe," she said, calling him by the familiar nickname that she hadn't used since before the war. "I'm not sure I could cook as well on one of those new-fangled things."

"Dear, you could make a feast over an open fire if you had to," Jorge chimed in. Marta beamed with pride.

Cabel went back to his list. "We should replace the sink and countertops, too, I think. Is there anything else you would like?"

Marta shook her head, amazement and delight shining in her eyes.

"Don't say no so quick, dear. What about that washing machine you were dreaming over in the McCall's magazine the other day?" Jorge turned to Cabel. "Doing the laundry outside in them big kettles is hard on her. Sometimes she has to get our daughter, Daisy, come over to help out."

Ashamed that he hadn't noticed how much Marta had aged or given any thought of what she might need, he nodded. "I'll add a washing machine to the list. I know you don't want to be late for Sunday dinner, so we can talk more about this later. Just think about what you need, and I'll make sure you have it."

Marta pulled a tat-edged handkerchief from the sleeve of her flowered Sunday dress and dabbed at her eyes. She hugged Cabel fiercely before walking down the hall, still wiping her away her tears. Jorge stepped up and patted him on the shoulder. "I never had a chance to say this when you came back, but welcome home." The old man followed his wife out of the room.

Cabel stood in the empty kitchen listening to Marta's excited voice as she headed toward the front door. He knew that the old couple thought that somehow between last night and this morning everything had changed, he had changed, but they were wrong. While he was glad that he could bring joy and ease to Marta and Jorge, he knew that the darkness still lived inside him and that it could destroy the world around him just as quickly and completely as it had five years ago in Chicago.

Cabel spent the rest of the morning looking at the condition of the house, really seeing it for the first time since his return from New Orleans. The roof needed repair if not complete replacement and much of the gingerbread trim was loose or missing. Paint peeled away from the siding in long strips, especially on the west side, which took the brunt of the strong winds off the lake. The side porch was giving way to rot, and loose metal railings on the second floor were likely to drop off, possibly killing someone, if not reattached soon. Marta and Jorge had seen to the yard and general upkeep as best they could, but these problems were beyond their abilities to fix. Cabel's lists grew.

While he walked around the house making his notes, he knew he was stalling. Answers to questions he didn't even know to ask could only be found at Silver Beach. His face flushed with shame as he remembered his collapse on the boardwalk. The people of St. Joseph had been waiting for him to come out of the house for months now, and he supposed he'd given them quite a show to go with the event.

His circuit of the house brought him to the front porch. He paused, looking out at the lake reflecting a cloudless sky. If he didn't return to Silver Beach today, he suspected he never would. With the resolution he had once drawn upon to force himself over the top of the trenches, Cabel put his paper and pencil on a table near the front door and stepped from the porch.

The morning had been cool, but by the time Cabel arrived at the base of the bluff, the mist had burned off, and the clean, wet smell of the lake filled the air. Blue water sparkled and families dotted the sand on the wide beach. Overhead, the roller coaster rumbled accompanied by shrieks and laughter. Church was over and it was time to play.

The boardwalk thronged with people, but Cabel knew that when the heat of August made Chicago nearly unlivable, Silver Beach would be bursting at the seams. He threaded his way through the crowds until he came to Bessie George's fortunetelling booth. Outside the concession, a group of girls, teenagers he guessed, stood near the partially opened flap, straining to hear whatever was being said within. Rather than interrupt, Cabel went in search of Joe George.

As he neared the game concessions, Cabel began to sweat. He shoved his shaking hands into his pockets. With clenched teeth, he continued down the boardwalk toward one of the many booths owned by Joe George. Bracing himself, he walked past the shooting gallery and didn't breathe again until he reached the duck pond game. Shots fired and the metallic smell of cordite competed with the aroma of fried onions. Another round fired, and Cabel was relieved to find himself still standing, still at Silver Beach. Now that he knew where the target game was and what to expect, maybe the spell was broken. He would hope, but he would also maintain his guard.

"There you are, Mr. Cabel." Joe George smiled and held out his hand. His grip was strong, his palms calloused. "I am happy you come back. Yesterday Mama worried you do not return and finish your quest, but this morning she said you would come."

Cabel smiled and shrugged. How Bessie George knew about his breakdown last night he couldn't guess, but he found himself absurdly pleased by the word "quest." *Don Quixote* had been one of his grandfather's favorite books, and he had insisted that Cabel read it. At the moment Cabel felt like a crazy man tilting at windmills.

"I do not understand why you want to talk about Kittie, but let us walk and see if I am able to help." He gestured to someone in another booth, and soon Daniela hurried forward, smiling at Cabel. Her smile wavered a bit when she learned she had to manage the duck pond booth for a few minutes, but she nodded to her uncle in good grace.

"I am glad you are better today," she said then darted under the counter that separated the public area from the inner workings of the booth. He nodded in acknowledgement but rather than linger and discuss his embarrassing incident, he followed Joe George to a booth farther along the boardwalk.

"Daniela is my niece. She come to us three years ago, after parents die, so you do not know her before."

"No, I think I would have remembered her."

Joe George grunted and stopped near the spill-the-milk booth he owned. "She is good girl, but she has strong will. I hope she make good wife for one of my sons, but she is more like sister to them, and so we arrange for them to marry girls from the old country. One will be here this summer and the other sometime in spring. This is good. It is time for boys to have families."

For a moment Cabel thought he had misheard the gypsy, but the satisfied smile on the other man's face told him he had not. His sons would soon be entering into marriage with complete strangers.

"Daniela," Joe George continued, "she is not ready to be good wife, but she is good girl and I take care of my own."

"I understand," Cabel said.

"I find husband for her, when time comes. But now, she should not think of man who is not of us. Such man should not give her reason to dream beyond her place." Joe George looked hard into Cabel's eyes.

A moment passed before Cabel realized that Joe George was warning him away from the girl. He almost smiled at the absurdity of the idea. "Don't worry, sir. Your niece is a beauty, but I'm afraid she's much too good for the likes of me."

Joe George's chest puffed with pride, but a glimmer in his eye told Cabel that the man thought the words were empty flattery. Couldn't the gypsy see past the Evans' family wealth to the damaged man before him? Certainly Cabel's collapse yesterday should have made it clear that he had nothing to offer anyone, especially a lovely young girl like Daniela.

Satisfied that Cabel would not distract his niece, Joe George continued to the spill-the-milk booth. Slapping the counter with affection he said, "When you are young, I own only this booth and high-striker game. Mama had fortunetelling booth. Now I have also duck pond and balloon darts. One son owns guess-your-age-and-weight booth. Very popular, though I do not understand it." He gave an eloquent shrug. "We give people what they want, what they spend money on, though this not same thing always, yes?" Joe George gave a booming laugh and slapped Cabel's back so hard the force almost sent him to his knees.

As he regained his balance, Cabel said, "I remember trying to show off on the high striker once when I was about ten or eleven years old."

"I remember too. You can only just pick up sledgehammer and not possible you make bell ring, but you try very hard. A young girl stand nearby, I think."

"Annabelle Carter." Cabel hadn't thought of her in years. The girl's family had rented one of Drake's cabins near the water for a few weeks that summer, and Cabel had fallen for the girl with the light brown hair and sweet smile. He had almost killed himself lifting the sledgehammer in an attempt to impress her. He had succeeded in that, at least, though he still wasn't sure why. The memory made him smile until thoughts of young girls and Silver Beach reminded him of his purpose. He felt a heaviness settle into his chest. "I need to ask you about Kittie Arledge."

Joe George nodded. "We have good summer, my family eats. We have bad summer, we have bad winter. At Silver Beach, always good summer. We work hard, and Daniela join family. Still there is more work than we can do. My sons tell me 'hire strong young men who will lift and carry.' But after booths are set up for summer, we carry only boxes, prizes. My sons can manage them." Joe George gave a negligent wave of his hand as if to dismiss his sons' hard work. "These prizes we make in winter. They always nice, I think, but people try harder to win now Daniela paints them. Hand me lion," Joe George said to a girl behind the counter. She brought over a large chalkware lion that looked as if he would leap from his stand to hunt zebras for his dinner. "Is beautiful, yes, and cheap to make. Tourists love them and spend much money to try and win them." He handed the lion back to the girl.

"As I say, sons want me to hire boys, but I say no. Boys spend more money, play more games, when pretty girl work booth."

The girl behind the counter blushed furiously. She turned and pretended to dust the prizes that crowded the shelves along the back of the booth.

Oblivious to the embarrassment he caused, Joe George continued. "Mama worries at first, but I say, 'Boys like them. Women more happy playing games when husbands are at shooting gallery.' And I am right," he exclaimed proudly.

"How did you come to hire Kittie?"

"Ah, poor Kittie." Joe George hung his head for a moment then looked up and continued his story. "When Mr. Drake build new ballroom, he mostly hire Germans from Pine Street. People up there"—he gestured to the top of the bluff—"call us sand bunnies, but Mr. Drake, he know better. We work hard. Ask them at mill, and they tell you how hard we work. So Mr. Drake, he hire the Germans; but Mr. Walter, his farm not do well, so Mr. Drake give him job, too." Cabel was shocked to hear of Arledge's problems. He never knew the man had owned a farm, but then there was no reason why he would have.

"Sometimes Kittie bring supper for father," Joe George continued. "Before she go home, she walk by booths. One day I ask if she want job. She say yes. This is last summer. The men finish ballroom this spring, ready for summer season. Kittie come back, ask for job. She work hard. I am happy to give it to her."

"What did she do for you, exactly?"

"She take money, give player ball to throw, and reset milk bottles if knock over. Not so easy, yes?" Joe George gestured to the girl again, and this time she brought over one of the targets. Although it was shaped like a milk bottle, it was made of padded leather. Joe George held it in his hand for a moment and studied Cabel. With a shrug he handed the target to Cabel and said, "Our secret."

The leather was worn and frayed in places. The milk bottle painted on the front was almost indiscernible from wear and use. Cabel took it from the gypsy and immediately felt the weight in the bottom. Now he understood why, as a boy, he had lost so many pennies at this booth. He looked over at Joe George who smiled and shrugged.

"We make no money if everyone win."

Cabel smiled and set the target on the counter.

"Kittie help make booths look nice," Joe George continued his story. "See. She hang our best prizes at top of booth. People see them when they play other games. They come to play here instead."

Cabel looked up at the rafter that ran along the front of the booth. A long line of chalkware kewpie dolls, horses, dogs, and other creatures hung from makeshift nooses made of bright ribbons and pieces of cloth. Some were figurines, others were banks, but all seemed cheerful in the face of their executions. Much of the chalkware looked garish and cheap, but others were charming. Daniela's work was unmistakable.

"What about boyfriends," Cabel asked, returning to his quest. "I understand that she was dating a musician from one of the bands that came through here."

"Ah, boys. Yes, Kittie like boys, and they like her, but she love one best. What is his name?"

"Gary Stevens," the girl behind the counter supplied. She darted a glance at Cabel then blushed again. Her fashionably bobbed brown hair seemed at odds with her clothes that, even to Cabel's untrained eyes, looked more than a few years out of date.

She had a nice figure, though, and pretty hazel eyes. Joe George was right; she would attract some players to the booth.

"Yes, Gary. She very sad when he die." Joe George hung his head again, though whether it was for Kittie or Gary Stevens, Cabel couldn't tell. Joe George lowered his voice and said, "Gangsters kill him in Chicago, near dance club he play at."

The girl behind him snorted and shook her head.

Someone called from the other end of the boardwalk, and Joe George turned and listened. "My son, Eddie. There is problem I must help with." He held out his hand and gave Cabel another bone-crushing shake. "You see Mama before you go. She want to talk with you." He left before Cabel could thank him.

"It wasn't a dance club, it was a speakeasy."

Cabel turned back to the counter. The girl who had seemed so industrious a moment before now pulled up a stool and leaned on the counter, settling in for a long chat.

"My name is Annette, by the way," she said, holding out a slim hand.

He shook it. "I'm Cabel Evans."

Annette's eyes widened. Cabel struggled not to flinch in the face of what was to come. She surprised him though. "You're that war hero who lives up on the bluff, the one that won't come out."

"That isn't quite true," he said, mentally balking at being called a hero.

She smiled and eyed him up and down as she played with a strand of her hair. "Well since you're standing here now, I guess it isn't." Her smile was coy, her eyes flirtatious. He chose to ignore the message they sent.

"You were telling me about Kittie and her boyfriend," Cabel said, trying to keep her on track.

"Boyfriends, you mean," she said, emphasizing the plural. She seemed pleased by his surprise. "She was a nice girl, and she really loved Gary, though I tried to warn her about him. But before she met him, she was walking around the park with Elmer Dupree.

Elmer's a real good dancer, and all of the girls, even the snooty ones from Chicago, want him to pick them for a dance. I don't care for him myself. He knows the girls like him, and he tries to take advantage." She sniffed in disgust then leaned over the counter, lowering her voice. "I don't know if its true but some people say that Elmer makes moonshine, mostly hard cider or berry wines, and that's where he gets his money for dance tickets and that leather coat he likes so much, as if anyone would mistake him for Charles Lindbergh!"

He tried to absorb this flow of information while thinking of the next question to ask but got lost in the details. Fortunately, Annette had more tales to tell so he left her to it.

"Now Gary, he played trumpet in the Wayne Sherman Band. They play at some speakeasies in Chicago, owned by Capone himself!" Her eyes widened in awe of her own words. Cabel wondered how she knew this or if she was simply repeating local gossip.

"Sometimes, the band plays here or over at the Crystal Palace in Coloma. They play in swanky places in Detroit and St. Louis, too. Once, they even took a train to New York City and played at some place there."

"But what about Gary Stevens? You said you warned Kittie about him," Cabel prompted.

She sat back on the stool and tried for a worldly pose as she shooed away a pair of teenagers who looked as if they wanted to play. She failed miserably in her attempts to seem mature, looking so young in fact that Cabel dropped his estimate of her age from eighteen to sixteen. "I told Kittie that any boy who traveled so much had to have girls everywhere and she shouldn't throw away a good thing with Elmer for Gary, but she wouldn't listen. Elmer was none too pleased to be set over for another boy, either, especially a city fellow."

Cabel decided he needed to meet this Elmer Dupree and take his measure. If even only part of Annette's description was accurate, Elmer may have taken his bruised feelings out on the one girl who had had the nerve to walk away from him.

"Well, thank you for talking with me. I appreciate your help."

"Well, I don't know what I'm helping you with, but it sure was fun."

Cabel was a few yards away when Annette called him back. "That band that Gary played in, the Wayne Sherman Band, they've been here all weekend. Tonight's their last show before they head back to Chicago."

"I might stop by and listen."

"They're a great band, so you'll want to do more than just listen." She motioned him closer. "I sell the tickets for the dances. Let me know if you want me to slip you a few extra." She gave him a wink then turned her attention to another group of boys who decided to test their throwing arms.

CHAPTER SEVEN

The night sky sparkled with stars, and moonlight gilded the waves that lapped against the shore. Silver Beach made good on its name. Lights from the rides and concessions glittered against the darkness of the bluff. The ever-present rumble of the roller-coaster mixed with laughter and music, creating a song as pure as summer.

Cabel risked scuffing the shine on his shoes to take the beach route to the ballroom rather than try to slip past Bessie George's booth on the boardwalk. Childish, he knew, but he had a newfound respect for the stories and rumors he had heard as a boy. Still tired from his earlier visit to the amusement park, Cabel wasn't prepared to face the woman who seemed to see him more clearly than he did himself.

Across the sand, near the point where the lake and river met, the Shadowland Ballroom glowed. The round building with its high, narrow windows mimicked the lighthouse that stood sentinel on the other side of the channel. Music, muted and indistinct, shifted into a recognizable melody as Cabel approached.

A large brown jug propped the ballroom door open. A group of young people mingled outside, chatting and fanning themselves with whatever was at hand. Cabel envied their carefree laughter and easy banter, wondering if he had ever been so young. In September he would be twenty-eight, which was hardly old, but then he didn't measure his age in terms of years, hadn't thought of himself as young in any respect since France.

No one gave him a second glance as he walked down the short path and stepped into a dream. The comfortable playfulness of Silver Beach was checked at the door, giving way to a sophistication that Cabel hadn't experienced since he had attended galas and other events at Chicago's premier hotels. The ballroom's high, domed ceiling, draped in silk, created the illusion of a pale pink sky while the polished wood floor gleamed below. There were no pillars or other supports, and it seemed as if the music itself kept the roof aloft. Although he had read about this architectural feat that promised perfect acoustics, nothing had prepared him for the graceful elegance of the design. Still looking up, he nearly collided with a young woman who smiled good-naturedly and asked, "First time here?" before disappearing into the crowd.

He nodded and continued to take in his surroundings. Deep leather booths with gleaming tables lined the far arc of the wall. Tables and chairs filled in the space between the wall and the cordoned-off dance floor. Along the curve nearest the stage was a booth selling dance tickets and a refreshment center offering fruit drinks, sodas, and snacks. The stage itself rivaled any he had seen in the dance halls of New Orleans. The band shell glittered with rhinestones and glass, perfectly framing the musicians on the stage. A glittering sign in front of the bandleader declared that the Wayne Sherman Band was playing tonight.

The music ended, and the dancers filed from the dance floor through a break in the cordons on the far end of the room while others lined up, tickets in hand, on the opposite side. Soon the dance floor filled again with couples and a few groups of girls who were tired of waiting to be asked. The band struck up a Charleston, and the crowd roared with appreciation as the dancers shimmied across the floor.

One young man stood out from the pack, dancing as if all eyes where on him, and they were, at least the female ones. The boy's dark hair gleamed with cream, and his clothes looked new and cared for in the way of a young man who intended to impress. His dance partner's smile was strained, and she struggled to keep up with his superior abilities. If the man had any class, Cabel thought, he would tone down his style to match that of his dance partner. Annette had been right, though, Elmer Dupree was at Shadowlands tonight.

Thinking of Annette reminded him that she, too, was here and decided to have her confirm that the young swank on the floor was in fact Elmer. He maneuvered his way through the crowd until he arrived at the ticket booth. Annette made change for a young man with an acne-pitted face and hopeful eyes. Without looking up, she snapped her fingers as the boy moved off, and Cabel realized that she was waiting for him to hand her money.

"Annette, do you remember me? We met earlier today."

The girl looked up, and Cabel was shocked to see she was wearing makeup. Her lovely face now looked tawdry and thick mascara hid her beautiful eyes.

"Do you like it?" she asked as she stood up and twirled before him. Gone was the outdated dress and heavy stockings. Barelegged and wearing a polka dot dress with a skirt that nearly skimmed her knees, she was now in fashion, and Cabel felt immensely sad. She leaned forward and confided, "My parents don't let me dress like this, so I keep this stuff at a friend's house."

He nodded, unsure of what to say, but she seemed to take this as approval and plunked herself back on the stool. "Did you want to buy a ticket? If you buy a couple, I could slip in an extra or two and no one would know."

"No, thank you. I just wanted to know if Elmer Dupree is here."

She made an effort to look bored. "Yeah, he's on the dance floor now. He's got money, but he gets the girls to buy the tickets and they're stupid enough to do it." She shook her head in disgust.

"Thank you," he said, moving out of the line. He had no intention of buying a ticket for the dubious honor of speaking with Elmer Dupree.

By the time the music ended, Cabel stood at the other end of the dance floor and caught Dupree's arm as the young man stepped passed the cordon. "I'd like to speak to you, if I may." They were nearly to the exit before the young man thought to complain about leaving his dates behind.

"Yes, I know that the girls are waiting, but that will make them even more anxious to dance with you when you return," Cabel assured him as he propelled Elmer out of the door and around the side of the building toward the river.

Elmer pulled his arm from Cabel's grasp as soon as they stopped. "Who are you, anyway?" he asked, eyeing Cabel while edging away. "You're not someone's brother, are you?"

Cabel shook his head, unsurprised that the boy needed to worry about receiving a beating over breaking a girl's heart, or worse. "No, my name is Cabel Evans. I'm a friend of Kittie's father, and I wanted to ask you a few questions about her."

"Oh, her." He tried to look disinterested, but even in the uncertain light, his eyes flashed with anger. "She thought she was too good for us yokels once a city boy noticed her. I tried to tell her that musicians were nothing but trouble, but she wouldn't listen."

"Were you angry when she started seeing the trumpet player?"

"Of course I was." Elmer paced, unmindful of the sand he was kicking into his perfectly turned pants cuffs. "Kittie and I had an understanding. It wasn't in writing or nothing, but she was my girl and she knew it."

"What about the girls inside, the ones you dance with?"

Elmer shot Cabel a look of distain. "That's just dancing. Those girls don't mean anything to me, and Kittie knew that. I don't love them like I loved her. Then she goes and takes up with some lying musician who used her to pass the time when he's in town and that was it. She said that he loved her; that he trusted her with his secrets but I knew the truth. He didn't care about her."

The hate in Elmer's voice resonated in Cabel. Here was a young man who was quite capable of killing if provoked. He began to wonder where Elmer was the night that Gary Stevens died. "How did you know that this man, Gary, didn't really care for Kittie?

"Because I heard him talking, that's how. You see that corner of the fishing pier?" Elmer asked, stabbing at the dark with a shaking finger. "One night when Kittie was working at her booth and the band was on a break, a bunch of the musicians sat over there talking." He gestured toward the fishing pier. "I was listening because I wanted to see what was so great about Gary Stevens, and I found out, too. Nothing!" Elmer kept his back to Cabel for a moment. When he spoke again, his voice held a barely restrained fury. "Gary was bragging about how he was screwing some woman who runs one of Capone's places in Chicago." He snorted in disgust. "Like a woman could do something that important."

Cabel thought of the nurses he had met during the war, many of whom, he was sure, could run the country if they were given a chance and certainly do a better job of it than Coolidge.

"He said how Kittie was sweet and all, but she was just a girl, and it was nice to have a real woman for a change. The other guys laughed at him and said that he shouldn't think he was too special, that this woman had a whole string of men. Gary sure didn't like hearing that," Elmer finished triumphantly. "I tried to tell Kittie, make her listen to me, but she said I was just jealous. I was so angry I could have…" His voice trailed off, taking most of his anger with it.

"Did you hurt her, Elmer?"

He spun around to face Cabel. "You mean like hit her or something? Hell no, I didn't hit her. What kind of a boyfriend do you think I am? I just wanted her back; then he gets killed and she dies and I don't know what to do." He reached into his back pocket, pulled out a hip flask, and offered it to Cabel. He declined. Elmer gave a philosophical shrug before taking a swig. "Just hard cider," he said. "I make it myself."

Cabel had forgotten what Annette had told him about Elmer's enterprises. The young man took risks and broke the law. He sounded sincerely indignant at being accused of hurting Kittie, but with all the girls he kept on a string, he had to be a convincing liar. He would never have survived this long without that particular skill.

Elmer tucked the hip flask into his pocket and wiped his mouth with his sleeve. "I don't know why you want to know about Kittie. She drowned in the river. I can't believe she would kill herself over that jerk, but I think she did."

"Don't spread nasty rumors about that nice girl."

Cabel and Elmer turned to find a man in his midforties or so standing near the ballroom's curved wall. "You get back inside, Elmer. You got a bunch of girls in there with broken hearts just waiting for you."

As quick as lightning Elmer changed from the angry boyfriend to the swank young man Cabel had first seen. The swagger was back in his step as he disappeared around the side of the building.

"Sometimes I want to smack that boy upside the head," the man said. He wore a light-colored shirt with an open vest over it that matched his well-tailored pants. "I'm Drake, by the way, Logan Drake. This is my park."

Cabel stepped forward and offered his hand. "I'm Cabel Evans, Mr. Logan. I've been coming to Silver Beach since I was a boy."

A smile creased Drake's weathered face. "I thought you were James Evans's grandson," he said, shaking Cabel's hand. "I heard you were at the park a couple of times in the last few days, and I was glad to know that you had come down here. I would have introduced myself at any rate, since I knew your granddad, but I wanted to try to catch you tonight. Bessie said you'd be here, and Joe George told me that I should have a talk with you."

A group of young people stumbled by in the sand as they headed for the lighted pier and cooler air. Cabel watched them pass before he spoke, organizing his thoughts and chastising himself for thinking he could pull anything over on Bessie George. "I'm not sure if there is anything that I need to talk to you about. I just need to know something about Kittie Arledge."

"Son, if you're asking questions about the people who work in my park, then you need to talk to me."

Cabel nodded, acknowledging his mistake. "I'm sorry. I just knew that the girl worked for the Georges so I started there." Unsure whether Drake was part of the coverup as to the cause of Kittie's death, he chose his next words carefully. "I knew Walter Arledge a long time ago, and he asked me to find out what I could about Kittie."

Drake scratched his scalp, looking confused. "I have daughters, too, and I know they can be a handful, but Kittie was a good girl. What did he want to know?"

"Why someone killed her." Cabel let the silence stretch between them as he had in Dr. Lewis's office. The response this time was very different.

"I don't understand. The doctor said she'd drowned. To be honest, I thought the same thing that Elmer did. That she…" He took a deep breath and expelled it loudly. "What do you mean, killed?"

Cabel hesitated but decided to trust his instincts, so he told the man what Walter had told him, leaving out Dr. Lewis's involvement. Drake listened then shook his head. "The mayor's a fool, and I don't care who knows I said that. If he thinks that lying about that girl's death will protect St. Joe, he's wrong, but I'm not surprised he'd do it." Drake pulled out a pack of cigarettes and offered one to Cabel. He nodded his thanks, lit it from

Drake's lighter, and inhaled deeply. Nicotine flowed through him, smoothing away an edge he hadn't realized was there.

"Mayor Delong thinks that St. Joe is his little kingdom and everyone in it exists just for the pleasure of serving him." Drake gestured, taking in Silver Beach and the ballroom. "This park brings in the tourists from Chicago, Indiana, Wisconsin, you name it. If they stay in St. Joe rather than go to Benton Harbor and the House of David, they stay because of me. You think Delong appreciates that? No, he does not." Drake threw his half-smoked cigarette into the sand and ground it out with a vicious turn of his heel. "He and all the others up on the bluff make money because of me, but they treat the people who live and work down here like they're nothing but scum. If he thought that the murder of one of the sand bunnies would hurt business, of course he'd lie about it." He stuck another cigarette between his lips and lit it.

"But what about Kittie? Would you have any idea who would have killed her?"

Drake shook his head. "No. Now if it were Gary who had been drowned in the river, I would suspect that Elmer did it, but I don't think he would've touched Kittie. Of course that boy's got a wild streak and a temper too. If he has had a drink or two in him, well, I guess anything's possible." He shook his head at the thought. "Thing is, I think he really loved Kittie. I can't see him killing her."

Cabel knew how much people could hurt, even kill, those they loved. Dark memories tried to push their way to the surface, but he shoved them back into the depths and asked, "If not Elmer, then who?"

"I don't know, son, maybe some vagrant, someone from out of town. We have a lot of people who pass through here. Most of 'em are good, but not all, and there are some that don't really belong anywhere and so they come here."

Like me, Cabel thought to himself.

Drake continued. "We get mixed-race couples sometimes and others who, well, let's say, they have more in common than most." He paused, waiting to see if Cabel understood what he was implying.

When it was clear he didn't, Drake gave a nod, directing his attention toward a pair of well-dressed men standing near the ballroom. Cabel still didn't understand until one man discretely reached over and briefly held the hand of the other. Ah. He turned back to Drake.

"Now, I don't want you to think I'm putting blame anywhere," Drake said, and it was clear that he meant every word. "Couples that are a bit different are quiet and they have their own problems, but they sure don't want any extra attention. I can't imagine any of them having anything to do with Kittie's death." He paused and looked out at the black depths of the lake. "Maybe I do want to blame them, or the vagrants that dig through the garbage cans after we close. It would be a comfort if it was someone like that rather than someone who knew her."

"Or who you know," Cabel added, finishing the thought.

Drake nodded. "I always know what goes on in my park, or at least I like to think I do. I know that Elmer has a flask of hard cider and some of my girls give dance tickets away to cute boys, but I also know who's trouble and who isn't. Still, I don't have a clue as to who might have killed poor Kittie."

"What about the musicians, guys like Gary Stevens?"

Drake leaned against the curved wall of his ballroom and sighed. "Most of the boys in the bands that come through here are nice young men, but some of the better-known bands or the ones that come out of Chicago, they tend to have a few bad ones in the group. I didn't like Gary Stevens, but I thought he was more spoiled than bad." He shook his head. "I didn't tell Kittie that. I thought the worst thing that would happen is that she'd get her heart broken, maybe learn something from it. I've been sick with the thought she'd killed herself over that young man. Of course, knowing someone killed her doesn't make it any better. If Gary had been alive when Kittie died, I'd have thought he'd done it. There was just something about him that wasn't right." He shook his head but didn't explain. "Since he was already dead, well, he couldn't have done it, could he?"

"No, I guess not." Cabel realized that he was holding the dead butt of his cigarette and let it fall to the sand. "I promised Walter Arledge that I would try to find some answers for him, but I don't think that it will be possible."

Drake smiled and held out his hand to Cabel. "You're an Evans, son, you'll figure things out. And please, let me know if there is anything I can do for you." His face grew serious. "I don't like the idea of a killer running around my park."

Cabel nodded in understanding but felt the weight of yet another person's expectations settle on his shoulders. Drake walked off, greeting people as he went. The band inside began another song.

It was time to go home.

CHAPTER EIGHT

On Monday Cabel spent a surprisingly pleasant morning with Marta and Jorge planning the kitchen renovations. Marta giggled like a schoolgirl over ads for any appliance or gadget that was new and easier to use than the near-relics that currently filled the kitchen. Jorge took a more thoughtful approach and had a broader view of the possibilities. His suggestions to expand the kitchen and add a mudroom were good, and in the end Cabel decided to leave the project to the old man and have him oversee the necessary repairs to the house as well. Jorge would do the job well and not take advantage of the situation.

Once Jorge stopped protesting and began to draw his ideas down on paper with Marta oohing and aahing over his shoulder, Cabel went to his favorite chair on the back porch and settled in with the paper. Stock prices were up again. Cabel had forgotten to call his broker and the delay had made him money, but his instincts warned that it was time to cash out as much and as quickly as possible with regard to that particular stock. He went to the hall where the phone hung near the parlor door, spoke with the operator, and waited for the call to go through.

Cabel was midargument with his broker when the doorbell chimed. Marta hurried past to answer the door. Cabel barely noticed as Marta held a lengthy discussion with the young boy who stood in the doorway until something about the look on his housekeeper's face made him pause. After issuing curt and decisive sell orders, he ended the call with his broker and turned to see what was wrong.

With one hand placed firmly on the boy's shoulder, Marta steered him into the house. The child looked to be about seven or eight, with large blue eyes that took in his surroundings with avid interest. His towhead swiveled in constant motion, reminding Cabel of a spring-headed toy he had played with when he was very young.

"He says that his father sent him to get you," Marta said. "And something about a burglary…"

"That's right," the boy said, abandoning his wide-eyed examination of the house to focus on Cabel. "Our house got broke into, it did! The window's smashed, and there's clothes and things everywhere. Ma's crying and Dad's yelling, and then he sent me to fetch you."

The boy nearly danced with excitement, giving Cabel a chance to look him over at greater length. His clothes were clean, though his pants were patched and the shirt frayed at the collar and cuffs. The shape of the boy's face and his general coloring helped Cabel finally place him. "Are you Walter Arledge's boy?"

"Well of course I am. Who else would I be?"

"Mind your manners when you talk to Mr. Cabel," Marta chided, shaking the boy's shoulder in rebuke.

"Yes, ma'am." The boy tried to look contrite but couldn't quite hide the gleam in his eyes. "My name's Nate, and Dad wants you to come right away. Sir," he added with a quick glance at Marta.

Cabel picked up his coat, straightened his tie, and motioned for the boy to lead the way outside. The stifling July day turned him back, and he handed the coat to Marta. Proprieties were eased on this side of the lake, and the heat made it a good day to take advantage of that fact.

The boy bounded down the street then hurried back to Cabel, like a puppy running ahead of its master before returning to make sure that the master was still following, only to run ahead again.

By the time they reached the Arledge house on Pine Street, Nate had walked twice as far as Cabel but covered the same amount of ground. If the boy was tired from his efforts, he gave no sign of it, which Cabel found annoying as he discretely used his handkerchief to wipe the sweat from his brow.

Walter Arledge stood outside a small clapboard house. Beach grass and a few hardy bushes dotted the front yard that was more sand than dirt. Beyond the house the crowded public beach started just a few scant yards from the back door. Scowling, Walter stood with his back to his home as he glared at the empty road that led to the top of the bluff. When he saw Cabel, he gave a sharp nod then sent the boy away to join his mother. "I told my wife and the girls to go down to the beach for a while. I didn't want them here when the police came, but I don't think they're coming."

"What? Why?"

Walter glared at Cabel and gestured to the top of the bluff. "Because we don't live up there, that's why." He stomped around the side of the house. Cabel followed. A window that faced the beach was broken, jagged pieces of glass still held tight in the frame. An upended bucket stood beneath it, used as a step, Cabel guessed, to climb into the house. Several footprints were visible in the sand. Walter Arledge knelt by one of them. Cabel joined him.

"I had someone from the Cooper & Wells factory call up the bluff and ask them to send the police down, but I don't think they've bothered. I bet they think we don't have anything worth stealing, and I guess they're right." Walter looked away for a moment, his body rigid, hands clenched at his side. Cabel waited, looking out over the sand and water, knowing the man would speak when he was ready. Walter turned back and pointed to a distinct footprint. "See that? No one who lives down here has shoes like that. We wear work boots, and most of them are patched on the sole, but these aren't patched and they sure aren't work boots."

Cabel looked down at Walter's shoes then back at the footprint. He was right. The print had a more pointed toe and narrower heel than a work boot, and the sole was intact. Cabel nodded and stood.

"People around here don't wear that kind of shoe except maybe to church, but most of us can't afford them." He glanced briefly down at Cabel's expensive half-boots then stepped around him, back straight as a rod, and led the way to the front stoop with its small, drooping porch and sagging swing "Whoever did this isn't from here, or at least from below the bluff."

"I'm sure you're right," Cabel said, suddenly embarrassed by his clothing and status. This was odd, given how little thought he put into either one of them. "What did they take?"

Anger colored Walter's face a deep, cruel red. "I wish I knew. The house is tore up from end to end, but the worst of the mess is in the room the older girls share, I mean shared." He blinked several times as anger warred with grief. "I don't think anything's missing, but whoever did this ripped up clothes and cushions. The dishes are broken, and I don't think my wife will ever get over this." He turned away again.

After a moment, Cabel asked, "When did this happen?"

"I don't know. We've been out in the countryside the last few days, picking vegetables. One of the farmers knew me from when I had my own bit of land and one of his sons drove into town to get me and the wife and kids. I've been out in the fields, along with my oldest girl." His voice caught for a moment, but he cleared his throat and pushed on. "My wife helped with the canning, and the little ones helped out where they could. We left on Friday and just got back. People around here look out for each other, but no one noticed the window broken until this morning, so I'm guessing that it happened last night."

Walter stepped into the house, and Cabel followed. Glass shards glittered on the scuffed wood floors near the broken window. Stuffing and bits of fabric covered most of the floor of the front room. What little the family had in the way of mementos lay shattered amid the wreckage. Pieces of a chalkware bank that had Daniela's unmistakable touch lay on top of torn strips of cloth that had once been curtains. A bit of glass arm here and porcelain petticoat there gave testament that more than one figurine had died a needless death. A glance into the kitchen showed more devastation. Dishes were smashed, and worse, what little food Walter's wife had been able to can for the winter now lay in a smeared mess in the middle of the room.

Wordlessly Walter led the way up a narrow flight of boxed-in stairs to the second floor. Clothes and scraps of cloth were strewn across the hallway. Each of the three small bedrooms had been pillaged, but the last one held the most destruction.

The girls had used whatever they could find to make their room cheerful. Scraps of bright material had been sewn together to make curtains and blankets but were now torn back into scraps. A chest of drawers had also served as a dressing table, but the few bottles of creams and potions that the girls had collected now lay smashed and ground into the floor. The drawers had been emptied of clothes that were ripped, shredded, and thrown about. Whoever had done this was very angry or very desperate. Cabel thought of Kittie and a cold fear settled in his belly.

Neither man spoke until they stood outside once more. "Do you think this had anything to do with what happened to my girl?"

"I don't know," Cabel said honestly, though his instincts told him that there was a connection. "I've been to Silver Beach a few times and spoken with the Georges and Logan Drake and a few other people, but I haven't learned anything yet that I think can help us."

Cabel paused a moment as the implications of this statement hit home, of how quickly his life had shifted from solitude to social. One week. It had been just over one week since Walter had disturbed his sanctuary asking for help. Ten days. Cabel counted them on his fingers as he recalled his actions. He'd seen Dr. Lewis, gone to Silver Beach not once but three times and had left the house this morning with Nate without a second thought. And somewhere along the way, Arledge had become Walter. Cabel shied away from the implications of these events only to find Walter looking at him with quiet confidence and great expectation.

Cabel wasn't an officer anymore, and Walter was no longer an enlisted man under his care. Couldn't Arledge see the present rather than the past? Whoever Walter thought him to be, Cabel certainly wasn't that man anymore. Maybe he never had been.

Taking a deep breath and running his fingers through his hair in frustration, Cabel looked at the mess around him rather than at the mess inside himself. "I'll have my housekeeper, Marta, gather up her daughter and a few of their friends. They'll come down here and give your wife a hand cleaning this up." Cabel silenced Walter's protest with a wave of his hand. "I'll make sure they bring some food down, too, maybe a picnic for your family. They can stay on the beach a bit longer while the women work on cleaning all of this up."

"Mr. Evans," Walter said in a voice that had turned hard and cold, "I sent my boy to fetch you so you could see what happened, see if it had anything to do with Kittie. I don't need your charity."

"And I'm not offering it," Cabel snapped back. "Maybe this happened because of Kittie or maybe it happened because I've been asking questions about her. Either way, I'm involved. You brought me into this, and I will see it through."

"That may be, but you don't have to—"

"Yes, I do. You don't want your wife and children wading through this mess, do you?" He took Walter's silence for assent. "Let me help you clean this up, and afterwards we can talk about what to do next."

Cabel waited for Walter to confer with his wife before heading back up the bluff. After a brief discussion with Marta, he was sure that she would handle the immediate needs of the family while he had a chat with the police.

|||||

The police department's red brick building trapped the afternoon heat as securely as it did its prisoners. Cabel's coat, retrieved from Marta when he stopped at the house, felt like a steam compress plastered against his body. All around him police officers worked in their dark blue woolen uniforms, and Cabel wondered how they could go about their duties without suffering from heat stroke.

The police sergeant stationed behind the large, scarred desk eyed Cabel as if sizing him up for a prisoner's uniform, an exercise the officer had been enjoying, on and off, for the past forty minutes. The promised appearance of the chief of police had yet to occur, and Cabel wondered if the man was even in the building. He stood and stretched, watching the police sergeant watching him, before making yet another round of the dingy gray room, looking at the wanted posters and reading notices of public hearings posted on the walls. He was reading one of the notices that wanted a city ordinance to bar children from eating ice cream on public sidewalks when a large, barrel-chested man swaggered into the room. Heavily adorned with medals, gold braid, and epilates wide enough to serve as airplane wings, the uniform announced the man. Steel-gray hair was cut in a military style and cool gray eyes completed the impression of a man of authority.

"So you're Mr. Cabel Evans." The police chief delivered a strong handshake with this pronouncement, clearly intending to intimidate.

"Yes," Cabel responded with an intentionally broad smile that caused the other man's to briefly falter. "I'd like to speak with you about a few matters, if I may."

"Of course, of course. We always want to help the public with its pesky little problems." The chief winked at his sergeant who smirked in response as Cabel walked past. He followed the older man down a dark corridor and up a flight of stairs to a large office. Through the small but blessedly open windows, the lake and sky leant color to an otherwise drab room.

"Please have a seat." The police chief gestured to a small chair on one side of a massive desk while settling down on a more comfortable-looking seat on the other side. A plaque on the desk finally gave the man a proper name, Mark Bradley.

"Chief Bradley," Cabel began.

"Please, son, just call me 'Chief.' Everyone does; well, those from up here, anyway." He gave a knowing smile and wink as if he and Cabel shared some private joke.

"Thank you, Chief. Now the reason for my visit—"

"Oh, I know why you're here."

"Really?" Was the chief in league with Bessie George?

"Of course I do. I understand you had some problems down at Silver Beach. Some ruffians pushed you down on the boardwalk a few days ago, and I heard you and young Elmer Dupree were fighting over a girl. I was a bit surprised at that, seeing how young some of his girls are, but darn, they sure are pretty, aren't they?" Another wink, more lascivious this time, made Cabel's skin crawl.

The mixture of fact, innuendo, and blatant lies momentarily stunned him into silence. He felt his face flush with a heat that had nothing to do with the temperature of the room. Head pounding, hands shaking, Cabel struggled for control. Fear and anger flared within him while glimpses of the war danced around the edges of his mind. As a boy and young man he had never been violent, never raised a hand in anger. And then he was trained to fight, to kill. But even then he used violence only against the enemy. Except for once. In Chicago. Against his own father. Shame flowed through him now, overpowering the fear and anger.

He took a deep breath and looked at Chief Bradley who was eyeing him with glee, pleased, apparently for having upset Cabel to such a degree. The man was a bully. That realization helped to calm him.

Forcing himself to sit back in the too-small chair, he stretched slightly, casually crossed his ankles. Shaking his head as if in sad disgust, he said, "I realize that I'm used to a different, shall we say 'standard' of policing, being from Chicago, but I am surprised at the poor quality of your information."

The chief's face, already florid in the heat, took on an alarming shade of purple. "How dare you."

Cabel slipped into his boardroom persona, the one best suited for when a company came to him with a subpar offering. "My dear sir, I am merely pointing out that your supposed information is inaccurate at best and possibly slanderous. As I would dislike marring my return to St. Joe by filing a lawsuit, let's assume that you had poor sources for your supposed facts and move on to the reason for my visit."

The chief did battle with some inner conflict. The big man's beefy hands flexed and clenched as if preparing to land a punch. He eyed Cabel, much as his sergeant had, but Cabel refused to drop his eyes. In the end it was the chief who looked away.

"You're right, of course," he said with false jocularity. "I should know better than to listen to gossip passed along by my men who patrol the beach front." He gave a shrug, his massive shoulders barely contained by the strained wool of his coat. Leaning forward, he folded his hands together on his desk and forced his face into an obvious parody of someone who wanted to help. "Just what can I do for you today, Mr. Cabel?"

"I understand that a call was placed to this department about a break-in at a house down on Pine Street. I was wondering why no one was sent down to investigate."

"Now, Mr. Cabel, you might have spent your summers here in your fancy house, but then you went back to your other fancy house in Chicago. You never lived here, not really, and you don't understand how we do things."

"Obviously."

If the chief caught the sarcasm, he chose to ignore it. "St. Joseph is a small town compared to Benton Harbor and Niles, but we still get a lot of calls from people needing help. Sometimes one or two of them slip between the cracks. It's unfortunate, but it happens."

"From what I've heard, calls from below the bluff often slip through the cracks unless it's from Cooper & Wells or Silver Beach."

"Now, Mr. Cabel"—the chief leaned back in his chair, arms folded across his belly—"I'm sure I don't know what you're implying, but maybe you're the one with the poor facts on this issue."

"Perhaps"—Cabel leaned forward, frustrated at the height disadvantage his small chair created—"but I was down on Pine Street earlier today. You see, the house that was broken into belonged to a friend of mine."

"And just how is it that you've come to know the Arledge family?"

"Well, I guess that call didn't slip too far down between the cracks after all."

The chief's face reddened when he realized his mistake, but he gave a small shrug and kept his smile firmly in place. "As I said, things get lost. But I'm surprised that you would know anyone from down there."

"Walter Arledge and I served together in France." Cabel kept his face impassive despite the whirl of emotions that always accompanied any reference to the war. "We've renewed our friendship recently, and I've taken an interest in him and his family. The loss of their eldest daughter has been hard on them."

"Poor little thing, drowning like that."

"He's not convinced that that's how she died."

"So I've heard." The chief gave a dismissive wave of his hand. "That little sand bunny slipped off the pier and died. You're not doing her family any favors by asking around about her death."

"So you do have some accurate information about my activities."

The chief's eyes hardened. He straightened in his chair and wagged a finger at Cabel. "You listen to me, Mr. Cabel. Leave that girl's death be, or something worse than a break-in might happen to that family."

"If I find out that you or your men had anything to do with—"

"Of course I didn't." The chief rose to his feet. Cabel did likewise. "I'm just saying that a lot of bad things have happened to that family, and it sure would be a shame if more misery was visited upon them. Stay out of things that don't concern you, Mr. Cabel. You never know when misery just might find you."

Although startled by the threat and the menace in the chief's voice, Cabel couldn't help but laugh. Misery had taken up residence in his life a long time ago, and the chief, for all of his bluster, was no match for that which already plagued him.

The chief studied him with concern and a bit of fear, obviously disconcerted by the response his threat had evoked.

Shifting back to his business persona, Cabel said, "I just want you to know, Chief, that the Arledge family has me watching out for them and if they need assistance from the police in the future, I expect them to receive it in a timely manner." Without waiting for a response, Cabel left the office and the stifling heat of the building. Stripping off his coat, he walked down the street smiling at the memory of the chief's stunned face. The smile faded as he realized that if the chief felt comfortable threatening a privileged member of the community, he must have the support of the mayor. The two had plotted to cover up the murder of a sixteen-year-old girl. What else were they willing to do to keep that secret?

CHAPTER NINE

Cabel trudged down the street, jacket slung over his shoulder, exhausted either by the heat or his encounter with Chief Bradley. What he needed now was a glass of Marta's lemonade, maybe a cookie or two, and the quiet solitude of his back porch. Reaching his home, he turned up the walk, debating whether to go through the house to let Marta know he was back or just slip through the side yard and settle into his waiting chair.

Shouts of laughter rang through the yard. Nate tore around the side of the house, followed closely by a slightly older girl whose dress flapped around her gangly legs as she closed the distance between them. For a moment Cabel felt as if he had fallen through a hole in time. He was ten, racing Jon across the yard to the large maple tree that served as home base with Jim tagging along behind. Another shout and he was back to the present, the weight of his life resettling heavily on his shoulders.

Nate's laughter turned to angry yelps of pain. Cabel ran to the side yard then slid to a stop. Nate lay on the ground, his sister on top of him, slapping at his arms and head with her open hands. Before he could intervene, Kaye Arledge appeared from the back yard and plucked the girl off of Nate before dumping her unceremoniously beside her brother.

"Belinda, I told you to keep that boy busy, not beat him to church and back."

Belinda Arledge stood and pointed down at her brother. "But he…"

"I don't care what he did. You're older and know better."

"That's right. You're older," Nate chimed in as he rose to his feet.

"Don't you get smart with me, boy." Kaye rounded on her son, shaking a finger in his face. "What would Mr. Cabel think, coming home to find you two acting like hooligans, fighting in his yard?"

"I think he'd find it very entertaining," Cabel said, stepping forward and offering Kaye his hand. "I know we met this morning but under such poor circumstances that I'd like to do it properly. It's a pleasure to meet you."

Kaye Arledge flushed a deep, becoming pink that showed off her wide blue eyes and light brown hair. Thin as the reeds that grew near the river, she was also strong and, Cabel guessed, very resilient. She let him take her hand and give it a brief shake before it fell back to her side. Nate's giggle brought her back to herself, and she gave a small laugh.

"Oh, Mr. Cabel, it seems to be my luck that you would catch me at my worst twice today."

"Mrs. Arledge, I doubt anyone has ever seen you at anything but your best."

Kaye Arledge flushed again, a pleased, shy smile on her face.

Cabel felt suddenly awkward in the presence of Walter's wife. The heat of the day seemed oppressive again, trapping him in this time and place. Kaye smiled down at her toes, bare and tanned against the green lawn.

"Is the lemonade ready yet?"

Nate's demand broke the spell. Kaye gave a nod and led the youngsters toward the back porch. Cabel followed, unheeding, until he reached the back yard. His footsteps faltered. Heart racing, he turned in a slow circle as his mind tried to comprehend the magnitude to which his sanctuary had been breached.

A ball, bat, and tattered glove lay abandoned under the sugar maple. Propped against its trunk, a worn cloth doll waited patiently for tea to be served in the small, chipped cups laid out in front of it. The laundry vat bubbled near the back fence, and clothes he had never seen before hung limp from the line in the breezeless afternoon. Two young women laughed together as they pushed sopping clothes through the wringer set up near the rinse basin. The porch, *his porch*, was strewn end to end with boxes and jumbles of this and that. His chair lay buried beneath a pile of torn and soiled bedding.

A band tightened around his chest, forcing the air from his lungs. The world started to spin and fade. Cabel leaned against the porch railing, holding one of the pillars for support, uncaring that he stood in Marta's flowerbed. Through a veil as thin as tissue, he could hear the booms of the cannons and the screams of the dying. Hours passed or maybe only seconds before the nearby voices eased him back to the world of the living.

Jorge and Walter stood together near the shed, deep in conversation, heads bent over a clipboard with one or the other occasionally looking up at the house. The men paid no attention to him, and he realized that his attack had gone unnoticed. Focusing on their voices, Cabel took slow, deep breaths. After a few minutes, his body stopped shaking and the world righted.

Observing the men standing side by side, Cabel realized that Walter was much closer to Jorge's age than his own. During the Great War, it was common for the lower ranking officers to be younger than the troops they led, but the burden of leadership had somehow confused Cabel into believing that he was older than those who had served under him. Once he had proved himself both as an officer and a soldier, his men had looked to him for more than orders and strategy, but for comfort and support as well. While he served as a surrogate father, uncle, and brother to men who faced daily horrors and near-certain death, his youth had slipped unnoticed beneath the mud and muck of the trenches.

The back door banged open as Marta backed through it carrying a tray laden with glasses and a pitcher of lemonade. Before she could negotiate the steps, Walter hurried forward, relieving her of her burden and carrying the tray to the table and chairs set out near the middle of the lawn. Shade from the large maple tree dappled the setting as it had during the summers of his childhood. For a moment Cabel could almost believe that his parents and grandparents would come out to join them.

Instead Kaye Arledge came onto the porch carrying a plate piled high with molasses crinkle cookies, Cabel's favorites. Belinda and Nate followed the cookies with hopeful expressions on their young faces, and together with their mother, they made a charming parade across the lawn. Jorge and Walter were joined by the two young women near the table. One was Jorge's and Marta's daughter Daisy, Cabel realized, and the other must be Anne, Walter's daughter, who was just a few years younger than Kittie had been.

As Cabel watched the two families mingle around the table, sipping lemonade and munching cookies, he began to feel like a bit character in a theatrical production. After a moment, Jorge noticed him and walked toward the porch. Cabel forced himself to stand and move away from his support pillar, meeting the elderly man halfway. Jorge held out a molasses cookie, which Cabel accepted. The sweet smell of sugar balanced the deeper notes of molasses. His mouth watered for a bite, but his stomach warned of dire consequences.

"I thought this might be a bit much for you, all of these people here and all, but Marta said you told her it would be okay."

Cabel remembered asking her to help the Arledges with the mess at their house and shook his head. "She has her own way of interpreting instructions, doesn't she?"

Jorge gave a small laugh of appreciation tinged with relief. "That she does, my boy, that she does. You know, your grandmother understood my Marta, letting her run things as she saw fit but giving very specific instructions on things Miss Evans wanted just so." Jorge sipped his lemonade. "Lots of opinions between the two of them, but in time your grandma learned to trust my wife's judgment on some matters. Things generally worked out for the best."

Cabel grunted then risked taking a bite of his cookie. The sweet crunch of the outside gave way to the soft, dense center. As he chewed, the tastes and textures blended to create perfection. Nodding in appreciation, he said, "She hasn't lost her touch."

"No, son, she hasn't." Jorge turned to rejoin the group around the table. Cabel followed, wondering if he and Jorge had been discussing the same thing.

At the table, Cabel learned that he had guessed correctly when he was reintroduced to Jorge and Marta's youngest daughter, Daisy. She had been ten years old the last time he had seen her. Married now and with a small child and, Cabel guessed, another on the way, she carried a bit of both of her parents in her face and manners. Her smile was open and welcoming, and if she held a grudge for the work she had done with her mother but for which she'd never been paid, she gave no sign.

He was right about Anne as well. Up close he could see that she was all of fourteen and had just begun the metamorphosis from girl to woman. Standing near her mother, she ducked her head whenever his glance passed near. Shoulders stooped and hair curtaining her face, she seemed the antithesis of the girl he believed her sister, Kittie, had been. He wondered if the awkward shyness was Anne's natural personality or a sad consequence of her older sister's death.

Marta pointedly ignored him, chatting with Kaye about gardens and food preservation with an exuberance that bordered on manic. When the refreshments were consumed and groups broke away to return to their tasks, Marta planted herself in front of him, arms crossed over her ample bosom and glared in defiance.

"I couldn't leave them down there, Cabe, not in that mess."

He opened his mouth to speak, but she wasn't through.

"They've lost near-everything, and Walter doesn't have a steady job right now. As soon as I heard that he had helped build the ballroom at Silver Beach, I knew he could help Jorge with all of the work that needs doing around here." She held up a hand to forestall an argument that wasn't forthcoming. "They need a place to stay while that house of theirs gets set back to rights, and they need to feel like it isn't charity. Their neighbor ladies are getting their house cleaned up enough to sleep in. I didn't think you could handle having them here full-time, but until they get their things sorted and that house organized, they'll be spending their days here."

He opened his mouth again.

"And, Cabe, you know I could use some help around here and Daisy's giving me another grandchild so she won't be much use, especially with her Toby walking now and getting into everything. Kaye's a hard worker and could use the money you'd pay her."

Cabel gave up trying to get a word in and waited until Marta finished having her say.

"I also know how much you like your back porch, but we need it right now so I've set you up someplace else."

She turned and marched across the lawn, arms swinging, back as straight as a soldier in formation. Jorge watched the procession, his face twitching as if to hide a smile. Cabel followed the woman who was supposed to be working for him until they turned the corner at the far side of the house. On the rickety side porch that had been slated for major repair stood an old wicker chair that Cabel knew from experience was anything but comfortable. A small table stood nearby, gently sloping with the floor. His newspaper awaited him on the sagging chair seat. No cushion had been added for his comfort, he noted, and wondered if this was an oversight or a subtle message from Marta.

"We'll work as fast as we can to sort through the things on the back porch, but it might take awhile. Clothes and such have to be cleaned and fixed or thrown away, and these folks can't afford to do too much of that. There are lots of decisions to make." She eyed him pointedly as if to imply that he was hindering this process. "I'm baking a ham for dinner tonight. I'll get everyone fed then send them home. There should be enough left over for ham biscuits for breakfast and maybe some sandwiches for lunch. That Nate can eat, and I don't know when he's last had a decent meal. Not that his parents haven't tried," Marta said, making sure that Cabel knew where the blame lay. "It's just harder for some to find work right now, and Walter's doing the best he can."

"You're right, of course," Cabel said. From the look of relieved triumph on Marta's face, he realized that she thought he had agreed to her entire scheme. Perhaps he had.

Marta knew better than to push her luck further. Wiping her hands on her apron, she started back around the house. "I'll try to keep the little ones away from this side of the house. It's not a safe place for them to be playing anyway."

No, but it's safe enough for me to be exiled to, Cabel thought sourly. With a sigh of resignation, he climbed onto the porch, wondering with every step if the underlying support posts had rotted through. The chair was as uncomfortable as he remembered and no amount of adjusting his posture improved matters. Sounds of work and laughter drifted from the back yard, making it impossible to concentrate on the paper. He held out for over an hour, more out of stubbornness than anything else. Finally he rolled up the paper and tossed it on the table only to have it roll off and hit the floor where it continued its progress until it disappeared over the edge of the porch.

Stepping gingerly, he made his way across the sagging planks until he arrived safely on the side lawn. As he came around to the back of the house, he found his gaze lingering with uncomfortable longing at his true refuge. Maybe Marta didn't appreciate how important the porch was to him, he thought, or maybe it didn't matter.

Anne sat on the floor of the back porch amongst the shambles of her family's life, sorting through a box with the earnest concentration of someone trying very hard not to cry. She didn't hear him until he reached the top of the steps and jumped nearly a foot when she realized she wasn't alone.

"I'm sorry. I didn't mean to startle you," Cabel said in the gentlest voice he could manage. The girl nodded but kept her eyes down. Unsure of what to do next, and as there were no chairs available, Cabel twitched up his pant legs and settled himself on the floor across from the girl. A smallish wooden box sat open between them, its contents partially sorted into small piles.

Anne selected another item from the box, a ticket stub of some sort, and after some internal debate placed it on one of the piles. She reached into the box for the next item, but her hand started to shake and everything slipped through her fingers. Tears showed in her eyes as she shoved her hand beneath her apron.

The drooping side porch suddenly seemed a paradise. Cabel could barely manage his own emotions, he doubted he could help Anne with hers, but he didn't want to leave the girl alone. He cleared his throat with a self-consciousness that reminded him of his eleventh grade physics teacher, only to find he had nothing to say.

The girl's hair had fallen across her face again, and he fought the urge to push it behind her ears. From the brief glimpses he had of her, he knew she would never achieve true beauty, but the foundation was set for a type of prettiness that would attract the attention of boys if she would just let them see her. He sighed and looked out over his yard, both familiar and entirely changed, and wondered what to do.

"This is her box, Kittie's I mean." Anne's voice was as tentative as her manner. "I know there are other things I should be doing, but..." Her voice choked. The sobs started softly but quickly became a torrent of tears.

With a panic usually reserved for nightmares, Cabel looked for help, but the crowd that had invaded the backyard had somehow disappeared. He looked back at the weeping girl. With a gesture more remembered than intended, Cabel reached into his pocket and brought forth a clean handkerchief. The girl accepted it gratefully, blotting her face and blowing her nose. The moment became more awkward when neither of them knew what to do with the now-soiled linen. Cabel rescued the situation by stuffing the thing back into his pocket.

He and Anne both stared into the box, less out of curiosity than out of necessity of something to do. The girl's slim hand reached in again and pulled out a folded piece of paper. She unfolded it with intense concentration, pressing the seams flat against the painted floorboards of the porch. She looked up and handed it to Cabel as if asking what to do with it.

The paper was a flyer that advertised the Wayne Sherman Band and listed each of its scheduled summer performances by date and location. The band played mostly at specific clubs in Chicago and Detroit, stopping in Grand Rapids, St. Joseph, and occasionally Coloma, as they traveled between the two larger cities. There were two dates when the band would play in St. Louis, but otherwise the schedule was a consistent loop between the Michigan and Chicago locations.

"Gary gave her that when he and Kittie first..." Anne's hand flew to her mouth, too late to keep the secret from escaping.

"It's okay, Anne, I know about your sister and Gary. Your parents know too."

She looked at him with an awe that children have for adults who seem to know everything. How quickly that would change.

"She kept everything he ever gave her, except a bracelet, but I guess she was wearing that when..."

"So what exactly is in her box?" he asked more to forestall another bout of tears than any real curiosity, though maybe a clue lay hidden among Kittie's bits of treasure.

"She kept everything, Kittie did. Mom always called her a little squirrel, storing away this and that." Anne gave a brief smile as her hand hovered over the piles then gestured to the largest. "This stuff is mostly from school, grade cards, ribbons she won, like that. Now this one is stuff that she saved when she was seeing Elmer." She poked a finger through the medium-sized pile, revealing tickets for dances at the old dance hall, passes to the House of David Amusement Park in Benton Harbor, dried flowers, bits of ribbon and cloth.

"What about that pile?" Cabel asked, pointing to the smallest one.

"That's the stuff from Gary." Anne shrugged as if dismissing the trumpet player as inconsequential. "I don't know why she left Elmer for that musician. Elmer's so much more handsome and nice and…"

"Is this all there is—from Gary I mean?" The last thing Cabel wanted to hear was a list of Elmer's dubious charms.

"Pretty much, except for a bank that Gary won for her at Silver Beach, but it got broken when—"

Nate flew out of the back door, banging it hard against the wall as he sailed through. Kaye followed quickly, yelling at the boy who had apparently stolen several cookies before disappearing behind the shed.

Cabel rose stiffly to his feet. It seemed that while he was starting to remember that he wasn't an old man, his body was reminding him that youth didn't last forever. Kaye abandoned her chase of her wayward son and came over to see what he and Anne were doing. Cabel quickly extracted himself from the scene. There was a possibility, however slight, that Marta would come out and give him the job of sorting through boxes.

He was in the house and halfway up the stairs before he noticed that he still had the Wayne Sherman flyer in his hand. Reading it again, he realized that the band had been in town the night Kittie was killed as well as this past weekend, when the break-in occurred. Of course it was playing in Chicago when Gary was killed, but what about the other two times? Was that a coincidence or something more sinister? He wasn't sure. They wouldn't be playing at Shadowlands again for another three weeks, so he would have to wait until then to speak with the band members, though he had no idea what to ask them.

A knock on the front door brought Marta from the kitchen. Cabel hovered on the steps, torn between the need for the privacy of his bedroom and his morbid curiosity to learn who else would appear on his doorstep today. Marta opened the door. The young paperboy gave Marta a gapped-tooth grin.

"I have a message here for Mr. Cabel. Mrs. Bessie George sent me up here and gave me ten cents!" The boy held up two nickels to be admired but quickly pocketed them in case Marta tried to do more than look.

Marta waited, tapping a toe on the floor, a sure sign that she wanted to get back to her kitchen. The boy stood, still smiling then looking confused over the lack of activity. His smile quickly returned as he dug into his pocket and pulled out a folded envelope.

"This here's for him, Mr. Cabel, I mean," he said, pointing a finger and bringing Cabel to Marta's notice.

All choices gone, he came down the stairs to take possession of the message. The boy's hopeful look had Cabel reaching into his own pocket and adding two nickels to the child's trove. After a quick smile and nod of thanks, the boy dashed down the walk toward the street. Marta trundled back to her kitchen, leaving Cabel holding the slim note that somehow felt heavy as lead.

He stepped to the study door, the knob turning in his hand before he came to his senses. His grandfather's presence would be keenly felt there, and Cabel's shame was too great to allow him to face even the ghost of the man.

The lowering sun made the front porch uncomfortably warm and bright, but Cabel was unwilling to risk life and limb on the side porch again, so he sat in the swing near the potted geraniums and broke the small wax seal of the envelope.

Mr. Cabel,

The time has come for you to travel across the lake. There you will find answers and more questions. Both will help you in your quest for justice. You are strong enough to face what must come.

Bessie George

His mind rebelled against the thought of returning to Chicago. There were times when St. Joseph felt too close to his family for comfort. He leaned against the back of the gently arching swing, and like falling through a tunnel, he tumbled into the darkness.

|||||

"Mr. Cabel. Mr. Cabel, you need to wake up. Miz Marta sent me to fetch you to dinner."

The persistent tugging on his arm brought him to his senses more quickly than Nate's voice. Cabel opened his eyes and squinted toward the west. The sun was lower; perhaps an hour had passed. Nate continued to tug.

"You know, my grandpa used to take naps, but then he was old."

The disgust in the boy's voice almost made Cabel smile. Almost. He shifted his weight, causing the porch swing to sway, and he fought against the wave of nausea. Slowly, carefully, he righted himself. Nate stood back, arms folded across his chest, waiting for an old man to stand.

After another moment or two, Cabel complied. As he stood, two pieces of paper drifted to the floor. The note from Bessie George landed on the flyer in such a way that it seemed to underline a date. Bending down, Cabel picked up the pages with care and saw that the dates that had caught his eye were for later this coming week. The Wayne Sherman Band would be playing at a place called the Charades Club in Chicago for the next several nights.

"Come on, Mr. Cabel." Nate resumed his tugging. "It's time to go."

CHAPTER TEN

Thick carpet muffled the measured steps of assistants and secretaries going about important business. Leather, glass, polished wood, and silk-hung walls bespoke of prosperity and expertise. This was a law firm you could entrust with matters both personal and professional. Here were men who would hold your future safe within their capable hands.

Sweat poured from Cabel despite the cool of the waiting area. Coffee sat untouched in the porcelain cup at his elbow, and he felt permanently attached to the leather chair in which he sat. He passed his damp handkerchief across his forhead yet again and wondered why he was putting himself through this torture.

The note from Bessie George might have been enough to rout him from St. Joe and across the lake to the city where dark memories held sway, though perhaps not. The next morning, however, a packet from the Evans' family attorneys had arrived, and its contents had also seemed to require a trip to Chicago. Still he resisted. The invasion of the Arledges proved to be the final shove needed to pry him from the house. Two days passed before he worked up his courage to book early morning passage on *The Morning Star*. The extra fee for the use of a small cabin during the five-hour voyage had been money well spent.

Away from the eyes of his fellow passengers, Cabel had paced the closet-sized room, six steps wide and eight steps deep, until he became dizzy and nauseous. A porter brought him tea, which he doubted he could drink, but in the end it had settled his stomach well enough. By the time the ship reached the Chicago pier, he was pale and shaky but able to walk down the gangplank on his own. Grateful that his condition was misinterpreted as seasickness, he shrugged away offers of assistance and hailed a cab, directing it to the law offices.

Cars crowded the streets, nearly twice as many as he remembered from five years ago. Most of the stately houses along Michigan Avenue were gone, replaced with towering office buildings with art deco facades. The cab turned westward before reaching the river and soon came to a halt in front of an older building, shorter than those around it yet somehow managing to look down its regal nose at its garish new neighbors.

Owens, Stanford, and Mills had managed the Evans family legal matters since James Cabel Evans had come to Chicago to open a new branch of the family's manufacturing business. After the Civil War had ended, James had found life in New England too constraining and had pushed his father to allow him to come to the still emerging city of Chicago to expand the business westward. Success had followed James to this new proving ground, and Jackson Owens held a significant role in achieving that success. His wisdom and experience in matters both professional and political had guided James to the right connections, paving the way for Evans Manufacturing to rise in stature and importance. It was said that Owens, Stanford, and Mills created many of the princes of the city and that the firm's power and stature rose with that of its clients. All in all it was a mutually beneficial arrangement.

That he, Cabel, had been left waiting for over twenty minutes, although in luxuriously appointed surroundings, was testament to how far he had come down in the world. Again he asked himself why he was there. The papers in his hand meant nothing to him. All he had to do was sign them and leave. Hell, he could have done that in St. Joe and sent them back by courier as was his normal routine. Yet still he sat, waiting, and berated himself as a fool.

A few minutes later, a matronly dressed woman with sensible shoes and conservatively coifed hair presented herself to him.

"I'm Margaret Leigh, and I'll take you to see Mr. Reynolds now. Follow me, please."

Cabel stood, relieved to find that the chair had not become a permanent attachment, and followed Miss Leigh past the receptionist's desk. Their route took them through a maze of hallways, past offices and conference rooms, a legal library, and other efficient-looking work areas. Halfway along an oak-paneled hall, Miss Leigh stopped before a closed door, knocked briskly, and then turned the handle, motioning for Cabel to enter. She left before he had a chance to thank her.

Steven Reynolds was everything a junior law partner should be, sleek yet serious, muscular but not intimidating, above average in height and intelligence with a pleasing countenance that was neither too handsome nor too stern. He rose from behind his desk, adjusting his expensive suit jacket as he stood, hesitating for just the briefest of moments before offering his hand in welcome while looking somewhere in the vicinity of Cabel's left shoulder. The lawyer ended the handshake more quickly than was socially acceptable. Here was a man who knew the worst that Cabel had done and judged him soundly for it.

A sense of exposure, so complete that Cabel felt naked, had every muscle tightened in preparation to flee. His forehead and palms were damp again, and his heart raced with a speed that he wished his legs could match. As if in a nightmare, though, he remained rooted in his hell.

Cabel barely heard the invitation to sit through the roaring in his ears and his graceless collapse in the chair was more a matter of necessity than social courtesy. Reynolds still would not make eye contact, and his expression communicated exactly how he felt about the man who had entered his office: disgust, hatred, and a modicum of pity that blended into a loathing that Cabel had long felt toward himself.

Continuing to focus on some point beyond Cabel's left shoulder, Reynolds said, "I must say I am surprised to see you. Usually you just sign where it's needed and return the documents. Your promptness and efficiency in these matters has always been appreciated."

You mean my compliance and absence, Cabel thought. The lawyer's condescending tone, as if he were speaking to an addled client or small child, allowed a sliver of anger to penetrate the shame that engulfed him. Cabel focused on that anger, encouraging it to grow a bit, just enough to crowd out some of the fear and humiliation that had taken hold. As his anger grew, his mind cleared and the businessman within stepped forward.

"I don't understand why my presence should surprise you. I called for an appointment and arrived at the specified time. It is I who should be surprised that you were so tardy."

The lawyer's lips thinned in response to the criticism. "I'm afraid another, rather important meeting went on longer than expected."

"I see," Cabel said, resting his elbows on the arms of the chair, tenting his fingers together and resting his chin lightly on their point. The pose had the duel benefit of giving him a serious air while also keeping his hands from shaking. "If your firm finds the business of Evans Manufacturing or that of any Evans family member to be so unimportant, perhaps Owens, Stanford, and Mills is no longer the right firm to represent our interests."

Reynolds smiled, bringing to mind the reptile that lawyers were reputed to be. "Strong words for someone with no authority in such matters."

Slowly and with great deliberation, Cabel straightened in his chair and stared at Reynolds until the lawyer was forced to meet his eyes. "I realize that I no longer take part in the day-to-day operations of the company; however, you should look more closely at the stock distribution before you make such a bold and irresponsible statement."

"You own less than ten percent—"

It was Cabel's turn to smile. "I *owned* less than ten percent outright, but you're forgetting that my grandmother left me her shares, another fifteen percent I believe. My grandfather left me his thirty percent in a trust that will end when I'm thirty, just over two years from now. You are speaking with the man who owns over fifty percent of Evans Manufacturing, so perhaps you might wish to reconsider your attitude."

Reynolds paled, and a gleam of sweat appeared on his brow. Cabel nearly smiled at the appearance of the man's handkerchief, thinking of his own sodden cloth buried in his pocket.

"You haven't taken part in any of the board votes in years. The directors vote the trust shares, and your mother voted yours until we succeeded in locating you in New Orleans."

That success probably feels like a mistake at this moment, Cabel thought with amusement. Though he had a modicum of sympathy for the lawyer, this was a business matter and would be dealt with as such. "Yes, my mother voted my shares for over four years. I'm curious what legal precedent exists that allowed her to do so."

Reynolds opened his mouth, but no words came forth, an unusual condition for a lawyer.

Waving the problem away with a small gesture, Cabel said, "It's probably best that we don't look back on that issue. The future is what is important and why I am here."

Relief and wariness clashed on the lawyer's face. "Yes, the future. That is exactly what the board of directors believes as well. That's why they want to expand the business, going into retail and moving into the western markets."

"Yes, I've read the reports." He still wasn't sure why, but he had. It had been a mistake, surely, but one that couldn't be rectified now. "I find the manufacturing expansions of interest, but the shift to opening our own retail stores seems a bit overreaching at this point."

"Your uncle Frank disagrees. The shift to retail was his idea and one he wants to succeed. Sears, Roebuck, and Company is moving into the retail business, to much success I might add."

"True, but they have been making personal-use products for years and selling them directly to the consumer through their mail order business. Evans Manufacturing builds parts that other manufacturers use in the production of their products and Sears is one of our biggest customers. What are we going to sell in these stores, gears and machine belts? And what will happen to the manufacturing arm, our core business, when Sears pulls its contracts because we now compete with them?"

Reynolds leaned back in his chair, his eyes again seeking some distant spot on the wall. "I'm sure your uncle and the other board members have considered these questions in great detail. Perhaps you need to speak to them." This last was said as much as a threat as a suggestion. Cabel's heart raced at the thought of meeting any of these men again, especially his uncle. "Your father agrees with the plan, at least that's what I've been told."

Cabel tried to conceal his shock, but this was too much. His father had regained his health enough to resume his place on the board? How long ago and to what end? He hated himself for having caused his father's extensive injuries, and now he hated himself again for doubting his father's motives, but the competitiveness between the two brothers had always existed. Failure by one brother would bring as much joy to the other as if it were a personal success. Did his father hope to see Frank fail so spectacularly that he would risk the entire company? Cabel wished he could deny that possibility, but his father's capacity for winning at all costs was limitless. Unfortunately, as a boy and young man, Cabel hadn't understood what prize his father sought until it was too late to mount a defense against his manipulations. The older Cabel grew, the higher the stakes were raised, and the more tragedy followed in the wake of his father's machinations. What was he up to now?

"It seems to me that while you *will be* the majority shareholder in Evans Manufacturing, at this moment, you aren't. Your father, uncle, and cousin own the other forty-five percent of the shares and currently vote the thirty percent held in trust. By the time the trust ends and you come into your shares, all of this will be over." Reynolds leaned back in his chair, hands clasped behind his head, smiling at Cabel and his predicament.

"You forget that I'm on the board as well. I have a say in how the trust shares are voted." His voice was as weak as his position.

Reynolds' smile widened. "True. But several members of this firm are also on the board as well as representatives from the bank. Then there's your cousin Jim. He is backing his father, but then *he* is a loyal son."

The jab was little more than a glancing blow, but combined with all of the others it was enough to break the last of Cabel's resolve. He rose and perversely offered his hand to Reynolds, forcing a physical contact that neither man desired. "I can't sign these papers," Cabel said, placing them on the desk. "They need to be redrawn with a second option of voting against the measures as well as for them."

"You must realize that the company will go forward with these plans whether you approve of them or not?"

"Perhaps, but I will not put myself on record as supporting a board resolution that will, in all likelihood, destroy the company my grandfather built."

"So now you care about your grandfather's company? You should have thought of it five years ago, before you nearly killed your father. You walked away from the business, leaving a mess for your uncle and cousin to clean up behind you. Why the sudden interest in the company? Why do you care about the choices the board makes? Why now?"

Why now indeed. How could Cabel explain his need to follow all manners of business endeavors as a way to maintain his sanity? This man would not understand why Cabel had retreated from the world, first to New Orleans then to his St. Joseph haven, nor could the lawyer appreciate the debt that forced him back into the world. Yet the question remained: why did he care what happened to the company? It was the worst thing he could do, and yet he found that he did.

With no explanation, no words, no fight left in him, Cabel walked stiff-legged to the door, leaving the victor to gloat over his spoils.

iiiii

On the recommendation of a cabdriver whose Model T he had flagged down on Michigan Avenue, Cabel was now ensconced in the luxury of the Drake Hotel. The cabbie had driven him north of the river to the hotel that had been newly built before Cabel had left the city and now seemed a permanent gem set along the sparkling shoreline of Lake Michigan.

The Romanesque fountain bubbled its welcome from the center of the large marble and oak-paneled lobby. The long polished wood and brass counter separated the posh, sophisticated guests from the courteous and helpful staff. Within a few short minutes, Cabel found himself following a bellboy down a thickly carpeted hall to a room whose elegant décor could not compete with the glorious panoramic view of the lake. Cabel saw this lake from its eastern shores every day, yet now, here, framed by wood and viewed through glass, it seemed remote yet beautiful, a painting created by a true master. Perhaps it was.

He tipped the bellboy. Then after arranging for his bag to be unpacked and his eveningwear pressed, Cabel stretched out on the bed in search of oblivion. As he closed his eyes, memories of the city, his family, of Jon and Elizabeth jostled for attention leaving him restless and edgy. Abandoning the struggle for sleep,

Cabel rose, picked up his jacket and hat, and rode the elevator to the lobby. Soon he found himself on streets no longer familiar yet forever a part of him.

Many of the homes that had lined Michigan Avenue north of the river were gone, replaced by towering office buildings and retail shops. Several of the landmarks of his youth had disappeared under the guise of progress. With no purpose or intent, Cabel wandered southward, stopping here or there to admire a window display or turn again toward the lake. After a five-year absence and the last eight months living in St. Joseph, the lake seemed to be on the wrong side, creating a slight disorientation.

A window display of embroidered aprons caught his eye, and he smiled, imagining Marta's reaction at receiving such an impractical gift. She would hem and haw, complaining that it was too pretty to use in the kitchen so what good was it? The apron would be tucked into a drawer only to be brought out for special occasions, like hosting tea for her friends or bearing the roast turkey to the table on Thanksgiving. She would wear it with pride.

Holding the door open for two ladies who were exiting the shop carrying parcels and bags, he waited for them to leave before stepping inside. Within moments a sales clerk approached, and Cabel selected an apron embroidered with cherry blossoms that reminded him of the tree in the back yard. A display of pots and pans caught his eye, and he decided that new ones were needed to go with the planned renovated kitchen. After a moment's hesitation, he ordered a second set to replace those damaged during the break-in at the Arledge home. Walter might complain, but if he didn't like it, he could bring the things back to Chicago and return them himself.

After making arrangements for payment and delivery of the pots and pans to St. Joseph, Cabel tucked the small package containing the apron under his arm and proceeded on his way. A toy store became his next stop where he purchased a picnic tea set to replace the chipped one Belinda used with her doll and a new baseball and bat for Nate, though he vowed to remind the boy that the bat was a toy, not a weapon to be used against his sister. He was about to leave when he saw a display of small trucks. After a few moments of internal debate, he selected a green one with yellow wheels, a small gift for the paperboy.

The helpful clerk arranged for all of his purchases to be delivered to the hotel, and Cabel continued down the street. He hadn't realized he was smiling until a group of young women in stylish, knee-length dresses passed by, giggling. Shaking his head in disgust with himself, he paused at a street corner, waiting until it was safe to cross. What did he have to smile about? Still, here he stood in this city that he both loved and hated, where he had once been loved and was now hated. He had survived and he had come home.

He considered the matter further as he walked down the next block. Whether in France, New Orleans, or St. Joseph, Cabel had always thought of Chicago as home, but now he realized that home had shifted. In spite of himself, the people who lived and cared for him in St. Joseph had become important to him. They were the ones who, despite his need for solitude, he looked forward to seeing again. He rubbed his hands over his face and gave himself a hard shake. This wasn't good. A dark violence lived inside him, and he needed, at all costs, to protect people from that destructive rage, especially people he cared about, so it was best not to... Damn it. How had this happened?

Determinedly he turned and marched back toward the Drake. His steps slowed when he realized he had purchased a gift for everyone but Anne, now the oldest Arledge girl. He felt obligated to give her something, which annoyed him greatly but also led to the question, what does a man, not a father or a brother or relative of any kind, buy for a fourteen-year-old girl? A gaggle of brightly dressed girls with matching purses and fashionable cloche hats passed by him, and Cabel knew what to do.

CHAPTER ELEVEN

With an efficient wave of his hand, the doorman of the Drake Hotel signaled to a cab from the line idling near the hotel's entrance. Cabel gave the man a tip then climbed into the back seat of the waiting car. Despite the heat of the evening, he felt chilled as if coming down with a cold, though he doubted he was ill. The same iciness had accompanied him to every board meeting since the war.

With a small tug, he loosed the tie that suddenly felt too tight. He hadn't worn evening clothes in over five years, and they felt more like a costume than anything he had a right to wear.

The cab pulled away from the curb and the driver asked Cabel for his destination.

"The Charades Club, please."

The cabby eyed him speculatively in the rearview mirror as if deciding if Cabel belonged in such a place then nodded as he turned onto Lake Shore Drive heading south. "You've been there before, to the club?"

Cabe shook his head. "I haven't been in Chicago for a while, and so I haven't yet had the pleasure."

The cabbie smiled. "I hear that's a real nice place but not one that most visitors know about."

The man waited for Cabel to fill in the missing information, but he just smiled vaguely as he looked to his left at the endless black expanse of the lake. This dark void contrasted sharply with the bright lights of the city that he could see through the windows on the other side of the cab. He'd always loved being on Lake Shore Drive at night, that narrow strip of road seemed to serve as a barrier between the dark and the light.

"You know the password, don't cha? There's a lot of places I could take you in town where you don't need a password. Capone and the other crooks own a lot of soda shops in the city, and you can walk right up to the counter and order almost anything you want. That's where most of the tourists go, and I could take you to one of them if you'd rather. My name's Hank, by the way."

Cabel shook his head. "Thank you, Hank, but I'd like to go to the Charades Club." Then more to be polite than from curiosity, he said, "I hear Capone owns the place."

"Yes, sir, he does, and most of the city, too. He has the mayor, the chief of police, and most of the aldermen in his pocket, if you know what I mean. But if you're expecting to see Capone, don't get your hopes up. The place is the biggest one he has in the city, but he doesn't like to go there himself, or so they say. Rumor has it that he's usually at the Lexington Hotel or the Green Door Tavern or one of the other places he owns."

"So it's a safe place to go, then?"

Hank gave the raspy laugh of a lifelong smoker. "Mister, there'll be more cops and politicians there tonight than anywhere else in the city. You couldn't be safer."

Cabel smiled but wondered all the same. When he'd left Chicago in 1922, prohibition existed, although often ignored in many parts of the city. He didn't think that there had been the same level of organized criminal activity then, but perhaps he had been too caught up in his own miseries to notice. "It must be nice to run a speakeasy and not have to worry about being arrested."

Hank laughed again. "Capone don't run a speakeasy, he owns more of them then you can count, and lots of other things, from what I hear." The cabbie made eye contact with Cabel in the mirror. "You hear a lot of things driving a cab in this city, and if you're smart you forget most of it before you get your fare." He shrugged and turned his eyes back to the road. The hour was late and traffic was light, but Cabel felt better when the man was watching where he was driving. "Anyway, Capone don't have to worry about the police. It's the other gangs he has to keep an eye out for."

"I'm sure it's a dangerous profession."

"Mister, you don't know the half of it. One or another of the gangs has tried to kill Capone at least nine times this year, and it's only July." The cab's wheels rumbled on the bridge as it crossed over the river. They were nearing their destination. "Bookies are taking bets on how many times someone's going to try to kill him by the end of the year. He's even placed some bets himself, so now they're betting on whether or not he'll be around to collect if he wins."

Cabel didn't know if he should feel shocked or amused. Today's Chicago was certainly different from the one he had known as a boy. "Please drop me off a few blocks from the club."

"Can do." After another turn, the cabbie slowed the car and pulled to the curb. Hank put his arm over the back of the front seat and looked over his shoulder. "You do know the password, right?"

Cabel handed over enough money to cover the fare and got out of the cab. Hank shrugged and pulled back into the street. A few blocks away, a streetlight shone down on a shabby awning, the entrance to the club. Now if only he could get inside.

ııııı

The pavement held the heat of the day, creating small swirls of mist as the night air cooled. The alleyway Cabel chose for reconnaissance smelled of vomit and urine, and he hoped the stench didn't cling to his clothes. Across the street, a group of young people in evening clothes gaily made their way down the sidewalk to a well-lit yet unmarked door. Laughing and talking, the girls clung to the boys' arms, sparkling gems against the gray walls of the city. One of the men knocked. A moment later the covering of a small window slid open, and words were briefly exchanged through the metal grate. A few moments passed before the door swung wide and the couples were ushered inside.

Less than ten minutes later more couples dressed for a night of dancing and entertainment made their way down the street. Cabel left the alley and slipped in behind the group's stragglers, adjusting his gait to match theirs. A young blonde woman with short, waved hair looked over her bare shoulder and gave him a welcoming, if slightly inebriated, smile. Cabel smiled back and stepped a bit closer.

By the time he and the stragglers caught up with the rest of the party, the door of the speakeasy stood open and inviting. Cabel slipped past the armed guard and followed the group down an inauspicious hallway. Faded paper hung in tattered strips, and a threadbare carpet covered the floor. Cabel began to think that he was in the wrong place.

As he and the group reached the end of the hall, they could hear music and laughter, muffled but unmistakable, leaking through the thick batting that covered a second door. Another guard opened the door, admitting them into a sparkling world.

Lights flashed, a band played. People talked and laughed, crowding each other to be heard over the cacophony. Disoriented, Cabel stood to one side of the door and braced his hand against a marble pillar, waiting for the confusing whole to sort itself into manageable pieces. The Wayne Sherman Band played on a sequined stage under a chandelier that bathed the room in shifting rainbows. Satin-draped women danced with coat-tailed men across the polished dance floor, swirling like petals strewn upon turbulent waters. Beyond the dance floor, round tables elbowed each other for space, and more glittering, beautiful people sat drinking and smoking, enjoying seeing and being seen.

An intricately carved bar stretched across the back of the room, its dark wood a sharp contrast to the gleaming brass footrests. Eight bartenders served the supplicants who came to worship at this altar.

A sharp jab from an errant elbow forced Cabel to move into the swirling depths of the room. Rather than vie for a table that he didn't want, he moved toward the bar, where a man alone would go unnoticed.

While in New Orleans, Cabel had learned that he was not one of the lucky ones for whom alcohol brought the blessing of forgetfulness. When he drank, his demons came out to play, and they were dangerous creatures indeed. At a speakeasy, though, a drink was required and a sip or two might help fortify him as he searched for answers. He still wasn't sure what he would find here, but it was possible that Kittie's death and the break-in at the Arledge home was linked to Gary, so he would learn what he could.

As Cabel neared the bar, a voice from his past reached out to catch him unawares, nearly choking him by its proximity. He turned and stared, transfixed at the sight of his cousin Jim in the center of a group of men. Through gestures and facial animation, it was clear that Jim held the group's attention with some story or antidote. His wild arm movements nearly upended his glass, its contents sloshing wildly. The other men smiled and laughed at the joke.

Jim seemed so alive as to be almost unreal. He'd grown up in the last five years, Cabel realized. Gone was the spoiled young man with the slicked hair and breezy personality, always ready for fun and a good laugh. In his place stood a businessman whose eyes held the weariness of responsibility and experience. Jim had always been outgoing, the center of whatever group of friends he had at the moment, but now he had an air of confidence and leadership about him that Cabel recognized, like seeing a well-loved jacket being worn by a stranger. Jealousy flared briefly then died. Cabel had no place in this world anymore.

Realizing that he had stared too long, he started to turn away only to have his cousin's gaze sweep past him then snap back. Jim's eyes widened with shock. The others in his group turned to see what had caught his attention. Time stopped.

The spell broke as Jim rushed forward, holding out a hand. Happiness tinged with uncertainty filled his cousin's eyes, yet he grasped Cabel's hand and pumped it furiously. "My god, it is you, isn't it?" Without waiting for an answer, Jim threw his arms around Cabel's shoulders and steered him toward the group of waiting men.

"This," Jim declared with a dramatic wave of his free arm, "is my long lost cousin, Cabel Evans."

Cabel studied the men as they heard this announcement. Most smiled pleasantly, if somewhat bemused by Jim's enthusiasm. Two of the men looked shocked and then stared hard, as if trying to examine his soul. Cabel didn't know these men but they clearly knew his history. Shame, swift and strong, flowed like a river, and he wondered why he cared. These were Jim's associates, not his. Not that Cabel had associates anymore, though Nate might volunteer for the post. The thought brought a smile to Cabel's face which in turn had the two men looking at each other in confusion. Their discomfiture pleased him, which was childish, he knew, but he felt he needed any victory he could manage.

"If you gentlemen with excuse me, I'd like to catch up with my cousin." The men nodded and drifted toward the bar. Arm still around Cabel's shoulders, Jim deftly steered him between people, tables, and other obstacles until they reached a small, high table near the far wall. Pushing his older cousin onto a tall, backless stool, Jim took the one opposite and stared at Cabel over the rim of his glass while a thousand emotions chased each other across his face. Studied amusement was the one to finally settle in place.

For his own part, Cabel found that it hurt to look at his cousin. He had his mother's dark eyes and light brown hair, but looking past those things, Jim looked so much like their grandfather that Cabel's heart ached. He wondered if the resemblance had always been there or if time and responsibility had somehow left their mark.

"I got a call from Steve Reynolds today, telling me that you were in town and here to cause trouble," Jim said with a sardonic smile.

Cabel opened his mouth to protest, but his cousin waved his hand to stop him.

"Steve's a good lawyer, unimaginative but useful in a midlevel sort of way. I wouldn't be surprised if the senior partners decided to move him over to wills and estates or tax law, something more plodding than business."

Jim sighed and looked into his now-empty glass. With a small flick of a manicured finger, a waiter was summoned, and Jim ordered another scotch. He raised an eyebrow at Cabel who shrugged in response and a second glass was ordered.

"All the Volstead Act did was to take the quality of booze down and the price up. Sometimes I think Capone and the other mobsters drafted the damn thing just to make money off of us poor bastards."

Cabel smiled at his "poor bastard" of a cousin in his hand-stitched suit and diamond cufflinks. Until that moment, he hadn't realized how much he'd missed Jim.

As if reading his thoughts, Jim said, "I was shocked when Steve told me you were in town, but not in a bad way. It's good to see you, Cabe, though it seems strange not to have Jon here too."

Grief hit hard and fast, etching Cabel with its acid mix of guilt and horror. He both prayed and feared that one day the pain would lessen, but that time had not yet come. A glass was pressed into his hand. He looked up to see his cousin watching him with sympathy as he raised his own glass. "To friends lost but never forgotten."

With a nod, Cabel raised his glass then welcomed the burn of the scotch down his throat that gave him an excuse for the tears that hovered too close to the surface. A second sip helped restore his balance. He looked his cousin up and down. "You're successful and it looks good on you."

Jim shrugged but his smile seemed truer and his shoulders relaxed. "Dad and I are working hard and the company is doing well. Dad wants to add some retail shops, but I guess you know that."

Cabel nodded but diverted his eyes, distracting himself with the whirl of activity from nearby tables. Cigarette girls, scantily clad and high heeled, moved among the tables with their boxes of wares. Everyone seemed to have a drink in one hand and a cigarette in the other.

"Steve says you don't like the idea."

Cabel shrugged, studying the contents of his glass as if answers could be divined within the swirls of amber liquor. "Did Steve also tell you that he neatly put me in my place?" He said the words with a smile, hoping to hide his shame. "He's correct, though. I don't have a right to interfere with the company anymore."

Jim waited patiently, a virtue Cabel hadn't known his cousin possessed. Finally, unable to stand the torture of wondering what he would see in Jim's eyes, Cabel raised his and saw... understanding. He blinked several times, sipped his false courage then looked again.

"Your father was a real bastard, you know that, right? Still is, for that matter." Jim held Cabel's eyes for a moment before looking for answers in the bottom of his own glass. "He was always jealous of you, you know. You were everything he wanted to be, smart and brave and strong. Just like his dad, dear old Grandfather. I think that was your big sin. You were the son our grandfather always wanted. God knows neither of our fathers ever achieved that goal." With a snort, Jim shook his head and smiled at some inner thought while Cabel's head reeled. He found himself shaking his head.

"You don't believe me? You poor bastard." Jim leaned forward, resting his elbows on the table. His half-empty glass hovered near his lips a moment before he took a sip. "I swear when he sent you off to war I don't know which he was more afraid of, that you'd come home a hero or not come home at all." He waved away Cabel's startled protest. "You really don't know do you, how much he's always hated you? I heard my parents talk about it, wondering what would happen when you came in to the rest of your shares in the company, whether your father would leave or demand that you sell him the majority holdings."

"But Father never..."

"Never what, said anything? How could he without admitting that he was jealous? Instead he pushed you to go to war, and afterwards he pushed you to act as if it never happened." Jim looked down at the tabletop and traced a small drop of moisture with his finger. "I'm ashamed to say that I enjoyed the fact that you came back...changed. Uncle Edward tried so hard to maintain the pretence that everything was normal, that the golden boy hadn't tarnished." A note of satisfaction slipped into his cousin's voice. He shook himself and glanced up at Cabel to see if he had noticed. Cabel kept his face neutral as emotions battered his soul.

"He needed you to at least *pretend* to be normal, so he wouldn't have to feel guilty. I heard my mother gossiping about you with her best friend, Iris. Dear old Mom hoped that Uncle Edward would drive you away, so Dad and I could take on a bigger role in the company. I never wanted it, never thought I would enjoy it but then... You finally had enough of your father's abuse and... Well, you left and your father was in the hospital. Mother got what she wanted, just not the way she expected, though I don't think she was displeased. For her, the only thing better than you leaving was you leaving in disgrace."

Disgrace, yes, and the shame that had come with it, but before that had come the pressure. Pressure to come back to the business, quickly rising to vice president of operations. Pressure to marry Elizabeth in spite of the fact that he could not think of her, be with her, without remembering Jon and his horrible death. Too broken to marry her and too much a coward to tell her why, Cabel had quietly released Elizabeth from the engagement that had been arranged for them as if they were no more than pieces on a chessboard. After the broken engagement had come the pressure to find a suitable girl and start a family.

Despite the anguish and despair that had taken up permanent residence within him during the war, Cabel's business instincts were as strong as ever. Under his leadership the company grew and expanded. Profits increased and the board of directors was very, very pleased. Had his father envied his son's accomplishments? Is that why he constantly shoved Cabel closer and closer to the dark abyss and finally over the edge? He knew his father was a master of manipulation, but most of his efforts seemed to be directed at besting his brother. Had his father really hated him? Memories, buried and forgotten, pushed their way to the surface. Stripped of familial considerations and viewed through the lens that Jim now provided, Cabel realized that it was true and wondered how he could have been blind to it for all those years.

Cabel's memories of his last board meeting were hazy except for his father's voice, prodding rather than praising, pushing and pushing until the pressure was finally released in a fury of fists and blood. He remembered being pulled away from his father's body, not knowing or caring if the man on the floor was dead or alive. Then came the taxi ride to the train station, the driver leery of taking a passenger with bloodied knuckles and a scratched face, regardless of how well dressed he was. Finally, the escape to New Orleans, selected in part because it was the farthest he could get from Chicago with the money he carried in his pocket.

Nothing Jim told him changed anything that had happened and yet…

A passing waiter was flagged to refill Jim's drink, and Cabel shook away the offer to top off his. Restless and uncertain, he wanted to leave and find a quiet place where he could contemplate this new perspective of himself and his father, but his cousin had other ideas.

"I suppose I should be sorry. I mean you probably didn't come here to talk about all this, but you need to know what a bastard your father can be. I honestly don't think I'd have lasted as long as you did before… Well, let's just say you're a better man than I am and talk of the future." He held his newly refilled glass aloft, and Cabe gently clinked his own against it. "So tell me, why do you think my father's plans are wrong for Evans Manufacturing?"

"Really, Jim, I don't want to interfere."

"Cabe, when we were growing up, I resented you and wanted to be you at the same time. You were always the best at everything, and you had Jon, so you didn't need me, no one needed me," Jim said with a bitter edge to his voice. "But look at me now, all grown up and running the family company." His smile held both irony and pride. "Still, damn it, short of Grandfather, you're the best businessman I've ever known, so please tell me what you think."

Cabel searched hard but found only sincerity in Jim's eyes. Taking his cousin at his word, Cabel began discussing his concerns about the expansion, going into greater detail than he had with Steve Reynolds. Jim listened well, asked insightful questions, and gently debated points of disagreement. Time and place disappeared while Cabel recaptured a small bit of his soul.

Finally Jim stood, stretched, and downed the last of his drink. "I need to get back to my friends, but it's good to see you again, Cabe." Jim hesitated a moment. "And thanks for your insights on the business proposal. It helped."

The cousins shook hands, and Cabel remembered how it felt to be accepted.

"By the way," Jim called over his shoulder. "You do know who runs this place, right?"

Cabel shrugged in confusion, but Jim was swallowed by the crowd before he could get an answer. Wayne Sherman announced that the band would be taking a break, and the energy in the room dropped as the musicians left the stage. Thirsty dancers rushed the bar. Cabel flattened himself against a pillar to avoid being crushed.

After the crowd had passed by, Cabel moved quickly through the maze of tables, trying to reach the stage before the band members disappeared behind the side curtains. He needed to find Gary's friends, to learn if the young trumpet player was involved in anything that might mean his death had been intentional rather than the result of being on the wrong street corner in the middle of a gang shoot-out. By the time Cabel reached the dance floor the only thing left on the bandstand were abandoned instruments and sheet music.

"Well, if it isn't the prodigal son," a sultry voice whispered near his ear.

CHAPTER TWELVE

The siren-red dress defied current fashions, audaciously display-ing voluptuous curves. A deep plunge of lace and satin provided a generous view of some of those curves, momentarily distracting Cabel from the woman's face. With an effort he raised his eyes to hers. His chest tightened and the room tipped as his mind tried to grasp what he saw. Blonde hair, brown eyes, dimpled chin, Elizabeth's face, yet not—too harsh, too worldly, too mocking.

"Rebecca," he said, more in relief than recognition. Elizabeth's older sister had been on the periphery of their lives, his, Jon's, and Elizabeth's. An unconventional girl in very staid times, she had scandalized her family on several occasions, though at the moment, Cabel couldn't remember anything specific.

"I go by 'Becca' now, darling," purred the woman in red as she linked her arm through his, steering him toward a private table tucked into a small alcove near the stage.

As he allowed himself to be led, he wondered if the woman he knew as Rebecca felt the slight trembling he could not control. Chicago was the city that held some of his best and worst memories. He worked hard to keep both firmly locked away, but here at the Charades Club that past was straining against the chains that held it so firmly in a dark, forbidden corner of his mind. His meeting with Jim had loosened some of those bonds, and he feared that his encounter with Rebecca would weaken those restraints even further.

Through the swirl of his thoughts, he realized that something was amiss. They had arrived at her table and she stood, waiting, watching, though it took a moment for him to understand and react. Brushing off dusty and disused manners, Cabel held out a chair for Becca. She sat, eyeing him speculatively, and he wondered how bad his lapse in attention had been. With an internal sigh, he took the chair across from her and waited.

Slowly and with great deliberation, she took a long drag on the cigarette that glowed at the end of a slim holder. The seams of her gown strained with the effort of containing her cleavage, but then she exhaled and disaster was averted. Though her actions were smooth and suggestive, they also seemed studied, practiced, as if her intent was to draw his eyes to her lush body. Was it habit, he wondered, or a display of genuine interest? He didn't know how to explain to her that her efforts were wasted on him. Intimacies of any kind threatened his hard-won control over his emotions, and he wouldn't risk that even to enjoy the comforts of a woman's body.

With the ease of experience, she removed the stub of the cigarette from its holder and replaced it with a fresh one. Long and sleek, the ebony and silver holder was very masculine in design, an interesting contrast to the woman who used it.

Becca studied him with her serious brown eyes. He wondered what she saw. After a moment she nodded to herself as if coming to some conclusion. Following a slight raise in her finger, a young waiter magically appeared, and Becca ordered drinks.

He used her momentary distraction to study the woman across from him. Her body was amply displayed, but he wondered about the woman who existed beyond the obvious. Although she was only three years his senior, she had lived in a world far beyond him for as long as he could remember. Looking past the drama and the rumors, Cabel had little memory of Becca from his youth except her skillful, flirtatious teasing that had left him feeling grown up and guilty at the same time. Where Elizabeth had been during those brief moments, he couldn't remember, not that there were many. Rebecca had rarely been home and was generally avoided by her younger sister and her group of friends.

Now they sat across from each other, strangers with a shared past.

As the waiter moved off to fill her order, Becca made a show of admiring the young man's physique before returning her attention to Cabel.

"Well, look at you, Cabe, all grown up. I always knew you'd be quite the looker one day, and I must say you haven't disappointed." Becca leaned forward, subjecting Cabel to the same demeaning assessment that she had given the waiter.

"I'm so flattered," he said, feeling like a mouse being toyed with by a cat. "If you keep eyeing me like that, I'm going to have to charge a fee." It was reckless to play along with her flirting, he knew, but that distraction was safer than risk facing the memories that stirred restlessly in the back of his mind.

Her deep-throated laugh matched her uninhibited demeanor. Brown eyes sparkled at him as she said, "And how much would that fee be? I wonder. Hmmm, I'll have to think about that." She eyed him again, and he wondered what price she would demand of him in return.

Bold, strong, slightly brash, she had had those qualities even as a young woman, but now there was also a sleek sophistication about her that suited her well. The wild daring he remembered was tempered, by age or experience he couldn't say. She sat across from him confident and poised with a hint of danger. An enticing combination but one he had no interest in pursuing. Becca would forever be Elizabeth's sister, and that wall would never be breached.

The prompt return of the waiter brought a welcome pause in their banter, and Cabel released a breath he hadn't realized he'd been holding. Becca raised her glass toward him, and he lifted his in return before taking a sip. The strong, peaty scotch was ambrosia compared to what he had sipped minutes earlier with Jim. Here was quality—powerful, seductive, dangerous, much like the woman across from him. He could lose himself in the contents of this glass but knew only too well where that could lead. With an internal sigh, he set his glass aside and focused on Becca.

She raised an eyebrow in surprise. "Don't you like it? I have my own bottle behind the bar, and I only share with very special people."

"Then I'm surprised you'd share it with the likes of me, the prodigal son and all."

"My dear Cabe, that's what makes us two of a kind." She smiled, leaning back in her chair. "Do you know why I go by 'Becca' now? When I was a child, maybe five or six, I wanted to be called 'Becky' and I wanted to call Elizabeth 'Beth.' I was delighted that our names would both start with the letter 'b.' Can you imagine me a little girl all excited to learn about letters and numbers and all?"

Cabel couldn't imagine her young and innocent. She'd always seemed mature and daring, ready for any adventure and to flout all of the rules. His mind balked at the thought of her as a girl in pigtails and pinafores. He certainly couldn't picture her in the role of a caring, older sister.

"Dear mummy explained that 'Becky' and 'Beth' were common names, and the Gishes were *not* common." Her eyes emptied as she traveled to the distant past. With a shake of her head, she returned to the present and gave him a malicious smile. "I legally changed my name to Becca Smith. Can you imagine anything more common than that?" She laughed like the girl she must have been while he fought back his surprise. Did her parents know?

She must have read the question on his face, because she said, "My parents know exactly what I did, though I'm not sure if they're relieved that they can distance themselves from me or

affronted that I would turn my back on their elevated status."
She shrugged, unconcerned. "Not that it matters. I've stopped
caring what my parents thought of me a long time ago. Besides
the present is much more interesting, for here you are, wild and
dangerous. I do like an unpredictable man, so much more exciting
than the bleating sheep that come here to drink." With a casual
toss of her head, she dismissed the wealthy clientele that surged
around her. "You are truly a welcomed change in routine."

Her eyes lingered on his face, more of a caress than a glance.
Cabel felt the heat of the offer that lay in her eyes and was
stunned when his body responded. He closed his eyes and took a
deep breath. Now was not the time to lose control.

"I love running this place, but with most of the top brass of
the police department here every night, I can't even count on a
decent raid to liven things up."

Distracted, it took a moment for her words to register,
and even then Cabel thought he had misunderstood until he
remembered Jim's parting comment. Shifting in his chair, he
looked at the club with a more discerning eye. Leather, crystal,
marble, and silk; money hung from the walls and dripped from
the ceiling. Darker, edgier than Shadowlands, the Charades Club
held a sophistication that only the forbidden could attain. When
he turned back, he found Becca watching him, chin raised either
in defiance or pride. He raised his glass to her. "Your place is as
magnificent as you."

A bright, natural smile briefly illuminated her face before it
was replaced with one of studied, careful amusement. "I have to
admit, Cabe, I expected you to be shocked, scandalized even. You
do surprise a girl."

Cabel shrugged, quietly pleased that he had momentarily
startled a sincere response from her. "The cabbie who brought
me here said this was Capone's place. I would think he would be
a dangerous man to work for."

"Every man is dangerous to work for." Her voice hardened and her eyes grew cold. Then she looked at him and smiled. "At least with Capone you know what to watch out for, and he was willing to give me a chance."

She leaned in, lowering her voice. He leaned closer so that he could hear, creating an unexpected and unwelcomed intimacy. "Dear old Mum and Dad decided that they had had enough when I ran up one too many gambling debts. They threatened to disown me if I didn't marry and settle down. Could you imagine?" Her rich laugh invited him to share her amusement. "Well, you can guess which path I chose. I soon found myself out of both money and supposed friends." Her voice became bitter, but she gave an elegant shrug of her shoulder, as if to throw off such disappointments.

"Through my connections in the gambling crowd, I met Capone, and I started managing one of his gentlemen's clubs out in Cicero. And no, I wasn't one of the working girls." Her hard stare dared him to challenge the truth of the statement. "I ran the place well; really cleaned it up and the profits soared. Still he wouldn't have let me run a speak like this, especially one of his best, if he hadn't lost a bet."

She smiled at his surprise, and her tone warmed though she kept her voice low and leaned further across the table, her breasts nearly spilling from the top of the gown. "He and some of his cronies were playing poker at the club one night. They let me join the game. Capone knew I didn't have a bankroll like the rest of them, so he changed the rules and we had to bet something other than money. He won the use of Larry Davis's airplane for a week." She laughed at the memory. "On one hand it came down to him and me. He asked me what I wanted him to bet, and I told him I wanted to run this place for a month, and he let that ride. I won the hand. That was three years ago." She sat back, a satisfied smile on her face. "You know, Cabe, you're one of the few people who know the true story. If I find out you've told anyone, I'll have you killed."

"My lips are sealed," he said.

She smiled, but the glint in her eyes suggested that the threat was not entirely facetious. Cabel was less concerned about her threat than he was curious as to what she had bet to call Capone's bid. Knowing he couldn't ask and doubting she would tell him the truth, he decided it was time to tell her the reason he was at the club tonight.

He leaned back to diminish the intimacy that her confession had created and was surprised by a sudden longing for its return. This was not the time, and she was Elizabeth's sister. He knew what could happen when he lost control. The arguments were strong but less persuasive than he had hoped. He forced his mind back to the issue at hand and took a sip of his drink, stalling for time as he tried to determine how best to approach the subject. His social skills were rusty at best, having been of little use on the New Orleans docks. Before that he had always been linked with Elizabeth, which meant he hadn't needed to learn to flirt or cajole. Looking across the table, he realized that nothing in his background had prepared him for this moment, this woman. He decided to be direct since he doubted he had the sophistication to succeed in any other fashion.

"I'm happy for your success, but I must be honest and tell you that it's as much for my sake as for yours. You see, I came here on a quest and I need your help."

Her eyes darkened. A slow, predatory smile spread across her face. She leaned forward again, displaying her cleavage for his perusal. "And what quest might this bold knight be on, and how can I be of service?" Her sultry whisper stirred his blood as her fingertips caressed the back of his hand in small circular motions. Again his body responded. Her eyes held promises he knew she would keep. But those eyes were too much like Elizabeth's for him to lose himself in their depths, and his own isolation kept him from seeking the intimacies she offered. While his body made demands, his head was clear. He knew where the danger lay.

Cabel turned his hand over and briefly squeezed her fingers before sliding his own out of her reach. Although his rejection had been gentle, her eyes flashed with anger, and her back straightened into a rigid, unbending posture.

"While I would love to allow you to continue your delusion of my gallant, knightly ways, I'm afraid the truth is more mundane." He tried for a playful tone, hoping to ease past her anger and convince her to help him. "During the war I served with a man named Walter Arledge. Recently his daughter, Kittie, died in a small town on the other side of the lake, over in St. Joseph."

"A tragedy to be sure, but it has nothing to do with me." Becca's voice, cold and unyielding, did not bode well for his success.

"I'm sure it doesn't," Cabel said quickly. "The problem is that the girl was murdered just a few weeks after her boyfriend was killed here in Chicago. His name was Gary Stevens. He played the trumpet in the Wayne Sherman Band."

Becca's eyes widened briefly in recognition of the boy's name. Another emotion flitted through as well, but it came and went too quickly for Cabel to do more than note its passing.

"Gary Stevens, now he was a loss to my stable." Becca leaned back in her chair, relaxing slightly as she picked up her cigarette holder and began to create a smokescreen between them. "That boy was young and much too full of himself, mind you, but he was trainable, I'll give him that." Becca smiled briefly at some memory before her face hardened. "I don't know anything about the boy, personally, other than details that I'm sure won't help you with your quest. Besides, Gary was caught in the middle of a gang shoot-out. It was just a matter of being in the wrong place at the wrong time." She shrugged with indifference as she crushed her cigarette out in a small glass dish. "I'm afraid that's all I know." She made as if to rise, but Cabel reached out and took hold of her wrist, halting her progress.

Her brown eyes flashed in rage, reminding him of the quick, volatile temper she had displayed as a girl. He released her immediately, raising his hands in surrender.

"I'm sorry," he said.

She stared at him like a cobra about to strike.

As he looked at the beautiful, angry woman across from him, he felt the absurdity of his mission. The weight of Walter's expectations suddenly pressed down on him. The taste of failure, bitter and strong, settled on the back of his tongue. He was a fool.

Cabel rose to his feet and offered Becca his hand. "I'm sorry to have bothered you. I'll be going now."

She remained seated and had taken his hand as a courtesy, but now gripped it tightly, refusing to release it. He wondered what she saw as she studied his face, but whatever was there caused her anger to slip away like wisps of smoke from her cigarette.

"What exactly do you want from me?" Her tone was coldly neutral, and he knew he had only one chance to redeem himself. She nodded to the chair opposite from hers, and he sat, grateful but cautious.

Taking a deep breath, he pleaded his case. "I'm trying to get a sense of the boy, Gary. The only person in Michigan who knew him well is the girl who died. I came here hoping that I could speak with some of the band members to see if they know anything that would help me. If you spoke to them on my behalf, I'm sure they would talk with me."

Becca studied him as she considered his request, calmer now, but the anger was still there, close to the surface. "You're so serious," she finally said. "The evening clothes are nice window dressing and you play the charmer quite well, but it's as if you're going from memory rather than what you feel. How sad."

Cabel felt himself redden as her words hit home. His exile and more recent isolation had marked him more than he realized.

Yet it seemed as if they were both playing roles this evening. He knew the cause of his and wondered at the reason for hers.

"I owe this man Arledge a great debt, soldier to soldier," he explained, hoping this last bit of truth would sway her, although it cost him to say the words aloud. "All I know is that Kittie was seeing the Stevens boy, and now they are both dead, murdered. I don't know if Kittie's death has anything to do with Gary's. I just need to know more about Gary so that I can find out who killed Kittie and repay my debt to her father."

Becca said nothing as she slipped another cigarette into its holder. She leaned forward and allowed him to light it for her from the book of matches on the table. Settling back in her chair, she considered him as if he were a problem to be solved, but one not worthy of much effort. With a nod, she came to her decision. "I thought you were joking when you said you were on a quest. Poor Cabe," she sighed. "Do you know what you're doing? I wonder where this might lead. Are you really prepared to find the truth for your friend? He may not like what you discover."

"He knows that and so do I. As for knowing what I'm doing, no. I feel like some detective in a cheap novel, blundering about and hoping to find a clue." He leaned forward and rested his elbows on the table. "I really could use your help. Please."

Her smile was more triumphant than pleasant, as if his repeated requests for help had satisfied some need within her. She nodded and with a small flick of a finger the young waiter returned, eager to serve. After a few quiet words for the boy's ears only, he disappeared again.

"The band will be back on stage in a minute so you won't have a chance to speak with anyone for a while. I've told Rob to let the band members know that you want to talk to them about Gary. During the next break one or two of his friends will stop by the table." She stood, smoothing her dress over her hips and the tops of her thighs, drawing his eyes to follow the movement of her hands. The motion was both sensual and calculated, though his body didn't seem to mind the later. "This is my private table," she continued. "You're free to use it for the rest of the evening, but don't stay chained to it. Dance, laugh, have fun. Do you remember how? I wonder."

"Thank you for your help," Cabel said, rising to see her off.

"Don't thank me yet. You owe me a favor, and I promise you, I will collect." Her cold smile left him to wonder if he could afford her price.

CHAPTER THIRTEEN

The band played, couples danced, and alcohol flowed freely, fueling the exuberant mood of the crowd. Ignoring Becca's advice, Cabel remained at the table, recovering from his encounter with her as well as with Jim. Taking slow sips of his drink, Cabel tried to relax and let the world manage without him. Although he'd never been in a Chicago speakeasy before, the people, the music, and the bits of conversation that floated by were familiar, reminding him of social events he had attended around the city over the years. Nothing had changed really, except him.

Speculative glances, some furtive, others bold, came his way time and again. He suspected that their interest was due to the fact that he sat at Becca's table rather than his own past, which made the scrutiny bearable. Cabel doubted anyone besides Becca and Jim would recognize him tonight, and as long as the crowd left him to himself, they were free to gossip. Nothing they imagined could be worse than the truth.

The Wayne Sherman Band played all of the popular songs, keeping the dance floor crowded. Except for his brief visit to the Shadowland Ballroom, Cabel hadn't listened to music for months and took the opportunity to become familiar with the current favorites. His foot tapped along with the rhythms as one song slipped seamlessly into another, but he had no desire to join the crush of people who chased the music around the polished wood floor. His hands shook slightly at the thought of bodies pressing into him from all sides. The stench of the trenches briefly filled his nose before it faded into nothing. No, he would enjoy the music from the safety of his hostess's table.

He spotted Becca a few times as she moved around the room, greeting guests, soothing ruffled feathers, and generally playing hostess to Chicago's elite. She fascinated him with her ability to tread a very narrow path, flirting with men enough to enchant them yet not enough to threaten their wives. Still, he couldn't help but notice the occasional lustful glance that came Becca's way when the women weren't watching, nor could he miss Becca's answering nod. These men were older, probably politically connected within the city, and he wondered what Becca's connection was to them beyond serving as manager of the club.

He also wondered how many of her parents' friends were in the crowd tonight. The place was popular, and he doubted that the upper crust would let someone else's scandal keep them away. Knowing the cruelties some of the wealthy were capable of, he was sure that at least some of the Gish's friends came here for that reason alone.

Wayne Sherman announced that the band would be taking another break, and the dance floor slowly emptied. As the minutes passed, Cabel wondered if the waiter had delivered the message or if Becca had given the young man some other instructions.

The curtains near the edge of the bandstand flared as someone on the other side made his way toward the break. A few seconds later, a slender young man with dark hair and an easy smile appeared at the gap in the curtain. Dressed in the bands' signature tuxedo and satin-trimmed shirt, he stopped near the edge of the stage and surveyed the room. After lighting a cigarette with an air of studied casualness, he sauntered over to Becca's table.

Cabel stood and held out his hand. "Hello. I'm Cabel Evans. Thank you for meeting with me."

The younger man studied Cabel with open interest before holding out his own hand. "I'm Pete Darcy. I understand you're a friend of Becca's." He gave Cabel a sly wink before sliding into a chair. Leaning back insolently, he eyed Cabel with speculation. "I have to say you're a little older than most of us, but I guess you're all right."

"I'm older than most of whom?"

The young musician gave a slanting smile as he blew cigarette smoke into the air. "You know, her stable, at least that's what she calls us. She likes having young guys in her bed the way some guys have mistresses or whatever." Pete smiled widely. "She likes to keep a couple of us around, you know, for when the mood strikes."

Cabel sat a moment, stunned by the young musician's words. He had thought that Becca's reference to Gary Stevens being part of her stable was for show or a joke. Instead she behaved much as men might in this situation. He didn't know whether to condemn or applaud her.

"You aren't one of us, are you?" Grey eyes twinkled with suppressed laughter.

"No, I guess not."

"Trust me, mister, you'd know if you were." The young man laughed outright then sat up straight, looking slightly worried. "Don't get me wrong, everyone here likes Becca, and frankly, you either show her respect or she shows you the door."

Cabel didn't doubt it.

"She's good to work for," Pete continued, in case Cabel misunderstood. "She takes care of her people, and she works harder than any of them. They say that Capone trusts her, and they don't say that about many people, especially a woman." He smiled and leaned back in his chair again. "And she's not like most girls. She stands up for herself. She likes to have a good time and isn't shy about it." He shrugged. "The thing is a lot of people know about us, her guys I mean, but mostly they think it's for show, an act, you know? And Becca likes that. She keeps everyone guessing but also keeps her private business private. Trust me, mister, you don't stick around long if you can't keep your mouth shut. That's why I was surprised that her note said to tell you anything you wanted to know." His eyes narrowed in speculation. "Who exactly are you?"

"I'm just an old friend of her family's," Cabel said, amused at the mixture of deference and bravado in the boy. "I knew her sister well at one point in time."

"Ah the beauteous and very proper Elizabeth," the young man said thoughtfully as he ran his hand over his oil-slicked hair. "Becca doesn't talk about her family much, but her sister's name was in the paper a few weeks ago, something about chairing some social committee or something. Anyway, from what Becca said, I don't think she and her sister are very close."

"I'm sure you're right." Cabel never read the society pages of the newspaper to avoid any mention of his family and former fiancée. "I'm not here to talk about Becca or her family. I'm here about Gary Stevens."

"Old news, mister. He's dead," Pete said, shifting uneasily in his chair.

"I know, I'd like to talk about his girlfriend," Cabel responded.

Pete snorted. "Which one?"

"How many did he have?"

The young musician tilted back in his chair, another knowing smile played across his face. "Look, mister. Some of the guys in the band are old, like you. They have wives, kids even. But the rest of us"—he held out his arms as if to encompass the world's youth—"well, we're young and single, at least as far as the girls know, and they sure do love us guys in the band." The smile shifted into a leer.

"And you take advantage of that," Cabel said in a flat, disapproving voice, suddenly feeling old again, or at least as old as Pete thought him to be.

The musician shrugged. "Of course. See, we're based here in Chicago, but we go over to St. Joe, Coloma, and Detroit. We always have at least one booking in Detroit every two weeks." His voice altered slightly as if to let Cabel know that the Detroit stop was significant in some way.

"So you're saying that Gary had a girlfriend in Detroit, too?"

Pete leaned forward, crushed out his cigarette, and gave Cabel a look that young men down through the ages bestow on their oblivious elders. "Of course he had a girlfriend in Detroit. He had one in each of our regular stops, but you really don't get it do you? We have a standing gig, one night only. In Detroit. Every two weeks. It costs a lot of money for us to go there, and if it were any other city, we'd be booked for at least three nights, maybe a whole week."

The boy paused. "You know Capone owns this place, right?"

Realizing that he still didn't understand, Pete shook his head at the depth of Cabel's stupidity and leaned further across the table, motioning Cabel to do the same. His voice lowered. "Most of the guys in the band don't know this, and I don't think Mr. Sherman does either. He thinks he's doing a favor for a friend of Capone's by playing at the Diamond Room in Detroit every two weeks during the season."

"But it isn't about a favor, is it?" Cabel had no idea what this was about but didn't think he could survive another pitying look from Pete without punching the kid in the nose.

"Now you're catching on." Pete nodded, like a proud parent whose child spoke its first words.

Cabel tamped down his annoyance and waited.

Pete continued, "The place is downtown, right across the river from Canada. After the club closes, our tour manager, Scottie, takes a few of us guys over to the riverfront. The Hiram Walker distillery is right across the water. Now do you understand?"

"You're a rum runner?"

Pete laughed quietly. "Its whiskey, actually, and depending on how you look at it, everyone on our tour bus is a rum runner. But, yeah, I help Scottie with the heavy lifting. Gary used to, too."

"Scottie?"

"Scottie Marks. He's Mr. Sherman's road manager, the guy who makes sure we have hotel rooms and a driver for the bus and whatever. Scottie also helps out Mr. Capone, and Gary and I help Scottie."

"Do you think Gary might have been killed because of this?"

Pete shrugged indifferently but gave the question some thought. "If it were anyone else, I'd say probably not. Capone's a big shot in Canada, flies in a lot of their beer, so no one messes with us, though anything is possible, especially on the American side of the river."

"So why would you think Gary might not have Capone's, ah, protection?"

"Look, mister, you had to know Gary. He was never happy unless he was doing something he wasn't supposed to be doing. I know he brought back some bottles of imported scotch a few times that never made it into the inventory."

"Was that enough to get him killed?" If this were true, Cabel doubted it had any connection to Kittie's death.

Pete leaned back in his chair, and Cabel did the same. "Probably not but you never know, especially with Capone. One minute you're in and the next you're out. From what I've heard, depending on his mood, he'd have a guy killed for a lot less."

Cabel thought a minute. "What else can you tell me about Gary?"

"You mean besides the girlfriends?" Pete considered the question. "Gary was a good guy, you know, always funny, ready to have a good time, but he could be a real jerk, too." Anger flitted across the musician's face.

"In what way?"

Pete looked uncomfortable and shrugged.

"Please, it would really help if I understood who Gary was."

"Look, he was a good guy, a friend…" Pete's voice trailed off.

Cabel suddenly felt sorry for the young man seated across from him and also curious. Except for the rum running and the girlfriends spread over at least two states, Pete considered Gary to be a good guy. What qualified as a bad one? Regardless, the real question was: did any of Gary's illegal activities get Kittie killed?

Pete checked his watch, and Cabel realized the band would be back on soon so he had to hurry. Unfortunately he didn't know what to ask so he went back to the beginning. "Before you go, what can you tell me about Gary and Kittie?"

"The girl from Shadowland? She's a sweet kid. I was a little worried for her when she took up with Gary, but he seemed to like her more than the rest." He smiled. "I should find her the next time we're back in St. Joe."

"You can't. She died a few weeks ago. Murdered."

Shock and horror replaced the smug satisfaction that seemed to be Pete's normal expression. For a moment he looked young, vulnerable.

"Who would do such a thing?"

"I don't know. That's why I'm here asking questions about Gary."

Pete shook his head slowly from side to side as if to deny Kittie's death. "Look, mister, I know I said Gary was a jerk, and sure he played the field, but I can't believe he'd have anything to do with Kittie, ah, dying."

"He died a week before she did so we know he wasn't directly involved but could the rum running have had anything to do—"

"No," Pete cut him off, his tone like the blade of a knife. His glance swept over the nearby tables, assuring him that no one was listening. He leaned forward again. "Becca doesn't like us talking about that, not with anyone. I only told you what I did because she said to answer your questions. But I know Gary wouldn't have told anyone about the running, especially Kittie."

"Why especially her?"

"She's sweet, like I said. Some girls like it, think its exciting to be with a rum runner, but I don't think Kittie would have. Gary knew girls. He could take one look at their clothes, their friends, and he would know just what it took to get her interested in him. He never would have told Kittie because she wouldn't have liked it."

Cabel considered this and realized that the young musician had implied that he and Gary *did* tell at least some girls about their side job if they thought it would serve as a lure. Still, although he'd never met Kittie, Cabel felt that Pete was probably right. She wouldn't have liked Gary if she had known what he was up to. But there was one woman who knew exactly what was going on.

"What about Gary and Becca? I heard that he used to brag about, well, being her boyfriend."

Pete laughed as he crushed out his cigarette. "Trust me, mister, she doesn't have boyfriends, but yeah, Gary liked to brag to some of the other musicians about it, until Becca heard and put a stop to it. It's not that the guys don't know, it's just that she doesn't like us to talk about her like that. Like I said, she keeps private things private."

"What did she do to Gary?"

"I don't know for sure, don't want to really. Becca can be scary sometimes." His face paled slightly at the thought, and Cabel could sympathize with the boy. Then Pete squared his shoulders and tried to reassert his bravado, but it now rang false. "I do know Gary sulked around for a week or so, and one of the other guys suddenly had a smile on his face. Then all of a sudden, he's back with Becca like nothing ever happened. I don't know what he did to make up with her, but it must have been really good."

Pete looked at his watch again, stood up, and held out his hand. "It's been nice to meet you, Mr. Evans. Hope you figure out who hurt Kittie. She was a nice girl."

"Just one more thing. Where can I find Scottie Marks?"

Pete shrugged. "We're based here so most of the guys have homes or apartments nearby and so Scottie doesn't have much to do except make sure the bus is ready for the next trip. We don't see him too much when we're here, just when we're on the road."

"So he's not here tonight?"

"Nope." He shook his head. "It really is a shame about Kittie."

Cabel stood and shook Pete's hand. The boy walked toward the stage looking serious and a little worried. Cabel felt a twinge of guilt at being the cause of Pete's new demeanor.

Before he could return to his seat, exhaustion hit Cabel like an enemy grenade. His body swayed and he used the table to steady himself. At that moment he could feel every penny of the emotional cost that this trip across the lake had racked up. He didn't have the energy to sit through another set. He needed to leave.

He had begun to make his way toward the door when the band returned to the stage. There was a sudden rush of couples moving toward the dance floor, and Cabel found himself caught in a tidal pool of taffeta and tails, buffeted from body to body. The room closed in around him as the stench of the trenches filled his lungs. Pain radiated from his chest as he fought to breathe when a hand gripped his elbow and pulled him from the current.

"You weren't going to leave without saying good-bye, were you?" Becca's accusing voice became a lifeline that drew him back to the speakeasy. He blinked twice then focused on her face. Her anger gave way to concern when she saw his face, and now embarrassment joined the panic and fear he knew she had seen there.

"Let me walk you out," she said softly. "I think you need a bit of fresh air."

He nodded his thanks and let her guide him through the padded door, down the dingy hallway and into the night.

"I really want to redecorate that hall. It's not as if the chief of police doesn't see it every other night, but the customers like to feel as if they are being naughty."

Cabel was too preoccupied taking in deep gulps of air to do more than nod. The speakeasy was in the heart of the city, too far inland to catch a lake breeze, yet the night air held a hint of its freshness.

He took another deep breath then braced himself to meet Becca's eyes, unsure of what he'd see. She stood in front of him, her red dress like a warning flare against the drab grays of the street and buildings. Her eyes held speculation but not pity. His breathing eased.

"I'm really rather cross with you, you know," Becca said. Her lips formed a beautiful, sexy pout. "You showed more interest in Pete then you did with me. Did your preferences change while you were off fighting for kin and country?"

Her question surprised a sharp bark of laughter from him. Then he laughed more, letting it ease the tension of the night from his body. Afraid that a hint of hysteria had begun to creep in, he forced himself to stop then wiped his eyes with his handkerchief. "No, my preferences have remained unchanged," he said. "But first of all, Becca, you need to recognize the difference between usefulness and fascination. The boy was useful, but *you* are fascinating." Dangerous, he added silently but also, undeniably, fascinating.

She seemed satisfied with his words but continued to study him carefully. "What's the second thing?"

"The second thing?"

"The second thing," she said with an impatient wave of her hand. "You said 'first of all.' So I want to know what the second thing is."

Cabel took her hand and held it to his chest, playing the part of the gallant knight she had accused him of being earlier. "The second thing, my dear lady, is that in your presence there is no other preference."

Her laughter echoed off the caverns of the buildings. "Cabe, it has been a true pleasure to see you again." She gave a quick flick of her wrist and soon an idling cab stood waiting at the curb. Her powers clearly extended beyond mere waiters. "As much as I have enjoyed our time, you look exhausted and I need to get back to my duties."

The cab driver jumped out and held the back door open. Cabel climbed in, unsure if he was being cared for or dismissed, either way it was a relief to be headed toward the solitude of his hotel room.

Through the open window, Becca said, "You will come back again, Cabe."

Were her words a command or a request? Another wave of exhaustion hit, and the question didn't matter anymore, so he nodded and sank back onto the seat.

As the cab pulled away, a sudden thought hit, and he yelled, "Stop!"

Becca turned back to him, her eyebrows raised in question.

He leaned out of the window and called, "I don't know the password."

Confused, she walked over to the cab "What's wrong?" she asked with impatience.

"I don't know the password to get into the club."

"Then how did you get in to begin with? Never mind," she said, waving away her own question. "The password should be easy for you to remember. It's 'Agatha.'" She stepped forward and spoke to the driver. "Don't stop again until you get him to his hotel. He's really not fit to be wandering the streets unattended."

"Yes, ma'am."

They pulled away again and the driver maneuvered his cab toward the north side of the city. As they bumped over the bridge that spanned the Chicago River, Cabel suddenly understood what Becca meant when she said that he should be able to remember the password to the club, though he didn't know whether to laugh or groan. Agatha, as in Agatha Gish. Her mother.

CHAPTER FOURTEEN

Heat, heavy and damp, pressed against him like an unwanted blanket. Cabel groaned as he rolled over trying to get comfortable, though it seemed an impossible task on the sodden sheets. Too hot to move and too uncomfortable to stay where he was, he decided that a cool bath would be perfect, but the bathroom was two doors down the hall and the heat had sapped his strength.

From the back yard came the sound of hammering, interspersed with the low rumble of quiet conversation and, once, a yelled curse. Cabel guessed that Jorge now sported a blackened thumb. There had been no obvious sounds of Nate or Belinda, and Cabel wondered idly what threats Kaye and Marta were using to keep them quiet.

The clock on the nightstand showed that it was almost three in the afternoon. He smiled, remembering Nate's disparaging views on napping and the elderly. Deciding that Nate was too young to appreciate the finer things in life, Cabel yawned and stretched then folded his arms behind his head to better contemplate the familiar ceiling.

Exhausted, he had returned to his hotel in the early hours of the morning, but sleep had eluded him. After a few futile hours on the too-soft bed, he had risen, showered, and shaved. A sleepy but well-mannered bellboy had brought Cabel a pot of coffee and a basket of sweet rolls. After the boy had left, Cabel poured himself a cup then stood by the window, waiting for dawn to tint the far edge of the lake.

When the first hints of color had appeared on the horizon, he packed, checked out of the hotel, and took a cab to the pier. Although he had booked a cabin on a larger ship leaving later in the morning, he found passage available on *The Cora Lee* and left Chicago before most of its citizens were awake.

Copies of both of the Chicago papers kept him entertained and distracted during the uneventful passage. Arriving home exhausted and empty, he was greeted by Marta, who had fussed over his bedraggled appearance as she ushered him up the stairs. Sleep had finally claimed him until the afternoon heat drew him back to wakefulness.

The doorbells chimed, though dully, as if they, too, were overcome with heat. Cabel yawned, knowing he needed to get up but unable to force himself to do so. In the years he had been away, he had forgotten the humidity of the Chicago and St. Joseph summers, just as he had forgotten the dryness of the air during the winter months. He remembered that his grandmother had purchased several electric fans in the years before his exile. When he finally found the energy to rise, he would find one and install it in his room before another night passed.

Even the thought of an artificial breeze could not motivate him to arise and go forth. He stopped fighting the sense that he should move and allowed his body to relax against the sodden bedclothes. His thoughts drifted with the scant breeze until a loud shriek shot him to his feet. Pulling on his pants and grabbing the shirt he had tossed over a chair, he struggled into it as he moved toward the bedroom door. Footsteps pounded up the stairs. Before he could reach the doorknob, Marta burst into the room. For a moment Cabel wasn't sure what shocked him more, that Marta had flung open the door without knocking or that she was capable of getting up the stairs so quickly.

"Oh Cabe, you shouldn't have. Oh my. Oh my. No. Jorge will want to send it all back for sure." She beamed at him even as she shook her head. "They're just too beautiful. How would I ever have the courage to use them?"

"I'm sure you're brave enough for anything you set your mind to," Cabel said, stalling for time. His overheated brain recognized Marta's words, but their meaning eluded him.

"You spent so much money, Cabe. And you bought a set for Kaye too. It's too much, though Kaye and her family could sure use them. I don't think they have a pot or pan left."

Pots. Pans. Ah ha. So much had happened in the few hours he had been in Chicago that Cabel had forgotten his impromptu shopping spree. Marta was as flustered and pleased as Cabel had imagined, more so even. Now on surer footing, he grinned as he opened his overnight case while Marta continued her excited babbling.

"I thought as long as we were remodeling the kitchen, we should get some new things to go in it," Cabel explained. "The pots and pans are for the kitchen, but this is just for you." With a flourish, he handed Marta the tissue-wrapped gift that had started it all.

With great care and reverence, she opened the package. Her eyes widened, and her mouth formed a perfect circle when she saw the embroidered apron. She looked at him with moist eyes before throwing her arms around him in a fierce hug and then rushing from the room.

Cabel stood a moment, nonplussed. He had expected her to be happy, pleased, but the tears surprised him. After further consideration, he decided that the gift must have been a greater success then he had imagined, but the slight disorientation he often felt when contemplating female behaviors followed him down the hall and into the bathroom.

With hair still damp from his bath, Cabel descended the stairs to find Nate waiting on the bottom step.

"You went all the way to Chicago, and all you brought back was dishes?"

Cabel fought back a smile at the utter disgust in the boy's tone.

"I suppose that's what's in the other box too. The one the hotel sent to you." Nate shook his head in commentary on the sad behaviors of adults.

"The box from the hotel?" Cabel couldn't imagine what the Drake Hotel had shipped to him. Nate headed toward the back of the house, clearly expecting Cabel to follow, which he did.

The kitchen was awash in brown packing paper. Copper pans gleamed on the old counter top. The two identical sets stood side-by-side but clearly separate, as if their respective owners had wanted to admire them but made sure that no pot of theirs somehow found its way into the other group. Propped against the wall near the back door was an odd lump of a package. After a moment, Cabel remembered the toys he had bought and had sent on to the hotel. In his sleep-deprived state this morning, he had left them behind.

"Well, Nate, I don't know about you, but that doesn't look like a box of dishes to me."

Self-consciously, Nate mimicked Cabel's stance, arms folded, one hand stroking his chin. "That's what I was thinking, but Mama and Miz Marta told me not to mess with it, so I've been waiting for you."

Ignoring the implied criticism, Cabel continued, "So what do you think is in there?"

Shocked, the boy stared up at him. "Don't you know?"

Cabel laughed out loud. Deciding not to test Nate's patience further, he found the kitchen shears and cut the twine. As the brown paper fell away revealing the bat, Nate's expression changed, becoming a perfect imitation of Marta's when she had beheld the apron. Fighting back another smile, Cabel picked up the bat, handing it to Nate. "Do *not* use it on your sisters."

For a moment the boy simply stared at the bat in his hands. Then, with a rebel yell that caused Cabel to jump a good foot into the air, the boy leaped toward the screen door. He shot through it with a bang, running into the deepening shadows of the late afternoon.

In the fragile peace of the kitchen, Cabel unwrapped the remaining items. The tea set in its wicker basket looked even more charming than he remembered. The hat he had finally decided on as the perfect gift for Anne now sat in a box, which had become slightly dented during its trip from Chicago, but he doubted the girl would mind. In the bottom, almost lost amongst the last shreds of paper, was the small truck for the paperboy. He tucked it into his pocket, where it would stay until he saw the child again.

A small sound, quieter than a chirp from a bird, came from near the door. Cabel looked up. Belinda stood with hopeful eyes on the other side of the screen, and he was profoundly grateful that he had thought of the young girl while on his unplanned shopping trip. Picking up the wicker basket, he opened the lid to show her what was inside. Her eyes filled with wonder as she slipped into the room. With a trembling finger, Belinda traced the rose pattern that edged the china plates then looked up to see his reaction, afraid he would be angry with her.

"I bought this especially for you," he said gently. "I noticed your doll was waiting for her tea the other day and thought the two of you might like some new dishes."

"Oh yes," she breathed. "Emily and I would love them."

Emily must be the doll, he thought after a moment's hesitation. "I'm sure the two of you will take good care of them." He held the basket out. Belinda looked at it, then at him, before reaching out to accept the gift.

"Thank you," she said softly, then turned to leave. As she reached the door, she turned back. "And thank you for Nate's bat too. I bet he forgot to say that." A shy grin followed this prediction.

"You're right," Cabel said. "And you're most welcome."

Another shy smile, then the girl disappeared into the yard.

Alone in the kitchen, Cabel contemplated the hatbox. Purchasing the cloche hat for Anne had seemed a brilliant idea until he walked into the hat store. He had left thirty minutes later feeling relief and embarrassment and a growing conviction that he had bought the wrong one. Doubt and embarrassment had now returned, along with a small nudge of anger. How had he gotten himself into this mess? Was a hat too personal of a gift to give to the daughter of a friend? And when had Walter become a friend?

He struggled with these questions until he decided to chuck the box in the compost heap and deal with Anne's disappointment later. His resolve lasted until he stood on the porch and surveyed the organized chaos of the back yard. He had personally witnessed the transformation over the past several days, but seeing it anew caused him to blink in shock. While the flowers still bloomed, the trees still leafed, and the garden still had its orderly rows of plants, gone was the peace, the haven that had been his refuge.

Planks of wood were stacked near the shed. Rails and posts leaned against it while sawhorses stood nearby with a pile of sawdust underneath. A rough workbench had been hammered together and held an assortment of tools, measures, and nails.

The younger children played under the sugar maple while Marta and Kaye hung clothes from the lines in the side yard. Voices led him around the far side of the house where Jorge and Walter inspected a hole in the porch floor.

"The whole thing's rotted through," Jorge said, like a doctor confirming a terminal diagnosis. "We should just pull the whole thing down and start over."

Walter nodded in agreement. The patient could not be saved.

Jorge looked up, spied Cabel, and shook his head just as sadly at him as he had at the hole in the porch. "Please tell me that the box you have isn't for Marta too. She cried and cried over that apron you brought her, and I don't think I can take any more waterworks right now."

"No, it's not for Marta," Cabel began, wishing he'd detoured by the compost heap on his way across the yard.

"Good." The old man stood, stepped down from the porch, and gave Cabel a pat on the shoulder as he walked past. "You did a real nice thing," he said in a voice so low Cabel almost missed the words.

"It better not be for my wife, either." Walter stood in front of him, hands on his hips and a touch of anger in his eyes.

"No, really, it's for Anne."

Walter's eyes grew wide as his fists clenched at his side.

Registering the threat of bodily harm, Cabel stepped back, holding one arm out to ward off Walter while hugging the hatbox to his side with the other arm.

"She's fourteen years old, you, you…"

"It isn't like that," Cabel said, backing up a few more steps. "I swear, Walter. It's just that I had bought the dishes for your wife and a bat for Nate and a tea set for Belinda and I needed to get something for Anne. I didn't want to leave her out."

"You didn't have to buy them things to begin with."

"I know and right now, I really wish I hadn't."

Walter seemed to hear the truth and unabashed desperation in Cabel's voice, for he paused a second, then his body relaxed. He shook his head, much as Jorge had done, then looked at Cabel and sighed. "When did you become Father Christmas?"

Cabel grinned a moment then sighed in return. "I was just walking down Michigan Avenue, and I saw the apron and thought of Marta. Then I went in and bought it."

"Well, there's your mistake right there."

"Exactly." Cabel rubbed the back of his neck to ease the tension. "Then I saw the pots and that place was right next to the toy store and so…"

Walter seemed to be fighting back a smile, which was better than fighting him, Cabel decided.

"So one thing led to another," Walter said, summing up the situation.

"Exactly," Cabel said again. "And now I'm stuck with this." He held out the box.

Walter stepped closer, tipped back the lid, and both men looked down at the simple blue hat that had caused the ruckus.

"So, do you think she'll like it?" Cabel was surprised at how much the other man's opinion mattered.

"You're asking me?" Walter looked up in alarm. "I'm not good at this sort of womanly thing." He backed away from the box as if it were a bomb.

"So what do I do with it now?"

"Give it to her, I guess."

"Maybe you should…"

"No, sir." Walter stepped around Cabel and headed to the back yard. "You bought that thing, you deal with it."

Coward, Cabel thought, but then so was he. It was just a hat, he reminded himself, and the girl either liked it or she didn't. He thumped the lid back on the box and followed Walter around the corner of the back porch. Kaye stood near the steps with a wash basket perched against one hip. With quick steps he made his way to her side.

She looked up and gave him a shy smile so much like Belinda's that it made him smile back. "Thank you, Mr. Cabel, for the pots and pans. They're too pretty to cook with, but Marta said I needed them, so I'll use them anyway."

"I'm glad you like them, and they're meant to be used. The clerk promised me that they were well made. Nate could probably use one of them for a drum and it wouldn't show any dents."

"Hush now. Let's not be giving him any ideas."

Cabel laughed then looked around to find Nate still under the tree, tossing a ball in the air and swinging at it with the bat. He missed and Cabel wondered if he should go toss a few to the boy. Surprised and uncomfortable at how natural the idea felt, he returned his attention to Kaye.

"Saying thank you doesn't seem to be enough," Kaye was saying, apparently unaware of his lapse of attention. "I wish there was something I could do…"

"There is," Cabel pounced before Kaye could rescind her offer. "I bought this for Anne." He held out the box for her inspection. "I'm not sure if it's right for a girl her age though the clerk said it would be fine. Still…"

Kaye set down the basket of clothes and took the box. Gently she lifted the lid, peering inside. Her smile brought a flood of relief.

"Oh, it's perfect." She looked up at him. "Anne will love it." She tried to return the box to Cabel, but he was already moving up the steps. "Wait. Don't you want to give it to her?"

"I'd really rather you did," he said, nearing the back door. "If you don't mind."

Kaye gave him a bemused smile and then walked toward the other side of the yard, presumably in search of Anne.

Cabel stepped into the kitchen feeling as if he had just dodged an enemy bullet only to find Marta waiting for him. Having known her since childhood he could tell by the set of her jaw and the look in her eyes that she was about to ask him to do something she knew he wouldn't like. He doubted his luck would allow him to dodge this bullet too. With a sigh of resignation, he waited to see what she wanted.

She bustled forward, an overly bright smile on her face. "Aren't you pleased with all of the work Jorge and Walter have done on the house?"

He nodded though most of the work seemed to be in preparation for the larger scale projects.

"They've ordered the shingles for the roof and some new iron work for the upper railings, just like you asked for." She paused then seemed to remember that no one had actually discussed the details with him, which was the way he wanted it. "They want to get the side porch done and maybe hire some men to help reshingle the roof before they start to work on the kitchen."

She seemed to be expecting something from him so he smiled and nodded. "Yes, that's fine." He tried to sidle around her, but she shifted her weight, continuing to block his path.

"The thing is, Cabe, they need the blueprints for the house."

"Sure, that's fine, but I don't know where they are."

"They're in the closet in your grandfather's study. He's always stored them in there."

Cabel's heart skipped a beat.

"Anyway, I know you don't want anyone to go in there, but Jorge and Walter need those plans, so you have to fetch them. They really can't do much more without them."

The ringing in his ears nearly drowned out Marta's words. Going into that room would be like facing his grandfather in person, and Cabel's shame was too great for that. Shaking his head, he tried to move past Marta, but she continued to block his way. Realizing he had to either shove the old woman aside or speak to her, he took a few deep breaths. Calmer, he dropped his eyes to hers and saw sadness and understanding in their pale blue depths. He looked away before he could see anymore. These he could accept, but not pity, anything but pity.

He felt Marta's hand on his arm. "It's just a room, Cabe. I know how you feel about it, but it's just a room. Besides, I think he would have understood, about things, about you, a lot more than you realize. He loved you the most."

And through my actions, I betrayed him the most, Cabel thought, finally easing around Marta and heading down the hall. His grandfather had died before the Great War, before everything changed. The grandson James Evans had loved was gone, destroyed in the horrors of battle along with so many others. Only the shell remained, and it was broken beyond repair.

Cabel walked down the hall, fully intending to march out the front door, down the street, and away from Marta's expectations. He managed two steps past the office door before he stopped, as if tethered to the knob. Taking several deep breaths, he willed his body to move, to continue on his intended course, but his legs shook, refusing to obey. After a moment, he leaned against the wall and waited, though he wasn't sure what he was waiting for. He tried to let his mind go blank, to retreat from memories both good and bad, all of which were now tainted by the war.

He found himself lost in a swirl of time, of people, of places. There seemed to be no order or meaning, just random bits of his life slipping through his consciousness. Childhood and adult events mingled with no thought to propriety. Horrors of war and holiday celebrations flowed together, mixing, churning. Regardless of what memories came forward, what year they occurred, Cabel felt his grandfather's presence, as if death held no sway in James Evans's ability to influence his grandson's life.

Cabel had tried to be a good officer, had felt the weight of the honor and duty of leading others into battle. Many died, more survived, and he prayed that this was due at least in some small measure to his skill and commitment. He had tried to do the right thing, even when he didn't know what that was. When he doubted the logic of his orders, he had followed them anyway, leading his men into hell time and again, wondering why but knowing that, in the end, it was the right thing to do. And his men had trusted him, followed him, surely the greatest honor of all. In his darkest moments, though, he wondered if they all wouldn't have been better served if he had just led them away from the bullets and the bloodshed. Not that that course of action had been possible, but at times it had seemed the only sane thing to do.

Shame, hot and full, descended on him at the thought of his grandfather somehow knowing these damning doubts. Would he have thought his grandson a coward for questioning his superiors, even in the privacy of his own mind, or worse, would he have judged Cabel as a coward for not standing up for his men in the face of the insanity that was the battle of the Somme? This question, this fearful doubt, kept him from sleep more nights than his dread of the horrors that awaited him in his dreams.

In the end he had been an honorable officer, a good soldier, and that, more than anything, seemed to be a damning indictment of his soul.

Deciding that the torture of staying out of the study was worse than that of entering it, Cabel reached for the knob. The door swung open, and beyond it was a room shrouded in shadows. Scents drifted toward him, wax, polish, and underneath it the spiciness of his grandfather's aftershave, the only real affectation the man had ever shown. Cabel smiled at the scent and allowed it to draw him in, turning on lights as he went. He crossed the room, noting the bookcases, the globe on its ornate stand, the deep leather chairs in front of the fireplace, but he kept his eyes diverted from the desk, his grandfather's seat of power.

Unfortunately, the closet lay just beyond it, but Cabel managed well enough. It took only a few moments to find the blue prints as well as two of the electric fans he had been wishing for earlier. Gathering the scrolls of paper and the fans proved awkward, and Cabel dumped the whole mess on the desk without a second thought.

His breath caught when he realized what he had done, half-expecting a scolding for risking the finish on the carved mahogany top. Instead, the silence continued. With a cautious hand, he touched the polished surface and was both pleased and disappointed that his grandfather's ghost didn't appear over his shoulder. The desk looked just as he had remembered it the last time he had been in the room. How old had he been? Seventeen or eighteen he decided. The greenglass-shaded lamp stood in the center, ready to spread its light on the leather and gilt-edged blotter. An ivory cup held pens and pencils, and a shallow oak tray waited for the day's work to be placed inside it.

The only addition was the battered box that now sat in the middle of the blotter. On top of it lay an envelope with his name written on it. The handwriting was both elegant and somehow stingy, a perfect description of the woman who had penned it. His grandmother had written him a message before she died.

He moved to sit in the massive leather chair and was surprised to find that it wasn't massive. His legs no longer dangled and the seat didn't feel as if it were about to swallow him. In fact, it suited him perfectly. Forcing aside these distracting thoughts, Cabel stared down at the cream-colored envelope and then picked it up, turning it over. The red wax seal was stamped with a stylized E in the center. He didn't have to look for the letter opener as it was still where it had always been, in the center desk drawer. A quick slice and his grandmother's words spilled out into his hand.

He kept the pieces of linen paper folded for a moment, wondering what condemnation his grandmother had felt necessary to bequeath him. Finally, he opened the letter and began to read.

My dearest Cabel,

If the world continues as it has for the past year, you shall be reading this after my death, for I doubt anything less than that would bring you home. I am sure I will not be mourned long within the family, but I do hope that you might hold some fond memories of me, though your grandfather was the center of the universe and those in his orbit could not hope to eclipse him.

I want you to know that I was adamantly opposed to your going off to war. Your father, however, refused to listen to me, and look where his stubbornness has taken us all. Although many things happened to bring us to this point, I have lain awake on many nights wondering if I could have spared you some of this pain if only I had given you this box sooner.

As you know, your grandfather served as an officer for the Union Army during the Civil War. He rarely spoke of this time and then did so only to honor the brave men he served with, many of whom had come from southwestern Michigan. This, in part, is why he chose to build his summer home here rather than on one of the fashionable Wisconsin lakes. As a young hostess, I was devastated by his decision, but he would not be dissuaded. Later I saw that this was very wise of him, for to follow our friends and associates to Wisconsin would have meant no break from his work or mine. Your mother and aunt felt much as I had when I was younger, and as soon as your grandfather died, houses were purchased on Lake Geneva, leaving this place to me and my memories.

I know I digress, but all of this is of importance.

Your father is in many ways a foolish man, and he always regretted that he had no war in which to fight. As if there is glory or honor in killing over ideals. James wanted to tell him, but he was afraid to speak of what he had seen and done in battle, afraid of somehow spreading those horrors to his sons.

The words blurred on the page. Cabel blinked back his tears as he set the letter aside and leaned back in the chair. How often had he felt as his grandfather had? When people asked about the war, it was clear they didn't want the truth. They wanted parades and uniforms and heroes, not stench and terror and meaningless deaths. Only a few of the boys he and Jon had been close to as they were growing up wanted to know, really know, what the war had been like, but how could he tell them? He wished with all of his soul that he could remove those images from his own mind. He did not want to be responsible for placing them in someone else's.

Yes, like his grandmother had written, his time as a soldier was like a disease of ugliness that he was afraid to spread. Even in New Orleans, working on the docks with others broken by the war, no one spoke of what they had endured except in drunken rages or drunken tears. Sobriety brought with it responsibility to keep the contagion contained.

With shaking hands, he picked up the letter and continued to read his grandmother's unexpected words.

> Your father refused to believe that war could
> be anything but a glorious adventure, and since he
> could not take the journey, he forced you to do
> so in his stead. Know that if your grandfather had
> lived, he never would have allowed this. He loved
> you and would have protected you, as your father
> should have done.
>
> While fighting the Confederates, he kept a journal.
> As far as I know, he never read it, never revisited
> his past. As soon as the conflict ended, he placed
> it in this box, along with his medals and memories,
> and shut it all away. War is powerful, though,
> and does not loosen its hold easily. Many nights
> he woke screaming and flailing, fighting battles of
> years past. On rare occasions something would

happen that seemed to bring forth a memory that would have him brooding for days. No one saw this but me, and although it lessened over the years, the war never let him be fully at peace.

Before you went to your war, I saw so much of my beloved James in you. Now, you are even more like him, but in such behaviors that weigh heavy on my soul. As with your grandfather, I know there is little I can do to comfort you or repair the wounds you have suffered. Instead, I offer you his journal so in the reading of it you might know what you hold in common with him. Perhaps knowing that you and he have trod the same path might bring you a measure of relief.

Although your actions of last year cannot be dismissed or condoned, I have an understanding as to their source. The past cannot be changed, so go forward in life and become the man you were meant to be, as your grandfather would have wished you to do. As I expect you to do.

Most lovingly,
Your grandmother
Katherine Coulter Evans

The pages fell to the blotter while Cabel tried to absorb the words he had read. His grandmother had never been a warm or loving woman. There was more genuine affection expressed within these pages than any he had received from her during her lifetime. He had to smile though. She couldn't get through the entire letter without taking him to task and delivering orders. And signing her full name, as if he could somehow forget who his grandmother was, was so like her that it brought an ache to his heart.

Pushing aside further thoughts of his grandmother, he studied the box on the desk. It was simple and well constructed but scarred from heavy use. His grandfather had probably carried it to war with him. There was no lock, just a simple metal latch, slightly rusted but easily released.

He ran his thumb along the edge of the lid and over the latch.

He would open it, but not today. Too many thoughts swirled through his brain, and he felt a need to sort them out before adding more to the muddle. Still, as he scooped up the plans and picked up the fans, he felt a sense of calm within himself, as if he had found something small but precious that he hadn't realized was missing until it was returned.

Fumbling a bit as he turned off the lamps on the way to the door, he was struck with a sudden thought. Marta had asked him to come here and get the plans because he had ordered that his grandfather's study be left undisturbed. Yet the shelves were dusted, the furniture polished, and the floors spotless.

He couldn't decide whether to throttle his meddling housekeeper or fire her but knew he wouldn't do either. He needed her too much.

CHAPTER FIFTEEN

Black met black on the distant horizon, the stars alone distinguishing sky from lake. On the sand below, Silver Beach glittered at the water's edge while on the north side of the river the lighthouse's beacon signaled safe harbor. From the bell tower of the Catholic church ten deep-throated tolls broke the quiet of the evening.

Standing at the edge of the bluff, Cabel let the cool breeze wash over him, cleansing away the heat of the day. After leaving his grandfather's study, he had kept to himself, unsure of what to say to Marta and not wanting the company of the hoards that now populated his backyard. The Arledges had left around eight o'clock, and shortly thereafter Marta and Jorge had retired to their small rooms at the back of the house. Cabel had heard their radio playing when he had snuck into the kitchen to pilfer some cold chicken from the icebox, as if he were a thief rather than the homeowner.

After his snack, he found himself wandering the main floor, passing through room after room, like a ghost in search of someone to haunt. On his third tour of the formal dining room, he knew he needed to find something more productive to do, even if it was just a walk to the bluff.

Since the walk to the bluff involved little more than crossing the street that ran in front of his house, he found the exercise unsatisfactory. Once again his eyes were drawn to the sparkling lights of the amusement park. With a sigh of both resignation and pleasure, he started down the sidewalk.

The cooling air had drawn St. Joseph residents from their homes, and many people nodded to Cabel in greeting as he made his way to the walking path near the Whitcomb Hotel. The breeze felt fresher, the air cooler as he descended the walkway to the bottom of the bluff. The rollercoaster rumbled on its tracks and the tantalizing scents of roasted nuts and frying onions mingled with the smell of water and sand.

Drawn toward the amusement park by a need for the company of others, even strangers, maybe especially strangers, Cabel stepped onto the boardwalk. Gone were the families with young children, probably already tucked into their beds. In their place, teenagers and young adults strolled along the walkway, though some older folk were intermingled in here and there. Cabel felt the familiar nostalgic excitement of the endless possibilities encapsulated in a summer's night at Silver Beach. He smiled at himself as a boy and, more ruefully, at the man who now stood on the worn planks of the boardwalk. This night held no possibilities for him, though it was pleasant to remember a time when it did.

Running the gauntlet of barkers trying to tempt patrons to their games, Cabel passed the carousel, its calliope playing a tinkling melody. Overhead, the airplane ride twirled to a chorus of delighted squeals. He remembered riding it happily when he was very young, then later with much embarrassment when chaperoning Jim. Tonight the planes were piloted by young couples who seemed quite delighted with the ride, or maybe it was the company they kept that made them smile.

The rollercoaster, with its flashing lights and wooden trestles, had been updated and moved since his childhood. While it looked to be a more exciting ride than it had been in his youth, he doubted that it had a name as romantic as the original, "Chase through the Clouds."

Past the rides, a few more games of chance tempted players to try their luck. People crowded three deep at the spill-the-milk booth, waiting for their turn to try and win a prize. Above their heads, the chalkware figures that Kittie had hung from the rafters bobbed gently in the evening breeze. Cabel wondered if Daniela worked at the booth tonight, but the crowd was too dense for him to see. Beyond the games, the high striker stood tall, its glowing apex marking the winning target. Next to it stood a souvenir stand selling trinkets and lemon drops. Past those amusements, the Shadowland Ballroom glowed against the dark backdrop of the lake.

Cabel stood listening to the music that drifted from the open doorway, watching the people mingling near the steps, and suddenly felt very much alone. A hand touched his arm. Looking down, he found Bessie George gazing up at him through thick lashes and heavily coaled eyes. She looked beautiful, mysterious, and timeless. Her makeup had been expertly applied to present a façade that one trusted yet slightly feared, though from his own experiences of her, maybe that wasn't a façade at all. He had a sudden vision of Bessie George seated at her vanity, watching in the mirror while Daniela painted her aunt's face much as she did the chalkware prizes.

"My niece has decided I must look more like a fortuneteller, like the ones they show in movies," Bessie George said, and Cabel wondered yet again if this woman could truly read minds. "I tell her, they are pretend, I am real. Who can look more like a fortuneteller than me? But Daniela, she is like a dog with a bone until I say 'yes.' Now I look like this." The old woman shrugged, causing her beaded shawl to slip from her shoulders, but underneath her denials, she seemed quite pleased with the results.

"You were fine as you were, of course," Cabel said, laying his hand on top of Bessie George's, "but if I may add, the effect she created brings forth your beauty. If only I were ten years younger, I would court you away from Joe George."

Bessie George laughed, a surprisingly youthful sound, and then wagged her finger at him. "Mr. Cabel, you are much too gallant for your own good, I think, but you know how to make an old woman feel young again."

Taking his arm, she drew him onto the sand, away from the direct glare of the lights that lined the boardwalk and began to study him, as if she could see him more clearly in the shadows. The thought both comforted and concerned him. With calloused hands, she reached up and cradled his face, gently tipping it down, allowing her to peer directly into his eyes. As before, he felt as if she were searching his soul.

She patted his cheeks as a grandmother would before releasing him and stepping back. "It is good. You are finding the answers you need."

Cabel gave a snort of denial before remembering his manners. "I'm sorry Miz Bessie, but all I've found are bits and pieces of nothing. I'm no closer to learning who killed Kittie now than I was when we met a few weeks ago."

Bessie George smiled, sad and knowing. "You have found more than you understand, but in time you will know your truth. It will make you unhappy, I think, but you will do what you must to help your friend. But remember, I said you are finding the answers you need, not the ones you want. In time, those will come, too."

Cabel frowned down at the fortuneteller. "Do you know who killed Kittie? Do you know why?"

She shook her head. "I do not know who did this evil, but I do know that you will find justice for your friend." With that, she turned and slipped into the darkness.

Unsettled, he stepped back onto the boardwalk, into the light, though it didn't seem as bright as it had a few moments ago. He had no answers and knew that there could be no justice or punishment great enough to balance the scales against Kittie's death. The magic of the night had drifted away like glitter in the breeze. Cabel decided to return home.

He glanced at the ballroom one last time, and then turned to begin the climb to the top of the bluff when his mind caught up with what his eyes had seen. Turning back, he saw a group of girls milling around the doorway. From this distance he couldn't make out their faces, but there was one thing he could distinguish quite clearly, a blue cloche hat.

By the time he reached the doorway, the girls had disappeared inside. Taking a breath like a swimmer about to dive underwater, Cabel crossed the threshold into a world of silk and music, dancing and laughter. After the Charades Club, Shadowland seemed wholesome and innocent but still sophisticated. It would never have the dark edge of the Chicago speakeasy, and for that he was thankful. Drake had managed to create a ballroom that was elegant and separate from the rest of Silver Beach yet somehow maintained the idealism and joy that was the park's foundation.

Since its band members were wearing suits rather than tuxedoes, the group was probably local. What they lacked in polish, they made up for with enthusiasm and lively music. Patrons elbowed each other for room on the dance floor while the line of those waiting for the next song snaked through nearby tables.

Although fairly tall, Cabel was no match for the crowded ballroom. The colorful array of constantly moving humanity made it impossible for him to find one lone girl, blue hat or no. The crush of bodies, the heat and noise battered Cabel's senses. Lightheaded and short of breath, he moved to the edge of the crowd, hoping to stem the tide of the horrific memories that lurked in his mind, seeking opportunities to attack. Leaning against the curved wall, he took deep breaths and focused on the music, grounding himself in the present. He was at the Shadlowland Ballroom, not France, he reminded himself over and over until the words dispelled his nightmares. No machineguns, no artillery shells, no cries of the dying, just a local band playing for local kids.

His heartbeat slowed, and his breathing returned to a normal pattern. Wrung out and exhausted, he wanted to leave but felt an obligation to check on Anne. He remembered her telling him that she wasn't allowed at the ballroom until she turned fifteen. With a groan, he pushed away from the wall, wondering what he would do with the errant fourteen-year-old if he caught up with her.

Elmer Dupree materialized from the crowd, holding out a hip flask. "You look like you could use a swig of this. It's hard cider. It's got a decent kick to it, if I do say so myself." The young man pressed the flask into Cabel's hand. "Turn to the wall and have a swallow. I don't want Drake to see you."

Obediently, Cabel turned his back to the ballroom and took a sip. The liquid burned the back of his throat and left a sharp, medicinal taste in his mouth. After the first shock, a surprisingly sweet apple flavor teased his taste buds, a reward for surviving the initial onslaught. Cautiously, he took another sip. Braced for the experience, it was somewhat more pleasant but not a way he'd want to get drunk.

Recapping the flask, he slipped it into Elmer's waiting hands only to watch it disappear with the grace of a magician.

"So what do you think?"

"I'll let you know when my eyes stop watering," Cabel said, taking out his handkerchief.

Elmer pouted, reminding Cabel of the immaturity of Kittie's former boyfriend. He had wanted to speak with the boy again, not antagonize him.

"You were right about the kick, though, and I liked the apple flavor."

Appeased, Elmer smiled. Cabel could see the charm in the boy but also the vanity. Life would be simple if he could prove that this young moonshiner had killed the girl, but he doubted it would be that easy.

"I use a blend of apples, not just one kind, and that's what makes my cider so special."

Special was one word for it. Lethal was another. "You must have quite a business going," Cabel said.

The boy's casual shrug belied his cunning smile. "I do all right and I plan to do a lot better. Yep, I'm moving up in the world. Soon my cider's going to be served in some of the finest speakeasys in Chicago."

Cabel coughed to cover his laugh. "Wow, that's great."

"It sure is. It's all about connections and I got 'em." The boy grinned then eyed Cabel appraisingly. "You aren't the only one who can ask questions and learn things, useful things."

"Like what? Anything about Kittie?"

"I wish. If I ever find out who killed my girl, I'll..." Fists clenched at his side, Elmer struggled to think of a punishment great enough to exact his revenge. Giving up the effort, he shrugged and said, "Anyway, I'm in with a guy who's going to make me rich. He'll help me sell my brew, and I'll help him run some other stuff he handles."

"Elmer, if you're dealing with rumrunners, you need to be careful. Are you sure..."

"Don't worry about me. I can take care of myself." Elmer puffed up like peacock. "I'm going to make it big, you'll see, and I won't need anyone's help to do it."

The boy turned and darted into the crowd, disappearing in seconds. Cabel fought the urge to go after him. *And do what?* he asked himself. *Advise a snotty young man on how to conduct illegal business dealings with thugs?* He had enough on his hands in locating Anne.

The music ended and the bandleader announced a fifteen-minute break. Hoping that the girl and her friends would want fresh air as much as he did, Cabel joined the mob at the door and finally, thankfully, stepped out into the cool of the evening.

Young people clustered in groups, mostly divided by gender, but some were mixed. Whether together or apart, young women flirted with young men, using their eyes, their gestures, even the toss of their hair to show their interest. In response, the men swaggered and preened, sending messages of their own.

He had never done this mating dance, Cabel realized. First and always, there had been Elizabeth, and she had joined him and Jon like a missing piece fitting into a puzzle. There had been no need to flirt, to gain attention, because he already had it. In one sense he had been lucky to escape the treacherous waters of youthful dating, but in another sense, he had missed out on the thrill of the unknown and the excitement of the chase. Even with the unspoken rivalry between him and Jon for Elizabeth's heart, all had been safe, maybe too much so.

Brushing away these disconcerting thoughts of his youth, Cabel scanned the milling crowd, looking for Anne. At the far edge of the masses, a group of girls clustered near a lamppost. A bit younger than most of the others, Cabel thought, shy, awkward. The blue cloche hat stood out like a beacon.

Deftly weaving through the clusters of young people, Cabel made his way toward the girls. Closer now, he could verify that, yes, it was Anne beneath the hat. She looked relaxed, happy even. Her face was animated in a way he had never seen before, her smile broader and more open then he would have imagined of her. She possessed a gentle prettiness that he had sensed would come, but here, now, it shone through. Away from her family, or maybe away from the realities of Kittie's death, Anne glowed.

Cabel hesitated near the group, knowing that she hadn't seen him yet. He hated the thought of ending her evening, which she was clearly enjoying, but he felt an obligation to Walter, and to Anne, too, if it came to that. Too many young men were noticing the girl, eyeing her, trying to catch her attention. She was either too naïve or too caught up in her friends to notice, but it wouldn't be long before one of the boys made his move.

Knowing he could procrastinate no further, Cabel stepped into the center of the group. Most of the girls looked surprised and stepped away from him, this odd adult in their midst. Anne, caught up in her conversation, didn't notice him until the voices around her silenced.

Her eyes widened in surprise when she saw him; her mouth opened then closed. Under the lamplight, even with the brim of her hat shading her face, Cabel could see where at least some of the illusion of Anne's maturity had come from. Mascara clumped on her lashes, and the dye creased her lids. Red smears stained her cheeks and lips. The heat of the ballroom had added a damp sheen over the girl's face, making it look clownish yet oddly adult. Absently, Cabel wondered if this was Anne's first attempt at using makeup.

She continued to gape up at him, which gave him time to notice her dress. Short by St. Joseph standards, and cut too low in the front, the color indistinguishable under the glare of the light. Dark red? Black? Either way, it was too sophisticated for a fourteen-year-old girl to be wearing at the ballroom, or anywhere else for that matter.

With a quick motion, Cabel removed his jacket and placed it around Anne's shoulders. He spun her around and began marching her down the boardwalk before she thought to object.

"Mr. Cabel, sir. Are you going to tell my parents?" Her voice quivered.

Unsure of what his answer would be, he continued past the games until he reached the ice cream parlor. He pushed her down a small alleyway, past the back of the building, and stopped in front of the restrooms. Handing Anne his handkerchief, he said, "Wash your face, and then we'll talk."

Head down, shoulders slumped, she was the epitome of dejection. Cabel fought back a smile as he watched her disappear behind the wooden door. How had he gotten himself into this? Leaning against the back of the ice cream parlor, he gave the matter much thought. Marta Voss was to blame, he realized. She had invited the Arledges into his home, his life. If she hadn't let Walter in that day, none of this would have happened. And he would still be sitting alone on his back porch, waiting to die. He shook his head. Throttle or thank? This question of what to do with his meddling housekeeper seemed to arise with some regularity.

Hinges squeaked. A freshly scrubbed Anne stepped out of the stall and made her way toward him like a penitent child. From girl to woman to girl again, she slipped between these worlds with head-spinning speed. Cringing at the memories of his own puberty, he studied Anne as intently as she studied her shoes.

Her hand lifted slowly, as if it held the weight of the world's burdens. Silently, she handed him a sodden and soiled handkerchief. Smeared with makeup, Cabel doubted even Marta could get it white again. There was also the question of what she would make of finding his handkerchief in such a state. Tossing the thing into a trash can, he placed his hand on Anne's shoulder and guided her toward the front of the building.

Opening the screen door to the ice cream parlor, he nudged her ahead of him into the brightly lit room. Most of the round tables with their cheerful red chairs were occupied with laughing, chatting young people. They seemed less self-conscious than their counterparts at the ballroom, except for Anne, who had pulled the lapels of his jacket up past her nose. He led her to the counter that ran along the back of the room. A chalkboard listed the day's choices.

Disappointed to see the word "peach" incompletely but definitely erased, Cabel ordered a chocolate cone. In response to his question, he thought he heard the word "strawberry" mumbled from within her burrow, so he ordered for Anne as well. After the business of purchasing the ice cream was complete, Cabel held the cones and used his elbow to guide Anne back outside. After a moment's consideration, he led the girl to one of the benches that allowed a view of the lake.

He sat and waited. Slowly, Anne emerged from her cocoon and accepted her ice cream. They both concentrated on eating their cones, racing against the warm summer night to finish before the ice cream melted. Cabel had forgotten to collect any napkins, and his handkerchief was in the trashcan, so he rested his elbows on his knees, letting his sticky fingers dangle a safe distance from his pants.

Daintily, Anne licked the last bits of ice cream from her fingers, innocent, yet sending an unintended message. Cabel understood Walter's desire to keep his daughter home for as long as reasonably possible. She was too naïve to navigate the world alone, yet how do you guide a young girl into adulthood? Anne needed her mother or older sister, not him, Cabel, a man too lost to find his own way let alone help another. He sighed. Kittie was dead, and Kaye was probably at home.

"Where do your parents think you are?" he asked.

Anne blinked at him. Whatever she thought he would say, this wasn't it. "I'm spending the night at my friend Peggy's house." She hung her head. "Her parents think she's staying at my house, but we're both staying with Violet. Her mother works the night shift at Cooper & Wells, and her dad's just…gone." She looked up at him, tears shimmering in her eyes. "I've never done anything like this before, I swear." She turned toward the water and shook her head. "I should have known I'd get caught. I always do. Not like Kittie."

Cabel sorted through what Anne said, trying to decide which of the many paths laid before him he should take. "You swear you've never done this before?"

"Yes, sir, I swear." She looked directly into his eyes for the first time since he had led her away from the ballroom. "I won't do it again, I promise, at least not until I'm old enough."

"By then you won't have anything to hide."

Her eyes dropped as she shrugged her shoulders. "I guess."

She would never make a successful poker player. He had to study her a moment, though, before understanding the depth of the issue. "Where do you keep your makeup and dress? I can't imagine your mother let you out of the house looking like this."

Anne sank into the folds of his jacket, her blue hat perched on the top. She didn't move or speak.

"Come on, Anne, playing opossum isn't going to make this go away. I'm worried about you and I need to know what's going on."

"I don't want to get anyone else in trouble," she said, her voice muffled.

Cabel nudged her with his elbow. "Come out of there. I don't want to make trouble for anyone. I just want to understand."

His coat heaved from the sigh she released. Anne lifted her face and lowered the jacket. "I'm so sorry."

"There's no need to be sorry, just tell me how this happened."

That final coax broke the dam, and Anne's story gushed forward. She and Peggy had planned to come to the amusement park for the evening and then spend the night at Peggy's house. Violet Baker, two years older than the girls and a friend of Kittie's, sought out Anne and asked her what she should do with Kittie's things. Anne knew that her sister had a stash of makeup and clothes that she kept at someone else's house, as did most girls with strict parents.

Cabel remembered that the young woman who worked at the ballroom, Annette, told him that she, too, kept her special dresses and makeup at a friend's house. He wondered if Violet ran a contraband storage business.

"Anyway," Anne continued, "Peggy and I went to Violet's, and she was so nice and showed me all of Kittie's things." Her eyes widened in wonder. "I had no idea how many gifts Gary had given her, dresses, scarves, and stuff. I know she had a silver bracelet from him, but she wore that all of the time, and Mother and Dad never said anything about it. I always thought that Gary was a big secret, but I guess not." She thought a moment. "You said that Dad knew about Gary. I bet he talked to Mr. Drake to check up on him."

Cabel nodded, impressed with her perceptions of her parents. He wondered if Kittie had been as observant. "What was your sister like?" he asked. "I never met her and no one speaks of her much, so I can't get a sense of her." He looked down into Anne's stricken face. "Oh, I'm so sorry. You don't need to answer that."

"It's okay. I'm just surprised, is all. None of us talk about her but all of us miss her, especially my mother, I think. They were very close." Her tone was wistful rather than jealous. She looked at the lake again, but he doubted she saw it. "Kittie was smart and funny. Prettier than me, you know, but she didn't make a big deal about it. She was always willing to help, even with chores, and she was good at keeping secrets." She turned to Cabel. "Once, when I was about seven or eight, I took a penny from my mother's pocketbook. I just wanted some candy, but she had said no. Anyway, Kittie caught me, I always get caught, and she made me put it back, but she never told. Nate would have."

Cabel stifled a smile. "He'd have to just to annoy you. I think its part of his responsibility as your little brother."

Anne scrunched up her nose in disgust. "Well, I'm just lucky that Belinda's younger, so he mostly picks on her."

He made a mental note to have a discussion with Nate about his treatment of his sisters before realizing that this was the second time in one day that he had thought to have a parental interaction with the boy. He was not Nate's father, brother, uncle, or cousin and should not get involved with this family any more than he was. With a rueful shake of his head, he reminded himself that he was sitting on a bench playing confessor to Anne, and later, probably tomorrow, he would have his talk with Nate. He wondered if this was what it was like to drown, but instead of water it was people, relationships, which had him in over his head. Maybe he should do what all good drowning victims do, stop struggling and accept the inevitable.

Anne sat, waiting. Cabel didn't want to upset her further, but he needed to know more about Kittie. "Did your sister keep anything besides clothes or makeup at Violet's house?"

"No, not really." The girl thought a moment. "She had a hat, though not as nice as mine." Her smile beamed up at him through the darkness. "Thank you for giving it to me. It's the best present anyone ever gave me."

"You're welcome." Cabel wondered if he should tell her that if it wasn't for the hat, she wouldn't have gotten caught. "Was there anything else that Kittie had hidden away, like letters or photographs?" Since he had no idea what he was looking for, he didn't know what to ask.

Anne shook her head. "There was some perfume, kind of spicy and strong. I don't like it, but it's in a pretty bottle that I want to keep. Oh, and there were some scarves and a shawl. Violet said they were silk, but I don't think Gary made enough money to buy something like that. Anyway, Violet took one of the scarves as payment for keeping the rest of the stuff for me. I didn't care because the color was too bright, and there was a tear in one end, though Violet said she could fix it."

There was no hope for it, he realized. He needed to see Kittie's stash. Rising from the bench, he motioned Anne to join him. "We need to go to Violet's house so you can change your clothes and I can see Kittie's things."

Anne's eyes widened. "I don't know, Mr. Cabel. I don't think Violet will like this."

"I'm not happy about it myself, but there really isn't any other choice." The finality of his words depressed them both.

CHAPTER SIXTEEN

Cabel and Anne wended their way toward the park exit that Anne said was the closest to Violet's house. Away from Silver Beach the streets were ill lit and poorly paved. Cabel kept a hand under Anne's elbow to help her over the rough cobblestones; though the closer they got to Violet's, the more he felt that the girl was dragging her feet rather than tripping over them.

The house that Anne led him to was in the beach slums, just a few blocks from the Arledge's home but a world away in appearance. Shabby was the word that came to mind. Overgrown bushes crowded the front stoop; unwashed windows with pealing frames created an overall sense of grime and disinterest. The walkway was broken and more hazardous than the street, and the stairs leading up to the door tilted at odd angles, creating a fun house effect.

Nudging Anne ahead of him, Cabel followed her to the door and waited while she tapped on its cracked surface so lightly, he doubted anyone could have heard it. The door flung open, as if those on the other side were waiting by the knob. Light spilled out, framing the two girls who stood in the threshold.

"Oh, you're here. Thank goodness. I don't know what I would have told your mother if I lost you," one of the girls said tearfully as she took Anne's hand and pulled her inside.

"I told you she'd be fine. Whoever that guy was, he was dressed too nicely to do anything bad," the second girl declared.

Cabel didn't realize that the girls hadn't seen him until the second one, Violet he presumed, started to shut the door. Stepping forward, he placed his hand against the door, preventing it from closing, and said, "Excuse me, I'm with Anne."

The two girls stared at him in shock, which gave way to fear in the younger one but a look of sly assessment in the other.

No one moved until Cabel said, "Anne, why don't you introduce me to your friends?"

"This is Violet," Anne said dutifully, pointing to each girl as she spoke. "And this is Peggy."

He had guessed correctly.

Violet studied him in a way that was disconcertingly similar to Becca, while Peggy continued to stare at him in frightened fascination. Anne stood between the girls, waiting, until a raised eyebrow from Cabel had her complete the introductions. "Oh, and this is Mr. Cabel Evans. He's, ah..." She looked at him helplessly.

"I'm a friend of Anne's father."

Violet gave a knowing sort of smile, as though the simple statement hid a darker, perverted relationship between him and Anne. Cabel tried not to picture the type of life the girl had led that caused her to assume such ugliness. He should feel pity for her, he knew, but instead felt dirty in her presence, as if he were somehow guilty of the imagined sins she had assigned him.

Wanting to leave as quickly as possible, Cabel jumped to the heart of the matter that had brought him to the girl's home. "Anne tells me that Kittie left some things here. I'd like to see them, please."

"Why? I don't think she has anything of yours in her box."

He blinked, surprised by the girl's challenge. Nothing was easy this evening.

Violet slouched against a paint-peeling wall in a room as shabby as the outside had predicted. Her eyes slanted, making her seem cunning and more experienced than she should be for her sixteen or so years. Maybe it wasn't the shape of her eyes, but the cold appraisal they held that made him hesitate. After a moment's thought, he settled on a near-truth.

"As I said, I'm a friend of Anne's father, and when I saw her at Shadowland, I knew she was breaking his rules, and so I tracked her down to speak with her about this. She told me that you kept some items for Kittie, and that you've offered to do the same for Anne, but I think it would be best if she changed her clothes, collected her things and came with me."

Violet eyed him thoughtfully, trying to sift truth from lie. Anne and Peggy stood together, staring at the floor, as if by avoiding eye contact, they would somehow be forgotten.

"Go change your clothes. Now," Cabel said to Anne in a quiet tone that brooked no defiance. It was as effective on a fourteen-year-old as it had been on raw recruits.

Anne left the room, and Peggy rushed up the stairs after her friend. Violet straightened from the wall and walked with a deliberate, hip-swinging gait to a beaten couch that sagged against the wall. Settling into a provocative pose, shoulders back, cleavage displayed, she sent a clear invitation.

Cabel ignored the message and sent one of his own. "Anne and Peggy are too young to be wearing makeup or going to the ballroom. I'll make sure that they don't go back there until they're old enough." *Thirty? Forty?* He sighed. "Until then, you will not hold any contraband items for them or help them break their parents' rules in any way. Is that clear?"

The girl leaned forward, dropping the flirtation in exchange for casual indifference. "I was just doing Anne a favor, you know. Her sister should be the one to help her with the makeup and stuff, but she's dead so I decided to take her place." The girl shrugged.

"For a fee."

Another shrug. "Of course. I have to get something out of this, don't I?"

"But Kittie already paid you."

Violet's eyes flared. "So what? She's gone and now Anne wants the same deal. New person, new rent. It's only fair."

Anne and Peggy clattered down the narrow stairs, both changed into simple dresses. Anne carried a fairly large cardboard box. Cabel stepped forward and relieved her of her burden.

"Is this everything?"

Both girls nodded glumly.

"Well, it's everything except the scarf Violet kept," Anne said.

Cabel turned to Violet. She must have read the determination in his eyes. With a huff, she rose from the couch and flounced from the room, returning a minute later with a red-patterned silk scarf. She tossed it at Cabel, letting it fall just short of his outstretched hand. Balancing the box, he leaned over and scooped it up, tossing it in with the rest of the jumble as he rose.

He nodded his good-bye to the older girl while ushering the younger ones out of the door. On the threshold he paused and looked back at Violet.

"Why didn't you just keep these things? Her parents didn't know about them, and Anne couldn't have forced you to give them to her."

Violet shrugged. "Kittie was a friend." She closed the door in his face.

At the end of the broken walkway, Anne and Peggy huddled like refugees, waiting to see what Cabel would do next.

He was rather curious about that himself.

CHAPTER SEVENTEEN

The following morning, Cabel rose early, dressed quickly, and then hurried to the small guest room at the back of the house. Empty. The neatly made bed gave no sign that the room had been occupied during the night. He sighed with relief.

Descending the stairs, the sound of voices drew him to the kitchen. Anne and Peggy sat at the old, scarred table shelling peas while Marta worked at the stove. The aroma of bacon and eggs wafted from her direction. His stomach growled in response.

The girls, he noticed, looked tired and chastised. While pleased that they seemed to have learned their lesson, he hoped they could pull off a better performance for Anne's parents than they were doing now. He didn't want to have to explain to Walter and Kaye how their daughter had come to be in his custody last night.

Marta turned away from the stove and saw him standing in the doorway. "Good morning, Cabe. Breakfast will be ready in a few minutes." She nodded in the girls' direction. "Anne stayed with her friend last night and they got here early to help with things, so I put them to work." She gave Cabel a quick wink before turning back to the stove. Marta didn't know exactly what had happened, but it was clear that neither he nor the girls had gotten away with everything.

His housekeeper motioned for him to sit at the end of the table and then placed a heavily laden plate of food and a cup of black coffee in front of him. Needing no further coaxing, he made short work of the meal. The girls, heads down and silent, kept their eyes on their task, not appreciating that their diligence broadcasted their guilt louder than if they had shouted it from the rooftop. He hid a smile behind the rim of his coffee cup.

With a sigh of satisfaction, Cabel rose from the table and refilled his cup from the pot on the stove. He and Marta exchanged glances over the top of girls' heads, and he left the kitchen with the certain knowledge that the girls had a busy day ahead of them.

He walked briskly down the hall but hesitated a moment before entering the study. The room still belonged to his grandfather, and he felt like an intruder.

Marta must have anticipated his actions as the curtains were open, allowing the morning light to dapple the carpet. The box he had placed on the floor the night before now sat on the small library table near the fireplace. He walked to the table and set his coffee cup on the coaster thoughtfully placed there for just that purpose. Although he appreciated his housekeeper's thoughtfulness, he felt disconcerted that she seemed to know his plans before he himself had made them. Maybe Marta and Bessie George somehow were conspiring against him, or maybe for him. The outcome was yet to be determined.

Ignoring those thoughts, he returned his attention to the battered cardboard box that sat on the table. One by one, he took out each item and set them on the table for further inspection. The collection was rather impressive for a poor girl from the beach slums of St. Joseph. Aside from the cheap makeup and hose, the items were of good, if not excellent quality. He found a decent tortoise shell comb and brush set and several scarves that he guessed were quite stylish. All were in rich colors with bold patterns, and three were made of expensive silk. A black Spanish-lace shawl, gently frayed and worn, came next, along with a straw cloche hat with drooping purple flowers. Someone had used pins to keep them in place, but it seemed a losing battle.

There were also two dresses in the box, the one that Anne had worn the night before and a second one that caught his breath. Its color was purple but of a shade so deep and rich that it seemed almost black. The dress looked like sin hanging from the tips of his fingers. The satin would slide over a woman's body, yet cling and define, and the deep slash in the front would answer any questions that might remain. Tossing it onto the table, he hoped that neither Kittie nor Anne had ever worn it, feeling that its mere presence could corrupt the innocent. What had Gary been thinking, giving a dress like that to a young girl? Cabel snorted at his own naiveté. Yes, what could a young womanizer like Gary possibly have been thinking? Anger, hot and swift, had his blood pumping, and his hands fisted. In that moment he was glad that the musician was dead, for both of their sakes.

After taking a deep, settling breath, Cabel looked into the box again. At the bottom sat a small, cloth-covered package, its weight surprising him as he brought it into the light. Dull brown fabric fell away to reveal a red lacquered box. Lifting the top back on its small hinges he found layers of tissue paper, which he carefully peeled away to reveal a cut-crystal atomizer filled with a pale amber liquid. This was the bottle that Anne had mentioned the night before. He doubted that the girl realized this perfume bottle cost more than her family made in a year. Cautiously, he sniffed the top. The scent was an intoxicating combination of citrus and musk, feminine yet aggressive. He wondered if Becca knew how much Gary had stolen from her.

Examining the other items on the table, he realized that the boy had probably helped himself to some of Becca's silk scarves as well, though a few had tears, just as Anne had said. Had they been plucked from the trash or ripped from dresses? Cabel doubted it would matter, from Becca's point of view. Then there was the purple gown. He touched it again and shook his head. If the gangsters hadn't killed Gary, Becca might have done so herself.

Returning to the dresses, he looked each one over with care, hoping to find pockets with notes or clues. Evening dresses, he discovered, did not have pockets, and there was nothing, not even a dance ticket, lying at the bottom of the box or within the layers of tissue. Sleuthing was more difficult than the dime novels had led him to believe.

With quick movements he sorted through the items as he packed them back into the box, keeping the purple dress and perfume bottle at the top of the pile. Most of the bounty he would hold for Anne until she was older, but the last two items he would return to Becca when he saw her again. While he inwardly flinched at the thought of going back to Chicago, he also knew it was inevitable. His only link between Gary and Kittie was Silver Beach, but Gary's life also connected him to rumrunners, the Charades Club, Al Capone, and Becca.

On this side of the lake, the only possible threat that Cabel could see came from Elmer Dupree. In Chicago, though, dangers were everywhere. While Elmer could be volatile, Cabel wasn't convinced he could be violent, where as violence was part and parcel for gangsters. But this left the question of why Kittie had been killed. Maybe Elmer had killed his ex-girlfriend, and Gary had just been at the wrong place at the wrong time. But why would Elmer wait to kill Kittie after her boyfriend had died? Presumably she would have been available again, maybe willing to go back to Elmer. And what of Gary? Could he have brought his secrets and dangers across the lake, placing Kittie in a killer's sights? This scenario felt closer to the truth, but maybe it was Cabel's own desire to keep Silver Beach a haven of innocence and fun that made this option more palatable.

The sound of voices in the kitchen brought Cabel back to his surroundings. After listening a moment, he realized that the rest of the Arledges had arrived to start their workday. Would he be able to find the answers that would ease their minds? Bessie George believed he could, and for now he would place his trust in her.

Returning to the task at hand, Cabel picked up the box and stored it on a shelf in the office closet. That chore completed, he walked over to his grandfather's desk, where another duty waited. Running his fingertips along the smooth, polished surface of the wood, he let a memory or two slip through before settling into the leather chair. His heart pounded as he eyed the rough wood box that sat in the center of the blotter. With a cautious finger, he touched the battered sides before slipping open the latch. The hinges gave a quiet groan as he opened the lid.

The first layer was a bundle of yellowed papers banded together with a frayed ribbon. Gently, and with shaking hands, Cabel removed the packet and untied the ribbon. Carefully thumbing through the pages, he saw that these were all government documents of his grandfather's time as an officer in the Union Army. Here was his notice of commission, decommission, and every other official paper that recorded the mileposts of a man's service to his country.

Setting those documents aside, he reached into the box again and brought forth another ribbon-bound packet, a thick stack of envelopes. Here was the gold to be found among any soldier's effects, his most treasured possessions: letters from home. Cabel didn't need to open them and read the words to know what they said. These tattered envelopes held love and hope, reminders of what life had been and might be again. During the fierce desperation of battle, a soldier didn't fight for ideals, or for his home or loved ones. All that mattered was his survival and that of the men who fought beside him. In the aftermath, when the horrors of the night bled into the boredom of the endless, waiting days, letters from home became a lifeline, granting a measure of sanity to an otherwise insane existence.

Gently, Cabel placed the envelopes to the side, having no desire to intrude on the intimacies they surely contained.

The next item in the box was a small, heavy bundle wrapped in a piece of dark-blue wool. The folds of the cloth fell open, revealing a collection of medals. Cabel gave his full attention to each in turn. Most were for valor, some recognized wounds received in battle. All spoke of bravery and leadership during times when both were so greatly needed. With guilt and shame, Cabel thought of his own medals, stored in a tobacco tin, shoved into the back of a dresser drawer. He had felt unworthy each time one had been awarded to him, the one that lived, when so many others, more deserving by far, lay dead in the desolation of the battlefield.

Using the scrap of dark wool, Cabel polished his grandfather's medals before lining them up along the top edge of the blotter. Each one represented a specific battle and act of heroism. Had his grandfather found pride in them, or did he, like his grandson, find that they only served as reminders of lives lost to fulfill a greater purpose?

Returning his attention to the box, he found the journal his grandmother had mentioned in her letter. Reverently, he moved the wooden box to the floor and placed the red-covered book in the center of the blotter. Light glinted off the gold letters embossed on the leather cover: James Cabel Evans. The gold script was ornate, almost feminine, and Cabel guessed that the journal had been a gift from either his grandmother or his great grandmother. On the flyleaf, though, the name was written again in the sure, bold handwriting that Cabel knew so well.

With tentative fingers, he turned the page.

June 14, 1861

Against the express wishes of my wife and parents, I have volunteered to serve as an officer in the Union Army...

Muted shadows drifted in the corners of the room when Cabel at last raised his eyes from the journal. Hours had passed while he had joined his grandfather in battle after horrible battle. Places that had no names and others that were known to all now had a firm hold in his heart and mind. He rubbed his eyes, knowing that nothing could erase the visions he had of a war in which he had never fought.

The places and names were different, but the brutalities of armed conflict remained constant regardless of the centuries in which they occurred. For all of Cabel's hatred of war and its devastating impact on the men who fought it, he felt pride in the sacrifice his grandfather had made and the better world that the war had left in its wake. Perhaps time would grant him the same grace.

Pushing away from the desk, he stood and stretched. The mantle clock chimed the noon hour. Hungry yet nauseous, Cabel found his way to a deserted kitchen. Voices and laughter drifted through the windows from the backyard scene of an alfresco luncheon. Rather than join the others, he rummaged through the icebox and cupboards until he assembled an oddly satisfying mix of beef, pickles, and cookies.

As he finished his meal, the sounds from the yard changed. Soon Marta and Kaye would come through the backdoor with dirty dishes and leftover food. Unprepared to face anyone, Cabel wolfed down the rest of his makeshift meal before hurrying up the stairs to his room.

The heat of the summer's day had risen, becoming trapped on the second floor. The small fan he had found in the office closet did little more than move hot air from one corner of the room to another. Lying on his bed, hands folded behind his head, Cabel listened to the sounds of construction and activity in the backyard. Restless and awake, he considered his options. Silver Beach held no appeal this afternoon, and a long walk seemed particularly unsatisfying.

With a grunt of frustration, he rose from the bed and changed into the set of work clothes he had worn upon his return from New Orleans. As he walked downstairs, he reminded himself that he owned this house, and if he wanted to fix the roof, he had every right to do so. He also made a silent promise. If Marta so much as gave him one smug or satisfied look, he would fire her on the spot.

In the end, he joined into the work with surprising ease. Jorge eyed his clothes then told him to pick up the other end of a post, which they then carried to the side yard. Walter seemed wary at first, but Cabel's years as a day laborer on the rough docks of New Orleans had taught him to work with his hands and soon his acceptance was complete.

At the end of the day, exhausted but satisfied, he fell into bed. That night his dreams were a melding of wars and battles, but he no longer fought alone. His grandfather stood beside him and Jon, too, was there. Although his heart ached to see his friend, the sharp pain had lost a bit of its edge. In his sleep, Cabel wept.

‖‖‖

That one day established a pattern for his life. Mornings were spent in the office reading his grandfather's journal, and in the afternoons he joined the other men to work on the house. The scaffolding was complete, and he and Walter replaced shingles while Jorge rebuilt the side porch. Marta's presence was surprisingly scarce, but after the first day, he forgot to wonder at the phenomenon.

The manual labor focused his mind and exhausted his body. His nightmares diminished, allowing his war-ravaged soul a long-needed respite. Somewhere between the roofing nails and tar paper, Cabel's obligation to the Arledge's slipped from his mind. At odd moments he would find Walter looking at him, not with disapproval, but a patient waiting. Kaye, too, seemed to be keeping a vigil, but he didn't know how to help them.

CHAPTER EIGHTEEN

After another long day, in the midst of a deep, near dreamless sleep, an annoyance disturbed him. Swatting at his ears to shoo the mosquito away did not stop the buzzing. With a grunt of frustration, Cabel forced himself awake. Although the buzzing stopped, he realized it had been the telephone that he heard. After a minute or so of silence, it began to ring again. Foregoing slippers and robe, he hurried down the stairs, hoping to answer the phone before the noise disturbed the Vosses.

He picked up the earpiece and waited while the operator to put the call through.

"Cabel? Is that you?"

"Yes, I'm here. Who am I speaking to, please?"

"It's Doctor Lewis. Something's happened. Elmer Dupree is dead."

"What?" Cabel shook his head in an attempt to clear it. "Kittie's boyfriend? How? Where?"

"I can't talk long," the doctor said breathlessly. "Chief Bradley is waiting for me at the Central Docks, but I wanted to call you first. From what the chief has said, I think you need to see this."

"Me? Why?" Shocked, Cabel wondered if death had somehow escaped from his dreams, and Dr. Lewis was holding him responsible.

"I'm sorry," Dr. Lewis said, his voice calming as if he were speaking with a traumatized patient. "I know you're looking into Kittie's murder, and while it sounds as if Elmer's death is different..."

Awake now, Cabel shoved his macabre thoughts aside and tried to focus on the doctor's words. "You think they might be connected?"

"I don't know, but I believe Chief Bradley is determined to hide the truth of this boy's death the same as he did with Kittie's."

"Let me get dressed, and I'll meet you at the docks," Cabel said, before remembering that he had no way to get there.

"I'm just down the street. Get dressed, and I'll meet you in front of your house. We'll drive down together."

The line went dead.

Cabel stood numbly listening to the hum of the phone until the operator returned and asked if he wished to place a call. He said no, replaced the earpiece and rushed up the stairs to change.

Dr. Lewis's car idled at the edge of the walkway, an old Model-T that sounded well maintained. Cabel opened the passenger door and barely had time to close it before they were rumbling down the brick-paved street.

"I'm sorry to get you out of bed like this, but I'm a bit shocked myself, two young people dead in such a brief time." The doctor sighed. "You have to accept death if you practice medicine, or you'll always be fighting an impossible battle. Still, old age is expected. Illnesses and accidents can be tragic, but to die at the hand of another..."

Cabel wondered if this gentle man considered how many men had died at the hands of his passenger. They drove past the Whitcomb Hotel. The young paperboy was not yet at his post.

"What do you know about Dupree's death?" he asked.

"The chief seems to think that the boy drank himself to death, but I find that hard to believe."

Cabel's throat burned at the memory of Dupree's cider and found he could believe it quite easily.

"I know Elmer brews his own stuff, but it tastes a lot stronger than it is. I swear that boy uses old socks for a filter."

"How do you know what Elmer's cider tastes like?"

"Hmm." The doctor cleared his throat. "There are a couple of moon shiners in the area, and I try to keep track of who's brewing what. It's not my job to uphold the law, and I don't want anyone to go blind or get sick, so I sample the, ah, product, just to make sure..."

Cabel was sure that the old man was blushing, but the darkness hid the evidence, as it did his own smile. "That makes sense," he said judiciously.

Dr. Lewis eyed him suspiciously, but Cabel kept his face serene. Finally, he asked the doctor, "Why do you think Bradley's trying to cover up the cause of Dupree's death?"

"He called to tell me that the boy died. Don't know why he bothered to call at all, except he knew it was protocol and there might be questions if he didn't. All in all, though, he didn't sound too upset about Elmer. Told me it was clear the boy drank himself to death and there was no need to get me out of bed for that and he'd take care of the paperwork for me." Dr. Lewis snorted. "The man must think I'm a fool. Anyway, I told him that, no, I was elected by the good people of St. Joseph to do a job, and I intended to do it."

"I bet he didn't like that."

"No, sir, he didn't," the doctor said with satisfaction. "But what really got me wondering was when I asked him where the body was found and he said it was by the Central Docks."

"You thought he was lying? Why?"

"Those docks are busy 'round the clock during the summer months, but it's especially at night. Men are loading crates of produce into the ships, welding things, and who knows what all. Anyway, wherever the chief was calling from, it wasn't the docks." The old man thought for a moment or two. "As a matter of fact,

I could have sworn I heard the Cooper & Wells looms in the background, like he was calling near…"

"Silver Beach." Everything seemed to come back to the amusement park. The thought made Cabel sad. Bad things shouldn't happen in the magical world that Drake had created.

The doctor nodded. "That's what I think."

"How are you going to explain why I'm with you?"

The doctor was quiet as he drove across the bridge that spanned the St. Joe River, linking the city of Benton Harbor to its poor relation on the other side. He turned onto a steep, but well-maintained road that led down to a marshy area and to the commercial docks beyond. Bright lights illuminated a scene of industrious activity, reminding Cabel of his own days working along side the big ships.

"I think I'll tell him that I was on my way here when I saw you out for a late night walk and asked you to come along." The doctor threw him a sideways glance. "You used to do that on a regular basis, you know, walking late at night, but I understand you don't do it as much these days."

Cabel didn't know which disturbed him more, the fact that his habits were so well known or that they had changed to such a great degree in recent weeks. "What about the telephone operator? Aren't you afraid she'll gossip or tell the chief that you called me?"

The doctor shook his head. "I make a point of knowing who's on each shift at the phone exchange. You can trust most of them to keep quiet about what they hear, but there are a few I'm sure will keep a confidence, so I ask for them when I'm dealing with patients. People don't need their private business discussed by strangers."

"True." Cabel thought a moment. "So that just leaves the problem of the chief. Do you think he'll believe your story?"

"I don't know, Cabe, but I really need you to help me convince him." The doctor's fate, and that of his son's, hung in the silent air between them.

Cabel didn't want this new burden, but they had reached the parking area and all other options were gone.

The doctor got out of the car and reached into the back for his large, black medical bag. Cabel followed more slowly, getting a sense of the world around him.

The air smelled of oil, diesel fuel, and peaches, slightly nauseating and sweet. Underlying that was the cloying odor of stagnant water from the marsh, which contrasted sharply with the scent of fresh water carried on the breeze from the river and lake. After his time in New Orleans, it seemed odd to Cabel to be on the docks and not smell salt water.

Next to him, Dr. Lewis stiffened, bringing him back to the present. Cabel followed the doctor's gaze and saw a barrel-chested man standing near a dilapidated storage shed that stood at the far edge of the loading area, away from the hubbub of activity and prying eyes. Even from across the yard, the man's anger was palatable.

"Chief Bradley isn't happy to see me," Cabel said, taking the heavy medical bag from Dr. Lewis's hand.

"No." The doctor shrugged his shoulders and started toward the shed.

They were still several yards away when Chief Bradley called out, "Hey, Doc, why'd you bring a citizen with you?"

"My nurse is off duty tonight, and I needed someone to carry my bag," the old man shouted back.

Cabel smiled and met the chief's eyes coolly.

"Why if it isn't St. Joe's protector of the sand bunnies, Mr. Evans," the chief sneered. "I thought you only worried about the goings on over at Silver Beach, or maybe it's just the pretty young girls over there. I heard you found yourself a couple of new ones last night."

Cabel let the breeze cool his temper before answering. "Your men just can't seem to supply you with accurate information, can they?"

The chief's back stiffened and his eyes flashed in anger, but there was curiosity in them as well that Cabel felt no need to satisfy.

Turning to the doctor, the chief said, "Why don't we let your assistant wait here so we don't upset his delicate sensibilities."

In response to a signal from the chief, a young uniformed officer stepped forward, hand outstretched to take the medical bag.

Cabel kept a firm grip on the handle. "I was out walking when I saw the doctor racing out of his driveway and flagged him down. He explained the situation, and I offered to help, which I intend to do." He shrugged, keeping his eyes steady on the chief's, daring the man to challenge him. "As for my sensibilities, after the war, I don't think there are too many things that could upset me."

Doctor Lewis turned to Cabel, shock and apology in his eyes. "Oh my, Cabe, I'm so sorry. I didn't think…"

Cabel shrugged again. "Don't worry, Doctor. I'll be fine." Shouldering his way past the young officer, he hurried toward the shed, hoping his lie would hold in the face of whatever lay within. He paused at the threshold and waited for Dr. Lewis.

"He's not in there," Chief Bradley said, pushing past Cabel and walking to the far side of the dilapidated building.

Dr. Lewis followed, and Cabel fell into step behind them. Turning the corner, he was surprised to see a police car parked there, completely out of sight from the dockworkers. Two more police officers stood nearby. The men had their backs to the shed, smoking in tense silence. Cabel had the distinct impression that they were trying to distance themselves from the chief's charade.

Elmer Dupree sat propped against the rough wooded wall, legs splayed, head lolled to the side. In the near darkness, some might suppose that the boy was merely unconscious or sleeping, but Cabel had seen death in too many forms to be fooled by a trick of the light. Bile rose in the back of his throat, and he swallowed convulsively to keep it there. His sweaty, shaking hands nearly lost their grip on Dr. Lewis's bag, which now seemed to weigh fifty pounds more than it had a moment ago. Only the knowledge that the chief was studying him, looking for signs of weakness to use against him and the doctor, kept Cabel standing. He hoped the darkness aided him now, and the chief would accept the illusion of strength.

The huge man heaved a sigh then stepped back. Dr. Lewis came forward, knelt, and touched Elmer's throat with gentleness more appropriate for the living, but also with the reverence that was reserved for the dead.

"My boys already checked, Doc. The kid drank his way right out of this world." The chief nudged a pint-sized canning jar that lay a few feet away, presumably having rolled from Elmer's dead hand.

Dr. Lewis picked up the jar and delicately sniffed its contents. "This is his hard cider, all right, but it isn't strong enough to…"

"Now Doc, don't make things more complicated than they have to be. This boy was practically born drunk and you know it." The unmistakable derision in Chief Bradley's voice made the young police officer cringe, and he, too, turned his back on the scene.

"You know me, Chief. I'll do my job, and I'll do it right." Dr. Lewis leaned closer to the body then back again. "Do the Benton Harbor police know that you're on their side of the river?"

Chief Bradley growled. The hair at the nape of Cabel's neck rose. He stepped forward to shield the elderly doctor from what seemed an imminent attack, but he had underestimated the chief's control.

Lighting a cigarette of his own, the chief puffed smoke into the air then smiled down at Dr. Lewis, still kneeling by the body.

"I didn't want to bother the Benton Harbor constabulary with a little problem like this. Elmer was one of ours, and we'll take care of him." His smile widened. "And how is that boy of yours, Doc? I hear the practice is doing real well…for now."

Dr. Lewis jerked back as if slapped in the face. Cabel glared at the chief before reaching down to help the doctor to stand. As he did so, the old man pointed down, wanting Cabel to notice something about the body, particularly Elmer's shoes. Although his eyes had become accustomed to the dim light, it still took him a moment to see what was wrong. Sand was imbedded in the seams where Elmer's heels were attached to the soles of his shoes. Standing up, still supporting Dr. Lewis with a hand under his elbow, Cabel looked back to the police car. Although the sand and beach grasses had been trampled by several pairs of feet, there was no mistaking the furrows made by dragging Elmer's body from the car to the side of the shed. The doctor was right. The boy had not died there.

Chief Bradley came forward, a large, ugly grin on his face. He clapped the doctor on his back so hard that the old man would have fallen had Cabel not kept a hold of him. "I'll expect to see the death certificate on my desk tomorrow. Accidental death, right?" Not waiting for an answer, the chief turned to his men and motioned for them to put Elmer's body into the back of the police car.

Cabel started to protest, but a hand on his arm stopped him. He looked down at Dr. Lewis, who seemed to have shrunk to the size of a child in the last few minutes.

"Don't bother. I know we should contact the funeral home, and they would come out with a hearse, but let's just get this farce over with."

Cabel nodded stiffly and helped Dr. Lewis back to the car.

CHAPTER NINETEEN

The night seemed reluctant to release its hold, or maybe it was Cabel's thoughts that kept the light at bay. He turned from the restaurant's window to study Dr. Lewis, who was slumped against the worn, padded bench on the other side of the shabby booth, its scarred wooden table between them. Exhaustion deepened the lines etched in the man's face and darkened the skin beneath his eyes. Cabel sighed, wondering what his own face revealed.

A waitress, smiling more from habit than pleasure, refilled his coffee cup then stepped away. Cabel took an appreciative sip. He would never confess this to Marta, but the Lake View Diner served some of the best coffee he had ever tasted. Although he had yet to sample the food, if the coffee was any indication, the meal would be worth the drive.

Dr. Lewis used his coffee cup to warm his hands but had yet to sip the steaming black liquid. The elderly man had spoken few words since asking Cabel to drive him to the diner. Cabel hadn't driven a car in almost five years, and it had taken a few turns on the crank handle to bring the engine to life. He imagined the elderly doctor standing outside in the wind or rain or snow, patiently coaxing the car to run. What Dr. Lewis needed, he had decided, was one of the newer cars that could be started from inside the cab, though he had no idea how to bring that about.

Following the doctor's simple directions, Cabel had driven through the deserted streets of St. Joe, getting the feel of the old Model T. He turned south when he reached the bluff and enjoyed driving the winding road that followed the curve of the shoreline, darkened houses and summer fields on one side, the endless black of the lake on the other. He drove until he spotted the lights of the diner spilling across the roadway. Given the man's line of work, all of the late night calls to bedsides and birthing rooms, he wasn't surprised that Dr. Lewis would know where to find hot food and strong coffee at 4:00 a.m.

The waitress brought their meals: platters stacked high with pancakes and toast surrounded by eggs, sausages, and potatoes. She deposited a plate in front of each of them then hesitated. Cabel looked up to find her staring at him. She nodded toward Dr. Lewis before turning away. He looked over and saw that the doctor, eyes closed and head back, had fallen asleep. Torn between letting the man rest and letting his food get cold, he finally reached over and gently shook Dr. Lewis's shoulder. He blinked and straightened; his eyes wide as if he were forcing them to remain open.

"I'm sorry I woke you, but I didn't want your breakfast to get cold," Cabel said.

Dr. Lewis nodded and cleared his throat before reaching for the salt and pepper shakers, applying a liberal dose of both to his eggs and potatoes. Cabel followed suit. Neither man spoke as they ate, slowly at first, then with increased gusto, as if they had found their appetites hidden among the onions and butter. Yes, Cabel vowed silently as he forked another bite of egg and sausage into his mouth, he would never tell Marta about this place, but maybe he could sneak Jorge and Walter over some morning. Nate, too.

Too soon, he found himself sopping up the last of the egg yolks with a crust of toast, sighing with pleasure. The waitress cleared their plates, smiling more warmly when she saw their empty state, and refilled the coffee cups. After she left, Cabel met Dr. Lewis's eyes and knew it was time to discuss the night's events. A vision of Elmer Dupree's body, pale and lifeless, skittered across his mind. His stomach turned sharply, and the wonderful meal threatened an unpleasant return. Swallowing hard, his mind cleared and his stomach settled. He looked across the table to find Dr. Lewis studying him.

"Cabe, I am so sorry to get you mixed up with this. I don't know which is worse, that I let you see that poor boy's body or that now Chief Bradley might threaten you too."

Cabel shrugged. "I was already mixed up with this, assuming that Kittie and Elmer's deaths are somehow connected. And as for Chief Bradley, well, he and I already had a disagreement that ended with him threatening me, and it had nothing to do with you. I can handle him." Brave words. "What do you think, Doctor? Did Elmer drink himself to death or was there something more going on?"

The doctor stared out the window and into the darkness before turning back to Cabel, his eyes troubled. "I wish I had had more time to examine the body. I can't say with certainty as to what killed him, but that boy did not die from drinking his cider." He paused as if trying to organize his thoughts. "I sniffed the jar and the area around the boy's mouth. The jar had held cider, no doubt there, but his mouth had a different smell, kind of sweet, like soda pop."

"How does soda pop kill Elmer?"

"By itself, it doesn't, but if something was mixed into it…"

"Poison?"

"If it's what I'm thinking, then yes, and no. If I had to guess, I'd say that Elmer drank soda pop mixed with denatured alcohol."

"Wood alcohol?" Cabel didn't know why the thought surprised him. While working on the docks in New Orleans, he had known several men who had stills, and many drugstores sold most of the ingredients needed to make liquor, if you knew what to buy. People made alcohol with everything from embalming fluid to anti-freeze, which was dangerous enough. But denatured alcohol was something else all together.

Even with prohibition, alcohol had its uses and several industries used alcohol for disinfecting and cleaning and other legitimate purposes. The government realized that this alcohol could be diverted for personal use, and so they ordered that methanol, or wood alcohol, be added to it, making it too dangerous for human consumption. Cabel remembered reading in the paper that more than 700 people had died in New York City while ringing in the New Year because they had spiked their drinks with denatured alcohol.

"But why do you think Elmer died from drinking denatured alcohol? No offense, Dr. Lewis, but I've had the experience of tasting his cider, and it seems pretty deadly all on its own."

A small smile played around the doctor's mouth. "I know, but as I told you earlier, it's strong but relatively harmless." He sighed and rubbed his hands over his face then rested his elbows on the table. "The thing that bothers me is the soda pop smell. Denatured alcohol tastes horrible, so most fools who decide to drink the stuff mix it with soda pop or juice to mask the flavor."

"So he might not have known what he was drinking."

"My guess is that he didn't. Oh, I'm sure he knew it was alcoholic, but not denatured alcohol. If whoever gave him that poison was smart, they would have shared a few swigs of Elmer's cider first, that certainly would have numbed his taste buds."

"Further masking the taste of the wood alcohol," Cabel said, finishing the thought. "But why do you think someone gave it to him? Couldn't he have gotten it on his own?"

Dr. Lewis paused while the waitress once again refilled their mugs then took a fortifying sip. "I'm sure you can get denatured alcohol around here, if you know who to ask, and Elmer was resourceful enough to get his hands on it if he wanted to. Still, I've talked to him and a few other young men about it and bathtub gin and a few other deadly drinks that are suddenly popular. I tried not to lecture, but I made sure those boys understood how dangerous these things were. Instead, I steered them to near-beer and homemade wines, then Elmer started making his cider. I know I can't keep these boys from drinking, but I hope to at least keep them alive."

Cabel smiled at the old man sitting across from him. Dr. Lewis was more pragmatic than he ever would have imagined. "So you think Elmer wouldn't have drunk wood alcohol if he'd known what it was?"

"I hope he was too smart for that, but he was eighteen."

"True," Cabel said, staring into the blackness of his coffee mug. Eighteen is what his grandfather had called one of the "idiot years." It was the time in life when young men thought they were immortal so they took stupid bets, drove too fast, or drank denatured alcohol—or went off to war. "So we don't really know if Elmer died from stupidity or malicious planning."

The doctor smiled sadly. "I think that about sums it up."

"What I don't understand is, if Elmer just drank some denatured alcohol, why did the jar have cider in it, and why would the chief care enough to move the body?"

"I don't have an answer to the first question, but it does seem to suggest that someone is hiding something, and I doubt it's the chief. If he thought that Elmer had died from drinking denatured alcohol, he would have waved that information in my face, proof that the boy's stupidity led to his death. As for the second question, I think it's like when Kittie died. Elmer died near Silver Beach, and the mayor doesn't want any bad publicity associated with the park."

"It seems like a big risk to take just to save the park some bad publicity." Cabel sipped his coffee and tried to understand.

Dr. Lewis sighed, suddenly looking older than his sixty-odd years. "As I told you before, St. Joe is having a hard time competing for business and tourists. Until Drake built his dock near Silver Beach, none of the passengers from Chicago or Milwaukee got off the boats on this side of the river. For many years, St. Joe was known for its sulfur baths and health treatments. People came from all over the country to stay at our fancy hotels and take different treatments. A lot of famous people came here, even Eleanor Roosevelt and Duncan Hines. About fifteen years ago though, interest in sulfur treatments waned and the baths closed. They've remodeled the Whitcomb Hotel, but it won't matter if there is no one to stay there.

"Now we also have those religious zealots of the House of David to compete with," the doctor continued. "They have their amusement park with rides and the train. Their baseball team does real well, too, and their orchestra is supposed to be phenomenal, so both draw big crowds. For a religious group, they sure are smart when it comes to business." He shook his head, a small smile playing at the corners of his mouth. "Mayor Delong was furious when their trolleys started meeting the boats at Drake's dock to cart the tourists out to their compound in Benton Harbor. Because of those trolleys, a lot of people come through here, but never spend a dollar in St. Joe." The doctor paused to sip his coffee. "Silver Beach is our biggest tourist draw, and Delong means to protect it."

Cabel nodded in understanding. He remembered the sulfur baths as a boy, though he'd never used them. What he had forgotten was how the strong smell of sulfur had permeated the downtown area. St. Joseph was picturesque, but for many years it had smelled like rotten eggs. As for the House of David group, they had been around too when he was a boy, but had not been as enterprising. No wonder the mayor was worried.

"Still," Cabel said, "the chief was pretty brazen about moving the body. He acted as if it was a big joke, daring us to challenge him."

Dr. Lewis nodded. "If I hadn't insisted on coming out to view the boy's body, the chief wouldn't have bothered with the charade. He just would have taken the body straight to Morton's

Funeral Home and written down whatever he wanted to on the death certificate."

"Probably, but why did he bring the body across the river and into Benton Harbor's jurisdiction? It seems like an unnecessarily dangerous choice."

"That was a mistake, I think," Dr. Lewis said. "When he called me and said that a body had been found, I asked him where it was. I don't think he had thought that through before he called, and so he said the first place that came to mind. It probably wasn't until after he said it that he realized his mistake, which is why he pushed me so hard to let him handle the paperwork, but I can get stubborn sometimes," he added with a rueful smile.

"But what about the Benton Harbor police, aren't they going to hear about this?"

"From who, the dock workers? More then a few of those men have had run-ins with the law, and I doubt any of them want to get involved in a police matter. As for the boy's family…" The doctor sighed then raised sad eyes to meet Cabel's. "His daddy ran off when he was about five or so, and his momma died a few years later. His uncle took him in and treated him more as a farm hand than a nephew. I doubt Henry Dupree's going to care one way or the other which side of the river that boy died on." He sipped his coffee then shook his head. "Even if the Benton Harbor chief of police does hear about this, I'm sure nothing would come of it. Chief Bradley has connections, and he'll use them if necessary."

Cabel nodded. "What I don't understand is the chief's openness in his lies and threats. Is he that confident in Mayor Delong's protection or does he have something on the mayor, too?"

Dr. Lewis considered Cabel's words. "First of all, you have to remember that he never threatens someone in the presence of an audience. Or at least not in front of an audience he can't control. He's a classic bully, and he has a badge, which makes him dangerous." He leaned back in the booth, resting against it as if the evening's work had suddenly caught up with him, but his voice was strong as he continued. "You haven't met Mayor Delong but my impression of the man is that he and the chief are well matched. They're both bullies but the mayor has polish so most folks don't see that side of him. Still, Delong has his work cut out for him, serving the people of St. Joe."

"How did he get elected mayor?" Cabel asked. "I wouldn't think the town fathers would put up with him."

"Delong promised to make things better, bring in new businesses and tourists, and to some degree he has, but I don't think it's enough. I'm hoping he's out in the next election." Dr. Lewis eyed Cabel speculatively. "Of course, the town will need someone to run against him."

Cabel almost choked on his coffee. "Don't look at me, sir. I'm barely managing my own household." He grinned with sudden inspiration. "Now Marta Voss, that's who should be running this town. She'd have everything sorted out and the dishes done by the end of the first day."

Dr. Lewis laughed. "I'm sure you're right."

Pleased that he had made the doctor smile, Cabel signaled for the check and stood up to pay, waving away the doctor's insistence that they split the bill. A generous tip brought another smile to a different face. The two men left the building and stepped into the balmy air. They looked toward the lake as the sun rose behind them, tinting the world with pink and gold.

Cabel helped Dr. Lewis into the passenger seat, started the car (only two cranks this time), and headed north. He had thought that the doctor had fallen asleep and jumped when the man spoke.

"Well, Cabe, what do we do next?"

"I wish I knew." Cabel thought a moment then asked, "Dr. Lewis, do you know if the Wayne Sherman Band played at Shadowland last night?"

"As a matter of fact they did. My son took his wife down there for a bit of dancing, so Mabel and I got to care for our grandson. Why?"

Cabel shrugged. He wanted to protect the doctor and his family as much as possible, but he also didn't know if the Wayne Sherman Band's presence last night had any significance. "I don't know," he finally admitted. "They were playing here the night that Kittie died and also the night that Walter's house was broken into. I know that Elmer thought he had a connection to sell his moonshine in Chicago, and I think it was through someone with the band, but I'm not sure. It just seems that a lot of bad things happen when that group is in town."

Dr. Lewis frowned. "If someone told Elmer that they could sell his hard cider in Chicago, they must have been pulling his leg. That stuff makes a better paint thinner than a drink." He looked at Cabel. "I've met the band leader, Mr. Sherman. He's a nice man. I can't imagine he'd have anything to do with illegal stuff, like rum running. That's what you're talking about, isn't it?"

"It is, but I don't think Mr. Sherman knows anything about it. I'm guessing most of the band doesn't either."

"So how did you find out?"

A fair question but Cabel didn't want to discuss his visit to the Chicago speakeasy. "Since Walter asked me to look into Kittie's death, I've learned a few things, but most of it seems irrelevant to my search."

The doctor nodded, respecting his reticence. "Just remember, Cabe, if Elmer was killed because he learned that people connected to that band are involved with something illegal, you could be in danger, too."

A metallic taste, cold and familiar, filled Cabel's mouth. Fear. He had lived with it every moment, waking and sleeping, during the war. A different kind of fear had come later. Fear of failing his family. Fear of letting people see how broken he was. Fear of losing control. In one form or another, the taste of fear had tainted his food and fouled his drink since his first day at the front, though it had receded in recent weeks. Until now.

"I'm so sorry, Cabe, I didn't mean to upset you, just warn you." Dr. Lewis's eyes were filled with worry and compassion.

Cabel looked away and concentrated on relaxing his grip on the steering wheel. "That's okay, Dr. Lewis," he said, trying to smile and knowing he'd failed. "I appreciate your concern and I'll be careful."

They had arrived at Dr. Lewis's house. Cabel drove up the driveway and parked beneath the carriage porch. He retrieved the doctor's bag from the back seat and escorted the elderly man to the door where his wife, wrapped in a colorful robe, anxiously waited.

"Thank you for seeing him home," Mabel said, relief adding emphasis to her words.

"It was my pleasure," Cabel said, setting the doctor's bag just inside the door. He bid the couple good-bye and began his walk home. Less then four blocks separated his house from the Lewises', but he made a small detour to buy a paper from the young boy who had probably stopped whistling now that dawn had arrived.

CHAPTER TWENTY

The motion of the rocking train car nearly lulled Cabel to sleep. Although he had slept most of yesterday and a fair amount last night, he still felt exhausted.

After leaving the Lewises' house he had gone in search of his paper. As he pulled coins from his pocket, he also found the yellow truck he had purchased in Chicago and gave it to the young boy. His gapped-tooth grin made the small expenditure worth every penny. The boy nodded his thanks, and Cabel left him admiring his prize beneath a streetlight. Upon returning home, Cabel fell into bed and slept deep and undisturbed, even with the noise of the construction work. Upon awakening he had done little more than eat and return to bed, though that sleep had been restless. Death had intruded in many forms, with many faces. At five a.m. he gave up on sleep, wishing he had a car so that he could drive back to the Lake View Diner.

Instead, he had waited for the day to start. He needed to meet with Walter to tell him about Elmer's death. The town was already abuzz with the news so Walter had known that the boy had died, but Cabel supplied additional information and shared some of the doctor's speculations. Walter listened, hands opening and closing into fists at his side, then looked at Cabel with steady brown eyes and asked, "So does this mean you're ready to get back to looking into my Kittie's death?"

Cabel had nodded, realizing how patient Walter and Kaye had been while waiting for him to return to his investigation. But what would be his next move? According to Kittie's flyer, the Wayne Sherman Band was headed toward Detroit. The road manager, Scottie Marks, was someone Cabel wanted to talk to, but at the moment he was out of reach. He wished, not for the first time, that he had paid more attention to the band's schedule, but there was nothing to do but wait. Talking with Chief Bradley would be a waste of time and might have dangerous repercussions for the doctor and his family, closing off that line of inquiry.

For the moment there was nothing he could do on this side of the lake. With dread and an odd bit of hope, he had realized that he needed to return to Chicago. Somehow things led back there, to the speakeasy. Besides, he had the dress and perfume from Kittie's stash to return to Becca, which afforded him an excuse to see her again and ask a few more questions.

With no ships sailing to Chicago at a convenient time, Cabel had walked down to the train station at the base of the bluff across the street from the Cooper & Wells factory. The Pierre-Marquette Railroad's schedule had included a run between Chicago and St. Joseph since the late eighteen hundreds, and Cabel had ridden it many times. The St. Joseph station was small and sparse but charming with its gingerbread trim and warm, red brick walls.

The conductor came through the car announcing their arrival in Chicago within the next fifteen minutes, forcing Cabel's thoughts back to the present. The conductor's news brought a flurry of activity as people rose to stretch or locate errant baggage or children. Cabel's stomach seemed to join in the fray, knotting and twisting until he feared he would be sick. Leaning back into his seat, he closed his eyes and took deep, long breaths. This sudden anxiety shouldn't have surprised him since it happened a few weeks ago aboard the ship that had taken him across the lake. This time though, the details of packing and purchasing the ticket, even boarding the train, had occurred with such ease that he wasn't prepared for this fierce attack of nerves.

As the train slowed, he opened his eyes to find a small child standing in front of him, swaying with the rhythm of the car. A boy, he thought, though it was hard to tell with the yellow curls and fluffy clothing. The child studied him a moment then held out a small tin soldier. Cabel took the toy and solemnly studied it, noting a few teeth marks and worn spots. He returned it to the child, who smiled before turning away at the sound of a woman's voice calling "Charlie." The gentle encounter calmed him, and he was able to walk with a near-steady gait to the doors and step down from the train without incident.

Chicago's new Union Station was light and airy, with soaring, arched ceilings in the Great Hall. Pink marble floors and walls seemed to sparkle in the light that filtered in through the high windows. Hundreds of people sat on the long wood benches, waited in ticket lines, or simply milled about waiting to leave or for someone to arrive. The room was large enough that, even with the crowd, Cabel easily maintained control of his frayed nerves. He followed a group of men in business suits to the taxi stand, where he briefly waited for an available cab.

He gave the cabbie the address of the Charades Club then settled into the back seat.

"Are you sure that's where you want to go?" the young man asked, looking over his shoulder. "I don't think they're open this early."

"Yes, thank you, I'm sure."

The driver gave a philosophical shrug then pointed his cab north. At midday the city thronged with people, businessmen, assistants, tourists, all easily identified by their various attire. The distance wasn't far and soon Cabel found himself on a busy sidewalk in front of the unassuming front door of the speakeasy. He tried the handle but found the door locked. A quiet knock, then a louder one produced no results.

"Maybe you should try the back door through the alley," a helpful passerby called out.

After two false turns, Cabel found the alley that ran behind the Charades Club. A large truck blocked most of the space between the buildings, its driver unloading barrels labeled "root beer," though Cabel doubted its veracity. The barrels were rolled to an open hatch in the sidewalk where men waited to lower them into a basement storage area.

Other men lounged near an open door, smoking and chatting. No one challenged him as he walked past. The doorway led straight into a large commercial kitchen. Its countertops and pots gleamed, awaiting a chef who had yet to appear. The club must also have a dining room, though Cabel didn't remember seeing one.

As he surveyed the empty kitchen, a door swung open and a young woman wearing a flowered skirt and a white shirtwaist walked in carrying a clipboard that held her attention. Cabel cleared his throat, and the girl jumped nearly a foot into the air.

Clutching the clipboard to her chest, she panted and stared. "Oh my, but you gave me a start," she said in a voice that hinted of the South.

"I'm sorry. I was looking for Becca, and the front door was locked so I came around the back."

She nodded as she tried to catch her breath. "I feel as if I've just run a mile. Oh my." She dabbed the cuff of her blouse against her brow.

"I really am sorry," Cabel said again.

The girl had gone pale, but her color was now returning, as did her curiosity. "So, are you a friend of Becca's?"

"Yes, ma'am. My name is Cabel Evans and—"

"Oh," she interrupted. "*You're* Mr. Evans. My oh my. You were here a few weeks ago, weren't you? Becca's very particular about who she lets sit at her private table, and we've all been wondering about you, especially since you left so early in the evening."

Cabel opened his mouth, then shut it, not quite sure how to respond.

"Does Becca know you were coming by today?" She let out a squeal when Cabel shook his head no. "Oh my, how romantic, you surprising her like this." The girl looked down at the overnight case in his hand. "And I bet you brought her a present." Her smile widened at the thought. "Well, now, Becca doesn't like to be interrupted when her office door is closed, but I'll bet she'd make an exception for you. Come with me."

Obediently, he followed the girl with the clipboard out of the swinging doors and down a short hallway. She pointed to the last door on the left and said, "That's the one you want," before hurrying back the way she'd come.

Cabel stood outside the door, debating what to do. He didn't want to interrupt Becca if she was working. From what he'd learned about her, there were a few other things he didn't want to interrupt either. His nerve slipped away, and he decided to find another cab, check in to a hotel, and come back after the club opened.

As he turned to leave, he heard Becca's voice, loud and angry, followed by a man's voice raised in fury. Without thought, Cabel burst through the door. Both occupants of the room froze, making an odd tableau. Becca stood on one side of a large desk, a heavy paperweight in her hand, prepared to defend herself, while a man, tall and menacing, stood on the other side, his fist raised. Both of them now turned, staring at him in shock. A red handprint was clearly visible on Becca's left cheek.

Between one breath and the next Cabel crossed the room, gripped the man's coat and slammed him against the wall. "Don't touch her."

The man's laugh was ugly and course. "Hundreds of men have touched her, what's one more?"

Cabel slammed the man against the wall again, sending picture frames crashing to the floor.

For a moment, the briefest of seconds, Cabel stood in no man's land, engaged in a fight to the death with a German soldier. Cabel raised his fist to deliver a killing blow. He blinked and found himself back in Becca's office. Cold sweat slid down his back, and his hand shook as he lowered it to his side. He kept the man pinned to the wall by the collar of his shirt until the echo of gunfire faded away, and he was certain that neither one of them would do anything foolish.

Broken glass crunched underfoot as he stepped away.

"Really, Cabe, must you always play the hero?" Becca drawled, stepping up beside him.

The man smirked.

"I'm sorry," Cabel said. "I didn't mean to intrude, but I heard…"

"A business discussion," Becca finished for him, adding a glare to be sure he received the message that his aid was neither sought nor appreciated. She stepped around him to address the man still hunched against the wall. "I'm sorry for my friend's intrusion. He really can't help himself. Are you all right?"

The man nodded and pushed away from the wall.

"Good." Becca reared back and slapped him hard across the cheek. "If you ever lay a finger on me again, I will have you killed." Her voice held cold confidence, and her eyes echoed the sentiment.

"Look, Becca, I'm sorry." The man sounded sincere and slightly pleading. "I just…"

"I know what you 'just.' Do you think before you act?" Becca laughed as if at her own joke. She stepped away and placed the paperweight on the polished surface of the desk, her eyes never leaving that of the man near the wall. With a flick of her wrist, she dismissed the incident. "I think we've concluded our business. Leave. Now."

With exaggerated care, the man straightened the collar of his shirt and pulled on his jacket to straighten it. One hand smoothed back his oil-slicked hair as the other tugged at the knot in his tie.

By the time he finished pulling himself together, his bravado had returned. "Look, sister, I don't take orders from you."

"This is my place, and if I tell you to leave, you leave. And let your bosses know that I expect them to send someone more refined for our next meeting."

With a harsh laugh, the man shook his head. "First of all, this is still Capone's place; and second, well, let's just say that you don't have as much power as you think you do, but you'll learn. If I'm lucky, I'll be the one who gets to teach you."

Cabel stepped forward, but Becca raised a hand to stop him. With slow, deliberate steps, she sauntered over to the man, who cringed and backed away. She smiled. Cabel hoped never to see such a smile again and never directed at him. Becca reached up and straightened the lapels of the man's cheap suit coat.

Looking up into his eyes, she said. "Dan, you are truly an idiot." She raised her hand and slowly grazed one long, red fingernail down his unshaven cheek. He paled. "If you raise a hand to me again, I won't have to kill you, your bosses will do it for me." Her voice was soft, almost gentle. "You are the one who is powerless here. Now leave." She turned away, going to her desk and began sorting through papers.

Dan's glare held hatred and a promise of retribution. He continued to stare at Becca, waiting for her to look up and see the manly threat in his eyes. She continued with her work, ignoring him, the greatest insult of all. Growing bored with the game, Dan turned away, deliberately grinding the broken glass and wood into the carpet as he walked to the far wall. A light touch on the wainscoting near the fireplace opened a cunningly concealed door through which Dan disappeared. After the door closed, Cabel stepped forward and ran his hand across the door and surrounding paneling. He doubted he could have spotted it if he hadn't already known it was there and wondered where it led.

"You're an idiot, too, you know," Becca said in a calm voice as she continued to sort papers and generally tidy the desktop, but it was a ruse. When she looked up, her face was a mask of fury. She came around the corner of the desk. Cabel backed away.

"What are you doing here?" she demanded, stalking toward him.

He stepped back.

"How dare you come rushing into my office like that? Do you realize what you could have done? I've worked so hard on this deal and you could have ruined everything." She continued stalking toward him. He continued backing away.

The doorknob pressed into his back, ending his retreat.

"You're not some knight in shining armor, and I'm not some damsel in distress. And if necessary this damsel can rescue her own damn self. I don't need you or any other man to do it for me. *Is that clear?*" She stood before him, standing on her toes so that their noses were mere inches apart.

He nodded, though he wanted to argue. She was strong, and successful at managing an illegal business. She worked for Al Capone and could deal with gangsters. Certainly she was more capable of violence than he expected, but still she was a woman. He looked at her red, swollen cheek. In spite of her protests, here was evidence that there were times when even she needed protection.

She stood with her arms crossed over her chest, waiting for a response. He decided to placate her rather than point out the obvious. "I swear, Becca, I'll never step in to try to help you again. If I see you drowning or trapped in a burning building, I'll just watch and wait for you save yourself, I promise."

Her lips twitched with a suppressed smile, and her eyes softened. For the first time since entering her office, he relaxed. Looking down into her lovely face, he felt the last remnants of his war memory slip away.

She touched his cheek gently then, with a coy smile, turned and walked away. Her unbound hair cascaded in a golden abundance down her back. The simple green dress she wore would have looked staid on any other woman, but on her it seemed to accentuate rather than diminish her sensual curves. Settling herself on a plush sofa that sat along the far wall of her office, she smiled again, warm and inviting. Her legs crossed, and the hem of her skirt slipped above her knees. With a manicured hand, she patted the cushion next to her.

Heat had risen within him, he couldn't deny that, and a warning bell clanged in his head, though it wasn't connected to his physical attraction to Becca. After a moment he realized what was wrong. Her anger had been real, but the shift from fury to seduction was too quick to be sincere, though he doubted most men would care. Then there were her movements. While sensual and arousing, they seemed more rote than genuine. The stage was set and her performance was flawless, but that's all it was, a performance. Was it habit, he wondered, or did she treat all men this way? Whatever she was plotting, though, it was clear that her true thoughts and emotions were tightly locked away. This was one thing they had in common.

Walking over to the sofa, he sat near her, but not close enough to invite any intimacies. Her eyes lit with amusement at his feeble attempts to distance himself from her charms. Shifting slightly to show off her body to its full advantage, she asked, "So, Cabe, what brings you to my office today?"

Through strength of character, he kept his eyes on hers. "I'm here to return some things that I suspect are yours but that have somehow wandered to the other side of the lake."

Her knowing smile let him know how transparent she thought the excuse to be.

"I also need to talk to you about Gary and Kittie again."

Amusement disappeared. "I don't know anything about the gangsters who shot Gary. Why do you keep boring me with this?"

Her denial was quick and angry. And she was lying. He could see it in her eyes, hear it in her voice. She'd been taken by surprise when he hadn't followed her script, and she didn't recover well.

Although he had no proof that she lied, he trusted his instincts and would try to find some answers. Perhaps a different tact would get him to the truth.

"I believe you, but there's been another death, probably murder. It was the boy who Kittie was seeing before she took up with Gary. This boy, Elmer Dupree, drank some denatured alcohol, probably without knowing what it was, and he died." He paused a moment, but she had nothing to say. "Elmer brewed moonshine and seemed to think he had a new market for his wares, a speakeasy in Chicago."

Becca laughed, though with little amusement. "And you immediately thought of me? How lovely. I can promise you, no home-made brew will ever be served here, I don't care how good it is."

"It was horrible stuff, to tell the truth," Cabel conceded. "At first I thought someone was pulling his leg. But the boy swore he had made a deal. His connection was through someone in the Wayne Sherman Band." A guess, but it was the only one that made sense. "Since they're based here at the club while they're in Chicago, I thought you might know something."

"Well, I don't," she snapped. "There are a lot of entrepreneurial young men in that band. I can think of several who might want to make a little money on the side by bringing over some hard cider, but if they do, it has nothing to do with me. Honestly, Cabe, do I look like some kind of a stage mother to you, keeping track of the musicians and making sure they're all getting a hot meal?"

"Becca, please."

"No. Go ahead and continue your quest if you must, but leave me out of it. If you want to talk to the band members, you're out of luck since they won't be back until Saturday. Beyond that, I can't help you." She stood and walked to her desk. "It was nice seeing you, Cabe, but I think you should leave now."

Focused on the papers in her hands, she didn't spare him another glance, dismissing him as thoroughly has she had Dan just a few minutes earlier. But Cabel had a card to play that the other man didn't.

He walked across the room and retrieved his overnight case. "Becca, I have something I need to show you."

Becca leaned over her desk, hands braced on the blotter, waiting.

Realizing that this was all of the invitation he would receive, Cabel placed his case on her desk. "I know I've told you about Kittie and Gary," he began.

"Cabe." Her voice held a clear warning.

"I know, but this is important." Cabel waited for Becca to give a resigned nod before continuing. "It seems that while they were dating, Gary gave Kittie several gifts."

Becca stood up straighter. He had her full attention.

"Her parents didn't allow her to have makeup or stylish dresses, so she kept her things at a friend's house. Her younger sister came across the stash, and I ended up confiscating it. When I looked through the things, I realized that some of it must belong to you."

Her eyes widened a moment before narrowing into angry slits. "I should have known. You've been playing me all along, haven't you?"

He blinked in surprise. "What? I don't understand."

She looked at him with an expression of confusion that probably matched his own. Finally she asked, "So what did you find?"

Cabel unbuckled his bag and reached inside. Becca watched his every movement. He held up the purple dress. She snatched it from him with such force that he checked to make sure he still had all of his fingers.

She held it up for inspection, looking for damage. "Well, at least the girl didn't ruin it."

"I doubt she even wore it. A dress like that would stand out in St. Joe, and given how young she was, I doubt she had the nerve to even try it on."

"You're probably right," she said, glaring at the dress and then at him. "There's something more, isn't there?"

Unsettled by her intensity, he hesitated a moment. "There were some scarves, a few were silk, I think, though most had small tears in them. There was also a black shawl, but it was snagged."

Becca nodded. "They were probably things I had thrown away or had put in the pile for the maid to mend." She eyed his bag. "What else did you find?"

Cabel pulled out the red lacquered box.

Becca was gentler when she snatched it from him, though it was only a matter of degrees. She held the crystal atomizer to the light, checking the level of the liquid it contained. "I guess the little hussy didn't like my perfume."

"Kittie wasn't a little hussy."

She swung around and gave him the full force of her wrath. "You're defending the girl? She had to have known that Gary had stolen these things, but she kept them anyway."

Cabel took a deep breath, wondering if he could explain the situation in a way that Becca would understand. "I never met the girl, but she comes from good people. She was young and naïve, and I doubt she knew the value of what he had given her. If I had to guess, she didn't like the perfume or the purple dress, but she kept them because they were from Gary."

Becca smirked. "Maybe she wasn't as sweet and innocent as you think."

"And maybe she wasn't as calculating or jaded as you want to believe," he snapped back.

Becca stiffened then gathered up the dress and the atomizer. "Was there anything else in this stash that I should know about? Anything valuable or important?"

"Important? No, nothing, and I looked carefully. I had hoped to find some clue to Kittie's death, but there was nothing useful. Why? Did Gary take anything else?"

She hesitated a moment too long. "No, but I didn't know he'd helped himself to these things, did I?"

"True." He looked at the dress and the atomizer. "If I come across anything else that I think might belong to you, I'll bring it back."

"You just can't help yourself, can you?" she asked. "You have to get involved and try to fix everyone's problems. Who fixes yours, I wonder."

Cabel shrugged uncomfortably. "It isn't like that. I made a promise to a friend to find out who killed his daughter, that's all."

"Have you found any answers?"

"No, but everything seems to lead back to Silver Beach…" He hesitated. "…and here." He braced himself, expecting her to be angry, but she just continued to study him as if he were some odd specimen that had crossed her path. Then she nodded, as if she had reached a decision.

Moving around the desk, she joined him where he stood. Her brown eyes twinkled with amusement, and he couldn't help but think that he was the brunt of some private joke. He stiffened when she reached up and smoothed his lapels, remembering the slap she had delivered to Dan. Instead, she tugged on the lapels, gently at first, then with more force until he conceded and let her draw his face down, closer to hers.

Soft and sultry, her voice was full of promise as she whispered in his ear, "Well, if all roads lead here, maybe you should take advantage of that."

He felt the warmth of her breath against his cheek, followed by a different kind of heat. Her moods changed so fast that he felt dizzy, though the lightheadedness could also be attributed to other factors. Regardless of her motives, he had to admit that if this was an act, she was very, very good.

Slowly, he stood, returning to his full height. Gently, carefully, he removed her hands from his jacket and stepped back.

She looked into his face and smiled, apparently satisfied with what she saw there. Closing his case and taking his hand, she led him to the door. "Where are you staying?"

"I hadn't decided, maybe the Drake Hotel. I stayed there the last time I was in town."

"No. Stay at the Blackstone. I know it's not as modern as the Drake, but she's a grand hotel and within walking distance. It would save you a cab fare or three."

"Three?"

She smiled, placed a hand on his chest. His body responded. "Come back tonight, Cabe. Let's see where your roads lead."

After a gentle shove, Cabel found himself on the other side of the closed office door.

CHAPTER TWENTY-ONE

Cabel lunched at the Blackstone's restaurant. As he ate a roast beef sandwich, he pondered his next course of action. The safe thing, the smart thing, would be to return to St. Joe and wait for the band to come through again. The road manager, Scottie Marks, was someone he needed to talk to. The man managed the illegal activities of Capone's rum-running operations, at least as it pertained to using the Wayne Sherman Band. Cabel wondered if there were other lines the man was willing to cross.

Then there was Becca.

The moment he had seen her at the club, he knew she was a danger to him. He couldn't look at her and not see Elizabeth, which inevitably led to thoughts of her and Jon and all that the war had taken from him, from all of them.

What he hadn't expected, what he hadn't thought possible, was his physical response to her. That fact that she was so enmeshed in his past should have been enough to keep him disinterested. Granted she was a master of the art of seduction, but he believed himself immune to such machinations. He was mistaken.

Becca was beautiful, lush, and dangerous. She could manipulate him with embarrassing ease. The only sane course of action was return to St. Joe.

But that was where the problem lay. He needed answers, and she could supply them.

He was certain that she was lying to him about Gary's murder, maybe Kittie's too. Was she protecting someone, or was it simply a matter of using what she knew as a means to control him? Was she involved in some way with the deaths of these two young people or did she just know something about them? Becca worked for Capone and knew thugs like Dan. As much as he'd like to think that women weren't capable of violence, he knew that Becca lived in a brutal world, though he couldn't imagine her committing murder. He thought back on the scene in her office and her cold eyes when she threatened Dan and revised that opinion. He could see her killing someone, but only if she felt threatened or maybe if there was something significant to be gained. Neither motive seemed to apply to Gary and certainly not to Kittie or Elmer Dupree. He didn't even know if their deaths were connected. That was the problem—there were too many things he didn't know.

Looking down at his plate, he saw the remains of a sandwich that he didn't remember eating. His coffee cup was empty, and when he looked up to request a refill, he realized that the dining room was nearly empty too. It was time to pay his bill and leave. He still hadn't decided whether to stay in Chicago or return to St. Joe.

Cabel stood and put his hand in his pocket, searching for his money clip. Instead, his fingers wrapped around a small metal disk. One of the medallions, he realized, his or Jon's, not that it mattered, for it had served its purpose of reminding him why he had come to Chicago today.

Kittie had been sixteen when she was murdered. He had never met her, didn't know what she had looked like, but he had a sense of her now, who she had been as a person. For the first time since her father had stepped onto his back porch, Cabel saw Kittie's death as the tragedy it was rather than a burden that had been thrust upon him. Standing at the restaurant counter, he grieved for a girl he had never known.

He let go of the medallion, found his money clip and paid his tab, leaving a generous tip for the waitress.

Then he checked into the hotel.

A bellboy stopped by his room to collect Cabel's evening clothes so they would be ironed and starched before he went back to the speakeasy to talk to Becca again. Too anxious to stay in the room, Cabel went back the lobby and out into the humid August air.

The Loop area, defined by the bend in the Chicago River, was the core business center of the city and home to the tallest skyscrapers in the Midwest. The Evans Manufacturing Offices were in the Monadnock Building on West Jackson Street, and Cabel carefully avoided that block as he wandered through the city where he had once belonged. Blending into the crowds but always aware of the masses, he kept as much space around himself as possible.

As he walked past the Marshall Fields Department Store, he remembered a time when he and Elizabeth had planned to meet beneath its clock, both of them forgetting that the store covered one square city block and that there was a clock on each corner. Separately, they had circled the store many times before giving up and going home alone. He smiled at the memory until they led to thoughts of Jon and a deep ache settled in his chest. Cabel attempted to distract himself by perusing the store's window displays, though he kept his hands firmly in his pockets. There would be no unplanned purchases today. He hadn't recovered from his last shopping spree.

After an hour or so, the oppressive heat drove him to seek refuge along the lakefront, where he found a bench and enjoyed a refreshing breeze as sailboats skimmed across the sparkling blue expanse. In July Chicago was hot, but August was worse. The combination of relenting sun and humidity turned the city into a sauna, and those who could afford to do so left in droves, seeking cool relief. Of course there were other reasons to leave the city.

Cabel found his thoughts returning to their starting point, Jon and Elizabeth, and shook his head to force them from his mind, focusing instead on the intense blue of the water.

The sun lowered in the sky. Tall buildings cast their long shadows across the city. Cabel would miss the sunset on the lake. Only those in Michigan enjoyed that sight, but the sunrise tomorrow would be just as spectacular. He rose with a sigh and returned to his hotel, where he found his evening clothes hanging in the closet, starched and pressed. His shoes gleamed from polish. His costume was ready, but was he?

After reading the paper, he bathed then went to the lobby barbershop for a trim and a shave. The decadence of sitting with warm towels on his face and an experienced barber at the razor was a luxury he hadn't afforded himself in years. Tension eased from his shoulders with every swipe of the blade, which seemed odd when he thought about the honed steel edge against his throat, but gave a mental shrug. Here was a forgotten ritual, one that held only good memories. Such things were few in number and therefore to be treasured. His tip was exorbitant, but he wanted to share his good mood and the stunned barber was most appreciative.

His mood slipped with each floor the elevator passed on its way up to his room. Tension returned, settling onto his shoulders. Resigned, he knew he needed to speak with Becca again, somehow convince her to confide in him. If only he had some clue, some link between Gary's death and Kittie's, he might have a way to persuade her to help him. To understand, though, he needed more information. This led him back to the Charades Club, back to Becca.

Circles within circles and he was lost in the labyrinth. He wondered if he would survive another encounter with Becca or if she would demand her pound of flesh.

Sunset failed to bring relief in either temperature or humidity. Sweat slipped in warm rivulets down Cabel's back and mingled with the starch of his shirt, creating a sodden mass beneath his evening coat. The air pressed on him from all sides, feeling like a solid, damp wall that required effort to push through. One last corner and the entrance to the Charades Club came into view. The dim overhead light and discrete awning could not conceal the glittering couples who waited at the stylishly shabby door.

Cabel gave the password to the burly gatekeeper who nodded with indifference as people filed past. The hallway was blissfully cool, and everyone seemed to pause a moment in pleasant surprise. Until that moment, Cabel hadn't appreciated the fact that the building was equipped with air conditioning and silently blessed the soul of whoever had thought to have it installed.

Beyond the padded door, a good portion of Chicago's rich and powerful drank, smoked, and laughed with the carefree abandon of the truly privileged. Every table was occupied, and more people crowded around them, talking and mingling. Those unable to secure seats stood in small groups, chatting and laughing.

On the stage, a big band played popular songs with professional polish and energy. A single microphone in the center of the stage suggested that a singer would perform later in the evening. The band's smooth transition from one song to the next kept the dance floor roiling with undulating bodies, though Cabel couldn't imagine dancing in the heat. The crowded room was several degrees warmer than the hallway; apparently even the new technology had its limits.

As he stood taking in his surroundings, people pulsed and moved around him, as if he were a rock in the river in which they flowed. Nodding to a few couples who had started to eye him with curiosity, Cabel headed toward the bar at the back of the room. The crowd was denser here but manageable, and he found himself ordering a scotch with ice with almost no tremor in either his hands or his voice. Pleased, he took his drink and moved away to seek shelter from the buffeting hoards.

He found a small alcove by a pillar, possibly the same one he had used on his last visit. The drink was cold, the alcohol burned, and Cabel nearly swooned from pleasure. Between sips of his drink, he scanned the room for Becca.

There were many beautiful women dressed in the height of fashion, most were bare-shouldered as a concession to the heat. Yet for all of the silk and satin, sparkles and feathers, none were Becca. She wasn't in the club tonight. Both relieved and disappointed, he debated his next move but realized that without Becca, there was no reason to stay.

The scotch was already watered down and as the ice cubes melted, it became a mere whisper on his tongue. Giving his glass to a passing waiter, he moved toward the exit. As he reached the padded door, it swung inward, propelled by a surging mass of humanity.

Bodies surrounded him, shoving him this way and that as an inebriated mob forced its way into the club. Caught in the maelstrom, there was nothing to do but flow with the current of the crowd. Soon they dissipated, moving off in different directions, leaving him like driftwood washed ashore after a storm.

Just as he regained his bearings and his breath, he found Becca standing before him and both were lost again.

She wore the purple dress he had returned to her that morning, and he found its promise of sin realized. A few moments passed before he was able to raise his eyes to meet her annoyed, slightly bored gaze.

"I bet your little innocent couldn't wear this dress as well as I do," she drawled.

"I doubt any woman is capable of that accomplishment." The truth slipped out before he could catch it back. She already had too much power over him, and he felt as if he'd just given her a bit more.

Her eyes warmed and a small smile played at the corner of her mouth. She gave a rueful shake of her head, as if faced with an unruly schoolboy who could charm his way out of trouble. "Follow me." She turned, knowing he would do as he was told. The crowds parted before her as she moved across the room.

And follow he did, realizing that he could manage the noise, the bodies, the inadvertent bumps of shoulders and elbows quite well when he had something to focus on. The purple satin caressed her hips as they moved with sensuous grace. One part of him knew that this distraction, however useful, was dangerous. The other part didn't care.

When they arrived at her private table, he pulled a chair out for her, but she placed a hand on his arm.

"I'm sorry, Cabe, but I can't join you right now. The ice truck didn't deliver today, and I'm trying to beg and borrow some from any place I can. Two of the waiters didn't show up, and one of the cigarette girls fell and sprained her ankle." She shrugged as if these problems were of no consequence, but he could sense her tension. This was the first glimpse he had of her as the manger of the speakeasy rather than the hostess. She understood her responsibilities to the club; would she respect his responsibilities to the dead?

"Is there anything I can do to help?" he asked out of courtesy rather than a belief that he could solve her problems.

She reached over and straightened his tie then smoothed his lapels into place. Giving them a satisfied pat, she smiled up into his eyes. "Be a good boy and entertain yourself for a while."

A waiter brought a drink, studying Cabel with open curiosity as he placed the glass on the table. The boy was young and handsome, apparent job requirements, though Becca seemed too distracted by her problems to notice.

"I don't know how long it will take to get ice delivered at this time of night, or even where I will get it from, so just relax and I'll join you as soon as I can."

"What about Al Capone? This is his place, right? If only half of what I've read is true, I'm sure he could get ice delivered here within the next fifteen minutes."

Between one blink of the eye and the next, Becca transformed from the warm hostess to a striking viper. "*I* run this place," she snarled. "I don't need you, Capone, or anyone else stepping in to do my job."

Cabel raised his hands, trying to calm her, but she would have none of it.

"I can get the damn iced delivered. It would have been done already, but Carlos didn't remember to tell me about the problem with the delivery until just before we opened. I swear sometimes I think that man is trying to sabotage me, but I won't let that happen." Her eyes blazed. "I'll have the ice here within the hour."

"I'm sorry. I never meant to imply that you couldn't run this place. I was just trying to solve the problem." He knew his mistake as soon as the words left his mouth, but it was too late to snatch them back.

"You son of a bitch," she hissed.

"I'm sorry," he said again, knowing it wasn't enough, at least not for Becca. She was proud and independent and apparently thought that receiving help was a sign of weakness. Maybe it was, in the world in which she lived. With an inward sigh and what he hoped was a charming smile, he added, "I'm an idiot, and I think I'll stop talking now."

"That's the smartest thing you've said all night." The fire in her eyes had banked, but he knew that even the smallest misstep would rekindle it.

He nodded in agreement.

The small smile returned to the corner of her mouth, but her eyes hadn't softened enough to allow Cabel to draw a breath of relief. She pointed a blood-red-tipped finger at him. "Sit. Stay. Behave yourself."

He sat.

Becca leaned down, letting the V of her dress gape open. He kept his eyes on hers rather than enjoy the view she offered. She took his demonstration of self-control as a challenge.

Her voice lowered, becoming husky and seductive. Warm breath caressed his ear, sending a jolt of passion through his body before it settled in his lap. "If you are a good boy, and I mean a very, very good boy, you just might get a reward." She straightened, turned away, and began working the room, greeting guests, smiling at strangers until she reached the bar and disappeared behind a discrete door. She never looked back.

Cabel knew she was playing him, punishing him for his stupidity. Maybe he deserved it, though not for the reasons that she thought. She had tempted him, producing the physical reaction that she sought, and he had been powerless to stop her.

She held all of the cards and had at least some of the answers. Could he pry the truth from her without losing a piece of his soul?

Toying with the book of matches on the table, he considered his dilemma. Sipping his drink, he replayed his meeting with her in her office earlier today, hoping to find some chink in her armor that he could use as leverage. Instead, a wisp of a memory slipped in and out of his grasp. She had said something today, something that was wrong, off. The more he tried to pin the memory down, the more it eluded him. Becca's secrets were still safe from him.

Music played. Around him people drank and smoked and danced. He sat at the table and sipped his drink, praying for the strength to deal with Becca and find the truth about Kittie's death.

CHAPTER TWENTY-TWO

People continued to pour into the already crowded club, yet somehow there was room for everyone. As midnight neared many of the older patrons made their way toward the door and were quickly replaced by energetic young couples for whom the clock tolled the beginning of the evening, not the end.

Cabel sipped his drink and watched the crowd. People talked and laughed, enjoying themselves. With a sharp pang of regret, he realized that he would never truly belong among the revelers who swarmed around him. Since returning from France, the only time he had felt accepted was when he worked alongside other war survivors on the docks of New Orleans.

New Orleans. The irony of their choice wasn't lost on him. He and many other veterans of the Great War had converged on the only city in the United States that held the true flavor of the land where they had lost themselves.

Knowing how dark his thoughts could turn, Cabel set his drink aside. This was not the night to remember, not the war, not Jon. In his heart he knew that as much as he missed his friend, he envied him, too. Dying was so much easier than surviving, especially with the guilt that came with it. Why him and not Jon or one of the other thousands of men who were sent home in coffins? He closed his eyes and tried to push away the heavy weight that threatened to pull him down.

A noise disrupted the flow of the evening, saving him from his thoughts. In spite of the loud, dense crowd, Cabel could hear someone yelling in anger. He stood, trying to see what was happening but other patrons did the same, and his view remained obscured. Still, above the noise of the crowd, the music of the band, he could have sworn that he heard his own name being offered up as a curse.

A tug on his sleeve caught his attention. He turned and found a young, handsome waiter standing before him, different from the last one, he thought, though it was difficult to be sure. The young man gestured for Cabel to follow, and so he did. They slipped around the edge of the alcove that was closest to the stage, walked up a small flight of stairs, then stepped behind the curtain. Rather than finding himself backstage as he expected, Cabel found a door. The stage curtain had been extended beyond necessity, allowing for its elegant concealment. Cabel wondered who used it and where it led but realized he was about to find out.

The waiter opened the door and stepped through, clearly expecting Cabel to follow. He did, closing the door behind him. The narrow hallway was dimly lit though richly paneled. The carpet beneath his feet felt plush and expensive. A long flight of stairs led to the second floor. Even before the waiter opened the narrow door at the top of the steps, Cabel's nose told him that he had found the dining room.

The door was in fact a gateway to a pasha's harem. The walls were painted in murals to resemble the onion-domed buildings of the Orient with the opulent gardens and lush interiors that belonged to men of wealth and power. Candles flickered on low tables set in front of deep couches, and oil-filled wall sconces supplemented their light, allowing safe passage through the room.

Careful placement of furnishings and plants assured a reasonable amount of privacy to those who dined in the shadows. Hushed music blended with subdued voices, though the occasional trill of feminine laughter added a bit of lightness to this muted world.

Scantily clad waitresses in harem outfits moved from table to table with catlike grace, bearing trays laden with silver-covered plates or trays with glasses and bottles of wine. The food smelled wonderful, and the setting was delightful. Cabel wondered why more of the crowd from downstairs hadn't come up to enjoy a meal.

A sharp elbow nudged his side. The young waiter pointed toward the arched doorway on the other side of the room. Cabel went as directed, respectfully keeping his eyes averted from the patrons dining in the dim light. A young woman stood at a small dais, her manner as aloof and polished as the alabaster bust that sat on a nearby pedestal. With a practiced smile, she welcomed an elderly gentleman in expensive evening clothes. A girl who looked young enough to be the man's granddaughter clung to his arm and gazed adoringly into his eyes. With a nod of acknowledgement to Cabel, the hostess stepped around him and led the disparate couple into the dining room.

The young waiter snickered as he watched the old man escort his companion to their table. He looked up to find Cabel watching him, and all amusement fled from the boy's face. Serious now, he led Cabel down a wide carpeted hallway and past a curved staircase. This was the entrance most of the guests used, Cabel realized, and wondered how many other hidden doors and passageways wended through the walls of the speakeasy.

The wide hallway intersected a narrower one that was lined with several doors. The waiter paused at one of them, gave a discrete knock before turning the handle. He gestured for Cabel to enter the room, which he did and found himself standing in a den of pleasure.

Satin pillows with silken tassels were tossed into corners and heaped onto a bed with a shimmering green spread that seemed to swathe acres of mattress. The walls were covered in a red silk cloth shot through with strands of gold. Every surface of the room begged to be caressed. The musky scent of incense filled the air.

He knew he was wide-eyed when he turned to the waiter, who shrugged and said, "Becca told me to tell you two things." The young man obediently held up two fingers. "First, you are here to wait only. Do not think that this room is an invitation of any kind. And two, even when you're not trying, you're more trouble than you're worth."

Before Cabel could open his mouth, the young man added, "Oh, she then told me to tell you to sit, stay, and behave yourself." He didn't bother to try and hide his grin as he shut the door in Cabel's face.

Cabel stared at the closed door for several seconds as his brain processed all of the information that had been flung in its path. Slowly he turned to survey the room again and found it to be even more sensual than his first impression. A small table near the bed held several slim bottles of colored oils and other small vials that contained mysteries that begged to be explored. The dresser and mirror were placed in such a way that those on the bed could watch themselves if they chose. Lamps had been carefully situated to create pleasant shadows and murky corners that could be enjoyed in a variety of ways. A long satin robe, deep blue and masculine, hung from the back of the door. This room held promises of sexual fulfillment, promises he was sure were kept.

A man could lose himself in this room. And it was that sense of shifted control, of sexual manipulation, that exposed the room for what it was: the boudoir of a prostitute. The musky incense couldn't fully mask the underlying odors of sex and sweat, and the small silver tray placed discretely on a shelf near the door served as a reminder that this was ultimately a business transaction. Although beautifully appointed, the room held a fecklessness that did not appeal to him. The feeling of sensuality faded, replaced by an impression of an empty stage that waited for the actors to begin their performance.

He shook his head at his own stupidity. The restaurant didn't serve the patrons of the speakeasy, but the brothel. Now he understood the odd couple he saw entering the restaurant and the young waiter's response. He looked around the room again and wondered how many men could afford to enjoy the services provided here.

A speakeasy below and a brothel above, it was not surprising that this building required so many hidden pathways. Knowing that the higher echelons of the Chicago police force enjoyed the Charades Club, Cabel wondered if the secrecy was a protection against raids or angry spouses.

"I know he's here, damn it."

Cabel would have laughed at the timing of the furious words if he hadn't recognized the voice of the man who had yelled.

"Frank Evans, if you raise your voice one more time, you will not visit this floor again." Neither the thickness of the door nor the distance of the hall could muffle the anger in Becca's voice.

"But that son of a bitch turned Jim, my own son, against me." His uncle's voice was quieter now yet still insistent.

Cabel had no idea what the man was talking about.

"I don't care what Cabel did or didn't do, you will not disturb my guests with your problems."

"Don't say that traitor's name in my presence. He tried to kill my brother, and now he's coming after me. That bastard won't be happy until he's destroyed us all."

"That's enough. One more word, and I mean even one, I'll have you escorted from this building by the police. And I promise you that I'll make sure your arrest makes the front page of the paper tomorrow morning."

The silence that followed held angry, unspoken words. Footsteps led away, and Cabel leaned against the doorframe, listening as they faded down the hall.

"Don't get too comfortable in there," Becca hissed through the closed door, causing him to jump. "Once I'm finished dealing with your uncle, you're next."

|||||

Cabel let the silken strands of the tassel slip again and again through his fingers. The pillow was large and comfortable enough, though his back was getting stiff from sitting with it pressed against the side of the bed.

After Becca had stalked away, he didn't need to see her to know that she had stalked, he found himself in a bit of a dilemma. Where do you sit in a prostitute's room when you aren't there to enjoy her services? Surfaces that had seemed enticing and fraught with possibilities now became a dubious place to rest his posterior. The chair and the bed were not options, and his imagination created too many scenarios for him to want to use the footstool or the small, cushioned bench that stood against the wall. Finally, he had pulled a pillow from the bottom of the stack near the window and settled himself in as comfortably as possible.

Fifteen minutes had passed before the door swung open. Becca stood in the hallway, hands on her hips, looking like a teacher prepared to deliver a harsh scolding to an errant child. Her face changed from anger to shock when she found Cabel sitting on the floor, legs stretched out in front of him. She burst out laughing, loud and full. Hinges squeaked up and down the hallway as people peeked out to see what she had found so amusing. Unable to stand, Becca leaned against the doorjamb as her chortles turned to howls of glee.

Wiping her eyes, she edged herself into the room and shut the door. She opened her mouth to speak but only laughed more.

Cabel squirmed on his pillow, uncomfortable at being the object of such unbridled amusement. Deciding he would have more dignity if he were on his feet, he stood, bringing the pillow with him. Becca found this hilarious. She pointed and laughed, holding her sides against the pain. Cabel glanced down at his tasseled pillow and realized it wasn't helping the situation, but didn't know what to do with it. As he glanced around the room trying to find a place to set the thing, Becca's shrieks reached a crescendo, and she crumpled to the carpet, a quivering heap of giggles and gasps.

He finally tossed the pillow onto the bed, where it slid across the satiny green cover and off the other side, out of sight at last. Looking down at Becca's tear-streaked, smiling face, he couldn't help but smile a bit, too, at himself, at the situation.

Becca held up a hand. Cabel grasped it and helped her to her feet.

"Cabe, of all of the things I expected to see when I opened the door, that wasn't it."

"Obviously." He knew he sounded like a sulky child but couldn't help himself.

She smiled broadly before trying to settle her face into a more neutral expression. Her efforts failed. "Now, don't be upset," she said. "Think about it. I leave a man alone in a room full of erotic things and rather than finding you looking through the dresser drawers or reading one of the naughty books from the cabinet, I find you sitting, just sitting, on a pillow in the middle of the floor." She shook her head as her smile widened. "I know I've said this before, but you do know how to surprise a girl."

"I would take that as a compliment if you hadn't pointed and laughed."

She tried not to, he had to give her credit for that at least, but she laughed again. Her breath came in pants by the time she was finished, and she was still smiling when she linked her arm through his. "Come on, let's get out of here."

"Where are we going?" he asked, happy to be leaving the boudoir.

"I've finished working for the night, so I thought we could head up to my apartment, if that's all right with you." She shot him a rueful glare. "Though I'm not sure you deserve to go, after all you've put me through."

"Becca, I swear I have no idea what my uncle is talking about or why he was looking for me."

Her look of disbelief shifted to surprise when she saw that he spoke the truth. Shaking her head, she led him further along the hall. "You really can't help yourself, can you? You cause trouble without even knowing it."

"But…"

"No, Cabe, no more tonight. I'm tired and just want to relax."

He nodded but hesitated. As much as he needed to speak with her, he knew his self-control was fragile. The brothel room had encouraged some heated fantasies, he wouldn't deny that, and now Becca stood next to him, nearly spilling from her purple sheath. His body responded to it all.

Knowing she wanted some measure of control over him, that she would use her sensuality as a weapon, did little to cool his blood. He needed to leave.

"Becca, you're tired and…"

She stared at him a moment. "Just a drink then, Cabe. You can at least give me that much of your time."

For the second time that day, warning bells rang in his head, but still he followed her. They walked to the end of the hallway and up another small staircase. She stopped in front of one of the two doors that opened off the small landing. Opening it with a flourish, she walked inside, knowing he would follow.

Her sitting room surprised him. The décor was modern, done in the art-deco style. Not his favorite, but it suited her. The smooth clean lines held none of the frills or embellishments that defined art nouveau. No, this room reflected the woman who lived here quite well. It was feminine yet strong, distinctive.

A painting of a female nude hung on the wall above the sofa, which seemed too clichéd for Becca's personality and at odds with the rest of the furnishings. Cabel walked over to study it further.

The picture was striking, though painted with an amateurish hand. Rather than reclining with her back to the viewer, gazing coquettishly over her shoulder, this woman faced her audience, challenging them with her nudity and her strong, unflinching gaze. The artist had perfectly captured Becca's essence.

She stepped up behind him and handed him a neat scotch. "Well?"

"He didn't do you justice."

"No, but what fun we had while he tried." She gave a brief, happy laugh. "Of course, that was painted years ago," she said more quietly as she stepped away and perched on a small couch.

The hint of vulnerability surprised him. Cabel turned to find her watching him closely. He remained where he was, unwilling to be seduced and uncertain as to what to say or do next.

She patted the seat cushion next to her in the same practiced manner she had in her office earlier in the day.

He stayed where he was. "Becca," he started. "I know you're tired and don't want to talk about what's happened to Gary and in St. Joseph, but—"

"Cabe, darling, I don't want to talk at all." Her husky voice washed over him like prime whiskey over ice.

His belly tightened in response to her invitation and lower still there was much anticipation. With a deep, ragged breath, he struggled to stay true to his course of action. "Becca."

"Shh," she whispered as she rose and crossed the room, the movements of her body bringing heat and promise. Standing before him, she reached up and worked at the knot of his tie until it hung free. Using the slim piece of fabric, she tugged his face closer until their lips were inches apart and hers opened invitingly, her eyes daring him to accept.

He almost did.

Almost.

As much as her eyes held promise, they also held exhaustion and a hint of calculation. She was playing her role, distracting him, expecting him to play his. And he wanted to. She pressed her breasts against him and the temptation grew.

Just as he began to dip his head toward hers, to start the dance, he saw the flash of triumph in her eyes, and that was enough.

Smoothly, he tilted her head and brushed his lips against her forehead.

Shocked, she stepped back, her body quivering with anger. "You bastard."

He held up his hands to stop the flow of her fury and was shocked when they did. With great care he searched for the words that would let her keep her dignity and, hopefully, let him keep his life.

"Becca, I'm sorry, but I can't do this right now."

She opened her mouth to protest, but he pushed on. "I've run a company. I understand how hard you work, and I can see the exhaustion in your eyes. From what you said, there was one problem after another tonight and you met every challenge, but now you're tired. I'm not going to take advantage."

"Maybe I want you to," she said, though without much heat. "Maybe this is how I relax after work."

"Maybe," he agreed. "But I don't want to audition to become part of your stable." He said the words with a smile, hoping to take out the sting.

She stilled for a moment, studying him carefully.

He held his breath.

With a small sigh, she shrugged her shoulders, and let the exhaustion she had been hiding show through her façade. "You just can't help but be a good guy, can you?" she asked with derision in her voice.

"Becca, I'm sorry."

"You should be." Her voice rose in anger, but it was short lived. "I don't make offers like this as often as you might think." Her smile was tight and cold. "I have to say I'm disappointed, Cabe. Did you really love her that much?"

He didn't need to ask whom she meant. "Elizabeth and I have been over a long time now. This isn't about her." Which was the truth, though it was a small lie as well. He would always see his past in Becca's face. "You're tired and I think it's best if I leave, though I'd like to talk to you again."

"No, Cabe." Anger flashed in her eyes and this time it did not cool. "You don't get to pick and choose what you take from me and what you leave behind." She turned sharply and walked across the room. Pausing on the threshold of a doorway that led deeper into the apartment, she looked over her shoulder and glared. "Downstairs the kitchen door is open, and a guard is waiting to see you out. Go. Now." She stepped into the room and slammed the door shut behind her.

Whatever answers she might possess were lost to him now. He had failed.

Before leaving, he glanced around the sitting room one last time, hoping for inspiration, a clue, anything. A basket of mending sitting near a chair caught his attention. He carefully sifted through the silks and taffetas, thinking about the things that Gary had stolen, but there were no answers there.

Quietly he let himself out of Becca's apartment.

With great stealth and care, he made his way down the stairs from floor to floor, making only one wrong turn on his way to the kitchen. A burly man sat at a table eating a piece of pie in the otherwise empty room. With a grunt, he stood and unlocked the back door. Cabel stepped out and heard the lock click decisively behind him.

Darkness enveloped the alley, making the trek challenging, but soon he found himself on the sidewalk. As he passed the awning that marked the door to the Charades Club, a large dark sedan pulled up alongside him.

A man dressed in a striped suit and a fedora stepped from the front passenger's seat and approached him. Cabel tensed.

The man stopped a few feet away and eyed Cabel as if he was something to be scraped off the bottom of a shoe. "You're Cabel Evans, right?"

Surprised, Cabel nodded.

"Good. Get in."

Another man opened the back door of the car and stepped aside, a clear invitation.

"Thanks, gentlemen, really, but I'm only a few blocks from my hotel, and I think I'll walk." Cabel attempted to step around the first man, who shifted his weight, effectively blocking Cabel's path.

"Well, aren't you a wiseacre. Come on, get in. The boss wants to meet you."

"Who?"

Both men laughed and the first one answered. "The boss, you know, Capone. He wants us to bring you to him, and he didn't say what condition you had to be in when you got there, so..." With that he opened his jacket. The gun in the shoulder holster gleamed in the harsh glare of the streetlight.

Cabel looked from the gun, to the man, then to the car. Slowly he walked forward and was given a slight push to help him into the back seat, where a third man waited. The driver looked back and offered a cold smile. The first man got in front while the other squeezed into the back. The doors closed with heavy thuds.

They drove through the darkened streets of Chicago.

CHAPTER TWENTY-THREE

The car ride took less than fifteen minutes. Cabel was relieved to know that they were staying in the Loop area, though he wondered why it mattered. Dead was dead whether it happened here or outside of the city limits.

His captors spoke not a word, either to him or each other, as they drove through the dark caverns of the empty business district. Occasionally one or another of the men eyed him speculatively then smiled as if they knew what horrible fate awaited him and they were pleased to be allowed to watch.

The barely leashed violence in the car brought forth Cabel's warrior instincts, and with them a soldier's memories. Outnumbered and with no weapon of his own, he knew he had no chance of survival if these men meant to kill him. For years, death had seemed like a gift, one that lay just beyond his grasp, and now it rode with him as they sped through the night, but the thought held no comfort. Sitting in the back seat of the car, surrounded by men with cold eyes, Cabel had to confront a truth that had been forming in the back of his mind for some time now—he wanted to live. He doubted he could stop the men from killing him, but he would put up one hell of a fight.

The car stopped in front of a low-slung building. Everyone but the driver stepped out, though it took having the muzzle of a gun shoved into his back before Cabel abandoned the dubious security of the car.

The building's bright green door contrasted sharply with the dull gray of the wood siding. Someone or something opened the door. The light spilling from the doorway made it impossible to say whether it was a large bear or an enormous man who blocked their entry.

"Hey, Joey," said the man with the gun. The giant grunted and stepped aside, allowing them to enter. Joey was the largest human being Cabel had ever seen. He wasn't particularly tall and certainly not fat, but was wide and muscle-bound, giving Cabel the impression of a boulder wearing a suit.

Before he could blink, Cabel found himself pressed against a wall, arms splayed out and his legs harshly kicked into a matching position. Rough hands explored his body for weapons. Satisfied that he was not a threat, Cabel was yanked upright by his collar then shoved behind the man who had first accosted him on the street.

The air smelled of alcohol and frying oil. Beneath those odors was the unmistakable stench of rot and death. Cabel shook his head, trying to clear it. There were no trenches here.

A gun was shoved into his back, and Cabel was forced to wend his way through a maze of tables that had their chairs placed upside down upon them. A scowling young man swept away the debris of the evening's custom, carefully avoided looking in his direction, as if he didn't want any part in what was about to happen. Cabel's hands began to shake, and he shoved them into his pockets.

Other men, large and dangerous, ringed the room, watching Cabel's progress as he followed his captor. All of the windows were barred and shuttered. No outsiders would witness whatever was to happen here tonight.

Beyond the next doorway men sat at round tables, drinks in hand, cigars in mouth, and piles of cash in front of them. Armed bodyguards stood sentinel in strategic positions around the room, machine guns slung from their shoulders by leather straps. The casual display of potential violence sent shivers down Cabel's spine. His fragile hold on the present slipped another notch.

Al Capone sat at the center table as a king sits on his throne, surrounded by his subjects and his wealth. The pictures in the paper didn't do justice to the man who dealt a hand of cards then waited for the other players to ante up before looking at his own. The scar was there, yes, and the dark hair and cold eyes, but a photograph could not convey the sense of power and menace that rose from the man like a noxious vapor.

Dread, such as he had not known in years, spilled over Cabel, leaving him cold and shaking.

Capone leaned his head to one side and listened as the leader of Cabel's captors spoke into his ear. Reptilian eyes shifted to Cabel then back to his cards, showing the same amount of interest in both. Then he nodded and motioned for Cabel to step forward, which he did, though his legs shook as they struggled to obey the command.

As he neared the table, Capone inclined his head to indicate that Cabel should take the spot now vacated by his kidnapper. When he stood beside the gangster, Cabel was almost surprised that the man smelled of cologne rather than brimstone. The gangster was expensively yet gaudily dressed in a pea green suit and a fedora with a matching band above the brim. His shirt cuffs were monogrammed, and diamond cufflinks flashed at his wrists. There were diamonds on his tie clasp, too, and large, glittering rings on his fingers. Whereas the man at the front door had looked like a boulder, the most powerful gangster in Chicago looked like a malevolent toad, though that could have owed more to the color of the suit than his squat physique. Cabel found it easier to notice these irrelevances than to focus on the butt of the revolver that was wedged into a pocket of Capone's suit coat.

Squinting his eyes against the cigar smoke, Capone looked up at Cabel then grunted, much as Joey had. He then turned back to the table and dealt out the requested cards to the other players. The game continued with bets placed, raised, and called. Eventually a man with slicked back hair and dark stubble won the pot.

Capone shrugged philosophically, but the coldness in his eyes deepened. Cabel was sure that no matter what else happened, at the end of the night Capone came out ahead.

While the next player at the table began to shuffle the cards, Capone looked up at Cabel and studied him for a long minute. Finally he said, "You're not her usual type. Becca likes them young, unless she wants something. What does she want from you?" His harsh New York accent made the question seem like a threat.

"I'm not sure." Cabel was shocked to hear the reedy sound of his own voice. Clearing his throat, he tried again. "We knew each other when I was a boy, and I happened to see her at the Charades Club the other night." The danger in the room, directed at him, was palpable. This was not the time or place to mention Gary or Kittie.

"You were engaged to her sister." The flat statement held a world of recriminations.

"Yes, a long time ago." Cabel licked his suddenly dry lips. "I haven't seen Becca in years. Actually, the last time I saw her she still went by 'Rebecca.'"

Masculine laughter rumbled through the room. Even Capone's eyes lit with a genuine smile. "That *was* a long time ago. You were in the war, right?" Capone didn't wait for a response. Didn't need one, as he seemed to know everything he needed to about Cabel. The question was, why?

As if reading his mind, Capone said, "Like I said, you're not Becca's usual choice in the sack, so I had some people ask some questions. You're pretty rich. Not as rich as some, but rich enough. And old, by her standards."

The comment elicited smirks and guffaws from the men around the table. Clearly Becca's choice of bed partners was a source of amusement to them. Would it improve his situation or make it worse, Cabel wondered, if they knew he hadn't slept with Becca? They probably wouldn't believe the truth.

Picking up his cards, Capone used his cigar stuck in the corner of his mouth to indicate the men at the table. "These guys think Becca's ah, style, is funny. I think she has bigger balls than most of the men in here." He paused to scowl at the other players. The men stilled like mice in the unexpected presence of a cat. "Becca runs my place better than a lot of these men run their operations, so I don't give a damn who she screws as long as the club makes a profit, which it does—a very, very nice one."

No one moved. No one coughed. The clang of a dropped tray in the other room caused everyone to jump, except Capone. The men around the tables gave small, self-depreciating laughs while the bodyguards re-holstered their revolvers or lowered their machine guns.

Cabel had jumped like everyone, and his already frayed nerves felt stretched to the breaking point. His chest tightened, and air seemed in short supply. He took a deep, painful breath and then another. He had dreamed of violence almost nightly since the war but here, in this room, he was surrounded by it once again. His body shook and his vision dimmed, but he had a lifeline and he clutched it tightly. He had been an officer in the United States military. As an officer, a leader, he had gone over the edge of the trench and into hell more times than he wanted to remember. He relied on that training, that determination, to force himself to stand straight and face whatever was to come.

Capone motioned to the guards and grunted. "There're a lot of men in this town who'd like to take over my operations, so I make sure that what's mine is protected." He nodded to the men seated at the other tables in the room. "At the end of the night, the take gets counted up, sometimes here, sometimes at my place at Hotel Lexington, sometimes other places. I like to keep my rivals guessing." His smile held more triumph than humor.

"I was going to ask if you know what it's like to have a gang gunning for you, but I guess you kind of do. That war, what a shame." He shook his head and then shrugged, as if to dismiss the devastation that the Germans had wrought. "Me, I have people trying to kill me all the time, trying to take over my business. Hey, Mick, what's the count up to now?"

A man at the table looked up from his cards. "It's up to ten for the year, boss."

Capone nodded and smiled. "But they haven't got me yet." He looked back at Cabel. "That war you was in was a terrible thing, but I've got my own war, see? The Irish mooks and the Sicilians are breathing down my neck, all wanting what's mine." Cold eyes looked up at Cabel again. "You don't know any of those bastards, do you?"

It took a moment for Cabel to realize that the man was serious. "No, sir, I've been away in New Orleans and have been back for less than a year. I spend most of my time in St. Joseph, Michigan."

Capone nodded and turned back to his cards. "That's what I hear, but I just want to lay my eyes on you, to make sure. I don't like new people showing up on my turf at the same time that I hear that one of the gangs wants to take over the Charades Club. Not that they're going to get their filthy paws on it. I have more police in there on any one night than you'll find on the streets."

Perfunctory laugh accompanied this statement, but Cabel knew the man spoke the truth. If the club was targeted to be taken over by another gang, Becca would be right in the middle of the fight. He didn't want to care, but he did.

"Becca does a good job, especially for a woman, but she is still a woman." Capone looked up at Cabel again. "That place is mine, and Becca running that place makes her mine too. I take care of what is mine." The man leaned back in his chair and enjoyed a long pull on his cigar before engulfing Cabel in its smoke. "I just thought you should know."

Rough laughter joined this statement. Capone made a dismissive gesture with his hand, and Cabel backed away from the table with the respectful caution shown to any dangerous, uncaged creature.

Cabel remembered little of the drive to the hotel and was more shocked than relieved to find himself still alive when the car stopped in front of the Blackstone's entrance. The men shoved him roughly from the vehicle, and Cabel counted it a small victory that he was able to keep his footing. He stood at the curb and watched until the car turned a corner and disappeared from sight.

After retrieving his key from the sleepy desk clerk, Cabel made his way to his room where he fell, fully clothed, onto the bed. Exhausted in mind and body, still he fought against sleep, knowing that the dangers he had faced this evening would bring forth the worst of his nightmares. In the end, though, his will failed and the blackest dregs of his memories came forth.

CHAPTER TWENTY-FOUR

Sodden sheets tangled around Cabel's legs as he thrashed on the bed, his own screams waking him from the nightmare that had held him captive. His chest hurt from the pounding of his heart. He couldn't catch his breath and began to panic, which sent his heart racing even faster. Staring at the ceiling, he concentrated on the play of shadows he saw there, much like he did at home. His breathing slowed and his heart rate lowered. He would live.

Staggering to the bathroom, he used the facilities and splashed water on his face before stumbling back to bed.

He woke an hour later, surprised that he had slept again, even for a short time, and that no nightmares had intruded. Not rested, but at least refreshed, he rose to start his day. After a shower and shave, he would pay his bill and head home. Last night had been a disaster. Becca would never speak to him again. He needed to look elsewhere for the answers he needed.

Before stepping into the tub, Cabel placed an order for coffee and rolls from room service. Lathering the soap onto the thick cloth, he scrubbed himself nearly raw, trying to wash away the stench of Capone and his henchmen. He knew it wasn't real, but he continued to scrub all the same. He shuddered at the memory of the guns, of the casual violence that seemed as much a part of the mob boss as his diamonds and gaudy suits. Rinsing off, he put on a hotel robe and answered the knock on the door.

"You son of a bitch."

Cabel's reflexes saved him from the fist that flew toward his face. He retreated into the bedroom with his uncle in fast pursuit.

"Uncle Frank."

"Don't you dare call me that, as if you're family."

"He is family." Jim now stood in the doorway. Behind him a bellboy looked on with avid interest.

Jim took the boy's tray and gave him a tip before shutting the door. He placed the tray on a small table while Frank gawked at this son.

"What the hell are you doing here?"

"Funny, Father, I was about to ask you the same thing."

Cabel cleared his throat. "I'm curious as well." He wished he was dressed rather than wearing only a bathrobe. This family reunion was going to be difficult enough without that disadvantage.

"You shut up, you, you…"

"Father's a bit upset," Jim said with a barely restrained smile. "I thought I'd better tag along and see what he was up to."

"What I'm up to?" Frank raged. "I'm trying to save our company from this ungrateful ass who should have had the decency to stay lost."

"You're the one who hired the detectives to find him," Jim pointed out.

"A mistake I regret with every fiber of my being." Frank had become quite portly since Cabel had last seen him, and his dark hair was thinner and shot through with grey. The man now pointed a sausage-like finger at him. "You almost killed your father, almost destroyed the company. I won't let you come back and finish the job."

"Cabel didn't kill Uncle Edward, and as far as I'm concerned, the bastard got what he deserved."

"No," Cabel and Frank said in unison. Surprised and confused to find Cabel in agreement with him, Frank seemed to deflate, like a balloon with a slow leak.

"Father didn't deserve what I did to him." Not that Cabel remembered much of what had happened that horrible day. His father had been goading him in front of the full board, that much he remembered, and it was not the first time. Many of the board members had become uncomfortable with Edward's treatment of his son, but none dared to intervene.

To this day, Cabel couldn't remember what his father had said that had finally pushed him over the edge. Since the war, Cabel felt as if he were standing on the rim of a dark precipice and knew if he fell, he would not return. His father had pushed and prodded him closer and closer to that brink, until he toppled in, dragging his father down with him.

"Your father is a prince of a man, and he deserves a better son than you."

Jim snorted. "You hate Uncle Edward and everyone knows it. Admit it, Father. You're not here because of what happened five years ago, you're here because of what's happening now."

"But he's turned you against me," Frank said, clutching a hand to his breast, the very picture of grief and anguish. "We have a plan, a brilliant plan, and now he's come along and is trying to ruin everything."

"He came along and talked sense," Jim corrected. "Father, the plan to open retail shops was wrong. I knew it from the first time you proposed it, but I didn't have the courage to stand up to you. I thought the board would stop you long before now so I wouldn't have to be the one to do it." He looked ruefully at Cabel. "Then you showed up at the Charades Club and we talked, and I realized that I should have trusted my instincts. You gave a voice to my concerns and the confidence that I knew what I was doing."

"But—"

"No, Father." Jim shook his head and gave his father a small, sad smile. "Cabel didn't change my mind, he helped me to see what I always knew, that this plan of your is a disaster in the making."

"How can you believe him? He's unstable. He almost killed his father."

"I'm sorry." Cabel hadn't meant to speak but the words, the truth, slipped out. "You probably won't believe me, but I don't remember what happened at that board meeting, but I do know that I was out of control and I hurt my father. For that I am truly sorry."

Frank squinted at him, as if suspecting that Cabel's admission was a ploy to confuse him.

"I was wrong to do what I did. I wish I could remember what happened, that I could take it back, but I can't." His eyes felt hot, and he looked out the window and blinked several times before he could continue. "I'm sorry that you don't like my advice to Jim, but I believe your plan would take the company in the wrong direction. If you don't agree, you can always vote against us."

"But between you and Jim, you hold the majority of shares." Frank crossed his arms across his chest, looking like a petulant child. "This was going to be my project. I know I can make it work." He turned to his son. "Jim, you need to trust me, not your insane cousin."

Cabel flinched at the words but couldn't dispute them.

"No, Father. I need to trust myself."

Frank looked from his son to his nephew and seemed to realize that this battle was lost. "I never thought I'd see the day when my own son would turn against me." He turned on his heel and stormed from the room.

"My father does have a flair for the dramatic," Jim observed. He smiled, but Cabel could see the hurt and sadness in his cousin's eyes. "Why don't you get dressed while I order us a proper breakfast? I think we need to talk."

As Cabel dressed his energy sagged. The burst of adrenalin that had carried him through the encounter with his uncle was spent, leaving him tired and unsettled.

He emerged from the bathroom to find Jim sitting at a table in front of the windows. Cabel had paid extra for a room on the lake side of the hotel, finding that the view calmed his nerves no matter which side of the lake his was on, though today he would need more than an expanse of water set things to right. He took the seat across from Jim.

On the table between them lay a breakfast of coffee and rolls, as well as their past and family ties. Better able to deal with the tangible, Cabel poured himself a cup of coffee and selected a roll from the tray. He looked over to find his cousin studying him over the rim of his own coffee cup.

"I'm sorry about my father," Jim said.

Cabel nearly choked. "Are you joking? I'm the one who should be sorry. I never meant to come between you."

Jim smiled ruefully and stared out the window for a moment. After he turned back he said, "Our fathers are alike, Cabe, both trying to outdo each other, both manipulating to get the upper hand and neither one caring who gets hurt in the process. I hear he was at the Charades Club last night, making a scene."

Cabel nodded then reddened when he remembered the conversation between his uncle and Becca.

"Ah, so I see you know that Father is a client." Jim's smile was bitter. "Don't worry, I've known for a few years now, Mother does as well, but that's a conversation for another time perhaps. Let's talk about the company."

"All right, but first, how did your father find me, and how did you show up here, too?"

Jim smiled and his shoulders relaxed. "Father was furious when I stopped his plans and is determined that everything is your fault. He has connections, especially at the club, and used them to find out when you returned. When he couldn't confront you last night, he found out where you were staying and decided to ambush you here."

"He's determined."

"He's saving face. I think even he knows his big scheme is a disaster, but he's too far in to stop without looking like a fool, at least in his mind."

"No man is more foolish than when he throws good money after bad," the cousins quoted together.

Jim raised his coffee cup. "To Grandfather."

"To Grandfather," Cabel repeated then took a lingering sip. Whatever he had imagined he would find in Chicago, he couldn't have dreamed of something as wonderful as this small, precious moment with his cousin.

"And how did you come to be here?"

Jim laughed. "There are many things Father is good at. Stealth isn't one of them. He did his version of sneaking out of the house at an early hour, including having breakfast, reading the paper, and calling for his driver. Since he never leaves for the office before ten and I knew the brothel would be closed in the morning, I thought I'd follow and see where he went." Jim smile held humor but also bitterness. "When he knocked on your door, I was expecting a mistress, not an errant cousin."

"Well, I'm glad you were wrong, on both counts. I needed you."

Surprised delight lit Jim's face, and for a moment, he looked like the boy Cabel remembered from so long ago. The smile faded and the adult Jim returned. "That's nice of you to say, Cabe." He nodded to himself as he refilled his coffee cup. "But let's get to it, shall we? Why are you back in Chicago, and what is this I hear about you and Becca?"

Cabel hesitated a moment, but only a moment. Jim deserved the truth, or at least as much of it as Cabel had to offer him, and so he told Jim everything. He started with Walter's appearance on his back porch and finished by describing his meeting last night with Capone. As he told his cousin of his amateur investiagation, other bits and pieces of his life slipped in, things he meant to leave unsaid. He told Jim about his shellshock experience at Silver Beach, his distress over the connections he'd made with Walter and his family, his own feelings of guilt and shame, it all poured out of him like fetid water from a broken dam. And Jim, bless him, just listened.

As the tale wound down, Jim looked at him in shock. "You met Capone at the Green Door Tavern?"

Of all of the comments Jim could have made, this was one that Cabel hadn't expected, though it was oddly safer than other topics his cousin could have chosen. "Yes. The man is truly terrifying."

"You don't remember the history of the tavern, do you?"

Cabel shook his head. He remembered that the door had been green, but under the circumstances, it hadn't mattered.

"Cabe, you've been away from Chicago too long," Jim said with a mock shake of his head. "After the great fire, everything in the city burned down. Before any laws could be passed that banned buildings from being made of wood, two structures were built in the middle of the rubble."

"I remember. There was a stable and a bar."

"The necessities." Jim laughed. "The stable is gone now, but the bar, the Green Door Tavern, is still there, and it's the only wooden building in the city. Capone says he likes it because it shows where Chicago's priorities are."

Cabel smiled, though not as broadly as Jim. "I remember now, but I have to tell you, Capone is a monster."

The light dimmed from Jim's eyes. He sat back in his chair and studied Cabel. "There are so many stories about Capone, most of them romanticized, I'm sure, but it makes you forget what a ruthless man he has to be to succeed in his chosen profession."

"He does have a certain style."

"And a gun. I'm sorry, Cabe, I wasn't thinking." He sat a moment. "Do you think Capone had anything to do with the musician's death or the girl's?"

Cabel shook his head. "If he did, I doubt he did the dirty work himself. Still, I can't see what killing Gary and Kittie would get him, but I can't let go of the sense that Gary is tied to Capone through the rum-running and to Becca through the club and her stable, and Kittie is connected to all of that through Gary."

"And don't forget the shady character in Becca's office yesterday. What sort of business is she into that the guy had to use a hidden door?"

"That's a good question." It was difficult to believe that he had walked in on the fight between Becca and Dan only yesterday. His exhaustion returned. It was time to go home. "Well, Jim, you asked what I was doing in Chicago, and there's your answer."

"Not the one I expected, though I can't decide if I'm relieved or disappointed."

"I don't understand."

"I thought you wanted back into the company."

"What?"

"You came back to meet with the lawyers, to stop my father from making a mistake. You came back and did the job I should have done." Jim kept his face tellingly neutral. "You're the best businessman I know, after grandfather. I figured that you were sounding things out, making your move to come back."

"No," Cabel said, the decisive tone in his voice bringing a look of guilty relief to Jim's face. "I wasn't lying when I said that I can't recall exactly what happened at my last board meeting, but I remember enough. I'm not going back."

"You're a shareholder and a family member, despite what my father said," Jim reminded him. "We have to give you a seat on the board, if you want it."

"I know." In his deepest heart, Cabel had dreamed of someday returning to the company, of being one of its leaders again. But it was just a dream and the reality of it would hurt the company, not help it. He wouldn't do that to Jim or to his grandfather's memory. Someday he might reenter the world of business, but not now, and not through Evans Manufacturing. "And the board would accept me because they had to, but I won't put them, or you, in that position. No, it's your company now, and you're doing a great job. Grandfather would be so proud." Cabel sipped his now-cold coffee in an attempt to ease the lump in his throat.

"Thank you," Jim said quietly. "Maybe someday…"

"No, but thank you for that." Cabel rose and offered his hand. "And thank you for protecting me from your father."

Jim's grin was wide and natural. "Any time, cousin, any time."

They parted ways at the doorway to the hotel room with much backslapping and promises, mostly on Cabel's part, not to wait so long to see each other again. After the door closed, Cabel stood a moment, feeling his soul shift as another small piece of it slipped back into place.

Shaking his head at his own imaginings, he packed his bag and checked out of the hotel.

Heat slammed into him the moment Cabel stepped outside. Although only midmorning, the heavy, humid air wrapped around him in an unwanted embrace. Cooler, fresher air awaited him in St. Joseph. This was a good day to be leaving the city. With that happy thought to spur him on, he joined the crowd on the sidewalk.

People seemed to be rushing everywhere, going to work, running errands. A mother walked toward him with one small child in a baby buggy and another dragging his feet, clearly not wanting to go wherever they were heading.

The baby in the buggy threw a toy onto the sidewalk. Realizing that the mother hadn't seen what had happened, Cabel bent over to pick it up.

"Gun, machine gun!" someone yelled. People screamed and scattered as shots tore into the bricks of the hotel at the precise location where Cabel had stood just a moment ago. A dark sedan raced down the street, the barrel of the machine gun disappearing inside the open window as it went.

Cabel watched the car disappear around the corner. He looked down at the toy in his hand and then at the marks left by the bullets on the wall behind him. Stunned and shaken, his mind worked to accept how close death had come once again. Slowly he got to his feet, as did the people around him. Others peeked round mailboxes or parked cars, assuring themselves that it was safe to come out. No one had been hurt, as far as Cabel could tell.

"Momma," a young voice called.

Nearby the young mother still lay on the ground, her small son beneath her. The baby in the carriage cried in fear, waiting for its mother's comfort.

"Get a doctor!" Cabel called as he reached the woman's side. Gently, carefully he lifted her up enough to turn her and for the boy to wiggle out.

"No blood," said a man, looking down. "She probably fainted."

Even as he spoke, the woman's eyes fluttered open. "My baby," she said weakly.

"She's all right," another woman said, jiggling the child on her hip. "I think the noise upset her."

Cabel stared at the woman holding the baby but couldn't find a trace of irony either in her voice or her manner. Shaking his head he stood and backed away, letting others step forward to help the woman on the ground. At least one of them seemed to know what he was doing.

The young boy now clung to the woman holding his younger sibling, watching wide eyed as the crowd surged around his mother. Sirens sounded in the distance, moving closer. The police were on their way.

The arrival of the police had brought some organization to the chaos on the street. The woman was cared for and sent home with her children. The police asked questions with a diligence that surprised Cabel. He had thought that the rumors were true, that Capone owned the city and the police did not interfere with his business. Maybe that rumor was exaggerated. Or maybe this had nothing to do with Capone, or him. Perhaps, like Gary, he had simply been in the wrong place at the wrong time. More questions without answers.

Many people on the street had pointed to Cabel, singling him out as the apparent target of the shooting, and Cabel found himself at the center of some very unwanted attention. A detective named Andrew Healy had questioned Cabel repeatedly, first on the street and later at a police station. With his close-cut salt and pepper hair and penetrating grey eyes, the older man seemed to know what he was doing, but the slump of his shoulders suggested that he doubted that his efforts would make any difference.

Without knowing whom he could trust, or even if he had been the target or an innocent bystander, Cabel insisted that he was a random victim. If the police were working with Capone and the mobster wanted him dead, then they already had their answers. If someone else had tried to kill Cabel, then he was as much in the dark as the police, though he doubted they would believe him.

Detective Healy grew tired of Cabel's reticence and finally left him alone in a small, drab room for over an hour. When he returned, his manner was more solicitous but also more suspicious.

"You didn't tell me you met with Capone last night," the detective began as he sat across the small, scarred table. "You didn't think that the fact that you work for Capone is important?"

Cabel stared at the man in horror. "I don't work for Capone," he finally managed. "I met him once, last night, because we have a mutual...friend."

The detective nodded. "Becca Smith. Yeah, I heard. Can you think of any reason why she'd want to have you killed?"

Cabel almost smiled. He could think of at least one, but he doubted that his rejection of her last night would cause her to hire someone to gun him down in the streets. "We knew each other many years ago and only recently became reacquainted," he said, choosing his words carefully. "We didn't exactly part on the best of terms yesterday, but I can't imagine she'd have me killed."

The detective nodded again. "Yeah, she works for Capone, so she couldn't put a hit on you without his permission. I'm told that didn't happen, but he's anxious to know why someone was shooting at you."

A moment passed while Cabel considered this information. Capone hadn't tried to kill him, Becca either, apparently, but the mob boss wanted to know who had. This was the reason for all of the questions, Capone wanted the incident investigated. Despite the heat trapped in the small, airless room, Cabel shivered.

"You said you were headed to the train station when the attack happened," Detective Healy said, watching Cabel closely. He nodded to himself as if he had decided something. Rising, he motioned for Cabel to do the same. "I don't know what you're in the middle of, and I have a feeling that you don't either. Let's get you back on the other side of the lake where you belong." He held the door open for Cabel to precede him into the hallway. "No offense, but if someone's going to kill you, I'd rather they do it over there than over here."

Cabel looked back at the detective. The older man's face was set in stern, uncompromising lines. He wasn't making a joke.

CHAPTER TWENTY-FIVE

Cabel stepped outside of the police station to find dark clouds scudding in from the west. A summer storm was brewing, promising lightning and wind as well as hard, driving rain. The weather matched his mood. Also waiting for him was the young policeman recruited to drive Cabel to the train station.

They were almost to the station when the storm struck. Driving rain pelted the city, limiting visibility and forcing everyone to seek cover. Wind lashed trees and whipped the lake into froth. Lightning bolts flashed through the heavy clouds, followed by deafening claps of thunder. God's fury unleashed upon Chicago.

Cabel arrived at Union Station and ran through the sheets of rain to the glass doorway. Thunder boomed, echoing in the high ceiling of the station. The sound was intense, resonating through his body and mind.

Behind the rain, past the thunder, was the distant sound of cannon fire. Cabel's chest tightened as he willed his mind to stay in the present, using the sights and sounds of the station to help keep him grounded.

Across the aisle, a few benches down, a pale-faced man clutched his briefcase as his chest rose and fell in rapid succession. Another survivor.

When the announcement came to board the train to St. Joseph, Cabel rushed to join the line of waiting passengers. There was little of this trip that he wished to remember, and he was relieved to be headed home.

Despite the weather, the train left on time, though the storm chased them around the rim of the lake. The heart of the gale had taken a more direct route over the water, and by the time the train pulled into the station in St. Joseph, the little city was held firmly in its clutches.

As the only person to disembark at the small brick station, Cabel found himself alone on the platform. The wind gusted, nearly knocking him off of his feet. The conductor seemed to offer condolences rather than a good-bye as he pulled up the steps and signaled the train to continue.

As it was past eight o'clock in the evening, the little station was closed. Everything was dark, even the streetlights, which made walking treacherous on the rain-slicked boards as Cabel made his way to the sheltered side of the building. Standing against the wall, protected from the worst of the wind and rain, he looked up and down the deserted street that made a mockery of his homecoming. Everyone was safely indoors, except for him.

He waited out the storm, listening as the thunderclaps became more and more distant, eventually fading away. The rain persisted, though now it was heavy and soaking, the kind that farmers prayed for to nourish their crops.

No cars or taxis drove past, and the rain showed no signs of abating. If he waited for the rain to end, he would be spending the night on a bench under the station's overhanging roof. The Arledges lived nearby, but it was late and he didn't want to disturb them. Pulling his jacket lapels up to protect his neck from the worst of the rain, he picked up his overnight case and began walking toward the path that would take him to the top of the bluff. He wanted a hot shower, warm food, and his own bed.

Behind the storm clouds, night was falling, and soon the darkness would be complete. He needed to get to the top of the bluff before that happened, or he might never find his way.

Past the last house, he caught glimpses of Silver Beach through the waves of rain that swept the landscape. The amusement park sprawled dark and empty on the sandy shores of the lake. Either the weather had knocked out the electricity, or Drake had felt it prudent to turn everything off. Either way, there was something slightly menacing about the deserted amusement park.

Shaking his head at his foolish thoughts, Cabel turned, head still bowed against the rain, and almost ran into a girl holding an umbrella. He jumped nearly a foot in the air, and his heart beat so loud in his ears that it temporarily blocked the sounds of the rain.

The girl spoke, but her words were lost in the downpour. Finally she pointed toward something and began to walk away. She turned back and gave him an impatient wave, making it clear that he was to follow and seemed satisfied when he began to trudge tamely behind her.

They hadn't gone far when they reached a set of stairs. Cabel looked up, surprised to see a two-story house in front of him. The gray sidings blended perfectly with the stormy evening, and without any lights, the building was nearly indistinguishable from its surroundings.

He followed the girl up the stairs and through the door she had opened and found himself on a small, enclosed porch. The girl shook the water off the umbrella before propping it up in a corner, then pulled off an oiled jacket and hung it on a waiting rack. She was slim, he saw, and about sixteen, he guessed, but in the darkness, it was impossible to know.

"You might want to leave your coat here, though the rest of you looks pretty wet too," the girl said.

Obediently he stripped off his sodden jacket and laid it over the back of chair, though there was little chance of it drying. After a moment's hesitation, he left his dripping case there as well.

The girl opened a second door, and they entered the house proper. "I got him, Mom," she called into the gloom.

"Good, bring him in here." The woman's words seemed welcoming, but he could hear undertones of exhaustion in her voice.

The girl picked up a lit candle that was waiting on a small table and led him through a maze of furniture to the back of the house. Cabel was conscious of the fact that he was leaving a trail of wet footprints across the floor, but there was nothing he could do about that. The girl stopped at a doorway that opened onto a kitchen. At the far side of the room, a woman sat at a large, scarred table and looked out at the night. An oil lamp offered dim but serviceable light in an otherwise dark house. There was enough for him to see the woman's dark hair pulled back into a bun, but there was not enough to see the color of her eyes, only that they seemed weary.

The woman rose and came to greet him. "Hello, I'm Mary. Mary Davidson," she said, offering him her hand. "I hope you don't mind that I sent Gert out to fetch you, but it's just too dangerous of a night to be wandering out there alone."

He started to take her hand when he realized how wet his was. He tried to wipe it dry on his pants, but they were soaked and the effort was futile. With a shrug of apology, he held out his hand so she could understand the problem.

Mary smiled and handed him a towel. After he dried his hands and face, he tried again. Shaking her hand, he said, "I'm Cabel Evans, and thank you so much for your kindness. I appreciate the shelter, though I'm surprised you saw me out in the rain."

She seemed to relax slightly upon hearing his name. "I've heard that you're a friend of Dr. Lewis. He's a good man. And I spotted you because I had just come down the outside steps after checking on the boys upstairs. My daughter, Gert, was with me so I sent her to bring you in. The power's out and I don't know when they will have it back on." She turned to the girl and said, "Please go check on your sister. She was sleeping, but you know how she can be when the weather's bad."

Gert nodded and left the room, her small flickering candle lighting her way.

"My oldest daughter has TB. She's not contagious, but she does need a lot of care." Mary tried to smile but couldn't quite manage the effort. She must have been pretty when she was younger, but those days had passed. "My goodness, here I am talking your ear off when you're wet and shivering in my kitchen."

Cabel hadn't realized how cold he was. It felt odd, given that he knew how warm the temperature was outside, even with the storm, but the wet had chilled him to the bone.

Mary bustled over to the stove and began to stoke the fire. Once it was burning to her satisfaction, she placed a kettle of water on it, then lit another candle and disappeared into the darkness beyond.

She returned with a bundle of clothes, which he gratefully accepted before following her to a small bathroom where he could change. She left the candle for him and gently closed the door behind her.

He presumed that the clothes belonged to her husband, who was slightly shorter and heavier than he was, but Cabel was appreciative of the warmth the rough work shirt and pants offered. Thick socks completed the outfit. When he returned to the kitchen, Mary had a steaming mug of coffee waiting for him. A drying rack had been set up near the stove. She draped his shirt and pants over it, then took his shoes, stuffed them with newspaper and placed them near the heat. Her ministrations were of such a personal nature that he suddenly felt uncomfortable in her presence.

"Please have a seat at the table. I'll see if I can find you something to eat."

"Thank you, but I don't want to be a burden."

Mary just smiled and donned an apron over her flowered dress. A muffled blast sounded above their heads. Mary glared at the ceiling. "I just got through telling that boy to stop shooting off that BB gun." She grabbed a broom and banged it against the ceiling. From the marks he could see, it wasn't the first time she'd done that.

A voice called out, young and masculine, but the words were indistinguishable.

Mary rolled her eyes, set the broom aside, and returned to the stove. "I run a boarding house for the bands that play at the ballroom and also up at the Whitcomb Hotel."

Her name and her boarding house somehow seemed familiar, though he couldn't quite place how. Maybe Walter had mentioned the woman and the bands, but he couldn't remember, not that it mattered.

Mary broke two eggs into a pan that had been heating on the stove. Suddenly the kitchen smelled of butter and bacon. Cabel's stomach rumbled in response.

Gert returned to the kitchen, but her mother sent her away, telling her daughter that it was time for bed. The mulish look on her face had Cabel revise the girl's age down a year or two. She was probably about Anne's age, maybe fourteen or fifteen. Gert rolled her eyes at her mother before stomping off into the darkness.

Mary sighed and rubbed her temples. "That girl's a handful, but she's a big help with the house and with her sister. I don't know how I would manage without her." She placed a plate with eggs and bacon in front of him. He tried not to fall on it like a starving man.

Between bites, he asked, "So you run a boarding house for the bands?"

She nodded. "Most of them are local or regional, usually college boys earning money over the summer. We put them up in the rooms upstairs and we've never had any trouble, but then Rick got himself a BB gun. I keep telling him to stop shooting the thing in the room. I almost broke an ankle trying to make the bed, slipping on those little round BBs."

Cabel gave what he hoped was a sympathetic smile, but his mind was skipping ahead to questions he wanted to ask.

"How long have you been taking in lodgers?"

"Since we moved into this house. My husband made the upstairs into seven rooms and put beds in. There are enough bedrooms down here for me and the girls." She read the question in Cabel's eyes and answered it before he could voice it. "My husband died last November. He was working on the new ballroom and fell from the scaffolding." She blinked hard, willing the tears away.

Cabel looked out at the rain to give her time to compose herself.

"Mr. Drake has been wonderful," she said, letting him know that she was back in control of her emotions. "He makes sure that the bands stay here, and he gave Gert a job taking tickets at the ballroom. When I have time between shifts at Cooper & Wells, he sometimes finds me something to do over at Silver Beach as well. He's a good man, and he'll make sure we don't starve." She smiled bravely, but the tears threatened again.

"Tell me about the bands. Do all of them stay here?"

"Well, most of them do. Some of the famous bands play here, you know, ones from New York and California. The ones you hear on the radio. They come here now that the ballroom is open. When it was just the dance hall, we didn't get those kind here, but now we get some really good ones. One of the conductors from New York tried to explain it to me a few months ago. Something about the curve of the ceiling and the perfect acustis, I think."

"Acoustics," Cabel offered.

"That's right." She smiled. "I don't understand it, but it helps keep body and soul together, so it's a good thing."

Cabel nodded as he pushed his plate away. Just a few hours ago, he had wondered what his next steps would be in finding Kittie's killer. Through happenstance and storm, he was now sitting with someone who might know something that could help, and it would certainly take his mind off of the attempt on his own life. He just wished he knew what to ask. Finally he decided to start with the obvious. "What about the Wayne Sherman Band? Do they stay here?"

Mary nodded. "Most of them, anyway. A few of them have family or girlfriends who live in town, and Mr. Sherman likes to stay up at the Whitcomb, but the younger ones stay here."

"Do you know a trumpet player named Pete Darcy?"

Mary smiled. "Now that one could charm the pollen from a bee, but he's a good boy."

"And what about Gary Stevens? Did you know him?"

Mary's smile faded. "The poor boy that was killed by gangsters, yes, I knew him."

"I'm sorry," Cabel said. "I don't want to upset you."

"No, it's okay." She sipped her coffee as she thought of what to say. "Gary was a good boy, but…"

"But?" Cabel prompted.

"It's nothing," she said finally. "No harm was done."

"Mary, I know the boy is dead and you don't want to speak ill of him, but if there is something you could tell me, I'd appreciate it." He waited for her to ask him why he wanted to know, but she just looked out the window as if there was shame in what she was about to say.

She didn't look at him as she started to speak. "Whenever Mr. Sherman's boys stayed here, I would notice things in the house were moved around a bit, mostly papers and books and such. I'd find that everything in the kitchen cabinets was slightly different than how I left things, but nothing was ever taken."

"Why did you think it was Gary?"

Mary gave a little shrug and looked at him. "I caught him, of course. He was in the living room, going through the mail. It was just bills and a letter from my sister, but still." Anger had come into her eyes. "I told him to get out, and he wasn't allowed downstairs again. They're only allowed down here to use the telephone, but not him, not again."

"Did you ever tell Mr. Sherman about this?"

"No, I didn't want to get Gary in trouble. He just seemed like the kind of boy who liked to know things, but I don't think he meant any harm. Still, I know a lot of the other boys didn't want to share a room with him. My place is small so that really isn't an option." She sighed. "Even then, Gary was still popular with his band mates, and he could be charming, make you forget that you were angry with him."

Cabel wondered if this is what Pete hadn't wanted to tell him when he said that Gary was a jerk. A boy who liked to know things could be dangerous indeed, especially in Al Capone's world. Forcing his attention back to Mary, he asked, "What about the road manager?"

"Scottie Marks," Mary said the man's name in a flat voice, looking as if she'd just bitten into something sour. "He doesn't stay here."

"Why?"

"He just doesn't." Her tone of voice told him that this was all she would say. "I see him of course, from time to time. After the band unloads their instruments at the ballroom, he drives the bus over here and parks it behind the house. All of the bands do, though most just have cars, not busses." She seemed to sag, as if the weight of the day had suddenly become too much to bear. "I'm going to go to bed, Mr. Evans."

"Cabel, please." He wanted her to stay and tell him more about Scottie Marks, anything to keep his fears at bay, but she was tired and he wouldn't be selfish.

A ghost of a smile flitted across her face. "Mr. Cabel, then," she said, making it clear that this was as much of a compromise as she would allow. "The lights are out on the bluff as well as down here, so I don't think it's safe for you to walk home tonight. Why don't you sleep on the couch? I'll get you a pillow and blanket. In the morning your clothes will be dry, and you'll be able to see to find your way home."

"If it isn't too much trouble, I would appreciate it."

"I have twelve young men sleeping upstairs. What's one more?" She rose from the table, taking the oil lamp with her. Cabel thought he heard a small scratch or scuff coming from the hallway and wondered if Gert had gone off to bed after all.

Mary led the way to the living room and indicated the couch he could sleep on. She lit a candle before disappearing down the hall and returning a few minutes later with a pillow and blanket. "Please make yourself at home, Mr. Cabel. I'll leave the lamp with you, in case you need it in the night."

"Thank you," he said. She had just turned away when another question occurred to him. "Mary," he said.

She turned to look at him.

"Do you know when the Wayne Sherman Band is coming back to play at Shadowland?"

Nodding, she said, "Of course, the day after tomorrow. Thursday. They'll play two nights then head back to Chicago."

"Thank you," he said again, then watched her walk down the hall, her small light disappearing behind a closed door. Picking up the blanket, he shook it out and began to make a bed of sorts on the couch, all the while wondering if Gert would make another appearance. A whisper of a sound, so quiet that it was nearly hidden by the sound of the rain on the roof, gave him his answer.

Without turning around, he asked, "Did you know Gary Stevens?"

He heard a small squeak, as quiet as a mouse, and knew he wasn't alone. He turned and found Gert standing by a chair, near enough to be seen but too far away to be touched. She was wiser to the ways of the world than Anne, and the realization saddened him.

The light was too dim to see her clearly, but her hair seemed to be blonde or light brown. The color of her eyes was impossible to discern. She was slim but gave the impression of strength, both of body and spirit, much like her mother.

Silence had stretched between them while he'd made his observations, and he realized that she had been studying him as well. He was suddenly tired and didn't want to play games with Gert, even if she had rescued him from the storm. He repeated his question. "Did you know Gary Stevens?"

Her serious eyes followed him as he retrieved the pillow that her mother had given him and set it upon the couch. She didn't speak until he sat.

"I knew him. Like Mother said, he liked to know things."

"You heard that, did you?"

She shrugged, trying to look uncaring but even the dim light could not hide the blush that bloomed on her cheeks. "Mother was wrong about the other thing, though."

"Which other thing? Did he steal from you?" Cabel asked.

"No, at least not that I know of. It wasn't that, it was about him not wanting to hurt people. I heard him talking once, to one of the other boys, not Pete, but another one. He said that he had something important that people would pay a lot of money for, to get it back."

Maybe Gary was a blackmailer, Cabel thought, though there were other possibilities. "Did he tell the boy what he had? Why it was so important?"

Gert shook her head. "He just said he'd be rich."

Instead of getting rich, Gary had died, just like Elmer Dupree. The question was, where was this important thing and had the young musician died because of it?

"What about Kittie? Did she have anything to do with this?"

Gert gave a small smile and shook her head. "Kittie was nice, sweet, you know. I don't think Gary was stupid enough to include her in his plans. If he did, she didn't tell me."

Cabel considered his next question carefully. "Did Gary ever give things to Kittie?"

Gert nodded again. "Sure, all the time. Sometimes it was clothes and things, but it all seemed like they were hand-me-downs. Still they were nice, and Kittie liked them well enough. He also gave her a silver bracelet. She was so happy when he did that." Her face fell. "I tried to tell her once, about Gary. That he wasn't nice like she thought, but she wouldn't listen and now she's dead."

Her sadness touched him. "It wasn't your fault, you know, her death."

She shrugged. "I know, but still…"

Yes, but still… Those were the thoughts that haunted you before you closed your eyes at night.

Weary in body and soul, Cabel tried to stifle a yawn but failed. In the ways of yawns, the girl followed suit.

"Thank you for answering my questions, but I think it's time we both got some sleep," he said politely, ready for the girl to leave.

Above them the muffled sound of the BB gun could be heard.

"Mother's going to kill him." With that pronouncement, Gert turned away and slipped into the darkness.

Cabel turned the oil lamp down then settled himself on the couch. Another muffled shot came from overhead followed by the patter of BBs rolling across the floor. Fortunately, this problem wasn't his to solve.

⁞⁞⁞⁞⁞

The couch had been cruel to his body. Worn springs had poked and prodded, while the cushions sagged and drooped. His complaining back woke him well before the sun. The few nightmares he remembered had been surprisingly mild, as if the demons that had followed him home from the war contented themselves with the punishment inflicted by the couch.

Having forgotten to wind his watch, Cabel had no way of knowing the exact time, not that it mattered. He sat up, lit the oil lamp, and made his way to the kitchen. His clothes still hung from the rack, dry but stiff. His shoes were still damp. Looking at the unappealing mess, he considered his options. His bag on the porch held a second suit and his evening clothes, but the only other shoes he had were his dress ones.

After retrieving his bag, he slipped into the bathroom where he proceeded to cobble together an outfit that would allow him to get home with some measure of dignity if anyone happened to see him.

He left a note of thanks and two silver dollars on top of the folded clothes he had borrowed before quietly leaving the house. The sun peaked over the edge of the bluff, providing enough light for him to safely make his way home, though he made a slight detour to buy a newspaper. The boy looked him up and down, making it clear that the outfit was a bit eccentric. Cabel rather liked the combination of his dress shirt, suit pants, and evening shoes. But apparently the paperboy had an understanding of fashion and, in his quiet way, let Cabel know that his outfit would not do.

Smiling, Cabel turned back toward the house. The boy's whistles faded into silence behind him. The streetlights were still dark and no lamps burned in the houses he passed. Soon enough, he stood in front of his house. As he walked up the stairs, he was surprised at his sense of relief, of homecoming. He sighed as he unlocked the door and stepped inside.

When he returned from New Orleans, this had been only a house, a place to wait until death finally came for him, having somehow missed him on the battlefields of France. Now, though... He shook his head. Connections, obligations, relationships, all had found their way into his life and those had transformed the house into something more. If only he could be transformed as easily. He had changed in recent weeks, he wouldn't deny that, but the war lived inside him, creating a darkness that would never allow him to step fully into the light.

Setting his keys on the small table by the front door, he listened. All was quiet. Marta and Jorge were apparently still asleep. Cabel was hungry but worried that he might awaken the couple if he went into the kitchen to forage for food. With longing, he remembered the wonderful breakfast he had eaten with Dr. Lewis at the Lakeview Diner. He really needed to buy a car.

In the end, he left his bag by the front door so that Marta would find it and know he was home. Then, with a sigh, he trudged up the stairs to his own bed.

|||||

He awoke to the sounds of a gentle rain and Marta bustling around somewhere down the hall from his room. Stretching, he reached over and found the bedside clock. Nine thirty. It was late enough for him to feel guilty but early enough that his body complained.

He managed to slip into the bathroom without encountering his housekeeper. His back demanded a long soak in a hot tub, but his stomach would not wait. His bath was brief, and he shaved without a care as to the final result. Fully dressed, he opened the bathroom door and turned to walk toward the stairs.

"Cabe?"

"Yes, Marta," he answered, swearing softly under his breath. His stomach grumbled in agreement

"Would you come here, please?"

"Yes, ma'am."

He followed the sounds of her labors toward the front of the house and found her in his grandparents' bedroom. Clothes were stacked in neat piles and bed linens had been set aside to be laundered. Marta had spread a quilt out on the large, heavy bed and was studying it intently.

"What's going on?" Cabel asked, trying to keep his voice pleasant, but in fact he was angry. This was his grandparents' room, and she was cleaning it out as if they didn't live there anymore. Which they didn't. But still… He sighed, sensing he was about to be the victim of another of his housekeeper's schemes.

"Good morning, Cabe," she said, trying to sound relaxed, but he could see the tension in her eyes. Yes, she was up to something and hoping he wouldn't be upset about it. "Come look at this quilt."

He walked over to the bed and looked at the quilt in question. It was large and colorful, with interconnected circles flowing across a cream background.

"Your grandmother had me make this for her when you were just a boy," Marta said.

"You mean Grandmother didn't make this?" He remembered her with needlework in her hands but never stopped to wonder what she was making.

"Oh my, no. Your grandmother did embroidery. She felt it was more fitting to her station and quilting was more fitting to mine."

Though words were lightly said, with no hint of resentment, Cabel cringed. "I'm sorry that Grandmother treated you that way."

Marta smiled and waved away the apology. "Cabe, your grandmother had very strict notions about how things should be, but she was a fair woman, in her fashion. We understood each other and that was enough." She smoothed the quilt with her hand then looked at him. "She came to me and asked me to make her a quilt, and I agreed. I was so surprised when she brought out a bag of old clothes for me to use. There were outfits from when you and Jim were babies and young boys. She also saved scraps from her favorite frocks that were either out of fashion or no longer serviceable, as she would say." Marta shook her head but smiled at the memory. "I guess your grandmother had a sentimental heart. It was just hidden away."

Cabel doubted his grandmother had a sentimental bone in her body, yet as he touched one of the rings made up of small pieces of cloth, he wondered. He smiled as his fingers found a swatch cut from a shirt he'd worn when he was about five or six, blue with thin white stripes. He had worn it until there wasn't much left. He looked up to find Marta smiling at him.

"People hold on to things that are important to them. Some things you can put in a box or a drawer and keep forever, but some things"—she touched a bit of lace on one of the squares—"things like babies and boys, weddings and parties, you can't save those. So you keep the scraps to mark their importance." She looked up at him to see if he understood. He wasn't sure if he did, but nodded and touched the quilt again.

"Well," Marta said, brushing her hands together as if she'd just finished a difficult chore, "let's get you some breakfast."

"That sounds wonderful." He let her get to the door before he added, "Before we go downstairs, why don't you tell me what you're doing in here."

Her shoulders sagged slightly, but then her spine straightened and she turned, ready to do battle. "This is the best bedroom in the house, Cabe. I thought it was time that it was cleared out and the new owner moved in."

He shook his head, unable to imagine such a thing.

"Cabe, your grandfather's been gone for almost fifteen years and your grandmother's gone now, too. Your father and your uncle never cared for this place, and your grandmother, for all of her faults, learned to love it simply because your grandfather did. You do too. I know you do."

Cabel nodded. Of course he loved this house, but to move into this room, no. He didn't belong in here.

"You belong in here, now, whether you realize it or not," she said, her words unknowingly countering his thoughts. Hands on her hips, she looked around the room. "I think it needs a new bed and curtains, maybe a fresh coat of paint on the walls."

"Marta," he said in warning, yet he knew it was too late. The woman had already had a plan and he needed to stop her. "Marta," he said more softly, "I know you mean well, even when you make me angry I know that, but this." He raised his arm to encompass the room. "I can't do this."

She gave him a sad smile, walked over, and patted him on his cheek. "I know," she said. She turned and got as far as the door before she added over her shoulder, "But, in time, you will and the room will be ready for you when you are."

He heard her walk down the hall then down the stairs, presumably headed to the kitchen to make his breakfast. After a moment he left the room, carefully closing the door as he went. Marta could make him do many things, but he wasn't going to use that room as his own and she would just have to accept that. His self-righteous resolve lasted until he walked downstairs and past the open door of the study.

CHAPTER TWENTY-SIX

He had given himself a day to recover from his jaunt to Chicago, but still felt exhausted. The Wayne Sherman Band would be playing at Shadowland that night, and Cabel knew he should go, but he didn't think he could muster the strength to do so.

After some internal debate, he decided he shouldn't pass up the opportunity to meet with more of Gary's band members. Because of Mary Davidson he knew that Gary had taken something and was holding it for ransom. He needed to track down the other boy and see if he knew what Gary had stolen.

Now, freshly showered and shaved, he stood in front of his wardrobe trying to decide if he should stay home or go to Silver Beach. There was so much he didn't know about Kittie's death, and what he did know was a jumble of seemingly unrelated facts. There was the band, the ballroom, and the speakeasy. There was rumrunning and moonshining. There was Becca and Capone and an odd assortment of gangsters. And there was violence. Gary had died, then Kittie. The Arledges' house had been burglarized, and then Elmer Dupree was killed. He himself had been kidnapped at gunpoint and taken to see the most ruthless man in Chicago and later shot at from a moving car while he had stood on a crowded sidewalk. These last details he kept to himself, shuddering at the thought of what Marta would do if she learned of the episode.

So why had Kittie died and how was she, a young girl in a small town, connected to what was happening in Chicago?

Somehow he would find the truth. But what had Bessie George told him? He remembered; he would find his answers, but they would make him sad.

Cabel thought of Walter and Kaye and their remaining children. For them he would risk being sad. He reached into the wardrobe and selected a suit. A few minutes later he stepped into the warm summer night.

At the top of the bluff, the air smelled of mown grass and honeysuckle. Below, it smelled of lake and sawdust, cotton candy and fried onions. This combination was as much a part of Silver Beach as the merry-go-round and the roller coaster.

The crowd in the ballroom was lighter this Thursday evening than it would be Friday and Saturday, but it was boisterous enough to please the band. Ticket sales were brisk, and dancers elbowed each other for a place on the polished wood floor.

A glance at the stage told him that Pete Darcy was where he belonged and was glad. The young trumpet player might know more than he was saying, but he didn't need to get mixed up in this mess any more than he was already. Still, he might be able to direct Cabel to other band members who Gary might have confided in. He also looked around the stage area, wondering where the road manager, Scottie Marks, might be. Since he had no idea what the man looked like, it was a futile effort, and he soon gave up the pointless activity.

Cabel spied Logan Drake near the food concessions and decided that another conversation with the owner of Silver Beach might prove useful. Drake smiled when he saw Cabel making his way across the room and waited for him to approach.

Standing next to him, Cabel could see that while the older man's smile was genuine, there was concern and sadness in his eyes. They exchanged traditional pleasantries while Drake led Cabel to an empty booth. Once seated, Drake went straight to the heart of the matter.

"I understand you were with Dr. Lewis when he examined Elmer's body."

"Yes, sir, I was."

Drake nodded. "Did he really drink himself to death? I have to ask because I can imagine Elmer doing some pretty stupid things. Dang, I've seen him do some pretty stupid things, but I can't believe he'd do that."

Cabel hesitated. If he told Drake the truth and the chief heard about it, Dr. Lewis and his son could be destroyed. He chose his words and tone carefully. "It appeared as if he drank himself to death, yes."

Drake studied him a moment, then nodded. "So the chief is hiding something. I should have known." He looked over the crowd, at the band playing on the stage, then back to Cabel. "I know what a bully the chief is, what he's capable of. Nothing you tell me will go any further."

Deciding to trust him, Cabel said, "Dr. Lewis thinks someone slipped Elmer wood alcohol."

Shaking his head, Drake looked away. Cabel left the man to his thoughts and wondered what to say next.

When Drake turned back, his eyes were slightly reddened and his face was set in a mask of fury. "Who did it? How did it happen? Do you have any idea?"

Cabel shook his head. "I'm sorry. I don't know anything except that the doctor suspects that soda was mixed with the wood alcohol to mask its taste." Again he hesitated then decided he might as well tell the man the rest of it. "It was also pretty obvious that Elmer died on this side of the river, probably near Silver Beach, and Chief Bradley had the body moved."

Drake's face hardened. "Of course he did. We have to keep the money flowing in. What does it matter if a young man dies?"

"And a young woman too," Cabel added. Responding to Drake's questioning look he said, "Kittie's dead too, remember, and the chief also lied about the circumstances of her death."

Drake looked stricken. "I'd forgotten about Kittie. I didn't know her as well as I knew Elmer, and I guess…"

"Please, don't worry about that. I came down here to look into Kittie's death. I don't know if there's a connection between her death and Elmer's, but if there is, I'll find it."

Drake nodded. "I guess that's the best we can hope for. Is there anything I can do to help?"

"The last time I spoke with Elmer, he was excited about a deal he thought he was going to make, selling his hard cider to speakeasies in Chicago. Do you know anything about that?"

"I heard the same rumors, or at least I thought they were rumors. You said that Elmer told you this himself?" Drake shrugged when Cabel nodded. "If that's the case, I'd guess that someone was having fun at that boy's expense. I can't imagine any place like that serving hard cider and certainly not the stuff that Elmer made."

Cabel thought a moment. There was something there, hidden in Drake's words, or maybe just connected to them. He shook his head in frustration. "Who do you think would set Elmer up for a joke like that?"

"That's the thing," Drake said. "I know that some of the bands that come through here, this one included," he added, nodding toward the stage, "play in some places in Chicago and Detroit that I suspect are speakeasies. But I can't believe that one of the musicians would have the connections to make Elmer believe he was getting a deal like he thought. The boy might have been a fool, but he wasn't an idiot."

Cabel suddenly felt like the idiot. He could think of someone who would have those connections, or at least could convince Elmer that he did. The question was why would he do so? Thanking Drake for his time, Cabel rose and shook the older man's hand.

"If you find out who did this, please let me know."

Cabel nodded before slipping through the crowd and into the night. He was almost to the Davidson's boarding house when he remembered that Mary had told him that Wayne Sherman's road manager, Scottie Marks, didn't stay at her place. His steps slowed as he came upon the large gray house. Maybe the manager was back at the ballroom, enjoying the music or working back stage. Cabel had no idea what the job entailed but decided that as long as he'd come this far, he'd at least look the bus over.

The nearby streetlights, along with the bright quarter moon, illuminated the parking area behind the boarding house enough for Cabel to find his way without tripping. Despite that bit of light, impenetrable shadows clung to the walls and the edges of the yard, making his footing unsure as he made his way around the building. In the sandy lot behind the house, the bus crouched in the near-darkness like a slumbering beast. The joyful sounds of Silver Beach, muted and distant, underscored the fact that the house stood between him and the amusement park, creating a bleak, separate world.

The evening suddenly seemed cold, though maybe it was just his own imaginings that made him feel chilled. Wiping his damp palms on his pant legs, Cabel walked toward the bus and began a slow tour around it, crouching now and then to look under the vehicle. Without a flashlight or lantern it was impossible for him to see anything that would indicate that the bus was used for rumrunning or any other illegal activity. Feeling like a bad actor in a worse play, Cabel wiped the sand from his hands as he rose to his feet.

"Help you, friend?" a voice drawled behind him.

Cabel spun around. Heart in his throat he searched the darkness for the man who had spoken. Obligingly the stranger stepped forward, separating himself from the dense shadows along the side of the house. Tall and muscular, these were the only details Cabel could discern of the man, that and the stout metal pipe he held in one hand.

"I'll ask again, friend. Can I help you?" The man stepped forward, slapping the pipe into the open palm of his free hand.

Stepping forward himself, Cabel kept one eye on the pipe while studying the man as much as the darkness allowed. Even through the shadows the man's smile was evident. Either he had enjoyed frightening Cabel or was pleasantly anticipating the violence that may yet occur, maybe both. Regardless, the man's smile reminded Cabel of Chief Bradley. This man, Scottie Marks, was a bully. He was also a rumrunner, but was he a killer? More questions without answers.

The man stood blocking the only reasonable exit from the parking lot, calmly slapping the pipe against this palm. Under the circumstances, Cabel decided that a direct approach would be best.

"I was looking for you, actually, if I'm correct in assuming that you're Scottie Marks."

The man hesitated, lowering the pipe a fraction before he stepped into the relatively lighter area away from the building. "Yeah, I'm Scottie Marks. Who are you, and if you're looking for me, why were you looking for me under the bus?"

Cabel ignored the reasonable question and answered the easier one first. "I'm Cabel Evans."

Scottie threw back his head and laughed. "Well, now, friend, I've heard all about you. Becca said you had an unfortunate habit of sticking your nose in places it doesn't belong."

"Becca?"

Grinning, Scottie stepped even closer and let the pipe rest against the side of his leg. "I work for her." Scottie shrugged and said, "Well, Mr. Sherman pays me to manage the band when it's on the road, but I do a little work for Becca on the side and that pays even better."

"So, do you work for Becca or Capone?"

Scottie laughed again. "Well, usually that's one and the same, but lately... Well let's just say that Becca's been branching out on her own a bit."

"That could be dangerous," Cabel said, more to himself than the road manager.

"Becca seems to think it's worth the risk."

"What is worth the risk, exactly?"

Scottie tensed then shrugged. Becca hadn't told him, Cabel realized. Whatever her larger plan was, she kept it to herself. She probably told Scottie bits and pieces, whatever he needed to know to do whatever task she set for him. Whatever she was up to, Scottie was useful to her, but not trusted. As always, she was a smart woman.

"Actually, I came here to ask you about Elmer Dupree, not Becca."

Scottie assumed a pose of great concentration, rubbing his chin while tilting his head to the sky, the picture of a man deep in thought. "No, friend, can't say that I can place him."

Liar, Cabel thought but decided to take a more diplomatic route. "That's odd. He told me that he had connections and would be selling his hard cider to a speakeasy in Chicago. As far as I know, you're the only person he could have met who would have the connections to make that happen."

"Ah, that boy." Scottie snapped his fingers as if his memory had been jogged and the correct information retrieved. "Well his cider was more kick than taste. That might work for the yokels on this side of the lake, but the people on the other side, well, they like to get more for their money than a burned throat and a bad hangover."

"So you tried his cider."

"Just to be polite."

"How friendly of you."

Scottie scowled.

"The last time I saw Elmer," Cabel continued, "he told me that he could ask questions, too, and he seemed to think he had learned something that he could use to encourage you to buy his cider. Did he try to blackmail you?"

Scottie swung the pipe so fast that Cabel almost missed it. Instinctively he jumped back, tripping over something and landing hard on his back in the packed sand, the fall probably saving his life. Scottie glared down at him.

"I caught that little bastard doing the same thing you were, looking under the bus, snooping in the storage compartments." He pointed the pipe at Cabel's head. "He seemed to think that he could force me to sell his cider, like Becca would ever serve that swill in her joint." His laugh was harsh, ugly. "I promised that boy whatever he wanted to hear to keep him in line, but then he died, and I didn't have to worry about him anymore, did I?"

Cabel inched back from Scottie then slowly rose to his feet. The man did nothing to either help or hinder the process. "Did you help him with that? The dying, I mean," Cabel asked, already knowing the answer but wondering if the manager's quick temper would lead to a confession.

With a shrug and a laugh, Scottie backed off, lowering the pipe and looking at Cabel as if he were a fool. "You ask some dangerous questions, friend. The kind that can get you killed."

"Like Elmer."

Scottie Marks shrugged, unconcerned. "You just need to understand that bad things can happen to people who get mixed up in things that don't concern them."

"But—"

"But what? You think you have all the answers? You don't know nothing, and you can prove even less. And besides, who are you going to run off and tell your made-up stories to, the chief? He doesn't care as long as he gets his cut, greedy bastard."

"Chief Bradley knows about the rumrunning?"

"He figured it out earlier this summer and doesn't care so long as he gets paid not to care." Scottie turned his back to Cabel and spoke as if to the sky. "That is one mean son of a bitch, but useful," he said, looking at Cabel over his shoulder. "Very useful."

"I'm sure he is."

Scottie resumed his perusal of the stars. Deciding he was as safe as he could be, Cabel turn and walked away. He'd reached the edge of the boarding house parking lot when he heard Scottie call out to him.

"Here's a piece of advice, friend," the road manager sneered. "Becca likes you well enough I guess, but she can't protect you, not from everything. And even if she could, don't expect her to save you if you get in the way of her plans."

Cabel turned back. "What does that mean?"

The parking lot looked deserted, and the shadows kept their secrets.

CHAPTER TWENTY-SEVEN

Sleep had come easily, but nightmares had been violent and horribly detailed. Wakefulness was his only refuge, and Cabel now studied himself in the bathroom mirror. His face dripped with the cold water he'd just splashed on it, and his hair stood on end as if he'd received a fright, which he supposed he had.

Nightmares were expected. He was more surprised when he didn't have one then when he did. But tonight it wasn't the war that invaded his sleep, but Becca and Kittie. In his dream he had tried to save Walter's daughter from an unknown assailant. Suddenly Becca had stood between him and the girl, distracting him until it was too late to save her.

Kittie lay face down in the water, her hair flowing with the gentle lapping of the waves against the pier, her silver bracelet shining on her pale wrist. He had stared down, horrified at the sight.

Behind him Becca had laughed. "She's not important, the little thief. She got what she deserved."

Cabel looked back to yell at Becca. "No one deserved this, especially not a sixteen-year-old girl."

A man stood behind Becca, but she didn't see him, not at first. She turned, though and raised her hands as if to ward off a blow. The gunshot was deafening, and Becca crumbled to the pier, blood spreading across her dress. Cabel ran to her and picked her up, but she just smiled.

"Don't worry," she said. "My maid can fix anything." She closed her eyes and died in his arms.

Cabel splashed more water on his face, hoping to wash away the last bit of his dream. Even now, awake and knowing it wasn't real, he could feel her body still as the last bit of life slipped away. He knew she was dangerous, and he suspected that she was involved in Kittie's death, but she was also Elizabeth's sister and a part of his own past. It was the truth that he wanted from this woman, not her death.

Back in his room, Cabel donned his robe. Although it was only 1:30 in the morning, he knew from experience that sleep was now an impossibility. He wanted to sit in his wicker chair and stare out into the night. The back porch was buried under the contents of the kitchen, but the side porch had been repaired. Although the view wasn't as nice, or the area as private as the back porch, it would have to do.

With the construction in the kitchen, it wasn't possible to reach the porch by way of the back door without making noise and risk waking Marta and Jorge. Instead Cabel stepped out of the front door and followed the porch around the side of the house. His chair waited, standing on boards that were now solid and level. Next to it was the rack that Marta used to air out linens that had been stored in the closet too long. Cabel stepped around it to reach his chair. As he passed by, he noticed that it wasn't covered with sheets or pillowcases, but with the quilt that Marta had made.

He reached out and touched one of the bits of cloth. The details of the pattern were lost in the night, but he could easily see the larger aspects, the dark, interconnected circles floating on the light background. As he traced one of the circles with his fingers, he thought about what Marta had said about using bits of cloth to mark special moments.

His hand stilled over the quilt.

Marking special moments. His grandmother had used the scraps to record specific times and events, ones that couldn't be saved by other means. However some things could be stored or even hidden, but they still might need to be marked.

Not fully grasping the idea that swirled within his brain, Cabel retraced his steps to the front door and let himself in. The house creaked, but in a known and comforting way, as he walked to his study. Turning on the lights as he crossed the room, he opened the closet door and brought down the box that held Anne's contraband.

Carrying it to the table, he set it down and opened it before carefully lifting out each item, studying it as he did so. One of the silk scarves caught his attention. Red with some sort of black swirled print, it was beautiful and sensuous, much like its original owner. He studied the scarf, letting the supple length slip through his fingers as he forced his brain to make the connections that were tantalizingly close but still just out of reach.

This was the scarf that Violet had demanded in payment of storing Anne's things, but he didn't think that was the connection. Frustrated, he spread the scarf on the table and studied it. There was a small tear near its center that was nearly invisible due to careful mending. The location of the tear made him wonder if the scarf had been attached to the dress and had been torn off somehow, damaging both. Satisfied with the logic, but not where it led, he examined the scarf further.

A few minutes later he found what he was looking for, though it was less of mending than an alteration. Placing the ends of the scarf side by side, he could see that one was different than the other, with hand stitching finishing one edge and machine stitching finishing the other. He wouldn't had noticed it if he hadn't been studying the scarf so closely.

Using a pair of scissors from the desk drawer, Cabel carefully snipped away the neat hand stitches and found a ragged edge folded beneath. It looked as if someone had torn a strip from the scarf then sewed the end to hide the frayed threads.

He held the scarf, knowing that he had seen a strip of this fabric somewhere else. Somewhere that was connected to Kittie, not Becca. He closed his eyes again in concentration, and when he opened them, he knew where to look for his answers.

IIIII

Silver Beach still glittered even though it was after two a.m. The rides stood dark and waiting, but some of the lights on the board-walk still shone in the night. A few of the concessions were lit as well. As Cabel walked along the wooden boards, he was amazed at how the park could feel so joyful when it was open and so menacing after it had closed. For all of its apparent desolation, Cabel knew he wasn't the only person at Silver Beach tonight. The sound of hammering came from the far side of the park.

After deciding it was best to know who else was around at this late hour, Cabel followed the noise and found himself in front of the old dance hall. The sign over the door now proclaimed the building as the "Fun House." With the Shadlowland Ballroom open, the dance hall was no longer needed and the building was being put to a new use. Someone was working late on Drake's newest attraction. Cabel tried the door and found it unlocked. He stepped inside.

The cavernous room held various rides and activities. In the far corner of the building behind heavy canvas curtains, the hammer stopped falling. Cabel stepped toward the curtain but was distracted by a large wood platform that stood in the center of the room. Round and wide, it stood about a foot off the floor, which was ringed with carpet.

"This is saucer ride," Joe George said from behind him.

Cabel jumped a foot in the air before turning to find the large man grinning with delight, though it faded a bit when he saw the anger in Cabel's face. "Ah, Mr. Cabel, do not be angry with Joe George. I just have fun. Come now, I show you how it work."

Although Cabel was tired of people sneaking up behind him and scaring him into next year, he had to smile at Joe George. "I'm glad to see you. I need to ask—"

"In moment. Come and see."

Joe George led Cabel to a small metal box that opened to reveal a lever conveniently marked on and off. "People come and sit on wood. Then we turn on." Joe George flipped the switch and the round platform began to rotate, slower at first, then it picked up speed. "Unless you sit in middle, off you go."

Cabel grinned in spite of himself. Nate and Belinda would love this.

"Some boys not ride. They stand at side and watch pretty girls fall off onto carpet." Now Joe George grinned. "It is fun to see."

Cabel nodded, imaging that as a young man he would have enjoyed such a sight. He shook his head to dispel these distracting thoughts and turned to the gypsy. "You're working late tonight."

The man thumped himself on the chest. "Joe George work late every night. After park close, Mr. Drake have me and Mr. Timothy fix broken things." He shrugged. "Here, always something broken, need to be fixed. But now we have also this." Joe George raised an arm to indicate the building around him. "Most is done, but there are few more things to do. Now we work on wooden slides. People use carpet squares to slide down." He used his hand in a wave motion to demonstrate. "Will be fun, yes, and boys will come to watch girls slide down. Is way of things."

Cabel smiled. *Yes, it is the way of things.* "I didn't expect to find you here, but I'm glad that I did. I need to go to the spill-the-milk booth. I think Kittie might have left something there."

Joe George looked thoughtfully at Cabel. "Booth is small. Kittie, she leave nothing there."

"Maybe not, but I'd like to look anyway, with your permission."

The gypsy looked at him a moment then shrugged. "If you think possible, go and look, yes. I must stay here. To get into booth, you go to back. There is flap in canvas, yes? Untie and you can get inside. Wait here."

Joe George disappeared behind the curtain and returned a moment later with a flashlight. "Booth covered for night. This you will need," he said, thrusting the flashlight into Cabel's hand. "Bring back when you finish." With a wave, he stepped behind the curtain again, and moments later the sound of hammering resumed.

Cabel appreciated the flashlight but would have appreciated the company even more. Obviously Joe George was comfortable at Silver Beach after closing time, but Cabel found it disconcerting, a gloomy stage waiting for its actors to reappear.

Shaking off these thoughts, he returned to the boardwalk and found his way to the spill-the-milk booth. Getting inside was as easy as Joe George had said. The lights of the boardwalk created odd shadows on the canvas walls, and Cabel was grateful for the flashlight. He shone its dim beam around the booth and over the row of chalkware figures that dangled from the rafter above. Joe George had told him that shortly before she died Kittie had reorganized the booth. One of the things she had done was to display some of the prizes from the rafters where people could see them better from the other side of the boardwalk.

Heart pounding, he swept the light again along the row of figurines, each one hanging from the wooden support by a strip of cloth or a length of ribbon. The one he sought hung near the center of the display, the red and black silk's distinctive pattern easily identifiable despite the poor lighting.

Standing on a stool, he untied the prize and carefully set it on the counter before jumping down onto the sandy floor. He shone the flashlight beam on the figurine. The dog-shaped bank had obviously been painted by Daniela; the dim light could not hide the superior quality of the work.

Cabel shook the bank, listening carefully, but didn't hear anything moving inside it. Holding it in his hand, he gave it a little toss. Nothing shifted or moved and the weight seemed right for an empty bank. The cork plug at the base stuck tight, either from damp or glue, not that it mattered. As far as he could tell, there was nothing there. He set the chalkware bank on the counter, feeling like an idiot to have raced down the bluff in the middle of the night on a fool's errand.

Climbing back onto the stool, he started to re-tie the bank to the rafter only to have it slip from his fingers and fall to the counter. He winced at the sharp crack it made as it hit the wood, knowing the piece was now chipped if not outright broken. Sitting on the counter, Cabel picked up the bank and studied it in the weak beam of the flashlight.

A large fissure started at its base near the cork plug and ran up the back to the coin slot. One of the dog's ears was missing and the other was chipped, the white of the chalkware a harsh contrast to the brown and black paint of the rest of its fur. Applying a light bit of pressure, the bank crumbled to pieces in his hand. Hidden within was a folded square of paper.

Without knowing what it said, he was sure that this was the thing that Gary had stolen and someone was willing to kill for. Whatever was written on that paper was dangerous enough that three young people had been murdered to find it. He wondered if this was also the reason someone had tried to kill him a few days ago. The piece of paper seemed such a small thing to die for, but someone was willing to commit murder to protect the secrets it contained.

Cabel's hand shook slightly as he picked up this prize within a prize. There was not one sheet of paper, but two, he discovered, as he unfolded the sheets and smoothed them against the side of the counter. Squinting at the typed words, he realized he was holding a contract. Becca's bold signature was easily read on the last line of the document along with a second, illegible one.

The sadness that Bessie George had predicted wrapped itself around Cabel in a bitter embrace. He took a deep breath and tried to imagine the series of events that led up to him standing there, in that canvas booth at Silver Beach.

Gary had stolen the document from Becca and given it to Kittie to hide. Gary's next move had probably been to blackmail someone, Becca or whomever she was working with, though Becca herself seemed the most logical choice. Hadn't Pete said that Becca had been angry with Gary, but suddenly he was back in her good graces? But something had gone wrong with Gary's plan and he had died. Cabel wondered if the boy had been killed on Becca's orders and, if so, did Capone know?

After Gary died, the search for the contract continued, and it had somehow been traced back to Silver Beach. This was why Kittie had died. Soon enough Cabel would learn the details of the girl's murder, but at the moment, all he could do was mourn a young girl who had lost her life because she had unwittingly crossed Becca's path.

Cabel refolded the papers and placed them in his pocket. He would read the contract after he returned to his study. Right now he just wanted to go home.

Cabel picked up an empty box from beneath the counter and swept the remains of the bank into it. As distracted as he was by his discovery, he didn't want to imagine what Joe George would do to him if the gypsy came to the booth and found a mess. Leaving the flashlight on a shelf and retying the canvas, Cabel returned to the boardwalk, bracing himself for the long trudge to the top of the bluff.

He crossed the boardwalk, headed for an exit. The track of the rollercoaster loomed overhead, its trestles and supports looking insubstantial in the darkness. Just as he reached where the empty cars awaited riders, a man stepped out from behind one of the support pillars.

"You found it, didn't you?" Scottie Marks asked.

CHAPTER TWENTY-EIGHT

The two men stared at each other, only a small strip of sand lay between them. Scotty playfully tossed his piece of pipe from hand to hand, his smile of anticipation bright and full, even in the uneven lights from the boardwalk.

Cabel slowly backed away from the man and the heavy length of pipe he held. They were at the opposite end of the park from the fun house. There would be no help, no witnesses.

"I asked you a question, friend," the road manager said, stepping forward, keeping pace with Cabel's retreat. "Becca wouldn't tell me exactly what Gary had taken, just that it was a couple of pieces of paper and she wanted them back. I searched his rooms, the bus, his instrument case, but I didn't find anything."

The gap narrowed. The metal pipe gleamed under the lights of a food stall. Cabel tried to focus on his escape, but Scottie's words entranced him.

"Becca told me to ask the girlfriend, but the little bitch was stupid enough to think she was special to Gary. When I told her to bring the important thing Gary had given her, she brought me a cheap silver bracelet instead of the papers."

Cabel's throat closed when he thought of the naïve girl Kittie had been. "And so you killed her."

Scottie's smile made Cabel's blood freeze. "Becca told me to make sure that the girl wasn't going to be trouble, and I have to tell you, it sure was fun."

Here was his truth, and it was uglier than Cabel had imagined.

Swinging the pipe, Scottie moved closer. "I went to her house, searched through her things, but I didn't find anything. I thought she might have hidden it in one of the game prizes Gary had given her, so I smashed them, but there wasn't nothing in 'em."

"Did you kill Gary, too, and Elmer Dupree?"

"I didn't kill Gary. Becca had someone else take care of that," Scottie said in a voice so matter-of-fact that Cabel knew he spoke the truth. Becca had ordered Gary's murder and Kittie's. Cold seeped into his heart. He wondered if it was now as cold as hers.

Scottie edged closer. "Now Elmer, he didn't know as much as he thought he did, but he was starting to make trouble about the rumrunning. Better to get rid of him before he figured out that I had killed the girl." He laughed even as he stepped forward. "The stupid fool still loved her even though she was dead and gone. But killing him was easier than it was to kill her. A few sips of a special drink I whipped up for him and he was gone."

He stopped a few steps away from Cabel and studied him as if he were a problem to solve, though not a particularly challenging one.

"Becca knew about that, too," Cabel said, thinking back to their last meeting in her office. He had told Becca that Elmer was a moonshiner, but not what he brewed. A moment later she mentioned Elmer's hard cider. She couldn't have known that unless she knew about Elmer from Scottie Marks. She had ordered Elmer's death, just as she had ordered the others. Lies upon lies, deaths upon deaths, all of which could be laid at her door. The coldness in his heart began to retreat, fanned by a flame of pure, white hate.

"You need to give me the papers you found, and then you can go home to your fancy house on top of the bluff."

Cabel didn't need to see the man clearly to read the lie in his eyes. "You're wrong. I didn't find anything."

Scottie laughed. "You don't lie too well, friend. No, when I saw you go to the booth, I realized how smart you were. It was the one place I didn't think to look, but you did and you found it."

"You followed me?"

"Nah. I have to meet someone in a few minutes so I was walking around, waiting, you know. Then I saw you come off the bluff path and into the park, so I thought I'd see what you were up to." Scottie smiled. "Becca's going to give me a nice bonus for finding those papers, so you need to give them to me. Now."

Cabel didn't move and had no words left to say.

The man waited then shrugged. "I guess I can go through your pockets after you're dead." He swung the pipe high and hard, springing forward, moving faster than Cabel expected.

He held up his arm to ward off the blow. Pain exploded near his wrist. He fell to the sand, cradling his broken arm. Still on the ground, he scrambled away from Scottie, who smiled as he stalked his prey, enjoying the terror he had created. Cabel tried to think through the haze of pain. There had to be a ride nearby, some dark corner where he could hide until help arrived.

Scottie swung the pipe again. Cabel rolled away, nearly passing out from the agony his movements caused. The pipe thunked against the sand, so close to Cabel's head that he felt the breeze of it passing. He pushed himself back until the hard side of a building stopped his retreat.

"Well, friend, it seems like you've got nowhere to go. Me, I've got a meeting to get to, so let's finish this so I can be on my way." He raised the pipe high above his head to deliver a killing blow.

Cabel raised his uninjured arm in a futile attempt to protect himself.

A shot thundered in the night. Scottie's eyes widened in surprise. His face went slack as he collapsed onto the sand.

Cabel watched Scottie's eyes grow dull. He wanted to look away but felt obligated to serve as witness while death staked its claim. Kittie's killer was dead.

Numb with pain and shock, he looked past the body sprawled in front of him, expecting to see Joe George. Instead Chief Bradley stepped from the shadows, holstering his gun as he moved silently across the sand. Grunting as he stepped up onto the boardwalk, he said nothing until he reached the other side and looked down, first at Cabel, then at the dead road manager.

Cabel tensed as the chief approached. Although the gun was holstered, Cabel wasn't foolish enough to think he was safe. Chief Bradley was a violent man who held a grudge, and Cabel lay defenseless before him.

"I have to say, Mr. Evans, you presented me with a difficult choice." The chief kicked Scottie's body. Looking back at Cabel, he said, "You've been a thorn in my side from the beginning of all this. First, you got mixed up in the death of that sand bunny rather than leaving it be, and now here you are, in the middle of this business."

The chief didn't seem to know that Kittie's death and Scottie's actions were connected, Cabel realized through a cloud of pain. It seemed prudent not to enlighten him.

The chief sighed, took off his hat, and scratched his balding head. Cabel heard Joe George yelling from the opposite end of the park. He would be there soon.

The chief also realized that a witness would arrive at any moment. He knelt down next to Cabel, grunting with the effort. Sweat poured down the chief's face, and his eyes glittered in the dark. He commanded all of Cabel's attention.

"I could have let the bastard kill you and then kill him, or let him kill you and walk away, but I didn't. No." He glanced down the boardwalk, gauging how much time he had before Joe George arrived. He turned back to Cabel and lowered his voice. "I had to choose, and I figured a dead road manager from Chicago will cause fewer problems for me and the mayor than a dead rich man from above the bluff." He looked hard into Cabel's eyes. "This man was trying to rob you, right? I just happened to be here and saved an appreciative citizen, didn't I?"

Cabel nodded, pleased to have the dubious honor of being the lesser of two evils in Chief Bradley's eyes. Knowing there wasn't much time and that he was risking the chief's wrath, he asked anyway, "Why were you here?" But the answer came to him before he'd finished asking the question. The band was finishing its loop from Chicago to Detroit and back. Bradley was here to meet Marks and get his bribe from the rumrunner.

Chief Bradley studied Cabel's face and seemed to realize that he knew the truth. "I guess you were just real lucky tonight. More lucky than you have a right to expect."

Joe George's heavy boots pounded on the boardwalk as he raced toward them, hammer raised as a weapon. The chief stood and stepped aside so that Joe George could see that Cabel was alive, at least, if not well.

"What has happened here?" Joe George demanded as he knelt beside Cabel. With unexpected gentleness, he took Cabel's arm and examined it. "It is broke. Dr. Lewis will fix." He looked up at the chief, wary but determined. "He will ride in your car, I think."

Chief Bradley shook his head. "I've got things here I need to take care of."

Joe George looked past Cabel to Scottie Marks' body. His eyes slowly traveled from the body to the chief's face, which he studied with great interest. Chief Bradley shifted uncomfortably under the gypsy's scrutiny and finally looked away. "I need to call some of my men and clean up this mess."

Joe George looked from Bradley to Cabel before answering. "Yes. This must be done. I will take Mr. Cabel to boarding house. Miss Mary will send for Dr. Lewis."

The chief nodded.

With great care, Joe George placed an arm around Cabel's waist and helped him to his feet. Pain engulfed him, and his knees buckled. Breathing hard and fighting against the darkness that threatened to drag him away, Cabel leaned against Joe George's strong body and allowed the man to lead him out of the park. Nearly unconscious, he realized that Joe George now carried him through the night, muttering under his breath something about the chief and how Mama should have warned him.

Maybe Bessie George had but no one had listened, or maybe she knew that some fates could not be avoided no matter what warnings were offered. Cabel's head nodded then fell against Joe George's rough shirt. Feeling like a child cradled in his father's arms, he closed his eyes and found peace.

CHAPTER TWENTY-NINE

Cabel woke to find that he was lying on a large bed in a strange room with no idea of how he had arrived there. He had a vague memory of riding in the backseat of a car. He remembered a doctor's exam room and seeing Dr. Lewis's worried face hovering over him. There had been another car ride, he thought, though he couldn't be sure, and now he was in this room. It was a place he knew, but he couldn't quite remember…

Sunlight filtered through the curtains, familiar yet not. He tried to concentrate, but the effort drained him. He would consider the problem later.

||||||

The room was dark when Cabel woke again, though a reassuring glow came from the hallway. The door to the room had been left ajar, allowing in enough light for him to make out vague shapes, but nothing more. Frustrated that he couldn't see many details of the room, and wanting to know where he was, he braced his arms on the bed to push himself up. He cried out as pain shot through his body. Looking down he was surprised to find his right arm encased in a bulky cast from elbow to wrist.

As the pain ebbed to a dull but constant ache, he realized that he was thirsty and hungry, but mostly confused. Afraid if he closed his eyes he would fall asleep again, he concentrated on the strip of light at the edge of the door, using it to focus his mind and sort through the fragments of memories that slipped away each time he tried to grasp them.

His memory returned with horrible and sudden clarity. Ignoring the pain in his arm, he leaned over the side of the bed to retch with painful, dry heaves. Clammy and dazed, he lay back on the pillows and closed his eyes. Sleep would be preferable to the knowledge of what had happened at Silver Beach.

Through the pain, past the horror, lay gratitude. Cabel was alive and glad of it. Yet his life had come with a price. He now owed a debt to Chief Bradley, and although he resented that fact, he would find a way to repay it.

Thinking of the debt reminded him of another one. The day Walter Arledge had stepped onto his porch everything changed. From that one step, all of the others had been taken. Cabel had resented this intrusion into his life then felt resigned to it, but now he realized how his investigation into Kittie's death had saved him.

Thoughts of Kittie brought him back to what had happened at Silver Beach last night. At least he assumed it was last night. He could now tell Walter who had killed his daughter, although he didn't yet understand why the papers she had hidden had led to her death. The fact that her murderer was dead as well might bring a small measure of comfort to the family though it didn't bring justice. Was that even possible?

He should be satisfied, Cabel told himself. In spite of the odds, the debt had been paid and Walter would have his truth. At least as much as there was to tell.

Satisfaction wasn't enough, Cabel knew, though part of him wanted it to be. The hatred he had felt for Becca as he learned what she had done still burned in his heart. With it came fear, for the white, pure hate was familiar to him. The last board meeting he had attended was still a blur, but he remembered his father's taunts, he remembered the anger that had grown larger, into something more, something too big to contain. Out of control, nearly out of his mind, he had almost killed his father and had destroyed what little life he had regained since the war.

Here was that hatred again, burning bright, leading him back into darkness. He needed to stay on this side of the lake, be done with his investigation. Becca could plot her plots and scheme her schemes in her lair in Chicago; it meant nothing to him.

Cabel closed his eyes, but it didn't help. The truth lay within him and could not be shut away. His stomach sickened when he thought of what lay ahead. He was stronger now, but this anger was intense. There was a very real possibility that his anger would be unleashed on Becca and neither one of them would survive.

The darkness he had lived in for so long was still there, but lighter now. There was so much more to lose than there had been five years ago.

In the dark room, Cabel almost talked himself out of going back but then he thought of Walter and his wife, of the debt he owed. He would live with the darkness or let it destroy him, but he couldn't live knowing that Becca succeeded with her plots at the cost of the lives of three young people. He would pay his debt and give Kittie what little justice there was in this horrible situation. Becca needed to be held accountable and in the murky world in which she lived, he was probably the only one who could do that.

Knowing his path had been chosen did not bring comfort. Becca would not make things easy for him or herself. With Scottie Marks dead, he doubted he could prove her involvement in any of the deaths, and with Capone's protection behind her, it wouldn't matter if he did.

The throbbing in his arm dulled, and he felt weary. He would read the contract that so many people had died for, and maybe he would understand. At the very least, he would know what questions to ask Becca when he saw her again.

Cabel yawned.

But for now he would rest.

As he settled more comfortably into the pillows, he wondered if Marta knew where he was, if she was worried about him.

Marta.

He looked around the dark room and groaned. The night could no longer hide where he was and the extent to which his scheming housekeeper would go to get her way.

His head rested on his grandparents' pillows that lay on his grandparents' bed, which stood in his grandparents' room. Cabel fell asleep plotting his revenge.

IIIII

The next two days passed in a comfortable fog of pain medication and tender care. His mind tended to drift with the breeze, and he found it difficult to focus on any topic or newspaper article for more than a moment or two. Dr. Lewis assured him that as soon as the bones began to knit, he would reduce the pain medication and Cabel would return to normal. In the end, Cabel had no choice but to flow with the movements of the days like a leaf caught in the current of a gentle stream. He knew there were things he should be doing but could not muster the energy to remember what they were.

Marta, always protective, was especially solicitous. She was anxious, Cabel was sure, for him to accept his new surroundings. With studied casualness, Marta moved more and more of his things into the room, always watching him out of the corner of her eye.

Part of him wanted to berate his housekeeper, or at least ask her why she tried so hard to force him back into the world, to take a place that was no longer reserved for him. Yet he knew the answer. Despite his stubbornness and despair, a spark of hope had been ignited, and she was fanning it for all she was worth, anticipating that it would become a permanent fire in his heart. He wasn't ready yet to tell her how well she had succeeded. It would only break her heart if he lost that hope again when he confronted Becca. He cared more than he expected to, as the darkness was not as comforting now as it had been a few weeks earlier.

Nate and Belinda, and even Anne, visited him in his spacious new room to tell him stories or otherwise keep him entertained. Belinda shyly brought him presents of pictures she had drawn, which he kept in a stack on the bedside table. Nate bounded into the room at least twice a day with gifts of oddly shaped rocks or small piles of the season's first crop of acorns.

Others visited as well, including Dr. Lewis and Jorge, though the one that touched him the most was the paperboy. The child never ventured upstairs but arrived at the house each morning after selling his papers to bring the ones that he had saved for Cabel. He refused payment at first, but Marta couldn't look at the small child with his patched clothes and worn shoes and accept the gift, no matter how sincerely offered. Instead she fed him breakfast and paid for the papers before sending the boy on his way. It was his housekeeper who learned the boy's name and the details of his family. The child's name was John, a fact that brought tears to Cabel's eyes.

He was becoming an old woman, he decided, laying about in bed and weeping over small boys. It was time to go downstairs. Marta found him on the landing and promptly shooed him back up again. He would have argued with her if he had had the strength, but instead fell gratefully back among the pillows.

On the third day after he'd awoken at home, Cabel persuaded Dr. Lewis to reduce the strength of his pain medication. Within hours he found his thinking to be clearer and the pain manageable enough, though the sling the doctor required him to wear was stiff and chaffing. Nate found the sling fascinating and asked to wear it. Cabel was tempted to make a gift of it to the boy but soon realized how much better his arm felt with the sling than without it. He tired of everyone thinking they knew what was best for him and adding insult to injury by being right.

That afternoon, just a few hours before dinnertime, Marta bustled around the room in a faded print dress, putting clean laundry in cabinets and drawers. She quietly slipped a furniture catalogue on top of the stack of magazines that sat on the side of the bed.

Cabel picked it up and noted that several bedroom sets had been marked, though one was circled and underlined, clearly his housekeeper's favorite. It was a classic design, not too modern or too old fashioned, and he had to admit, it was his favorite too. Still he had to ask, "Do I really have a choice or have you already ordered the set?"

"Now, Cabe, this is your room, not mine. You need to decide what you want in here." She tried to look indignant, but her guilty conscience seemed to tweak her, for she walked nearer and started to smooth the blanket across the foot of the bed. Without meeting his eyes, she said, "This room is a lot nicer, Cabe. It's bigger than your old one, and sunnier, too. You can see the lake from the window, and I thought we could put a small table and chair out on the little balcony for you. All you need is some new furniture, and it'll feel like yours, not someone else's."

"When is it being delivered?" he asked, unable to keep the sarcasm from his voice.

She hesitated a moment. "Next Tuesday, unless you want to change the order."

First he was shocked, and then he grinned, then smiled, and then started to laugh.

Marta was smart enough not to join in, but there was a twinkle in her eye as she finished her unnecessary chores.

She turned to leave, but he stopped her. "Do you have my clothes from the night I was hurt?"

"I have the jacket and pants, but not your shirt. I'm sorry, but Dr. Lewis had to cut it off of you so that he wouldn't hurt you any more than he had to. I still don't understand what crazy scheme took you down to Silver Beach that late at night. If you want to go for a walk, there're plenty of places above the bluff where you can wander around without tripping over the boardwalk and breaking your arm on a bench."

That must have been the story the chief had created and Joe George had agreed to it. What Cabel didn't understand was how Scottie's death had gone unnoticed, but felt it was prudent to let the lie stand. He owed Joe George that much. And of course he owed Chief Bradley his life. No one mentioned Scottie Marks. There was no reason for anyone at the house to do so, but Cabel was curious to know what the chief had done with the body.

Pulling his thoughts back to Marta, he said, "There were some papers in the jacket pocket."

She nodded. "They're on your desk. Do you want them?"

He considered this a moment. "No. I'm going downstairs tomorrow, so I'll look at them then."

Marta looked about to protest, but then she studied him a moment and nodded. "I guess this is your last night to have dinner in bed."

"Would you please send Walter up to see me before he leaves for the day?"

His housekeeper nodded, but a worried look crossed her face. She knew there was more to the story than she was being told and she was concerned.

A few minutes later, Walter knocked on the door. Once his friend was seated, Cabel told Walter the truth as he knew it, as well as his guesses and surmises. There were some things he did not share, especially the obvious pleasure that Scottie Marks took in killing Walter's daughter. This was one thing that Kittie's parents did not need to know.

Walter also didn't need to know how difficult the investigation had been for Cabel on a personal level. So he left out of the story his own nightmares and the episode of shellshock he had experienced at Silver Beach. As a fellow soldier, he knew Walter would understand, but the man carried his own burdens and Cabel would not add to them.

The issues with Becca were more complicated. Cabel told of her role in his past as well as in Kittie's death. He omitted any mention of his attraction to Becca as well as the extent of his anger, afraid of what either one might reveal about himself.

So Cabel told the story as best he could, protecting them both to some degree. Still, it had been a relief to tell someone the truth of what had really happened at the amusement park, and Cabel told Walter about Chief Bradley's role in the matter.

After Cabel finished his story, Walter nodded then walked to the window. He drew a handkerchief from his pocket and wept. Cabel looked away, as much to hide his own tears as to give his friend some privacy.

Without turning back to Cabel, Walter asked, "Are you done with this business then?"

"No."

"But this woman, Becca, you knew her as a boy. You have a tie to her."

Cabel nodded, though his stomach turned. Here was treacherous territory. He couldn't let Walter see how much he would risk when he confronted Becca. He tried to keep his voice neutral. "Yes, but I also have one to you." He shifted uncomfortably in the bed. "When I was a teenager, Becca existed on the periphery of my life. I was focused on her sister and my friend Jon. Becca was always there, always noticed, but not a part of things." He took a deep breath as he decided how to explain. "When I saw her at the Charades Club, I knew she was dangerous, but I thought just to me. It was difficult to see the true Becca because she looks so much like Elizabeth. When I was around Becca I had to fight against my memories, against myself. I didn't want to remember all that I had lost." His voice broke and he took a sip of water to cover the lapse in the story.

Walter nodded, waiting patiently for whatever else was to come.

"I kept going back because I knew she was keeping things from me and I wanted the truth." Cabel felt his anger rise and fought to contain it. "Becca sent Scottie Marks after Kittie and probably knew that he would kill her." Cabel's vision blurred and narrowed until he was able to swallow his anger. His voice shook slightly as he continued. "I don't think it's possible for her to pay for this crime, but I need for her to know the cost others have paid for her schemes, though I can't promise you that she'll care."

"Cabe, you don't need to do this. This woman is involved with criminals and not just petty thieves or moonshiners." Walter returned to the chair next to the bed and sat down. He looked Cabel in the eye. "We're talking about Al Capone, Cabe. This woman works for Al Capone, and who knows what she and that man have done?"

"Yes, but…"

Walter shook his head. "No, it's too dangerous. You found out who killed my girl, and the man who did it is dead. It's enough. Kaye and I will let it be enough."

Cabel nearly broke under the weight of the compassion he saw in the older man's eyes. Quietly he said, "But it's not enough for me." Walter started to protest, but Cabel continued to speak. "I need her to tell me the truth. I need her to explain why all of this happened. It won't change anything, but I need to know."

"And you think you can force her to tell you the truth?"

"I have what she wants, what all of the deaths and lies have been about. She will bargain for it, and my price will be for her to tell me the truth."

"Or have you killed like the others. Maybe she was behind what happened to you on the street corner. Did you think of that?"

Cabel nodded. Even through his drugged haze, he had thought of that. There was no hiding from the things that Scottie Marks had told him; the man had no reason to lie. Was Becca capable of ordering the death of another human being? The horrible truth was, yes. Did she order his? He thought not, but perhaps his pride kept him from seeing the truth. She had lied to him, tried to manipulate and distract him, but did she hate him or feel threatened enough by him to kill him?

"I need to finish this and I can only do it by talking with her." Again he felt his hatred rise up like a snake preparing to strike. Knowing how dangerous he could be in this state, he was risking his sanity by confronting Becca, but she needed to be stopped.

"Your pride could get you killed, and it's a foolish thing to die over."

"I know, but then there are a lot of foolish things to die for."

Walter shook his head at that statement. "Kaye and Marta will never forgive me if something happened to you because I asked you to look into Kittie's death."

Cabel felt a small smile tug at the corners of his mouth. "Then you better hope nothing happens to me."

Walter studied him a moment, then nodded, accepting that Cabel would not be dissuaded from his path. The older man sighed again and rose heavily to his feet. Holding out his hand, he shook Cabel's and said, "Thank you for all that you've done." He paused and cleared his throat. "I'll tell my wife what you've learned. I'm sure it will bring her some comfort." He crossed the room and opened the door before he added, "I don't think I'll forgive you if you go to Chicago and get yourself killed." The door shut quietly behind him.

Alone, Cabel considered Walter's words and knew that the man was right. He also knew, regardless of the possible dangers, he would see this through to the end.

CHAPTER THIRTY

The Charades Club was a chaotic mass of humanity. After a conversation with a passing waiter and a few false starts, Cabel finally located Becca laughing and smiling at a group of men who devoured her with their eyes. She flirted with them in a studied manner, a hand on an arm here, a sideways glance there. The men didn't notice her lack of sincerity as they competed for her attention. Even from across the room he could see the calculating glitter in her eyes. These men were well connected, either in business or politics or both, and somehow Becca used them in one fashion or another, of that Cabel had no doubt.

They were not his problem.

After Dr. Lewis had reduced the strength of his pain medication, the horrors of the war had invaded Cabel's sleep with a clarity and ferocity he had not experienced in years. Nightmares had plagued him since the war, but after meeting Capone, the attempt against his own life, and witnessing Scottie Marks die on the boardwalk, his dreams were as detailed and ghastly as they had been when he first returned from France. He had awakened each morning exhausted and edgy.

Cabel knew that he was not ready for his confrontation with Becca, but it didn't matter. After reading the papers he had found in the carnival prize, he knew she would act soon, and he intended to stop her. Even with the urgency he felt, three more days passed before he had the strength to travel to Chicago.

Now he watched Becca flirting with her guests and felt cold but in control, at least for now. As she spoke to the men, she glanced over the crowd. Her eyes swept past him then returned to his face. Whatever she saw there caused her to excuse herself from the men and hurry to his side.

"Cabel, I thought you were smart enough not to come back here, or didn't I make myself clear?"

"You made yourself very clear, but we need to talk."

She gave a short, harsh laugh. "There is nothing more to be said. You're the war hero, the honorable officer, and I'm too tainted to deserve your attentions." The bitterness in her voice surprised him.

Cabel looked over her head at the people packed into the room, trying to stem the rush of anger that fought against its reins before dropping his eyes back to meet hers. "Do you really want me to believe that I've hurt you somehow, that you're the victim in this?" He shook his head. "You've lied to me from the moment I walked into this club, and I know why. Unless you want your secrets shouted to your clientele, to Capone, we will go to your office and talk."

"You found it," she whispered, her eyes filled with both relief and dread. "It's not what you think."

Cabel grabbed her arm with his good hand and yanked her toward him. "I know exactly what it is, and I'm tired of your lies. Do we discuss this here or in your office?"

Still she hesitated.

Keeping hold of her arm, he steered her toward the bar. She struggled against his grip, but his determination was stronger than hers and he drew her across the room. "Cabel," she hissed, "let go of me, now."

He looked down into her lovely, lying face. "No," he said. Becca continued to struggle as he led her around the edge of the wooden bar and to the door he had seen her use on a previous visit. The bartenders stood wide-eyed, but none of them intervened as they slipped through the door. As Cabel expected, the door led to a utilitarian hallway. Becca tried to jerk her arm away, demanding her release, but he retained his hold as he got his bearings.

Two burly men in cheap, ill-fitting suits stepped into the hallway behind them. "Need help, Miz Becca?" one of them asked, pulling back his jacket to reveal the butt of a gun.

Becca hesitated, looking from her bodyguards to Cabel.

He leaned over and whispered in her ear, "Who pays them, you or Capone? Do you really want them in our meeting, because I don't mind an audience if you don't."

She looked up at him with a hatred as pure as his own. "No, David, thank you. I can handle this fool."

Cabel waited for the men to return to the bar before following the sounds of food preparation. Once he reached the kitchen, he knew his way, and soon guided Becca into her office, freeing her immediately after closing the door.

She rubbed her elbow, glaring at him. Never taking her eyes from his, she marched to her desk and opened a drawer. The gun she now pointed at him was large and heavy, but she handled it with confidence. "No one touches me like that. Ever."

He leaned against the closed door and waited. She seemed surprised at his lack of concern for his own well-being and, after a moment, lowered the gun, placing it on the desk blotter.

She opened her mouth to speak but closed it as her eyes widened in surprise when she saw his cast. "Who clipped you?"

"Scottie Marks."

"That lying, cheating bastard." She came around the desk and stepped toward him. "Do you know where he is?"

"No" was all he could manage, which was true enough since he didn't know what Chief Bradley had done with Marks's body. Now, he wondered what else the chief had done.

"He stole the last shipment of whisky from the tour bus then disappeared, the bastard," she said, unwittingly supplying the answer to Cabel's unspoken question. "Scottie's useful, but he isn't all that bright. It won't take long for Capone's men to find him, and he won't survive long after that." She gave a cruel laugh.

Cabel closed his eyes and rested the back of his head against the door. The chief had stolen the shipment then buried Mark's body where it would never be found. All it would take was a word from Cabel and Chief Bradley would be dead, killed on the orders of the most ruthless gangster in America. He opened his eyes and found Becca standing before him. He owed the chief his life. That debt was now repaid.

He raised his injured arm up slightly as if to show off his cast. "Marks did this to me when he tried to get the contract for you."

Becca's eyes turned wary as she considered this information. "I see. May I have it back?"

He shook his head. "I read it, the contract."

"You're no lawyer."

"No, but I am a businessman. You made a deal with someone named George Malone. You help him with something, and if it is successful, he gives you the deed to this place."

"So?"

Cabel shook his head in disgust. "So he doesn't own this building. Capone does. The only way he can give you the property is if Capone is dead."

Becca gave him a cold smile. "That's right. The only way I'll ever get my hands on this place is over Capone's dead body." She gave a shrug and turned away.

He grabbed her shoulder and forced her to face him. She flinched under the strength of his grip on her shoulder, and he loosened it slightly. She jerked away.

"I told you not to touch me."

"I don't care. You need to explain this to me. Tell me why a sixteen-year-old girl in Michigan had to die so you could own this place."

"She died because she was a greedy little bitch."

Cabel's vision began to narrow, focusing only on Becca's face. He fought against his reaction. After a few deep breaths he said, "No. Kittie was a foolish young girl who was in love with the wrong boy. You're the greedy one here, not the girl."

Becca shrugged. "She shouldn't have gotten into the middle of this."

"She didn't know that she was getting into anything. She was just doing a favor for Gary."

"Well then, it's his fault the girl is dead, not mine."

"No," Cabel said with deliberate calm. He didn't come here to kill Becca, but he did need to stop her. Calling on every bit of strength he had, he focused on that goal and prayed for the control to keep his violence leashed. "Kittie died because you sent Scottie Marks after her. He didn't need to kill her. She didn't know anything."

"I couldn't take that risk. Do you know what's at stake here?"

The matter-of-fact tone of her voice sent chills down his spine. Despite what Scottie Marks had said, even though Cabel knew he spoke the truth, he still hoped that somehow he was wrong. Now the last wisps of hope slipped away like smoke in a breeze. At least now the lies had stopped, though the truth could be more dangerous.

"No, tell me, tell me what's at stake here," Cabel said, his voice calm, his vision clear. "You run the best-known, most-exclusive speakeasy in the city. Why isn't that enough for you?"

"Why should it be enough? Why can't I have more?"

"But people have died…"

"People always have to die. How do you think Capone got most of his businesses? I'll tell you. He used violence, threats, and yes, even murder to get what he wanted, just like every other gangster in this city. I'm just playing by their rules." She stood before him, eyes wild and chest heaving as she panted as much in excitement as in rage. "Capone killed a business partner to get the deed to this place. Why shouldn't I do the same to get it from him?"

"Because you're not him."

She shook her head in mocking disbelief. "Are you really that big of a fool? My God, Cabe, grow up and see the world for what it is." She crossed the room to stand behind her desk. "I've had to fight and scrape for everything I have, and I don't intend to lose it," she said, pounding the desk for emphasis. "As long as Capone owns the Charades Club, I manage this place only at his whim, and there are a lot of men out there who would gladly take my place. I've worked my ass off getting this club known, making it special. This place turns more profits in one weekend than half of the other speaks he owns combined. And yet do I have any real control? No."

She turned her head away from him and blinked hard. When she turned back, any hint of tears had vanished. "He books the entertainment and tells me what drinks to serve. Oh, he lets me decorate and run the brothel as I like, but I could do so much better if I ran the whole thing on my own.

"Do you know how many aldermen I have to sleep with to keep them happy? And the chief of police, well, he takes his bribes in the form of sex as well as money." She glared at Cabel, and he felt her revulsion for the men, for Capone, for herself. "I hate that, I hate being Capone's whore. Why do you think I flaunt my stable of boys in everyone's faces?" Her chin rose in defiance before giving him her answer. "When I tell those powerful sons of bitches that they're handsome, pretend that they're studs, it makes me ill. And they're so stupid that, for the moment, they believe me. But they can't ignore the fact that when I *choose* to have a man in my bed, it isn't them. It's never them."

"Becca—"

"Don't, Cabe, don't tell me you're sorry for me. I'm not. It's my own fault really, a sign of my success. If I wasn't so well known, if the club wasn't so popular, the bastards would be happy screwing one of the younger girls upstairs. But no, they want me, and I make them pay for the privilege." Her twisted smile nearly broke his heart.

"Now do you understand? I'm literally putting my ass on the line, and I want to get the reward. All of it. I'm sick and tired of working harder than any member of Capone's gang, being more successful, and still having to get his approval for everything from hiring a dishwasher to buying new glasses for the bar."

"And people have to die just so you can get what you want?"

"Yes," she hissed. "That's the price, and I'm willing to pay it."

Cabel thought of Kittie and her family, of Elmer. "But you're not the one who pays."

"I don't care, as long as I get what I want."

"Even if a sixteen-year-old girl and a seventeen-year-old boy have to die?"

"Whatever it takes, Cabe, whatever it takes."

Becca stood behind her desk, bitter, ruthless. Gone were the charm, the humor, and any hint of vulnerability. All shreds of humanity had been stripped away.

"You really don't care, do you? People have died, a young girl died, and it doesn't matter to you." He stared into her cold dark brown eyes. "Scottie told me, but I thought I knew you. I didn't want to believe…" His hands fisted, and the need to use them strained his control.

"Believe it, Cabe. And just so we're clear, I don't want or need your approval. I know what I'm doing and it doesn't fit in your perfect view of how the world works, but I don't care. I don't live in your world, I live in this one."

"What about Kittie and Elmer? They weren't a part of any of this. They deserved better and now they deserve justice." He almost choked on the last word as his vision blurred and narrowed. He felt the violence rising and fought against it, for his sake, not hers.

"Really, Cabe, justice? We both know how little of that truly exists, and I promise you, there isn't any to be found here." The coldness had returned to her eyes. "I will own this club and run it as I see fit. You can't stop me. I won't let that happen."

She picked up the gun from the desk and leveled it at him once again.

He stared at the gun, knowing she would use it. The first time she pointed it at him, it was more for effect than desire to kill. Now, though, he threatened her future, and he believed her when she said she wouldn't let that happen. The tension in his body eased, as if her demonstration of brutality diminished the need for his own.

"So you're going to kill me yourself rather than let Capone's goons do the job, or was it Malone's men who tried to gun me down?"

"That wasn't my fault. Malone's thug, Dan, knew you were asking questions about Gary and had been taken to see Capone. He decided to have you taken out. I didn't know until it was over."

He studied her face a moment. "I almost believe you."

She shook her head, whether in denial or acknowledgement he couldn't say.

"From the moment you walked into the club asking questions, I knew you would be trouble, I just had no idea how much."

He was suddenly tired. Knowing the truth changed nothing. She expressed no remorse or even excuses, simply a statement that she took what she wanted without any concern for those who were caught in the web of her lies and schemes. His trek to Chicago was the fool's errand that Walter had predicted. His hatred toward her faded, not to pity exactly, but a calm acceptance of the ugly reality of who she was. She would live out this day, he would keep his soul, and justice would be as unobtainable as she predicted.

The gun was heavy, and she shifted it slightly, tightening her finger on the trigger as she did so. An unnatural calm came over him. In the years since the war he had forgotten this feeling, this knowledge that death was close and it would find him or it wouldn't. This time, though, he fought against the quiet acceptance of whatever would befall him. The apathy that marked his days for so many years was gone, and he would fight to live.

"How do you know that this man, George Malone, will honor the contract?"

"Because it will be good business for him, and he is nothing if not a businessman."

"I don't understand." Cabel wanted to keep her talking, hoping the heavy gun would waiver so he could take it from her. He just needed time.

"Cabe, Cabe," Becca said, shaking her head in mock disappointment. "I thought you were a businessman yourself, but I guess you don't know how things get done in my world."

"I guess not."

She lowered the gun, resting the tip of the barrel on the desk blotter, ready to raise it at any provocation. "Capone is a lucky bastard. Everyone's trying to kill him, but he just won't die, which is good for me." She smiled. "I saw an opportunity, and I took it. That's good business, right? Seeing an opportunity and having the nerve to take advantage of it? So I went to Malone and made him a proposal. I'd get his men close enough to kill Capone in exchange for the deed to this place."

Cabel nodded. "I understand, but I still don't see—"

"You really are an innocent, aren't you?" Becca shook her head in wonderment. "Do you realize that when Capone dies, this city will be in chaos? He owns the mayor, the chief of police, and most of the aldermen. Malone thinks he can just step in and take over Capone's empire, but there are a lot of men in Capone's organization who won't give up without a fight. Then there are the other gangs, especially the Irish, who will join in the battle."

"There will be a bloodbath," Cabel said. His mind raced as he tried to understand all of the implications of what would happen if this powerful gangster died.

"Yes, the streets of Chicago will run red with blood. And while everyone else is fighting, I'll take over this club and run it as it should be run, with decent alcohol and better bands. Capone always books the black groups for his place in Cicero. I want them to play here."

Her words were void of emotion, merely simple statements of the facts as she saw them. Capone's death and the ensuing gang war were all factored into her business plan. He wondered if she was insane, or maybe it was the world that had gone crazy and he was the one who didn't belong.

"Bugsy Malone knows that Chicago's elite won't give up their entertainment just because there's a turf war. Given that most of the upper brass of the police department is here on any given evening, this will continue to be the safe place to come, and I'll need to serve drinks, cigarettes, provide entertainment."

"And Malone will have a guaranteed buyer for his illegal alcohol," Cabel said, starting to understand.

Becca smiled at him as if he was a slow student who finally answered a question correctly. "Exactly. Chicago is Chicago. Even the fire couldn't keep this city down for long. No matter what's happening in the streets, there's going to be a party somewhere. It might as well be here."

"Malone could still double cross you."

"He could." She shrugged then smiled. "But I'll take that risk. Soon Malone is going to be fighting for his life along with every other gangster in this city, and no one's going to pay any attention to me. I'm just a woman."

And a cobra's just a snake, Cabel thought.

"Prohibition isn't going to last forever," Becca continued. "Even the fool reformers who got us into this mess have seen that it isn't working. When it's over, I'll still have this club and the gangsters are going to have to crawl back into the sewer where they belong."

"So you'll win."

She squared her shoulders, smiling proudly. "Damn right, I'll win."

"But who loses?" Cabel asked, softly. "An innocent girl was murdered. And Gary Stevens…"

"That bastard. This whole thing is his fault."

"He found your contract," Cabel guessed.

"Yes. I'd hidden it behind the painting of me in my sitting room. Somehow Gary found it and tried to blackmail me. I couldn't admit to Malone that I'd lost it. He hadn't wanted to put our agreement in writing to begin with, but I insisted. It doesn't offer any real protection, but it showed him how serious I was. Also, I could have used it against him, early on, telling Capone that Malone had come to me, using the contract as proof."

Her smiled faltered. "If Malone knew that Gary had stolen the contract, he would have had me killed."

"So you had Gary killed instead."

Becca shrugged. "I just told Malone that Gary was asking too many questions, which was true enough. So Malone's men took care of the problem."

"They killed that boy."

Her eyes held his. "Yes."

"Becca…"

"This is the world I live in. This is what it takes to get what I want. You want me to feel sad because people have died, but I won't. I can't. It's just their poor luck that they got in my way."

"So you killed them, Gary and Kittie and Elmer." Cabel felt his anger rise again, felt the need to destroy her any way he could. He let the emotion wash over him, clearing his mind. "You are a murderer."

"What I did wasn't the same. I just gave the orders. I didn't actually kill anyone." The gun shook. She fought to steady it.

"So you're going to start with me?"

She steadied the gun, aiming it with deadly accuracy. Their eyes met and he saw the moment when she finally acknowledged the truth. It didn't matter if she pulled the trigger or not. There was already blood on her hands. The gun waivered then slowly, carefully, she set it on the blotter.

Tears fell, slowly at first, then she started to sob. Cabel rushed around the desk and pulled her to him, carefully setting the gun out of her reach as he did so. Becca clung to him as he held her to his chest and let the tears flow. His throat burned from his own unshed tears, though he couldn't say exactly who they were for.

Her tears slowed and she pulled away, turning her back to him as she dabbed at her face with a handkerchief. When she turned back, her eyes were red, her makeup nearly gone, but she seemed composed. "You need to leave, Cabe. Now."

"I can't. You need to stop what you're doing."

"It's too late for that." Her shoulders slumped, and her voice became weary. "If I don't help Malone, he'll kill me. If I warn Capone, he'll kill me. The only chance I have is to see this through."

"No, you could leave, walk away."

She gave him a small, sad smile. "And go where? Do what? Will you run away with me? Marry me? Protect me?" She read the truth in his eyes and smiled sadly. "Don't worry, Cabe. I told you before I don't need anyone to rescue me. I'll manage it on my own. But you need to leave, now."

Cabel stood before her, uncertain and confused. The fury that he had felt when he read the contract, the anger that had driven him across the lake to confront Becca had all but disappeared. He had come here to force her to look him in the eye and tell him the truth. She had given him what he sought, but there was no satisfaction in it. There were no winners in Becca's game, no justice. He stood before her, empty and exhausted.

"Cabe, I'm serious. You need to go before—"

"No, don't go now, the fun's just about to start."

Cabel turned to find the the hidden door in the wall ajar. Standing in the opening was Malone's goon, Dan. Here was the man who had probably killed Gary, slapped Becca, and shot at him on a street corner. With his cheap suit and greased hair, he looked more like a parody of a gangster rather than the real thing. He would have looked comical, but the effect was ruined by the expression of anticipation on his face and the heavy revolver he aimed at Cabel's chest. "You're a hard man to kill, but I think that's about to change."

CHAPTER THIRTY-ONE

The dark, narrow passageway that lay behind the concealed door pressed against him like a living thing, stealing the air from his lungs. Since the war, Cabel avoided crowds as well as tight spaces as the memory of the trenches was always a breath away. But as with the trenches, here, too, he was surrounded by violence. He was ignored by the men who stood on either side of him. They were too intent on the conversation taking place on the other side of the door to give him much thought. Apparently the cast on his right arm gave the men the impression that he was either helpless or incompetent. Either way, he was dismissed as a needless burden, one which would soon be tossed aside.

After Dan had walked into Becca's office, he had demanded that Cabel join him and his men in the hidden passageway, one more assurance that Becca would do as Malone wanted. Dan didn't seem to realize how close Becca had come to killing Cabel herself, limiting his effectiveness as a hostage. Dan had also made it clear that if Cabel didn't cooperate, Becca would die. Cabel was feeling ambivalent about that at the moment. He still didn't know if Dan had been acting on Becca's orders or Malone's when he tried to gun him down in the street. It shouldn't matter, but it did.

Over an hour had passed since Cabel had been forced into the passage with the other men, who had spoken in low voices until they had heard Becca open her door and welcome Capone into her office. They now waited in silence, breathing the stale air, listening for the signal that would call them to action. One of Malone's men jabbed the barrel of his gun into Cabel's side at random intervals, reminding him to stay quiet. Cabel considered the absurdity of the man threatening to shoot him if he made any noise. He let this irrelevant thought slide through his mind to keep him grounded in the present. The pull of the horrors of his past were strong in this dark and narrow place. Though his present was fairly horrific, as well. Whether by Malone's men or Capone's, Cabel knew he would be dead before morning.

The murmur of voices from the office continued. The tension in the passageway grew as the men waited for the signal from Becca that Capone and his men would be vulnerable to attack. Dan stood at the head of the line, his machine gun ready. Seven other gangsters made up the murder squad, and then there was Cabel himself. The plan seemed to be that at the appointed time, Dan would burst into the office and take out as many men as possible with the machine gun. The others would follow, picking off any survivors of the initial onslaught. Cabel had no idea how Becca expected to live through the ambush.

The man behind Cabel shuffled his feet then shoved the muzzle of his gun against Cabel's side, as if blaming him for the delay. The man at the end of the line stifled a sneeze.

Without any signal that Cabel could discern, Dan threw the door open and leaped into Becca's office, firing the machine gun as he went. Cabel was propelled into the room by the man behind him and knocked to the floor. He nearly passed out from the jarring pain in his arm as others rushed in to join the gunfight.

One of Malone's men had managed to block the office door. Capone and his men were trapped within, fighting for their lives. Men on the other side of the door pounded on it, and the wood was beginning to splinter. Soon it would give way, and Capone's reinforcements would arrive. Malone's men needed to finish their job soon or die.

The noise of the machine guns was constant and near deafening, punctuated here and there by shots fired by handguns. The smell of cordite filled the air along with the screams of the injured and dying. Images of barbed wire and the stench of death surrounded him, but Cabel fought against those memories. A body fell in front of him, and for one horrible second, he didn't know if the dead man was from the past or the present.

The war within and the battle in the office continued to ebb and flow into a bizarre whole. Dan fell to the floor, his machine gun giving a last few bursts of deadly fire before going silent. German's slithered through no-man's land as Capone's men took what little cover they could in the office.

Two German's crouched behind a rock, their backs to Cabel. The rock became a desk, and Cabel could see that someone hid behind it. From what little he could see of the spats and the suit, he was sure it was Capone. Did he fight for the Germans or the Allies?

A gun skittered near his hand as another body fell. Cabel's hand closed around the hard grip of the weapon, and he found himself in a stand of shattered trees. Fog covered the ground, swirling around his legs. The air held the stench of decay and poison from the last remnants of the deadly mustard gas that had passed through in the night. Disoriented from the fog, lost from his unit, he had no idea which side of the battle line he was now on.

Creeping forward, hoping safety lay in that direction, he heard a faint sound. Cautiously he raised his head above the fog to find two young German soldiers stripping a dead body of its possessions.

He rose, aimed his gun, and told the soldiers to stop. They looked up and Cabel realized that they were boys, dressed as soldiers, yes, but still boys. Across the witch's cauldron of fog, they stared at each other. He hoped they would be smart, surrender and live, but one of them reached down for his weapon.

"I said, put the gun down."

The hard muzzle of a gun pressed against the back of Cabel's head. His vision tilted and blurred until it finally settled and he found himself in Becca's office. Someone reached around him and yanked the revolver from his hand. Two men cowered next to a desk. Capone stood on the other side of it, watching Cabel with cold, assessing eyes.

"When I saw you come out of that door with Malone's men, I thought you were with them. I'm glad I was wrong. You're a good man to have on my side in a fight."

Cabel would have laughed at the absurd statement, but nausea burned in the back of his throat so insistently that it was all he could do to keep from vomiting at the gangster's feet. Instead he nodded as he struggled to remain standing, afraid that if he fell to the floor the gangster might suspect the truth.

Capone studied Cabel a moment longer then walked away, issuing orders as he went. Malone's men were rounded up, two seemingly unharmed, three more injured but alive.

"Take 'em down to the stockyards, boys. You know what to do."

The captured men looked horrified. Cabel wished he could do something to prevent futher death, or even care about the fate of these strangers, but at the moment he felt nothing but horror at his own actions.

With a final nod, Capone surveyed the destroyed office and left the room, closely guarded by several of his men.

Capone gone, Cabel gave into the shaking in his limbs and sank to the floor, uncaring of the blood and gore that covered the carpet. Men worked around him, ignoring him, for which he was grateful. Several minutes passed before he could sort out what had happened in the past and the present and how the one had inadvertently saved him now. Thinking of how close he had come to dying, all those years ago and again in this office, he began to shiver as horror and exhaustion overtook him.

Someone kicked his leg. Cabel looked up to find a hard, angry face.

"Are you deaf or something?" The gangster looked exasperated. "I told you, Becca's over by the fireplace. She's asking for you."

Becca. How could he have forgotten about her? At least she was still alive.

Cabel gripped the side of the desk and pulled himself to his feet. With careful steps, he made his way across the room to where a man crouched near the fireplace, speaking in low tones to someone hidden by the edge of the bricks.

As Cabel approached, the other man looked up and saw him and nodded in acknowledgement before moving away. The man's serious demeanor was the only warning Cabel had of what he would find.

Becca sat against the wall, blood pooling in her lap from the wound in her chest. She looked up at him and gave a wan smile that broke his heart.

He knelt and took her hand, already so cold. "Becca, I'm sorry. I didn't know what to do. I couldn't help you."

"You had to be the hero. It's all right. You can't help yourself." She struggled for her next breath.

"I'm sorry," he said again.

"No," she said softly. "You couldn't save me, Cabe." She coughed. "But I'm glad you tried."

Cabel gathered her into his arms and held her close. He didn't understand her. He couldn't forgive her. Still, in this moment, she needed him, and he wouldn't deny her the small comfort of his presence. He rocked her in his arms as she closed her eyes and took her last breath. He held her a moment more.

"Mr. Evans, over here, please."

The man who gestured to him could have been a bank manager except for the shoulder holster that was visible through his open coat.

Cabel was amazed he was able to stand and make his way across the room. Bullet holes had gouged the plastered walls and ceiling and left deep fissures in the wood floor. The sofa and chairs disgorged their stuffing. Lamps lay shattered amid the wreckage of broken furniture. Cabel focused on these banalities rather than the blood and gore that covered the carpet and spattered the walls. His stomach lurched. He swallowed quickly and tried not to breathe as he made his way across the room.

When he reached the door, the man who wasn't a banker courteously touched Cabel's uninjured arm and led him to the kitchen. The room was empty of its normal occupants. Instead, Capone sat at a table in the far corner surrounded by a squad of heavily armed men.

A few of the men parted, making a path for Cabel. He walked unsteadily toward the gangster and after Capone nodded toward a second chair, sank into it. Despite his shock, Cabel knew that he was still in mortal danger. Capone only had to raise a finger, and Cabel would become one more body to be disposed of.

Capone leaned forward and stared at him with soulless eyes. "What were you doing with Malone's men?"

Cabel hesitated, then realized that there was no one left to protect except Chief Bradley, so he told Capone most of the truth. He started with the deal between Becca and Bugsy Malone, the contract, the deaths of Gary, Kittie, and Elmer. He told the gangster how Dan had tried to kill him on the street corner and failed. Although he told Capone about finding the contract, he left out Scottie Mark's involvement, instead repeating the fiction of falling and breaking his arm, the only lie he told the gangster. He finished by explaining how he had come to stop Becca, but ended up captured by Malone's men instead.

Capone listened carefully, his face a cold mask that hid his thoughts and feelings. At the end of Cabel's recitation, he asked, "Do you still have the contract?"

Cabel started to reach into the inner pocket of his coat but froze when he felt the muzzle of a gun against his head. Someone behind him reached in and retrieved the document, handing it to Capone before removing the gun barrel from Cabel's skull.

With care and deliberation, Capone unfolded the contract and read it through several times. He grunted and looked up at Cabel. "This Kittie girl died in July, right?"

"Yes, July twelfth." Weariness threatened to pull Cabel under, but he fought against it, knowing that one wrong word could mean his death.

Capone looked at the contract again. "This was signed in late June." He looked at Cabel again as if trying to divine the truth. "And you're saying that you weren't involved in any of this at that time?"

"That's right," Cabel said. "I haven't been in this city for several years. Your businesses, your wars, they mean nothing to me. As for Becca…" He paused and cleared his throat. "I knew her long ago, but she'd changed since last we met. But then, so have I."

"That's right. You went crazy and almost killed your father, then took off, right?"

Cabel nodded, deciding that Capone's summary was close enough to the truth that he had nothing to add.

"But you've been over in St. Joe, Michigan, for a while, right?"

"Less than a year, and until fairly recently, I've kept to myself." Cabel almost smiled at the inadequacy of the statement in expressing how his life had changed over the last several weeks.

"Maybe you should have kept on keeping to yourself," Capone observed before he shrugged and changed the subject. "I'm disappointed in Becca. I thought she liked working for me."

"I don't think Becca would ever have been satisfied working for anyone." He wondered why he felt the need to explain her to Capone.

The gangster shrugged. "I know she didn't like helping out with the bribes, you know, sleeping with who I told her to, not that Becca was a deal breaker or anything, more like a bonus, really. Besides the men didn't brag about it, I wouldn't let 'em, and of course they didn't want their wives to know. If word had gotten out that they were seeing Becca, those women would have known by suppertime and all hell would have broken loose." He sat back and fingered the diamond pin in his tie. "Yes, I am disappointed in the girl."

"What about Malone?" Cabel asked, unable to mask the anger in his voice. "Are you disappointed with him, too?"

"Watch that smart mouth of yours. I haven't decided what to do with you yet." He glared at Cabel, and some of the men moved restlessly, prepared to kill when the order came. "As for Bugsy, this isn't the first time this year he's tried to kill me. You know, on some days I feel like people should just line up to take a shot at me, there's been so many that have tried." He laughed ruefully. "When they started taking bets on how many times someone would try to off me, I put some money down. I picked ten, but we're past that number now." He smiled then sighed. "Malone's men killed Becca, just so you know. Planned to from the start, given how things looked."

"From what she said, they were supposed to protect her."

"Yeah, well, they didn't. Malone, well, you just can't trust that bum. The first one of his men that popped out of that sneaky little door started spraying bullets, but he was looking for someone. Becca was against the fireplace, trying to hide behind the side of it when the mook shot her. If he had gone for me first, I'd be dead right now, but he went after Becca so I had time to get behind that desk." He shook his head. "I complained to hell and back when she wanted me to buy that thing. I asked her 'What does a little girl like you need with a big desk like that?' I'm glad she won that battle. It saved my life."

Cabel had mixed feelings on the subject so he kept his mouth shut. He was becoming giddy with fatigue and reaching the point where he wished that Capone would just shoot him and get it over with.

"I've got the contract, Becca's dead, and I'll deal with Malone, but what do I do with you?"

Cabel opened his mouth and found he had nothing to say, although he was remembering an adage about being careful what you wished for.

Capone looked at him and started laughing. "You're so tired you don't know which end is up, do you?" He laughed some more then grew serious. "The thing is, I believe you. I don't think you were part of this deal, and I do think you came here tonight to stop Becca." He stared at Cabel. "I guess I'm wondering why you got involved at all? Once you found the contract, you had to know how it would end."

"I just don't like seeing people hurt," was all of the explanation he had to offer.

"I'd call you an idiot for coming here, but you pulled a gun on Malone's men, ended the fight. If you hadn't decided to help Becca, I'd probably be dead right now."

Cabel shrugged. He hadn't intended to help Capone, hadn't cared who won or lost. He had picked up the gun, got lost in the past, and inadvertently ended the fight. His personal armistice.

The gangster looked down at his fingers, as if admiring his manicure, then he took off one of the many rings he wore. It was a plain band with a few small diamonds set down the middle.

He handed the ring to Cabel. "Look inside it," he said.

Cabel took the ring and did as he was told. Capone's name was etched inside the band.

"I like to mark my property, so everyone knows what's mine."

"Seems like a smart thing to do," Cabel said, wondering why they were discussing rings.

Capone smiled, but it didn't reach his eyes. Cabel wondered if it ever did.

"I owe you, Mr. Cabel Evans. You aren't one of my men, but you stopped Malone's goons and you protected me. I usually pay for protection like that." He held out the ring. "You keep this." Cabel protested, but Capone waived it away like he was swatting a fly. "Don't make me tell you again. You don't want to insult me."

Cabel swallowed hard and accepted the gift.

"I'll want that ring back someday. Sometime you're going to need something, a favor that no one else can deliver, something you want done that no one else will do. You get that ring to me, and I'll take care of whatever it is you want. Understand?"

Cabel nodded again.

"Good, now go get some sleep before you fall down in a gutter. Hey, Henry," Capone called. The man who looked like a banker appeared at the table. "You make sure that Mr. Evans here gets to his hotel in one piece, and get that suit of his cleaned, too."

Cabel looked down at himself. Until that moment he hadn't realized he was covered in blood. Feeling ill, he rose unsteadily to his feet. Capone remained seated but held out his hand. Prudently, Cabel shook hands with the most feared gangster in the city before following Henry out of the back door and into the night.

CHAPTER THIRTY-TWO

The ship docked just as the sun slipped above the edge of the bluff, bathing the beach and water in pinks and golds. Silver Beach looked as pristine as one of its postcards, with its rides and amusements waiting for people to come and bring it to life.

Cabel walked down the gangplank wearing the new suit that Henry had somehow unearthed for him at three o'clock in the morning. Wanting to leave Chicago as soon as possible, Cabel had decided to forego a hotel in favor of finding his way home. After boarding a ship, he had gone to his cabin, where he dozed on and off with the sound of gunshots ringing in his ears and battle after battle played themselves out in his mind.

Now, awake and back in St. Joeseph, he looked at the sparkling waters that separated him from Chicago. If only the water could distance him from his memories as well. He sighed and squinted at the rising sun. Becca was dead, Capone was in his debt, and through some capricious twist of fate, he had managed not to die. His soul felt raw and scraped, but he could live with that, with what had happened last night.

That was enough for now.

As he stepped from the pier, a shadow moved in a small alley that ran between two of the buildings that fronted the river. A moment later Bessie George stepped forward, and Cabel's only real surprise was that he was surprised at all.

The fortuneteller walked toward him. He met her halfway. She looked into his eyes, placed a hand against his chest, and then nodded, much like Dr. Lewis did after a satisfactory examination.

"You are sad, yes, and there was death, but you are healing. This is good, Mr. Cabel, very good." She smiled then sighed and patted his cast. "There is much yet to do, but this is good."

He opened his mouth to ask her what more he could do, how much more was expected of him, but she shook her head. "We talk later. Now Dr. Lewis is at top of bluff. He goes to breakfast, I think. You go, too."

Cabel watched her walk away, wondering what Dr. Lewis had to do with anything before he realized that she meant that the doctor was going back to that wonderful diner. Cabel didn't care how Bessie George knew what she knew. He believed her and rushed up the bluff path to flag down the doctor and join him for a meal.